NO ONE DIES YET

Kobby Ben Ben

NO ONE DIES YET

Europa
editions

Europa Editions
27 Union Square West, Suite 302
New York NY 10003
www.europaeditions.com
info@europaeditions.com

Copyright © 2023 by Kobby Ben Ben
First publication 2024 by Europa Editions

Library of Congress Cataloging in Publication Data is available
ISBN 978-1-60945-756-3

Ben Ben, Kobby
No One Dies Yet

Art direction by Emanuele Ragnisco
instagram.com/emanueleragnisco

Cover design and illustration by Ginevra Rapisardi

Prepress by Grafica Punto Print – Rome

Printed in Italy

CONTENTS

Part One - 17

Part Two - 95

Part Three - 253

Acknowledgements - 381

To Aspecialkindofdouble. Everyone deserves to see themselves immortalised in fiction at least once in their lifetime. This is you and me kiki-ing in the DMs forever and ever.

0

Harry (1969–2018)

Independence came and left. Colonisation left and came. Harry came and left. It was we who killed Harry.

We saw him the moment his flight squatted and spilled its stairs across our tarmac. Birthed this man hauling little luggage of silver spoons and swaddled in that milky, not-from-here scent. Passed from one immigration officer to another, fussed over. Eyes, an innocent blue, beheld this motherland as if some prenatal prophecy permitted him possession of her. Cocky and colicky, the result of a disturbance that rammed his head farther up his ass. Tossed onto us after some white land's postpartum disappointment.

We listened to his slow, deliberate, *dumdum* footfalls creating gaping wounds in the skulls of our brothers buried beneath. Whenever his kind stepped on our soil, we cried from unrest, we slammed the roofs of our graves like disgruntled kids kicking up a fuss. If only we could puncture the earth's surface and wrench him down here with us. But we are powerless.

So we watched him sit in his arranged car. We watched him watch the sights in awe, listen to the city's noises, breathe in our smells. And scoff. And sneeze. He struck his nose as though it had smelt evil. *What in the bloody hell was that shite smell!* "Cor, blimey," we said back at him, not as useful as our *onye aye gbemi*, but we did the hand gestures to fill in the semantic gaps their languages left. *E le akɛ gamɛi ji wɔ!*

Harry's eyes had never met Africa. Still, he and his kind

came with their conceptions passed down from old sailors' songs. Songs about indigenous peoples whose lives were dissected wing after wing, one antenna after the other, like an insect tortured at the hands of a fascinated child. Songs with ludicrous lyrics: *Oh what bare land and deep, evil forests, oh what dark men swinging from the branches of trees, clothed in leaves, hooting at each other and hunting wildlife, running amok then jumping onto the saddles of elephants gifted them at birth.*

Finding no evidence of the above accounts, Harry needled his ancestors' narratives into the men who walked the streets with their hair matted, their dicks hanging and swinging, their ashy, dusty buttocks revealed through a pair of pants that looked like they'd survived the Chinese's galamsey dynamites. Yes, he confirmed, this was Africa; where women hooted while carrying loads on their heads; where fowl and dogs ran wild or were run over and over until their innards mingled with the tar. His expectations met, he awarded himself a look of horror and disdain, relaxed into the back of his taxi and placed a liver-spotted hand on his chest. No more a baby to this city, his dramatic skin had visibly aged. His real age now evident. Fifty. But could be younger, given his kind—all things white like *mã*—moulded rather rapidly.

As though things couldn't get any worse, and he could no longer be shocked at the sights Africa had to offer, he found himself spying on a mob in action. Those armed pedestrians jaywalking through the streets, swinging from lane to lane and picking up their victim the way a butcher's knife swoops down on obnoxious bone. His heart, it lurched. "Christ," he muttered as he watched the apprehended thief being slapped and stamped and stoned. The novelty of this experience, unreported in all of his ancestors' songs, filled him with genuine dread. His driver, unfazed by the incident, whistled on and wheeled on as if violence was a default setting of the city. "My God, who are these people?"

Onyɛ aye gbemi.

Violence is what built this city. Violence was the navigating ships teeming with the Harrys of this world. Violence was the vice that infiltrated our culture. It was the spices and the re-sources stolen. It was the mice that scurried across the indigenes piled one on top of the other. Dead. When the locals sought to push back the invaders, violence raised the buildings, the trade routes, it raised the funds to build torture sites for them.

Yet Harry sat back in his hotel, oblivious to the violence that had preceded him, as those too were exempted from the gospels of the sailors. The images of men being beaten to death would scar his memory. Savages, he might have called us.

Do we need to give more reasons why we killed Harry? Is Violence not what begets violence? What more motivation did we need? Maybe if you considered Harry a symbol and not human, the violence, like hungry canines, we unleashed on him would be stomachable.

Here are more symbols we'd like to be rid of: acne-ridden volunteers who step on our heads with their mud-encrusted boots and summon their saviour-complex to save our earth, pasty-looking employees of MNCs who take jobs in Africa from Africans. All of them, taking a break from their cold, capitalist weathers, daring to swim in our seas, and buying out our lands to build their embassies.

For Harry and the other symbols, we could not act quickly enough; the "neo" part of this stage as deadly as its forbearer. Before we knew it, they had almost outnumbered us. Again. For every Black dreadlocked man on the streets, there were five white women looking to birth mixed kids with superior genes. We could not watch our children commit the same mistakes we did, inviting them in and letting them take over. Yet, we could do nothing on our own.

We are dead anyway. We need vessels to act on our behalf. We need you. Maybe if it were your hands holding the kerchief that did the smothering, or your eyes spying the lids of these Harrys surrender consciousness, you'd be more forgiving, eh? If you heard our pleas in your dreams, would you refuse us? Who watches his brothers cry in agony and refuses to help? We would drown you in our pain, shock you with our voices. You would try to resist. We are stronger.

It was to our burial site that we lured Harry. Always our burial site. The swanky resorts. The clean beaches.

Harry's eyes were his weak point; little mirrors, which gave easy access to his wits. We saw our sea, our food, reflected in them. We also saw her. Our vessel. Dancing in them. Who could resist a shapely, voluptuous vessel? *Yoo ni damɔ shi.* Meatier than their women back home. The kind all of them would dabble in, anything to take a break from their predisposed desires. For what is a fling if not an opportunity to invest in an object different from your usual pursuits? Wasn't that what Africa was to the Harrys of this world? A vast land ripe with adventure begging to be juiced; mangoes falling off trees and rolling towards white feet.

She, this vessel, worked as a server in the resort's restaurant. He watched her sashay towards him, like one of those exotic palm trees bordering the coast, as she brought in a tray piled high with our remains. "Why don't you feast on our fathers' pain?" she said. He was bewitched. He wouldn't look at the tray and its contents. He ignored the sharp-toothed aroma of decay that snaked into his nostrils. His senses were directed at her even as he devoured, cutting through our skulls and spooning our marrows into his mouth. Nom. Nom. Nothing like a four-century-old microwaved meal. He chewed and chewed. We are tough, we are painful, our stories are hard to ingest, but he washed us down with the preservative ethanol, without choking, without crying, without acknowledging four centuries of pain presented to him on a silver platter for a tour fee of gossamer value charged against the violence wreaked and yet some of them gawked at the prices anyway, because they assumed Africa would be cheap.

Buulu. Onyε aye gbemi.

Our vessel smiled at him and asked if he was enjoying his trip. "Not until now," he answered with the devious charm of his kind, wiping away the cobweb that dribbled onto his chin. "What's your name?" he wanted to know. Our vessel gave the Harrys of this world a different name every time. Harry rose when he was done with his meal. He staggered. "I think I should walk you to your room," she offered.

We've managed to convince the locals to live by a set of taboos. Taboo to not pray to us before fishing. Taboo to harvest more than enough fish. Taboo to fish on Tuesday. If disobeyed, they believe we will reveal ourselves to them in haunting shapes.

On Tuesday, we all rose to the occasion as our vessel brought in Harry who'd been shackled and stripped naked to reveal his fat. Good, industrial fat. Not even the seagulls that squawked at us in the mornings were around to witness this feast. The waters were silent, as were the winds, which were our breaths held in anticipation. We raised our hands for the sacrifice. We sang the song of dentists asking little kids to open their mouths for observation. *Ahhhh.* We swallowed Harry into the depths of our new home—where they had dumped us to file insurance claims and returned with wreaths for our corroborative silence. *Gbemi, gbemi, gbemi!*

PART ONE

The role of narrators in stories can be best described by alluding to the wind. Narrators move with stealth, sifting through tiny openings. They're everywhere. Yet won't attract attention to themselves.

Through them stories breathe, or fly as kites, pacing and plotting and twisting this way and turning that way. A howling voice.

Through them dust can be thrown in the eyes of the reader: they lie, withhold, or omit.

Yes, they're everything that's crooked in a narrative.

But without narrators, a story will simply not begin.

Sample Entry for Column
(*written by Kobby on 13 December, 2019;
13 days after the friends arrive*)

How do you begin a murder story starring a curious foreigner and an opportunistic local without giving away the entire plot—who died and why? You start with the obvious villain.

The friends and I meet during twilight, when Accra staggers after long hours of enduring the earth's spinning, when inhabitants conditioning themselves for the violent degeneracy of the city's unending nightlife observe preliminary rest. Watch the novel resident on an evening stroll, humming to the rhythm of his footfalls, oblivious to the crime that stealthily advances from behind and taps him on the shoulder.

I am not the obvious villain. I am not the first opportunistic local the friends encounter.

Nana's are the hard features often found smoking in a halfway house that police constantly raid for stashes of weed, tramadol, and little schoolgirls who've been tied up and messed up. That ebony skin, yanked over protruding cheekbones and jawline, possesses a mummified aspect that leaves little flesh for other emotions to absolve his perpetually disgusted countenance. He inspires both fear and security. The bodyguard in the movie who kills to protect.

His hands are something for conversation too. Scarring on the insides of his palms to show that he's done one too many odd jobs. Nothing with insurance, only the promise of quick cash exchanged in the back-alley kitchens of fufu chop bars.

Elton or any of his companions may have mulled over these textured palms, and the hardship greased into them, after Nana sieves through the throng at the airport and clasps each of their hands into his own possessively, shakes them, then proceeds to collect their luggage without apologising for being late—a detail that confirms his Ghanaianness. This makes me chuckle despite the friends' visible irritations as they recount the hours spent in the airport worried sick that the first gay escort they'd trusted would leave them stranded in a country like this. Like this—a phrase so loaded it should be italicised, even if it is expressed in a casual tone that eschews insinuation, that offers no room for regrets or hurried initiatives to touch up their prejudices in my presence. I grin placidly; their tale continues without a hitch.

The three exchange curious glances before following Nana out of the airport, given he looks nothing like those pictures Elton had perused online before sending a Friend Request. They will discover (per another of my invalid assumptions) that Nana exemplifies the demographic for whom Facebook is for sharing Otabil sermons and hounding job postings. For this reason, men like him on the app wouldn't consider selfies, only studio-shot photos that air-brush their scars and struggles into something that resembles innocence. A crime scene wiped clean.

"Nah, that's not it." At the bar where the friends and I convene, Elton bats away these assessments of Nana. "His looks aside, I was only getting scared 'cause something 'bout him didn't sit right with me—"

"—and come to find out," one friend butts in with suggestive candour, a gush of Kokroko spewing out of the lips of the other, whose laughter splinters the hushed ambiance in which Gyedu Ambolley's Bon Adooso is a serpentine accompaniment, hissing through the background chatter of neighbouring patrons. Though I did not spend so much time douching (in one of those public bathrooms with vile disinfectants that made it clear you were not welcome) just so these three could rant about this stranger and the supposed danger he posed—no matter that I too was a stranger with intentions unknown, I swallow my frustrations with a swig of Savanna, and, in my most exaggerated accent, implore, "Tell me EVERY-TIN."

Outside the airport, the sun bakes Nana purple, his teeth and eyes become a burnished gold. At the circumventing taxi drivers quoting exorbitant fares, he yells, "*Chama* for there!" They're relentless all the same, tussling with one another, and with Nana, who refuses to hand over the friends' bags, because he wants the "local price," he insists "local price, *kraa!*" The other drivers already booked for airport pickups look on this scene with contempt, aware that their commercial counterparts are the first scammers tourists will encounter upon entering a country like this. Even so, they remain mute as a matter of accustomed connivance. We have all had our moral compasses poisoned, inventing clever ways to rid foreigners of a few bucks. Nevertheless, some unsuspecting travel writer takes one look at this eagerness for service—this hunger to assist tourists with their luggage, their transport, recommendations for this, that, or some other dilemma—and grows spellbound by this elaborate performance. Oh, we locals laugh, and clink our beers—*kpa kpa kpa*—after another global paper is duped into spreading the gospel of Ghanaian hospitality. *E dey be kɛkɛ!*

"We're going to take an Uber." Scott—the lightest among the three, husband to Vincent, who hasn't yet discovered he's now white, and thus assumes the race's privileges and curses—announces impatiently. But Uber! What's Uber to Nana who takes *troskis* and considers taxis a luxury for the ever-aspiring lower middle-class? What then could be said of Ubers, which he's heard are private taxis servicing those who can afford not to ask for a price reduction?

"No," Nana squeezes his grip on the three's luggage. To a

taxi driver, he switches from his pidgin into the local dialect of his people.

If you are dark-skinned and of Nana's height (something between 5 feet and 5' 7"), the mean height for which coffins in this country are made, anyone would rightly guess you're Ashanti. The ethnic group at the beginning of every story on Ghana's opposition to colonial rule. It's this history of strength, coupled with a long-standing perception that people of his ethnic group are stingy, that Nana forces on this driver who finally concedes and ushers the foreigners into his car. "*Akwaaba!* Welcome! In this country, your eyes have to be hot!" The driver tells them in broken English and laughs bigheartedly, warning them too that he has no air-conditioning. Nana tells him to shut up and drive. He drives through the airport gates, past the topiary of letters that say "Year of Return." He speeds into the thick of the Ghanaian heat that sits on the skin like a heavy conscience. He honks at the jam of vendors and beggars plastering their pasty faces over the car's windows. "*Obroni. Obroni. Obroni*," they chant at Scott, who looks into his folded fist, refusing to give in.

That's how the friends enter the country. That's how they enter their hotel. No one dies yet.

The friends and I meet at an alfresco bar in Accra called Republic, known to be a favourite tourist and expat spot. More than enough white people to make locals like me sit up. "Nana isn't gay as Elton thought," Vincent and Scott announce over the surrounding din of clashing beers, their own lips torn between draining their liquors and finishing this tale. At the hotel, Elton reaches in for a kiss, and Nana steps back, jumps back, backs off. Takes off.

"Kobby, you should have seen Elton's face!" Scott and Vincent finally conclude, after several intermissions of gasping, can't-breathe, lord-help-me laughter, the latter slapping my thighs and letting his palm linger, an action that is at once painful and tender, mimicking the spicy and savoury traits of

a friendship long-lived—an untimely occurrence for our relationship too early in its infancy to suffer such intimate man-
handling, and this makes me uncomfortable, makes me direct
a nervous laugh to Elton, who wears a lopsided smile over his
embarrassment even as he nods to validate this story.

Elton is a bear of a man, tall and beefy, the kind whose hugs
entrap you whole, caught in the warmth of skin and strength.
I'd thought of American rapper Rick Ross—the beard, the
vaunting display of layered necklaces (wouldn't be surprised if
he'd tattooed every inch of skin below his neck)—the first time
we met through Man4Man. I couldn't have guessed he plays
Corinne Bailey Rae on repeat, collapses into a bout of pleading
giggles when his overly sensitive nipples are sucked, and knows
all the lyrics to "Like A Star"—these three words his only tat-
too, inked over his rear deltoids. I should tell him to take his
picture off Man4Man, since that's a sure way to get killed. I'd
be lying of course, but he wouldn't know.

No one dies yet. In this unusual murder story where no one,
not even its narrators, is who they say they are.

Nana and I are two local guides with differing ideas of how
stories are to be told. I, the first of the guides in narrative order,
relays his story in the English of our newspapers. Nana tells his
in the tradition of our cultures, of grandmothers dancing and
clapping and telling tales by the fireside. It's a conflict of languages, between the old culture and the new, the oral and the
written. Newspapers and drums. Nana and me. Who dies first?
No one dies yet.

The next part of the story begins with blood. In the hotel.
After Elton and I have had great fucking sex, the kind of sex
that makes you want to fight orgasm, push it off, so high on that
mountain of pleasure the world sinks beneath, deaf to your
surroundings and invested in making your lover cuss and curl
and cum. Hearts panting, dicks throbbing, grunts and throats
throttled, asses spanked and spat on and smashed. A bloody

I

Kobby
(On the day the friends arrive)

O n certain days, Accra decides it's going to burn with such fury that it hopes its inhabitants get a taste of what Hell feels like, and repent as the roadside pastors instruct. It's as if the city is angry about some slight committed against it. Burning, into rooftops of cars in traffic, through the shielding umbrellas mothers wield to hide the babies wrapped against their backs. Fires erupting on pavements into the shoes of pedestrians and peddlers who yelp, *Awurade ɛdeɛn na y'ayɛ na wo teetee yɛn sa ara!*

Still, nothing, not even the coconut oil bleeding down my hairline and stinging my eyes, deters me from my Saturday routine. To be born in Accra is to have the thick skin needed to survive her tempestuous moods. Even if the city batters and slaps you around, you have no other bosom to turn to. So you lean into the heat like you endure a mother's tough love, convinced she'll have a change of heart. Then at some grown age, you wonder why maternal hate isn't as touted as maternal love. God knows having such language would free a lot of children. From expecting love to materialise where hate is festering. From expecting Accra to love us, when she's only capable of hate, of heat scorching our sensitive napes, our hyper-pigmentations and our ageing skin, our cracked lips chorusing *Black don't crack* when Accra cracks her whip over our backs.

Accra hates us, hates us all.

Even with all this hate, being such an enterprising people,

we inhabitants of Accra create love. We sell love. Out in the open, on the labyrinthine streets of Jamestown. Hawkers yell, *Come, come, come buy my love*. There's no love greater than the love you find on Accra's streets, a love that makes life a lot more liveable on a low-income salary. All Ghanaians know if you want to purchase love without having to chip in on the rent of some exorbitant store, get love on the streets. Mothers and fathers can take their children all through primary school to university with the earnings they make on the street because Ghanaians do support local, even if local is a supply chain that begins in a Chinese warehouse. All things imported from China are love, it don't cost a thing.

I find shelter in the shade of the old Kingsway store which used to be Ghana's premiere shopping centre in the twentieth century, the former prime shoplifting grounds for British and Irish expat wives whom it became store policy to hound owing to the increasing cases of pilfered sugar and flour holstered into the waistbands of their panties. The building—dilapidated the only way time and terrible maintenance assaults walls, erodes hues, summons mildew—sits with a prestige not dissimilar to a run-down Grecian arena. Once a year, it is repurposed into a mural gallery to attract thousands of art enthusiasts around the world for Ghana's largest street art festival, Chale Wote.

On Saturdays, it's these streets of Accra I spend my afternoons browsing, looking for love, buying love from independent bookstores on table tops. At Kingsway, there are rows and rows of books mounted on sloping slabs of wood, on mats, on the arms of men who wave their wares—their love, in the faces of pedestrians. *I'm the Richest Man in Babylon, hey! Buy my Richest Man in Babylon, hey!*

Accra's streets are the best places to stumble on some prehistoric Harlequin romances, Silhouette bodice-rippers, and bestsellers from old white writers—the stuff that always made it to *The Sunday Times* bestseller list two decades ago. Anyone fooled into walking into a shop labelled "bookstore" would be surprised to find only outdated diaries and stationery. True bibliophiles know that to find their next read they've got to approach these streets as though it were their oyster farm, searching for undiscovered gems among pirated copies of *Becoming*.

One seller accosts me the moment he figures I'm someone who might read a book, who might need a little love. He lures me to his religious stall, recommending Benny Hinn, who would "speak to my spirit." I am tempted to ask if he's got anything that'll keep me from masturbating when night comes and my past creeps in with its metallic taste on my tongue. What about those times when masturbation alone isn't enough, and I have to resort to other invented rituals, perhaps AESMA, Auto-erotic Sadomasochist Asphyxiation? Would you happen to know of any writers who have written extensively on this strange exercise that cinches my throat and fucks with my air-supply? Am I the only one who finds pleasure from imagining, in gory detail, the many ways I might be murdered?

"Those," I say, pointing at old, in-surprisingly-good-condition paperbacks beneath the religious books.

"John Grisham?" he asks in rapid-fire speech. "You like John Grisham?" He begins speaking in pellets. "Dean Koontz? You like Dean Koontz? Sandra Brown? I get plenty-plenty crime." We share a brief look, a smile stretches his wind-chapped lips, happy he's figured what this customer loves.

I pick up a sunburned James Patterson hardback and press it to my nose. Interesting thing about old hardcovers: if you rip off the book jacket and sniff at specific spots on the cloth-bound cover you might catch a whiff of its old home or owner. That some of these books are acquired from dead readers delights me. Used books delight me. I imagine that once they were treasures of a dying man, given away to some charity organisation determined to ship them to Africa for underprivileged kids.

Unfortunately, these ones found themselves in the wrong hands and now here they are, sold at rather affordable prices. The library information in a few of them—*Our Nig, The Autobiography of Malcolm X*—makes me wonder what their stories are, how they escaped the libraries of the West to find freedom in the streets of Africa.

"Oga, you go buy?"

"How much for all?" I ask him. I do not bargain. He hands me my plastic bag of new acquisitions. He scratches my palm before we separate, and winks at me. I wonder if his subtle flirtations are inspired by my penis etched along the inseam of my jeans. The offending sight that has caused some elderly citizens to sidestep me, as though my apparent lack of underwear indicates an ungodly fondness for heinous perversions. As we are wont to say, *Show me you're not wearing any underwear and I'll show you your character*; these onlookers (pretending they're looking elsewhere) may have already gained access to the intimate recesses of my brain. They've discovered endless scores of compromising data, including the NSFW photos of Elton. And BrooklynDude2. And PeckhamLad5. All Year of Return tourists whose Airbnbs will be temporary enclaves from Accra's homophobic climate—if my messages to meet are responded to. If, like these pedestrians, these returnees haven't already concluded that I fit the profile of Ghanaian whose paths they'd rather not cross.

"See you soon o!" the man shouts at me as I walk away without acknowledging his advances.

At the "Tema Station" lorry station, with its parked buses and swarming flies feasting on littered trash, there's a crowd circumventing the newsstands plastered with news about the "Sasabonsam Killer." From my vantage point, I scan the grim front pages, the magnified pictures of corpses with perforated bodies: heads bearing tiny red holes; intestines, unbarred from the carnage, leaking, bursting forth like foliage. I smile, entranced.

Everyone but me refuses to see the poetry in dying. To imagine the sounds: of necks snapping like fires sinking their teeth into the crevices of wood; of bodies being knifed—squishy as the sound of feet stepping into mulch; of mouths writhing for air as poison seals off gullets. I could watch these macabre presentations for hours. But someone has decided this is the right time to interrupt my reverie, brushing past me to witness the Sasabonsam Killer's handiwork.

Every newspaper is a cawing crow lamenting this serial killer in the eschatological style of evangelical outreach. Yes, a person capable of such violence may also possess Christ's grace to turn himself in. Yes, a few biblical verses are all it takes to cause such a person to repent and refrain. How delusional these publications are.

It comes to me that the newsprint collage could be a perfect backdrop for an Instagram photo showing off my recent purchases, an idea not far off from the current theme on my grid which has books captured against my brother's obituaries. The photo turns out sinister with the chosen filter. I upload it to my stories instead, because this new aesthetic fucks up the prevailing ambience of my grid. For a caption, I write: *Book Haul #52, Crime Fic on Newspaper Crime, John Grisham, Dean Koontz, Sandra Brown*. Within seconds, someone reacts to my story. They're neither friend nor follower; they're also not that one person for whom all my posts are written. They're just another of those #like4like, #follow4follow, #share4share accounts whose sole talent is to repost content from smaller, smarter bookstagrammers. I mask my disappointment with a smiley emoji.

The rest of my Saturday routine, consisting of visits to the pharmacist and the loctitian at Kaneshie, would have still ground to a halt if the police hadn't shown up with bats, if the newsstand owner along with everyone else hadn't run helter-skelter. My Saturday routine grinds to a halt the moment my Man4Man phone pings.

In my pouch, I thumb through the tattered copy of *American Psycho*, a hardback of *My Sister, the Serial Killer* gifted by my boss, who scribbled onto its endpapers: *Saw the title and immediately thought of you <3*, to retrieve the sad, cracked Android lit with **1 new message from Elton**: *Hey there, would you mind us meeting tonight, to see how things go? ;)*

I rummage for my other phone, and, under the watchful eyes of a possible pickpocket, I quickly fire my dad a text: *You can lock the gate, won't be sleeping home tonight.*

My father's reply is instant: *The olanzapine, did you buy it?*

I purchase an enema from a market woman who calls me *Bra*. She claims I have got the prettiest ɛgyerɛ she's seen and wants to know which parent I got this diastema from. Neither of them, I answer, adding, that in between my mother's teeth are several gaps that are man-made. But the details of this disclosure aren't important to her; what she really wants to know is if I will buy some of her ginger to go with this enema she's convinced I'll be using on my disobedient child—the same purpose for which my own mother had used her enemas. I shake my head no. I have plenty ginger at home, I tell her, *medaase*. A taxi conveniently stops by her stall, I slide in, and ask the driver to take me to Accra City Hotel, where they've got good bathrooms.

II

Nana
(On the day the friends arrive;
Nana's first meeting with Kobby)

Before I speak the English, I think in Twi. Before I can understand English, I bring it into Twi. And even if I wish that I can make one language be separate from the other one, so that when I speak people can understand me, I know that a man like me, with the face I have, with the school I go to, no one takes anything I say to be the truth even if I swear on my father's grave.

Why should anyone believe me when even my grandmother don't? When every time I speak, she shout for my top and say, *Nokware deɛ ɛyɛ baako pɛ!* Like the time her chest grow and her eyes make red like the pepper chicken my sister steal from her soup inside, and even when I told her that I didn't take her chicken and eat it and that my sister is the one who take and eat her chicken, grandmother shout for my top again and again, *The truth is only one!*

In Twi, "to take and eat" can be the same as to believe: *gye di*. So hear my story, but please don't be like my grandmother. Please, take and eat:

They call me Nana. I am thirty years. I live in Accra, but I come from a village in Mampong. My mother was a housewife and my father a very small farmer. They die. This is how my teacher teach me to write *Myself* composition. This is how you begin *Myself* essay if you want to get five-over-ten, which is not a bad mark if you can never get six-over-ten. It is not a bad mark if you cannot *conshugate*, if you cannot do concord, if you don't know difference between noun and *adjetief*, if your teacher say that you'll stop school at Primary 6 and his prophecy come true. In your composition, you do not say: *They call me Nana, I am a big person in my village. Where I come from, they call you Nana if you are a king. Where I come from, I have a big cocoa farm because what is for my mother's brother is also for me and not my cousins.* You do not say all this because over in this Accra, when you go to job interview to talk about yourself and you say that, people will laugh at you. So I talk about myself the English way—the way my teacher teach me. Nobody laugh. Nobody listen too. So I really become happy when on Facebook Elton listen to me when I talk about myself. And then he told me that he and his friends will come to Ghana to visit me because I'm so interesting. If only I knew that he was coming all the way to Ghana from America to kiss me . . . *hmm.*

Adwuma biara yɛ Adwuma, we say where I come from. Every work is work. I am happy to get a job now even if I didn't go to JSS. Facebook help me. Jesus help me. My pastor help me. My pastor speak to Jesus and Jesus listen. I chat with *Obroni* and America people on the internet. I talk about how God love them, how we are poor, how they should send us money to help poor children like me. And sometimes I have to send them a naked picture for them to send the money. At first I didn't want to do all this: send my pipi to collect money. But Pastor told me this is how I'll leave Ghana and go to America. The Lord gave my pastor Prophecy that someone from America, a woman, will give me visa and come take me to America.

So on the Tecno phone when I say hi to Elton and he say hi too, I ask him if he knows my brother-in-law, that he lives in America with my sister and that he is black like Elton. Elton laugh and tell me he don't know him. But Elton and me become good, good friends. So good that he told me that I should send him naked picture. And then he sent me his big brown buttocks. He like my black pipi and that is when he say that I'm so interesting and that him and his friends will come visit me.

I go and pick Elton from the airport when he come. The security men in the airport look me up and down and let me enter to meet him. I see plenty *obroni* coming to Ghana, people holding names on paper.

Plenty Ghanaians want to do quick-quick to leave Ghana to *aburokyire* to see *obroni*. Ghana is hard so I don't understand why plenty *obroni* come here. I don't understand why Elton and his friends come here. But I take their bag and shake them. They ask me how I am. I say I am fine. I turn my back and carry their bags out of the airport. The taxi driver we meet outside look behind me to see white man and say a bad, high price. I get angry at him. My face get hot and my chest grow and I do as if I am going to walk away with Elton and his white and black friends. But he call me back. Call me by my name, Nana, which you also call any stranger you respect, like *oga* like the Alata people say, or *bossu* like the people here in Accra too say. The taxi driver tell me to take it cool and then he agree to my price. Elton and his white and black friend sit in the car. We drive to the hotel.

I am not a bad man. I no kill anybody since I become Born Again. But they are afraid of me. I can see them talk quietly in their ears, and it sound like they are snakes. I tell them Ghana is peaceful place. Better than Alata where everybody does 419 and Boko Haram kidnap people left and right like they say on TV here. Even if they have better film than we have here, Ghana is better than there. I tell them that we are Christian here, God-fearing people. The taxi driver too tell them plenty nice things. They start asking plenty questions. I can't understand all of them when they talk. I keep quiet a lot, the *kaka* in my mouth make it smell I know, so I brush my teeth well, even use mouthwash my pastor give me and when I spit it out all I see is the blood colour and not the blue mouthwash. Sometimes, I can taste blood in my mouth, not today, but I still don't like talking plenty. The taxi driver tells me what they are saying because he tells me in Twi that he has seen Elton's black friend in a film before. "*Titanic?*" I ask him. That's the cassette film sellers sell to me when I come to Accra. My life begin to sink like that ship the moment I meet that Elton other black friend, with the hair like plenty snakes. The moment I shake his hand is the moment I shake hands with the devil. *Obonsam*, that is how we call the devil. You can bring it to English and it will mean someone who beats hands.

We stop at a traffic light and all the refugee Niger and Chad small-small children run to our car to beg when they see Elton white friend.

"*Obroni, obroni,*" they say. Sometimes, I don't know how these people learn Twi. They speak Twi better than some Ghanaian people who have gone to school plenty. Twi is slowly dying with some Ghana children, but seeing this children speak Twi, the language of my people, make my eye collect. The taxi driver like many Ghanaian hate this children. "*Monkɔ, monkɔ,*" he shout for their top, "*dabiara adeserɛ nkoaa na aka mo!* I tell him, *Yesu se mo ma nkwadaa no mmra menkyɛn.*"

"Please sirs," some man that have dress in suit come to our car window, "can you kindly give me some money to buy some cool water?"

"Herh, you too you are who?" the taxi driver shout at him.

"Please, friends, my parents came from Michigan and left me here to take care—"

Everybody in the car is laughing.

"*Firi hɔ,*" the taxi driver roll up his windows. "*Wo ho fin sɛ* Michigan! Michi-ghana *wai, nnyɛ* Michigan, Michighana."

"Nana." It's the first time I hear Elton's black friend voice. I look at him with the mirror that make you see what happen in backseat. "What's the meaning of *obroni?*"

"White man," the taxi driver say before I can say.

"So these (folks) (basically) calling you a white (dude), Scott," Elton black friend say to the white man and laugh. "*Obroni. Obroni. Obroni.*" He bring his head to the white man face and shout in his ear, as if calling someone *Obroni* is a bad thing. Elton laugh too. The taxi driver laugh too as if he understand them. In Twi, to understand someone mean to sit under them, the taxi driver has gone low to their level. I haven't. *Obroni* is a good word. You can use it to call someone and their eyes will not die. But Elton white friend eyes begin to die.

"Vince, quit playing," the white man say. Elton and his black friend laugh louder.

"(Coloniser)," Elton say.

"Okay, now you're pushing it." The white friend bring his fingers up as if to hit Elton.

"*Obroni* is not a bad word." I speak. They all go quiet and look at me with straight face. "We called white people that because of their hair. Their hair was like corn hair, *aburo* hair. Why we call America *Aburokyire*. Because from the back of the corn came the white man. Calling someone a white man is not bad. Over here we love white people. More than Chinese. White people do nice-nice things for this country." I smile like when I answer math question correct in school.

Elton's friends look at him, then look back at me. They all look like harmattan have catch their face. Like they don't pomade Queen Elizabeth Cocoa Butter before coming to Ghana.

"Alright," Elton say. "Thanks for explaining." I feel like I have done myself fool. All three of them look at me as if I am a fool. Like when I'm translating my pastor English to Twi during sermon and I say it so wrong the old woman in church who make herself like Queen of England get up and shout that I'm fool. I know I'm not fool. The *kaka* in my mouth begin to fill with blood.

"*Kyerɛsɛ w'aka nkwasiasem o,*" the taxi driver say to me and laugh small. I tell him that he should shut up and drive the car *na* the traffic light is green.

"Well, that was from a place," Elton say, we hear the zip of his bag opening.

"I need a joint too, these Africans be (on some other shit)," the white man say. The black friend hit him on the thigh when he see that I'm looking at them through the mirror and I make my face like the sky when the rain about to fall.

We hear a sound like *shh* from the back, me and the taxi driver turn to see Elton has light *wee* and has start smoking.

"Hey o, please o," the taxi driver start shouting at Elton top. "You smoking *wee*? Do you want police to catch me?"

"What? Why?" The three of them look confuse.

"*Wee* is illegal," I say to them as I tell the driver to shut up again and that police is not around. I turn to Elton and ask him to hide the *wee* and is not good to smoke here. He listen to me and smile small. I smile back. Elton and I will be close. *Ata ne Ata.*

"Imma hide this real quick then, even though that's some bullshit. We in Africa."

"Right? Don't they grow the stuff here?" black friend say.

"*Ei, ei, ei,*" the taxi driver say to me only. "*Year of Return foɔ yi beku yɛn. Omo bɛkyerɛ yɛn mma nneɛma bɔne.*"

I want to laugh, but I don't. He's telling the truth. When the government, when my President Akuffo Addo—the president from my hometown, announce 2019 is Year of Return and that plenty black Americans will be coming to Accra to go and see Cape Coast Castle, all Ghana become happy like Asamoah Gyan have not miss penalty at World Cup finals before. Everyone say that this will bring money into the economy. Osu Oxford Street sellers have already started making so many things with Ghana flag: shoe, boxers, even lipstick that you can put it on your mouth once and it will paint the red, gold, green, and star in the middle. Only school children are annoyed that

GTV won't show *Home Alone* again this Christmas, just Kunta Kinte. My God, no one suffer in life more than Kunta Kinte. That is when you see white man of old days can be very wicked. The new white men are nice. They bring us plenty Bibles from abroad and my pastor and I sell them when it's supposed to be free.

The black Americans on the street will be speaking that their English which the sellers on the street copy so they can get them to buy more things. Who will tell them that Ghana people can trick you? So far, if money has come in the economy, we the poor people don't see. All we see is the plenty *wee* and cigarette that they have smoke finish and throw on the floor. Pastor say that we should try to bring plenty Year of Return people to church to repent. Maybe I can help Elton stop smoking *wee*.

"Your phone keeps vibrating, Elton. Already on (Man4Man)?"

Elton laugh at what his black friend say. "I joined this Year of Return page on Facebook, for events happening in the area. I get an alert every time someone makes a post. So many posts. Unsurprisingly, there are no (queer) Year of Return events."

"I'm not sure this place is going to be as open as SA," white friend say. "Isn't it illegal here? Jails and killings, that sort of stuff?"

"I bet Nana's gonna know (queer) events happening in the area."

"Err, I wouldn't bet on it, he doesn't look (queer) to me." Black friend say, his eyes squeezing to look at me in the mirror on the front.

"He sent me a pic of his . . . (willie)."

I try to increase the radio volume so that it fills the quiet in the car, but I turn it down quickly when I hear what's on it. As if Elton and his friends will understand the Twi Kokonsa FM presenters are speaking. Everyone is talking about the Sasabonsam Killer, this man who they have called like that because of the holes he chook-chook into people's bodies, and how he leave the dead people looking like Satan *ankasa*. The government have told the radio to stop talking plenty-plenty about it so that it will not spoil Ghana tourism and the Year of Return. At first, I was angry with the president for wanting people to keep quiet about it. But now, I don't want Elton and his friends to hear about them, to know sometimes Accra become dangerous. Over here we say, *M'ɛnhohoro wo ntoma a ayɛ fi wɔ abɔnten*. I think the English have a similar proverb that say don't let outside people see you wash your dirty clothes.

Soon, the taxi driver stop at the hotel and I get down to carry their bags quick-quick. The white man want to hold his own bag but I'm stronger than him and take his bag from him. "My mother raise me well, okay?" I tell him.

A nice woman come from inside, walk to us and push the security man away, smiling big to Elton and his friends. "I'm the (receptionist)." She walk in front of them, leading them to their room as Elton's white friend speak to her. She likes the white man well-well because her smile become bigger and bigger and she talk to only him. She is the kind of woman Pastor will call Beelzebub because she is wearing coat and trousers like man.

We step inside some small room that open and all of us enter and the woman press something that look like bell but it didn't ring and the room start going up-up like a hawk after stealing baby hen before it vanish. I sweat, *paa*. I look hard on a sticker in the moving room that say, Year of Return. Elton smile at me. He ask me how to say thank you in Twi as the woman talk loud to Elton's black friend and white friend. I tell him *Medaase*.

You see, this is why I hate English. Something strong like *Medaase* which mean to bow your head can become Thank You which do not mean anything and do not show that you respect and come from good home. English die pass. I teach Elton to pronounce *Medaase* good. I talk in his ear like his friends do in the car, like a snake, and he laugh, *kikiki*, as if I'm tickling him and he hold my hand tight. The room stop, and I say *Yesu*

Medaase like they teach us to do at Sunday School when we arrive to a place safely without accident.

We go to a door. I watch the woman press some numbers on the wall like it is a phone. And the door open. All of us walk inside. The black and white friend laugh. Wow, they say. I mention God's name. The room is so white you think it is for Angels. The woman say bye-bye to us and go away. Elton's black friend and white friend go room to room. This house is like plenty chamber and hall and I see from the window that we have come up up. Elton come close to me and hold my hands, his hand big around mine. He say *Medaase* to me. I laugh because he sound funny. His friends come back and they take money from their pocket to give me. I become sad. "No, no." I shake my head at the dollars.

"You want cedis?"

"No, no." They look very shocked and their eyes die small. I tell them I don't want their money. I want to tell them over here you work before you get payment at end of the month but Elton smile and tell his friends to relax. "Relax," I tell them again too. The white one look at me funny. Elton say something to them and that is when he turn and kiss me. His beard scratching-scratching my chin, his hand lying on my buttocks, his tongue doing *fekyere-fekyere* to enter my mouth that I've press together tight like 1-cedi church offering. *Jesus!* I jump back.

I almost kill him.

III

KOBBY

(Kobby's meeting with the friends;
his first encounter with Nana)

It's one of those Accra nights with humid air pooling perspiration wherever fabric kisses skin. We're still at Republic, where our European-seeming neighbours keep ordering, yelling drunken slurs at the waiter. They, these whites, are quite the spectacle, demanding everyone's attention just as they demand their drinks. The waiter, a man with pinprick starter locs and the lankiness of a Fulani, looks like he might kill them. But as stories like this go, he's polite, and serves them, even curtsies when he does, laughing. He catches my eye on one of his runs, we smile.

I've already informed the group that these Germans are a sight when drunk. You must wait to see them dance! How do you know those are Germans? To most Ghanaians, you're German if you're white; something to do with the 70s and the boom in Ghana–Germany migration resulting in the emergence of German borgas, and the inclusion of *ja* in local dialects. Also, you can easily tell those are German from their appropriation of our culture without compunction, without caring about the politics of their actions. They wear our clothes, wear our hairstyles and fuck our men.

Our conversation moves from the Germans to white expats gentrifying suburbs of Accra.

"They come in, and we watch the beginnings of a thunderstorm eclipse our communities. Dark clouds swallow up the non-gentrified areas. Buildings are coated in gloom waiting for the lightning to strike. Some birds fly out before the storm of prices and high cost-of-living hit, some birds remain nesting until they are forcibly expelled. We are the birds. We are also the sky that darkens, the mood that shifts, the fist that clenches. We may have accepted the idea that if you were a local, what you used belonged to them. Tenants in our own land, we lot. We're still waiting for the signal to descend on these gentrifiers, peck and pluck out their eyes. It may never come. Our loose feathers materialise on their *Akwaaba* doormats, an attempt to forewarn. They interpret this shedding as an absit omen, a cause for joy, our plumes fashioned into feathered juju mirrors for their foyers."

I immediately take a swig of my Savanna, the subtle equivalent of slamming a palm onto my mouth to rein in my reckless loquacity, which makes me worry I'm putting too much effort into appearing charming under Scott's intense scrutiny. More so after he's caught my gaze darkening in response to the vibrations from Elton's phone.

When the Germans have broken into the offbeat hip-thrusts of white people attempting Afro dancing, Vincent and Scott, tired of my severity perhaps, begin the conversation about Nana.

Nana this, Nana that.

They're almost obsessed. My smile wavers as I listen, but I keep it nailed in place. Though, with every passing second, it rots into a grimace. Elton is too busy squeezing my thigh to sense that I am uneasy. He is the kind of tipsy that makes one horny enough to forget they are in a country where there's popular conception that mobs are waiting to ambush men caught walking hand-in-hand. It's all an exaggeration, the way foreign media depicts homophobia in countries like ours. Still, on the wrong side of town, if no elderly samaritan stopped to plead on your behalf, you'll be found bleeding into sewage systems, among all the litter and faecal matter of the populace.

"So what are your thoughts on Nana?" Vincent slaps his mug of foamy Kokoroko on the unpolished tree bark fashioned as a table, conveying an abrupt malice, which startles Elton's buzzing phone and wrests my irritation from the device. He is stout, a heavy look that makes you aware at first encounter that he likes his food fast and his morning runs short, a body type that is canonised by many women here as Mr. Otua. He is the oldest among the three, who are perhaps in their forties while he is in his early fifties, gifted with a cleft chin bulbing through the deposits of fat along his jawline, jittery fingers which may be alluding to a quick shortness of breath, and tiny punctures for eyes that give him the look of Forest Whitaker without the subastral lustre of celebrity. Despite all his peculiarities, he radiates an assuredness I've often perceived in the older men my boss fancies; the result of moneyed flashes of obscure jewellery resting on his index finger, wrist and neck, the sightings of which spark momentary twitches in my groin. He's also the most curious and asks me all sorts about anything that pops into his line of sight. And when he catches the outline of a hardback in my faux leather bag, he wants to know what my all-time favourite book is. "No one should ask a bookworm that," I respond tritely. "What is your favourite novel?" I return the question with confrontation. "*Go Tell It on the Mountain,*" he answers without missing a beat. "Obvious," I say, turning to the others, hoping that it isn't also obvious that I have never read Baldwin.

Scott, his husband, gave up speaking to me when he realised I had difficulty understanding his LA drawl, especially now that alcohol tediously drags it against the floor as one would a lifeless body. His tipsiness fizzles out minutes after downing each bottle of Shandy, allowing his eagle-eyed squint to follow my every move—not in a way that insinuates mistrust, but an introvert's manner of finely combing a stranger's gestures and features for familiar idiosyncrasies before opening up. His is the light skin that at night could be mistaken for white, making him insist to the waiters who supply his Shandy that despite his aquiline nose and his bad-spine-posture both his parents are Black. "Even my low tolerance is a testament of my Blackness," he adds with a drunken sway. We get looks from the Middle Eastern patrons at different tables, who are probably trying to come up with explanations for our unusual group of three locals and one white man, all of them angling towards us in case there's a business deal to be disclosed. Scott, his guard finally let down, now leans in to me and eagerly awaits my response after Vincent asks for my thoughts on Nana.

"Na-Na." I finally speak, after seconds of faking pensive silence, when I'm only steeling my nerves against Elton's fingers currently tracing the groin of my jeans—at the exact spot my balls are resting. "You all are pronouncing it wrong. It's Nana," I say. Vincent and Scott look deflated.

"How do y'all say that again?" Scott asks.

"Na-Na. Think of Rihanna's song, *Na-na-na, c'mon, Na-na, c'mon . . .*" The reference is lost on them. "It's not said the way you guys say 'granny' in the states."

"They play Rihanna here?"

Vincent sibilates his disapproval at his husband's question. "What do you mean by tha—Of course they do."

"I was just asking, Vincent," Scott says, a bit miffed.

"It's not a necessary question." They break into a mini-argument, which makes me slide a look to Elton. He shakes his head in a manner that suggests conversations between the two often veer into endless bickering. He winks at me—placatingly or flirtatiously, I can't tell—and moves his hands farther up my thigh. Into my underwear. Finds what he's looking for. Swipes it, this pre-cum, with his finger, which proves that I may be enjoying this *flick-tease*. He winks. His phone vibrates, interrupting this telepathic correspondence we've built over the voices of his friends. He lifts the device to his face, and the incoming notifications illuminate his private smile. Even at this table, I'm in competition with other Man4Man candidates for his bed.

"So back to Nana." Elton interrupts his friends' scuffle. "Is that right? Is that how you pronounce it?"

"Close," I concede. "I've not met Nana but he sounds quite the character. He cooks and cleans for you, you say?"

"Does our laundry, picks up stuff for us . . . it's like we're living with a host family," Scott continues. "And he doesn't want to be paid. He's not taking our money."

"Where did you find this guy again?" I ask Elton, with all the humour I can muster, managing to bottle up my rising anger.

"Facebook. He reached out to me. I thought he was cute—"

"—and gay." I grab his hand off my crotch and set it on the table. He and the others become silent for what seems like a minute, contemplating my gesture that turned out more brash than I'd intended.

"In our culture it's impolite to bring up matters of money. It's a Ghanaian thing: we're more concerned with people paying us what they think we're worth than stating our worth." I like what I represent to them: a local opinion they can trust. They are in Accra for two weeks as part of their Africa tour. ("We say Africa, but we're only seeing two countries," Vincent said mockingly earlier). I would be their eyes to a city that needed help navigating, and a brain to help them unravel the enigma that is Nana. "You'd have to give him what you think he deserves. What does he do anyway?"

"Nothing at the moment," Vincent answers. "He said his dad is a prison officer, along with his brothers. He's the only one who hasn't found his way into that service—"

"And now he's cleaning and making sure tourists are safe," Scott cuts in. All three laugh half-heartedly. I try joining them but fail, so I smile on the sidelines instead. One of us breaks the moment by looking at his watch, and we all scramble for our phones. Elton calls for the end of the night. They settle the bill.

"Hey," I call out to Starter Locs Waiter as the others leave to call a taxi.

He looks much younger on closer inspection, no signs of those strenuous lines on his forehead from a while ago.

I dig into my pouch, manoeuvre around the paperbacks. The waiter looks away politely although expectantly. "It's a tip. For all the hard-work."

"Tank you o, bros." Nigerian. He quickly grabs at the folded note. An object he misses makes a pinging sound over the tar. He picks it up, slides his fingers over the rather sharp tip of the instrument the money had been concealing. I only realise now his nails are painted. The faded red of dried blood.

"For your hair. Retwisting." I stare at the European patrons. "It's also very . . . multipurpose." It takes a moment before my intent is furtively slipped under the dim of the moonlight, into his mind. He smiles at me, wider. At this moment, the DJ plays the haunting "Suro Nnipa Na Gyae Saman." The switch from Afrobeats to old-school highlife is so unexpected, I can't help but wonder if the song is some sort of shade aimed at me.

"You're so kind," Elton tells me on my way back, throwing his hand over my shoulder. It takes a lot of fidgety resolve not to slide away from him.

In the taxi, Elton runs his fingers in circular motions over my collarbone, sliding them further into my shirt to locate a nipple. The buttons' resistance is no match for his willpower; he simply pops a few. Scott and Vincent keep the taxi driver engrossed in conversation—accomplices, buying their friend privacy so the driver won't notice what's going on in his car with its Jesus swinging on a crucifix against the rearview mirror.

"Finally! A driver that can speak English!" Scott bursts out.

"Yeah, the Year of Return has been kind to us Uber drivers. It's nice having you all around. Plenty work, plenty food to feed our wives and kids, pay school fees and everything. Please, come every year."

"We sure will!" Vincent is over-enthusiastic.

If I didn't have my mouth full with Elton's fingers, I would have managed a grunt for the Uber driver's take. The government has persuaded millions of people from the African diaspora and other curious travellers into the country to commemorate four hundred years since the first slave ship sailed away. The city feels full, engorged like a soaked, germy sponge awaiting disposal. It's rather horrific, that a year with programmes not meant for us locals is affecting us. For city dwellers like me, the Year of Return is a silo's worth of weevils boring holes into our savings. Uber prices have gone up, which is the only reason drivers are less cranky. Restaurants have hiked the prices of jollof, as no one wants to come to Ghana without trying the infamous dish Nigerians won't quit squabbling with us over. On the streets, cheaply manufactured technological accessories like earphones and chargers are now pricey owing to their high demand—which could be tied to the increased cases of pickpocketing.

I'm not complaining though. The Year of Return has brought me more lovers on Man4Man, where I've talked intersectionality, Black Lives Matter activism, and Bayard Rustin's role in the Civil Rights Movement, and gained a fuck. I've found I can be political when desperate to be thrown against a wall, or in turn can exert power over some Black Brit with toxic masculinity issues who only reinstalls Man4Man when he travels out of Peckham. *I can do both*, this man tells me in the secrecy of his hotel room. *Well, so can I*, I reply and pull out my penis, smiling wryly as we both watch it thrash about like a fish out of water.

On the app, I go off like an academic: *All you men journeying across continents to commemorate this significant event in history, only to get here and realise you've got to strip yourselves of certain identities, place your race before your sexual urges. Black queer men have been compartmentalising, proportioning their identities all their lives. Over here, we're made to navigate our lives in ways that obliterate our queerness. Over there, your Blackness is at stake, to be swallowed and limited and constrained. In all cases, we're practicing that dance of self-preservation, dancing, or rather, dangling at the edge of the oppressor's canines.*

My rants are mostly acknowledged with curt responses: *nice, interesting, kul.* As if their recipients were irritated that I'd let what could have been a great Medium post interfere with the desires of sojourners looking for a quick fuck with a strapping African male. In any case, such orations move me to the front of the queue, bypassing all the men who currently vibrate between mine and Elton's thighs.

The Uber reaches its destination in a few minutes. "What am I?" Scott asks the driver, "white or Black?" Vincent searches his wallet for the fare.

"White." The others laugh at the answer given.

"Well, for speaking good English, here's a tip," Scott sulks.

The friends are on the fourth floor of one of the apartment complexes in Ridge, an old-money Ghanaian neighbourhood with families of diverse Middle Eastern heritage who've been here as long as the Ghanaians have. As we enter the building, a congenial security man wishes us goodnight in a manner that makes it distinctly obvious that he knows what acts we will be getting up to. Either the others are clueless, or they ignore his tone. Being gay in a city like this, there are few moments I don't assume everyone's out to get me, so I keep my spine straight, my walk rigid, each step calculated. These hormonal surges of masculine energy rise to the occasion like a trusty handyman, screwing down loose limbs that need stiffening, my swinging waist that needs hammering. I become a different man; what men from Nana's ethnic group would praise. *Barima mu Barima.*

We exit the elevator into a corridor swathed in coffee wallpaper and synonymously brown carpets—"a poop dick": Scott voices his thoughts on the decor, which causes Elton to take my hand and squeeze it, winking at me before asking in low tones if I'll need to douche. And because I'd rather not watch Scott punch in the code to their apartment—the way one pretends someone's password isn't of interest and looks away—my response to Elton is a kiss on the cheek. He's caught off-guard by the gesture, smiles tightly at me, ruffles my locs and quickly scans the corridor, checking if we're alone. We are not. The cameras are an extension of the homophobic eyes of those who installed them.

"I think Nana knows the code," Vincent says once inside the apartment. I survey the minimalist open-plan living area slash kitchen. As expected of buildings like this, the interior lacks individuality, impersonal in its whiteness, harsh for the air-conditioning blasting on high, predictable for the smell of sandalwood that oozes out of an invisible diffuser. Very western, very industrial, very empty. Similar to apartments I've had to sneak out of on Monday mornings, pregnant with intestinal gas, having offered company throughout the weekend to bored, depressive expats who like to cuddle, display their collection of Annie Leibowitz photo journals, and argue—insist—on the relevance of Madonna to Lady Gaga's career. A part of me hopes Nana will spring out of this whiteness, a dark barrel of a gun staring right up my nose, adding character to this boring blandness.

"He's not around," Elton says as though sensing my stiffness. He directs me to a couch, moves to the kitchen as the other couple says their goodnights. He takes a stash of weed out of a cabinet, smiles at me the wicked smile that often follows the exhibition of something illegal. Someone, maybe Nana, must have informed him weed is prohibited here. He pours a glass of something alcoholic and offers it to me. I saunter to the counter, take the glass, and lean into him. There's an air of awkwardness that slithers around us, like it has business here. It's as though we both know what's going to happen but have no idea how it's going to start, which is characteristic of hook-ups that can't decide if they are just flings or something more. I down my glass, bang it on the counter. He takes a long pull of his weed, passes it to me. I blow smoke onto his face. "Naughty." He grins and takes my chin in his hands. For a brief moment, he is distracted by the thin scar above my brow—a relic of a bad collision. I quickly plant my lips against his. Our kiss is nothing noteworthy, two tongues scrambling for entry into the other's mouth, too many glitches before we separate. Somehow, I had been expecting this.

"Ready?" I croon hoarsely, suggesting an urgency for things to move along. Elton crosses the counter, unzips my pants and goes down on me. My bag falls off the counter, and all of its contents, including the paperbacks and pill box my boss gave me, are vomited all over the tiled floors. We take things to the room. We fuck and flip, fuck and flip. Where his nails have dug for blood, his lips follow. I spank him even if he doesn't insist. He grunts when I cum before he does. I watch him finish himself off, listening to the *fap-fap* sounds from his difficulty in busting a nut.

"Where you going?" He begs me to stay as his cum still froths over his dick and I'm hopping off the bed to search for my clothes. We lie in bed, holding each other in an odd silence. I may have heard him say *Medaase* before a heavy snore slips out of him. I sleep. And that's how Nana lets himself into my dreams. I wake up panting before he gets the chance to stab his knife into my, then Elton's, chest. I don't sleep for the rest of the night, kept awake by Elton's laborious snores and a dark presence that hovers around the apartment. My eyes constantly twitch, registering all the sounds of the night, listening for more than the crickets and the croaking frogs, until morning comes with its mundane noises. The singing birds. The crowing roosters. The momentary vrooming of cars on the quiet street below. *Brodo hyew!* The sound of bread sellers singing out their stock.

Ako balm, n'akyi yɛ ne ya, Ako balm, ne nan yɛ ne ya. Ako balm,
n'akyi yɛ ne ya ne nan yɛ ne ya, ne mfe yɛ ne ya. Then noises
more internal, more invasive. Doors bang. Blinds swing open.
Ominous footsteps muffled against carpets. I see the dark ob-
struction of feet behind the tiny space underneath our door. I
imagine ears pressed onto the thick wood, listening for sounds
of life. Then light sifts through the opening under the door
once again. I exhale. Reach for my phone and frown when my
Gmail as well as Instagram Messenger is empty. I scroll through
my timeline listlessly.

In reality, he's shorter than I expected. It's after a short sleep
that I meet him in person. Elton and I are stumbling out of the
bedroom, attempting light pre-breakfast conversation. Even
though somewhere from the apartment, Corinne Bailey Rae's
"Trouble Sleeping" streams, he keeps a steady humming of
"Ayeyi Wura" as he labours over the kitchen counter.

"Nana," we both say. If he's surprised I know his name, he
doesn't show it. He hands Elton a mug so effortlessly I get the
sense that I am witnessing a routine, that I am seated front row
at the domestication of a wild thing.

"Kobby, have you met Nana?" Vincent says, walking out of
his room with Scott in tow. Nana hands them their mugs.

"You want Nescafé," Nana asks me, without the high in-
flection one would normally end a question with. I'm not sure
I have enough words to refuse, he's already making me one. I
grab the thin glass he fills with the instant powder and watch
him pour hot water into it. I keep my eyes on him. I barely notice the liquid sliding over the edge of the glass until it sears my
skin. He moves away. I step back. I can't take my eyes off him.
Something metallic coats my tongue.

Then it happens, impossible to know when and how it begins, like mornings woken up on peed sheets. I hear it before I
can stop it. A silent crack. And then a much louder one. Burning liquid caressing my toes.

"Hey, are you okay?" Elton wrests my glass or what remains of it, the rest shattered on the floor. Nana immediately rises to the occasion and begins swiping at the blood in my hands with a white—not what I'd go for—dishrag.

I still can't keep my gaze off his face. He's more gentle with his coarse hands than I imagined he would be.

IV

KOBBY
(4 days after the friends arrive)

A ccra hides its deeds like a cat going out to fuck. Come, come. *Akwaaba.* What's ours is yours. It's welcoming to foreigners, ushering them towards stairways where they cannot see the crime and killings. I once ran into one man squeezing his hand around the throat of a girl. I stood there, seconds spent studying a rat stringing through the assailant's construction boots. Peace, I said. Shalom, he said. I walked away. Have you ever come close to being the victim of a cold-blooded murderer?

Elton doesn't seem to be interested in the stories I tell when I'm high.

"Blessed," he says, before passing me the blunt, "y'all are blessed! Too many dicks, too little throats, so many tops on y'all's damn sites." His only concern is making it to the last row of Man4Man's Hot Singles Near You page, while I too pretend I'm invested in this moment. My meandering tales are lacklustre answers to his sporadic questions about the city.

"So when are you inviting me to your place?" he asks.

I tilt my head towards the swamp of insects camping next to the patio's lightbulb and blow smoke into the dark night sky. "I live far from the city," I reply.

"You live alone?"

"Yes," I say, paying him as much mind as one would a whining fly too out of reach to swat at. Because there are bugs that don't require immediate extermination. And there's Nana, who is just as eager to see me gone.

It's been two days since Nana and I met. And—like Corinne Bailey Rae's concerns in "Enchantment," a song which has been on repeat in this apartment—I'm still obsessing over him; his hands in particular. Twice a day, to treat my lacerated palm, he manipulates the coarseness of his hands in a way that renounces all the lifetime of hardship they've endured. Once, while he was at it, I experienced a hypnosis brought on by a sense of bilocation; I was back in an ENG 601 Introduction to Nobel Laureates class, rendering the following excerpt:

What could his calloused hands produce to make her smile? . . . What could his heavy arms and befuddled brain accomplish that would earn him his own respect . . .

Nana carried on, as if reciting course material was the most natural thing to do while having one's wounds dressed. As if he didn't find disturbing my dreamy expression when he lubricated my hands with his ointment. When he asked if it was "paining me" or if he should keep going, he never considered the implications of his concern, or realised he could be fuelling my unsavoury desires. We have both transacted the stories of our lives through and into our palms by risking this intimate contact. Since this exchange between people of differing values wouldn't happen without a surcharge, without some ensuing judgement, I'm guessing he already thinks—given my soft, unmanly palms—that I'm not one to be trusted; that Ashanti way of labelling anything foreign dubious. Well, should I be following my tribal prejudices too, I'd tell you Ashantis aren't trustworthy either. Those fuckers, according to my mother, would betray flesh and blood for soup with ample meat—vampires, backbiters, all of them. Elton, are you listening? I hear Nana cleaning as you and I smoke weed out on the patio. The running tap. The dishes clashing against the sink. The chafing of the dishrag over the wet plates. He's staring at us, yes. I sense it. Elton, do you not?—

"Take me to your place. I want to see that bookshelf where your nudes are staged. Do you write too?"

"No. Where did you get this weed from? It's fucking mind-altering. One minute I'm whispering gibberish to myself, the next I'm addressing you in language that makes me doubt my sanity."

"Ha! Got it from here, actually. Through an old friend of mine's contact. This old friend used to live in Ghana, lived quite large too—I mean open, not large. He frequented this gay club called 10 Pounds and there was some other gay night at a club he called Epo's. He kept telling me Accra's as free as New York before Giuliani. Though for a fuck, he'd still pay money boys or whatever you call them here. One of them is this weed guy who asked if I wanted other services after handing me the package. That made me laugh, considering you were sprawled up in my bed that minute, like a mistress, a satisfied one too. I told him that'll be all . . . this weed works wonders, doesn't it . . ."

The image of Nana languishing in my peripheral vision obstructs what little attention I've given you, Elton. But you push your lips into my neck to regain my focus. That wetness against skin, I feel it in my groin. And Nana feels it through the tiny cleavage in the glass partition's blinds. Nana, what are you? Why have you got beguiling eyes? Why can you not—

My chin is forced about its axis and I am staring into your eyes now, Elton. You ask: "Are you high yet? You zoning out already? Tell me more about yourself."

"I'll tell you a story about cats, a story about growing up. Won't you be lucky to know a story about my childhood? I never think about my past, but I'll tell this story because it's relevant for you to understand who Nana is, Elton."

"You just be chatting shit when you're high," Elton laughs.

Knock. Knock. The blunt falls from my hand to the floor.

We are interrupted. Elton's fingers go limp on my thigh. The faint odour of something my olfactory senses can't place and that lemony dishwashing detergent which sticks to Nana's clothes mingle with the smell of weed, almost overpowering the latter. We're made to feel guilty for our seamless, carefree lives as he labours in the background. Since our meeting, the vicious opening of Slimani's *Lullaby*—a novel investigating the murderous motives of Louise, its psychotic maid—has been on constant loop in my mind. I see Louise in Nana anytime I watch him summon an orderly cleanliness into the mess we leave behind. In my nightly AESMA rituals, I find myself fantasising about the moment Nana snaps. Like Louise. His choice of weapon digging into our bodies as he splatters the messy art of our lazy lives onto the white walls, painting an entire apartment with our privilege.

"I go now." Nana says this without looking in our direction.

"Thanks, Nana," Elton says, and attempts to close the patio doors. But Nana plants his foot in the way.

Odd silence, in the background of which permeates the *shhh* sounds of a spattering shower and an off-key vocal impression of Diana Ross's "I'm Coming Out"; Scott yelling at Vincent to shut up and asking Vince if he isn't aware he's putting Mama Ross to shame.

"You going out tonight?" Nana asks.

"No." Elton rises and stretches his hand to him. "We'll be fine." Nana doesn't take the hand immediately. A dog, can't shake him off. In the two days we've been touring Accra, he would not let Elton and his friends leave his sight. Around me, he growls under his breath, attempting a bark. Back off. Last night, as I stood rinsing my face in Elton's bathroom, lingering over the scar above my brow, I noticed, through the mirror, a sliver of yellow reflected against the bathroom's white tiles, a foreign light. Elton's and his friend's voices rang loud with laughter on the balcony so I knew none of them could have opened the door I was sure I had banged shut. No one besides Nana could have been hounding me. I allowed him to watch. As I tucked an olanzapine under my tongue. As I spat the deformed tablet back into my boss's old pill box. And then I grinned at the mirror. Before kicking the door shut. I wouldn't trust Nana if I was Elton. I wouldn't trust me if I was Elton.

Nana flicks his gaze to me. "Your hand, issokay?" I nod after a while, feeling odd that he's repaying my glares with kindness. His eyes find my hand and what looks like a smile curves his lips. This smile isn't directed at me, just a sense of pride at his own work. I'm struck by a sudden cognisance, realising a newness to the bland modifications of his face. But those facial muscles quickly default to their usual impassiveness, leaving me wondering if there was ever a smile at all. My phone lights up. I turn to it. Caller ID says **Dad**. I turn from it.

"We are ready." Vincent and Scott come out of their rooms, the former tugging a shirt over his belly. Nana looks at them, then looks back at Elton. Nana looks at me. My phone vibrates. I put it on silent.

"Don't keep long, o." Nana speaks in an authoritative voice, a parent announcing a curfew. "Something bad happening in the night these days . . ." He tosses a frown my way. "There's . . . there's a Ga mantse that have die. It's not good thing to stay late in the night—"

"I am sure we'll be fine, Nana." There's an edge to Elton's voice.

"I will buy fish tomorrow to come cook," Nana announces, walking proprietorially towards the door as if he's showing someone out. And with that, he leaves. Yet his aura, the parts of him he has sealed into every pore of this apartment he's cleaned, seeps into the air, displacing the air-diffuser's aromatic breath. We all inhale his absence in our silence. Fish. That's it: fish. That's the smell he leaves behind. Suspicion.

"Who is this guy?" Scott asks no one in particular, then turns to me, "What did he mean by the death of someone?"

"When a chief dies, he's buried with human heads." All three flinch. "No chief's died, I would know. He just wants you to stay in."

"Oh, well then. We are late." Vincent announces jovially. "Kobby, we are ready to see Gay Accra."

My phone pings. **1 new message from Dad**: *Am locking the gate. Take your medicines.*

V

NANA

(4 days after the friends arrive)

Wo feefee efunu ani ase aa wo huni saamaa.* When you look-look into the eyes of a dead person, you will see maggots. My grandmother used to say this proverb to me whenever I want to look-look things plenty. My teacher say, curiosity killed the cat. Tell me now, which make more sense?

I am telling you, English is dead, no aroma. Even if some like it more than Twi because it sweet from the white man mouth. Me, I'll tell you that it's sweet as the aroma coming from this gutter.

I have to say that the whole of Accra, this gutter I'm standing by, smell like a place people can sleep inside. I sleep inside some bad gutters before because I come to Accra and no family member will answer my call. And I will tell you this, Accra is not a nice place to sleep outside. If mosquitoes don't kill you, life itself will pity you and kill you. Zoomlion wake you up even before 6.00 A.M. wanting to sweep the road as if it is their living room. And if somebody is nice to you, it is because they want to steal from you or want you to vote for them in assemblyman election. Eat one food a day and you will be lucky. But if you want to eat more than once, you have to use your empty stomach to work in a chop bar and pound big fufu. If you live on the road in Accra, you will see things. You will see things even God cannot see. Bad, bad people doing wicked things you cannot think of.

Right now, I know I am looking for trouble. My body and mind don't feel right. But I don't trust the guy with the hair like snakes. I have to protect my friends. My pastor say they need me plenty so they don't go to hell. That's why I am here, near the nicest gutter of my life by the nicest hotel I will ever see.

Ambassadorial Hotel is the name of the hotel. It is bigger than Elton and his friend's place, so many cars and so many people walking out and in. Not bigger than my uncle cocoa farm, but close. You will never think a place like this is in Ghana here. But Accra is different from Ghana plenty-plenty. Accra is like America, where the people are rich and they accept gay-gay things. I don't know why Elton and his friends decide to come to this hotel with the guy who has snake on his head. Every hotel is a prostitution background, my pastor say to us in church.

My pastor decide that I should put my eye for ground when it comes to Elton and his friends. When Elton kiss me, my pastor get angry that I didn't kiss him too, because kiss is nothing. He show me a video of the Roman Father who is old kissing people and I understand. We'll be having Harvest in the church too, so my pastor is afraid that if I don't kiss Elton he will not give me money to put in the envelope they make us share to people who are not even members of the church, so they can put money in to help build the church. Maybe Pastor want church big like Ambassadorial Hotel, because we been building and building and building plenty times. I was going to listen to Pastor, and kiss Elton well-well. But when I come the next day, the guy with the snakes on his head already coming out of Elton room.

Over here we say *suro nnipa, na gyae saman*. Fear man and stop fearing ghosts. One day, I was walking to my house when I saw this Rasta who was walking alone, from the back she look beautiful, *paa*. I follow her until she pass some dark corner. I don't stop walking faster-faster. She walk faster-faster too. I think she vanish from my eyes. But I saw her again. She was walking to two people now. A man and woman. The man have all to fly and knock our heads against the makeshift polyvinyl ceiling. In the heated car, someone on my row popped open a rubber-sealed window, and another passenger seated by me exclaimed gratefully, "*Ah oyiwala doŋ!*" I turned to this person, finally facing the old man who kept dozing off on my shoulder. He was a tiny human, his feet never touching the woodboards that made up the car's flooring. Smelt of ayelɔ and baby oil, a scent that was both sweet (in the first few seconds of taking it in) and sickening (after an hour of sitting in it). His salt-and-pepper hair had enormous bald patches, a maplike scalp which appeared honourable, conferred by time and genetics to imply the man's awareness of colonial and present-day geographies, hence his irredeemable prompts to attempt unknown routes steering our lorry further into the city's treacherous vehicle-infested swamps.

A chorus of ululating voices stole my attention from this old man. In the rural community the vehicle was held up at, two men were being paraded by an army of civilians who all held sticks and canes. Forgetting our traffic distress, all of us passengers leaned towards the windows. We were grateful that our slow-moving car was tailing the procession, offering us a perfect view of the scene unfolding. We all thought these men thieves, but the group's murmurings, which crawled in tandem with our *tro-tro*, told otherwise. *Koo Bee. Gbeei. Gay.* The words chanted over and over again as the two men were commanded to kneel. The mob began what they assumed a form of discipline, lashing these men. "*Bo no, bo no,* beat him, *me kraa me tumi si firi car yi mu ara mɛ baa bɛ bo ɔmo bi.*" The people in my vehicle sang, a Greco-Roman audience offering support for the brutal violence unleashed in an arena. The moment flesh gave way to splotches of blood, I turned away.

"Hey, hey," a hand tapped me on the shoulder. "Hey," another hand swiped across my vision. It was the old man, speaking through the noise. "Where do you do your hair?"

His fingers invaded my locs then drew my chin so I faced him. "Hey, I'm talking to you, you don't hear?" he said louder, snapping his fingers in my face, twisting his head to the musicality of his remonstrations.

Transformed he did before my eyes, becoming a nebulous thing with mannerisms stretching across the boundless jurisdictions of some gender identity yet to be disclosed. Enthralled by him/them, I pushed away the violence which soon became a distant memory, a trauma I would occasionally grapple with and smooth under my skin as if I was attending to something as simple as an itch, associating it, this trauma, with the warm tactile memory of the most acute interlocking needle pressed into my palm, along with the voice of its mythical owner saying, "This needle can be used for anything you want, not only for hair, but to protect yourself, fa bɔ wo ho ban, be safe."

This was my first encounter with the old, gender-defying loctician who owns a salon at Kaneshie. At their insistence, I always carry the interlocking needle in my pouch. It would become my only harness for a life that could so easily be taken away in one, wrong, sealed fate.

place to be: a cultured event. And right here at the Ambassadorial Hotel, right here at this opening-night exhibition of some famous artist, one can find the culture and the cultured.

The Culture: the glasses of wine you, your friends, and I are greeted with at the swivel doors. "Oooh," you push your meaty face into mine and swoon. I have to visibly recoil when the security men give us a funny look at our closeness and for your carelessness, Elton. I briskly usher us all into the building. "Swanky," Vincent says upon entrance. We're accosted by another server before we can take the whole place in. You ask what this is, pointing at a ball-like treat that has a shiny brown coating. "Looks like shit," Scott whispers. "*Adaakwa*, gluten-free, taste it." I say. "Spicy," Scott yelps, and returns what's left to the tray. The server picks up the remainder with a tissue and folds it away. He doesn't hide his irritation. "I like it," you smack your lips, "I like it a lot." I smile. I like you a lot, Elton. We walk through the foyer. You palm the walls and ask about the *adinkra* that are embossed on them. "Akan hieroglyphics," I answer. "What does this mean?" Vincent asks, pointing at one symbol shaped as a comb. I stutter. "Let's take a picture, maybe Nana would know," you offer. I leave you three to it and head out into the grand lobby. The chandeliers look like fangs suspending from the vaulted ceiling. The walls are teeming with horrifying shadows of the giant sculptures of Ashanti warriors frozen in battle. I watch you brush your hand against the tip of one woman's sculpted gun. "Yaa Asantewaa," I say. "Be careful, she bites." A doorman of sorts sporting an off-white suit with a bow-tie, his hair shiny and permed—which is the butt of Scott's joke: *Y'all got Benson here serving creamy crack*—curtsies, and asks if we came to see the exhibition. He takes us through a simulated Moroccan-style door painted over the walls and says, "*Akwaaba*," to which Vincent responds, "*Medaase*." We are greeted by loud instrumentalists playing Osibisa's "Welcome Home." "Oh, that's from *Coming to America*," Vincent pipes up, taking out his phone to record them. I do not tell him he's wrong. "Accra is bouuuugieee," you whisper to me, your hot breath tickling my skin and making me giggle.

The Cultured: Everyone in Accra's art scene is the same people in Accra's literary scene, also the same people in Accra's academia scene. We've all seen one another at some point and behave like distant relatives who have to endure conversation with each other. You watch me air-kiss a couple of people. I make a few shallow introductions (name, occupation, known-for), and these close strangers and I talk about the artist and how we are so excited Google commissioned her. "Google?" Scott inquires, looking at the art hanging over our heads with a cynic's interest. "Nice meeting you, darling," person after person says to me, "let's have coffee sometime and catch up." You note all the differing accents with a curiosity that shoots up a brow. Accra too is like that, it's like all cosmopolitan cities in the world. *Amigo, just 'cause we're all très chic and elite and bougie from all places in zhe world don't mean it got to be expensive and shit, it's all kak, innit?* Slang-ccents swirl around us like we're straws in an elaborate cocktail. And because Accra's so small, I spot my boss among her group of friends and duck.

On and on we meander through the packed gallery, through all of Accra's art scene. You move away to study the art on the walls. "06.03.1957 Galleria." Vincent reads out the name of the gallery lettered bold and black, high up the white walls. "That date is familiar," he says. "Now don't tell me, I will remember, always been a genius in history class, still a genius. I'll remember." Scott interrupts Vincent's infantile glee: "I hate it here, it's so crowded." Vincent tuts. "You shouldn't have come then," Vincent says. "Well, if I knew it was going to be this crowded . . . is it always this much?" Scott turns to me. I usher them towards an air-conditioner in a spacious spot. "Better now?" I ask Scott. He shrugs. "It's our date of Independence," I say to Vincent. He frowns at me for offering the answer to his self-imposed quiz and says, "That's right, the first country to attain independence in Africa."

Elton, I have noticed strange habits in your friends. They are good, even nice people, kind and tolerable. They are armed with their Pleases and Thank Yous and their tips—traits realised less and less in foreigners. But, in the same way old paintings have craquelure, often considered as works of art themselves, your friends are not without flaws. Flaws so bearable others may look on them as delightful quirks. I know I have got my own delightful quirks. Delightful quirks so questionable others may look on them as flaws, giant red flags to avoid. Better for you not to see them. Or if you have seen them, I wouldn't know. I still think you like to believe the good in everything and everyone, just as you have for your friends—to love them despite their flaws; a trusting little puppy buried in the hulk of a man like you. Your own flaw, so contrary to Scott's.

Scott observes everything with such creased brows and a wrinkling of his nose that you'd think he was a disdainful mother-in-law hunting for a film of dust. In the first days of meeting him, I wanted to believe he was getting acquainted with the scents of Accra, which sometimes can be a lot to take in, I must admit; whether it is the spicy scent of ground pepper that hits the back of your throat in an effort to choke you, the ubiquitous smell of sewer, the *borla* cars that drive by and make you hold your breath for seconds. But we are at the Ambassadorial Hotel, one of the few places in Accra whose scents are a pleasant set of floral and fruity notes, and yet, he's got this expression. With this same look, he picks up menus at restaurants, tosses them away in seconds, deciding he's not ordering anything. He's the archetype of that tourist who views different places under the lens of his home country. As though to him travel is for discovering and continually affirming that one's culture, his culture, is superior to others'. I imagine this will be why Nana will want to kill him: those two little condescending holes for eyes. Stab little knives in them and leave them tearing. I cop a glass from a passing tray and push it in his direction. He's caught off-guard by my gesture. He hides his irritation with a smile and accepts the wine. I turn to you, Elton, a big bear of a man in another version of your large t-shirt and sagging baggy shorts look, drawing eyes everywhere you go. I must tell you why market women in Accra are drawn to you, but I love watching your puzzlement as woman after woman walks up to you and asks for your number. Your attention has never left the art pieces. You are so caught up in the worlds these paintings offer, you haven't yet noticed that all around you is Accra's gay scene. This really is why I brought you here. We live in a country where gays can only express themselves through art, only coming out of their hiding places during art exhibitions.

Spot the fashion gays who totter around speaking in high-pitched tones that beg for everyone's attention. "I fucked the guy that just walked in," you hear them tittering. They are only here for the free wine and the nibbles and, of course, to out other supposedly hetero men. Spot the muscle and Rasta gays who are paired up with older white men they're chaperoning around town. They say to these white people, "I love art too, in my home I have got lots of pieces." They're lying: the only artwork they've got are the Jesuses framed with Bible quotes from Matthew. They're escorts, paid to be given a blow job. Vincent leans in to me and says, "Man4Man has nothing on this," so I know he's paying close attention. If you do too, you'll spot the DL gays, the ones standing at the outskirts of it all, unfitting sociopaths, here to scope out other discreet gays. They spot each other and they nod. They see the fashion gays and they look away. I smile. Vincent smiles. Scott huffs like the air-conditioning above. I look your way, hoping to see you blinded by a painting, but I catch you looking at me. Your gaze, needling through Accra's elitist-cum-pretentious folk, is intent, as though only I matter. It's this habit of yours that I find uncomfortable. Just like those times I search vast, busy streets for you; worried about your whereabouts; worried I lost you to peddlers who scream and shove their wares at foreigners like you; worried I lost you to peddlers who aren't really peddlers, who lie about wares that may interest you in faraway mazes of shops. Me, speaking Twi to hawkers, speaking Twi to everyone, anyone—*Paakyew w'ahu man yi*. Then I find you watching me, like now, in my unguarded moments. You smile. My lips quiver.

"Who knew all you needed to do to find the gays was walk into an art exhibition?" Vincent says, diverting my attention from you.

"Now's a good time to match the mysterious torsos on Man-4Man with their real faces," Scott quips.

As the gay scene augments and becomes more conspicuous in the gallery, like a gushing stream of water piling around a boulder, I stand on the periphery and wonder which group I fit into. I wonder into what category other gay men will place me, spotting me with three older year-of-returnees. I never try to fit myself into these stereotypical labels that I nonetheless foist, like preexisting regnal names, on other queers. This delusional othering of myself disassociates me from the community. As if all the known alphabets (from the L, to the G, the B, the T, even the Q) fail to address my identity. As if I'm holding out for another letter, a new sexual-behavioural ethnotype—yet to be discovered—for someone who loves sucking the dick of travellers and delights in ephemeral trysts.

The Bougie: The crowd weaving through the loud band which everyone ignores and regards a nuisance is extra pretentious, given the abstract art pieces, too, could lend themselves to whatever absurd interpretations. I consider asking the others if they want to ditch Elton and head out into the lobby. Having had enough of the conversations that dart right into my ears as though I have offered them as a bullseye target. But I see my boss still wedged at the exit. Tall, thin, tittering among her people. I'm not surprised she is here. This is the circle to which she belongs. This same diaspora and subaltern been-to crowd she constantly harangues about on Mondays after these events, her gum-wrapped tongue sliding out of her obsidian lips in scintillating animadversions about *New Yorkers who are in fact just from the Bronx and not Manhattanites as they claim, Hackney-based mixed-race artists whose only connection to East London lay in that deadbeat Ghanaian dad and we all know—draws airquotes—Hackney-based which ideally follows BAME, is deffo strategically placed in a bio as a currency to access grants, residencies and such. And bruv, don't even get me started on the Swedish and Ukranian trained doctors, the Taiwanese and the Chinese ESL teachers, coming back to Ghana on their annual leaves just so they can turn up at DLT and be ballin' with all the other March or December Returnees.* Every one of these kinds of guests has a chin tilted upwards, holding themselves upright and uptight as if they might unravel if they loosened up. They sometimes speak with a foreign accent or a fake one (LAFA, we call them—Locally Acquired Foreign Accents), exchanging contact cards and swapping smiles that often resemble soundless snarls. Tigresses. It's not easy spotting the sore thumbs, the lambs. Everyone excels at performing a uniform choreography of ostentatiousness. That game of frivolous, pretentious, auto-generated small-talk often gleaned in tea-party scenes in Austen-esque novels. Albeit this is a very Accra kind of pretence; as in "I have read *The Beautyful Ones Are Not Yet Born* and Fanon," and, "I love Osibisa and Fela," and, "I have visited Marrakech and Mombasa." There are times I've wanted to play the deviant during these scenes, the Darcy abstaining from the superficiality, waiting on an errant guest to launch into a tirade: *Fuck this. Fuck this. Fuck this repetitive strain of draining refrains. Let's deconstruct the symbols of trauma, heartbreak, grief in these art pieces and how they mirror our own trauma, heartbreak, grief. Tell me who taught you to die on the inside while fake-laughing on the outside. Show me the sides you cover up in public bathroom mirrors. Are you also dark? Were you also abused by a neighbour, or a family member? How old were you before you knew that hand on your lips and that hush weren't signs of affection? How long did it take for you to hand over the pearly-whites of your childhood glee in exchange for this nicotine-tainted anxiety society calls adulting? What Blue Mondays have you masked with Mona Lisa's smile?*

The Poverty: I can barely thrive in companies like these, who relate their wanderlust in an attempt to compete with one another. To stretch out their flamboyance and soak up the sunlight at the expense of disadvantaged weeds like me. The spotlight is only reserved for the few tall enough to access it, their diaspores light enough to be dispersed into foreign lands. It turns out that I am the sore thumb, the shrivelled piece of stump axed by my obligatory budget cuts to survive an exorbitant city like Accra. I watch everyone else bloom, as I wait for the piercing of new shoots. And as my gaze weaves through the disentangled leaves which float as their trees gesticulate their self-importance, it settles on a familiar figure. Another shrivelled piece of stump. Hardened and browning amongst the sea of green. Nana.

Someone hits me on the shoulder. I turn.

"Kobby!" My name is hurled like a punch.

"Oh, hi!"

I make the introductions: "Elton, Scott, and Vincent, meet Brian." I search the room for the stump and you are not there anymore. Did I imagine you, Nana? I admit that I am obsessed with you. My own little stalker. I fancy that idea sometimes. Maybe my kink is being jumped in the dark and fucked senseless. You, Nana, look like the type who could help me realise my desires. It's no secret I'm obsessed with you. More than I am with Elton. Even when he makes me cum, it's the thought of you hovering next to the patio's glass partition that readies my dick for the avalanche. You're the pre-cum. You're watching, always watching. I wring my neck to check for pockets of air. I square my shoulders. I make my stance more impressive. I'm putting on a show for you. If you're really here, I hope I'm a delight to watch.

"You are being a stranger, Kobby," Brian says after giving my company a once-over.

"I actually came to the opening because I knew you would be here."

Brian theatrically tosses his loc extensions behind him, revealing one of those crucifix earrings. I have already informed Vincent and Scott of the one giveaway for knowing someone might be queer in Accra: If they have extensions, they could be queer. A wearer of extensions myself in the past, I hated the rubbery feel of the synthetic locs on my neck, felt like tiny ants crawling all over. I once scratched my skin sore until I couldn't take it anymore, I had to take them out. I walked around for a week caressing the scars with pleasure, as if they were serrations from a lover's nails.

"I like your shoes," says Vincent.

"Thank you! You know, I have a saying: All good animals go to heaven, unless they're exotic—then I want them for shoes!" Brian quips. "Can you guess what animal these are from?"

"Looks like . . . some dog?" Vincent suggests.

"God," Brian rounds his shoulders and arranges his limbs and features into a portrait of gay shock. "Do not make the mistake of associating me with my family's business in Lawra's dog-meat market! I've been disinherited! Take another guess!"

Finding out which sad creature decided Brian's shoes made a good graveyard isn't the problem here. The problem is Vincent. He is far too eager. That's his flaw. His words invariably wedge themselves into others' conversations. He plays the role of the keen tourist, wagging his tongue at everything, pushing his head down to get petted by the locals. He has picked up a plethora of local phrases to surprise his Uber driver and lower-class service personnel, so trusting of everyone he doesn't mind engaging anyone in conversation. "That's how you learn, Kobby!" He guffaws anytime he catches me staring through creased brows after doing something I've warned him against. I wonder if it's this flaw Nana would take advantage of, too easy to trust that Vincent wouldn't see the brick coming down on his skull. I look at him now, thrusting his hand toward Brian. "Vincent from LA; we're all from LA."

"Y'all came here for the Year of Return too, right?" Brian looks at Scott, who regards him with those condescending eyes of his, sweeping his gaze over the former's mudcloth tunic and deciding to remain unimpressed even though all he's been asking for since his arrival is an African tailor who will sew him all the traditional outfits he spots.

"Yes," Vincent answers for Scott.

Elton, you are so bored you have stuffed your hands into the pockets of your baggy shorts, flicking your eyes between Brian and the art in an effort not to appear rude.

"I am looking to invest here though. Love it."

Brian rolls his eyes at Vince's remark. "You Black Americans." As Vincent asks what he means by that, Brian turns from him and says to me, "You still got my number?"

"Yes, I do."

"Okay love, see you around." Brian flashes us a wide smile, his way of showing off the little piece of gold installed in his teeth, but unwittingly reveals a canine sullied with *adaakwa*. He almost leaves.

"We were hoping you'd take us to the more private places," Vincent says before I can stop him.

Brian looks at me, "Well, of course, that's the only reason you'd be here."

"Not," I say almost too quickly and bite my lip. "Elton here loves art. He wanted to be here."

Brian sighs and turns to the others. "Go back to your hotel, darlings. Nothing will be happening tonight." He kisses his teeth and walks away.

I follow briskly. "Brian. Brian." His heels make cringey sounds against the tiled floors, a little child whacking at a silver utensil with a spoon. "Brian." All efforts to get him to halt are useless and I follow him out of the gallery and into the lobby, dodging the trays of the servers and narrowly avoiding my boss's gaze.

"You know what your problem is, Kobby?" Brian whirls to face me in the secluded entryway to the bathrooms. "You are such a fucking slave to exotic cock." Right there is my categorisation, right there's my label: *Slave to Exotic Cock.* "Always inviting these outsiders into spaces reserved for us."

"I am just always so busy. That's why we haven't seen each other in a while." Wish I could avoid him forever, but Brian is my access to the underground. I have never been a part of the community to be privy to its rhythms. Elton and his friends need Brian.

"Same excuses as always," Brian hisses.

"I finally got a paying gig—"

"I know. For four fucking years, the only evidence I had to prove you are living is that deathly job you do. Where were you when we needed you?" He yanks up his tunic, showing me a deep scarring on his shin. "This is all your doing. You are never going to get access to us." He enunciates every syllable of his next verbal punch: "Cow-ward." He moves around me and heads into the night's outline beyond the hotel's exit.

I turn to the throng of people in the hotel lobby. Everyone's too caught up in their little conversations to have witnessed the scene. And then I see you, sticking out like an end of a carpet that hides something dark underneath. The wound under the bandaging on my hand flares.

"Hey." Elton comes into the empty bathroom aisle. I look over his shoulders to confirm if it was you I saw, Nana. "He's a bit of an ass." For a second I wonder if it's you he's talking about. "I don't mind if we don't see Accra's secretive gay scene. I'm in this country to have fun, and I'll have it either way, my way." He's pushing his meaty head into my face now, and even though I swear I saw you a while ago, all I see now is him.

"He'll come around." I finally mouth, not sure if I am indeed talking about Brian.

"He seemed really annoyed."

"He has every reason to be."

"Oh?"

"I have been avoiding him since . . ."

"You avoid people a lot." He smacks my ass.

"We are in Ghana." My rebuke is swift and razor-sharp as if I am chiding someone who should know better. Maybe if I quoted the statistics of deaths caused by homophobic attacks he'd be more careful. But I do not. So he takes a step further, begins rubbing his groin against mine, while nosing hesitant kisses against my neck, my chin, on the contours of my lips, a dog sniffing another's heat. I finally budge. My mouth parts for his tongue. It feels like I have let go of the handles of a playground slide, uninhibited and free.

We don't only kiss. Things escalate quickly. He pushes me into the bathroom, where the harsh orange candescent lights reveal his features crumpled into something like a fist. He slams my back through the swing door of an empty stall, where there's a blob of poop trying to stay afloat in the pool of yellow. There's no going back now, we've breached the point of no return.

During public sex, foreplay isn't a forgotten formality. Rather, it's elusive, measured by infinitesimal fractions of a second, or just plainly edited out to make for a racier porn clip. Foreplay is in the thrill of being caught; the song of one's heart's palpitations. It's in the eyes; the silent signals sent to each other—*Pull down your pants*—because talking becomes an even riskier venture than the sex itself. Bent over, waiting with bated breath, listening to the belt buckle's jingle or the zipper's whine, is foreplay. Also, the glitches, the silent howl and the hasty retreat after a dick's first stab, the harvesting of spit to lube up for another attempt. Deciding on a tempo: *You good?* Fucking. Foreplay over. Clip starts.

With each thrust, Elton kneads me into subservience, forces my cheek onto the cold tile, next to the tiny opening under the stall. I am so distracted by my body's seamless ductility that I spend a few seconds marvelling at this feat of contortion. It takes a while to catch the odd whiff of fish snaking through all that bathroom disinfectant. I brush off my paranoia, choosing instead to indulge in this heady moment plucked right out of the playbook of Hollywood gay sex scenes.

I don't doubt you're watching us, Nana. Your voyeurism doesn't bother me. Imagining you, separated by thin walls, or climbing onto a toilet to peer into our stall, fuels my excitement for this risk I'm taking.

Here, look at me.

When I look behind, Nana, it's your ebony skin I see—your groin wiggling its way into my ass, your dark hands clamping my mouth shut as I whimper from the force of being taken without lube, without another bout of spit. What this springs up is a memory of a Facebook post by a major local news outlet propositioning yet another non-neutral debate on the legalisation of homosexuality in Ghana, providing a platform for airheads and one quasi-academic commenter who, after outlining his degrees—which included one dubious doctoral event at LSE, declared that "gayism" must remain criminalised because the gays import way too much lube in a country where decreasing imports may be crucial to rescuing its failing economy. If only he and his cronies could see us now, playing our part in nation-building. Although this brand of self-denial and patriotism doesn't come without cost, without excruciating pain—the reason I gnaw at your salty fingers with a ferality whose reward is a thundering fist flung into my spine. I gasp. For your extremist

Pentecostal faith, it's highly likely this may be your first time indulging in the paradise that is anal sex, so your inexperience, your selfishness, your disregard of my humanness I let slide. In doing so, I am transformed into your object. Diminished to nothing but a hollow hole, which you must

Keep plunging,
Shove all of you into me,
Recklessly,
Hurt me with intention.
Don't spit,
Split me.
Treat me like your fucking little whore.
Do you like that?
Do you like it when I call myself a
Whore
Slut
Bitch
You like it when I emasculate myself for you, don't you?
Fuck yeah
Don't stop even as I cum.
Even as it gets painful.
Give me that cock, Daddy.
When you feel me clench,
That's my prostate singing.
I'm about to nut.

You hoist me up and spin me round to face you. When I see your eyes, the fantasy is broken. Reality stinks.

Elton.

I watch jizz splatter on me like I'm a workplace men's bath-room tile during lunch-break. My smile is feigned as he laughs and brings his face into mine for a closing credits kiss. "Was it good?" he asks. He scoops the cum spiralling down my chin and smears it onto my lips. I turn away, reaching for my clothes to put an end to the performance. "It was good," he repeats, "wasn't it?" There's a lingering jab in my ass; it's possible his dick has left a mess of open wounds which may grow into tumorous cysts. To appease my hypochondria, I have to visualise chugging down any of the over-the-counter antibiotics/painkillers I've been stockpiling for when I'm struck by that perfect mix of boredom and courage, and the light above feels too bright.

"You were noisy," I tell him. I walk out of the stall as I hear the bathroom door open, avoiding the eyes of the white stranger who walks in.

Elton remains trapped in the stall, granting me a few minutes to regain my composure before I head back to his friends.

VII

PRAYER REQUEST FOR THE PRAYER BOWL FOR PRAYER
WARRIORS OF JESUS LOVES ME CHURCH TO GIVE TO GOD
(written by Nana; 5 days after the friends arrive)

D ear God,
How do you start to write a prayer request that is not
easy like Break and Go miracles and Travelling Mercies? But Father Lord, your word say we should come to you
when we are weary. So please take my prayer request which
come in the form of a long story.

Stories like this start like all good Anansesεm. First, you see
Ananse, a man walking into a car. Not *tro-tro*. This Ananse does
not like to sit with poor people and listen to us talk politics or
find one man get up and preach in the car so that the driver
does not ask him to pay and he gets money from the passengers
in the *tro-tro* as offering. Father Lord, You are an all-knowing
God, and You know why they call the lorry *tro-tro*—because
first it cost *tro*, very little, to board it. But I also think that they
call it *tro-tro* because, first-first, when it move, you will hear *tro-
tro* from deep inside the engine-engine. But now, plenty cars
that they have write Dutch and German on the body have become *tro-tro*, nice-nice 207 cars, cars so proper you can't hear
the engine choke-choke when they move. Which is why we say
that a name will never go away; a good name stay with you, a
bad name will also stay with you. Just like Ananse, who will
forever be Ananse in my eyes even if You, oh God, do not answer my prayer and use me as your vessel to kill him. It's as if
the Uber driver already knows that this Rasta is going to Osu.
That's where all the Rastas like, where the *obronis* are there

plenty. This Uber Driver only care about Rasta name, and his name according to Uber Driver phone is Kobby.

But we'll call him Ananse, because we don't know where this Kobby is from, where his clan takes their powers, what is his people's animal, where his people go when they die. We know nothing about him. Where I come from, if no one knows your last name you are not a person. You are a thing. So we will call this Kobby, Ananse.

I have not met this Ananse yet. By this time Elton and his friends have come from the airport. How Elton find out about Ananse, no one knows. I thought I was his only Ghanaian friend. But maybe, because I don't want to kiss him, he found someone else, Ananse. Maybe with Facebook. Or Hi5. Or one of those things that help you talk to people you don't know when the world wake up one morning and say that Facebook and Hi5 is *tete-tete* so we should all join another place. I don't know. All I know is, Elton and his friends have made me go home. They told me they are tired from going to the market and seeing Oxford Street. I even took them to Art Centre and I help them get things at good prices when the sellers want to cheat them. After all this, all I have done for them, they are ungrateful and find another friend just because I didn't kiss Elton. Well, one of us will die. Let's wait and see.

Let's wait for Elton and his friends to play hide-and-seek with me and leave their house at night to meet Ananse. He'll be here in ten minutes, he says to Elton in WhatsApp. And when the driver arrive at Republic and Rasta alias Ananse alias Kobby, all the names they will put on his obituary, aged 27 or something, get out of the car without causing trouble like Rastas do—even though the Uber get stopped by the police and Rasta gets searched for *wee* (he does not have *wee*)—the driver thank Jesus and drive away quickly.

So here is Kobby, standing in Republic, looking exactly like his Facebook picture because Elton wave at him to come join them. He walk to join them on their table outside, passing by *obronis* and waiters running around. "Hi, my name is Kobby," he tell Elton's friends, who already like him because he's Ananse. He looks good, doesn't look hard like me. They tell him all they have done since coming to Ghana. And because they think Kobby will know me, they decide to tell him about me.

Elton and his friends don't know anything about Kobby, but over here in this Ghana, your dressing and your hairstyle judge you. No one would take Rasta, who wear tight clothes like his parents didn't raise him well, home. But Elton do so.

I know all this because I don't hurry-hurry to leave. I wait outside in the bush in front of their big storey building and watch. Remember this bush, take note of it, *paa*. I will kill someone here. That person will be Rasta Kobby Ananse. Who my heart burn me the moment I see him with my friends come out of an Uber and walk into the building.

I leave the bush and follow them after a while, pressing the knife in my pocket to check if it's there and feeling blood from my *kaka* fill my mouth. If this Rasta man try anything on Elton and his friends I'm going to kill him, and then Elton will know how dangerous it is to invite Rasta people to his house. Or anybody you don't know honestly. This Ghana is not safe. Rastas are not safe. I reach their room on fourth floor and type the code. I make my feet move quiet-quiet as I step inside. On the kitchen counter—the kitchen which has become my own and I cook and fry fish with different food for Elton and his friends, I see a glass and raise it to my nose to smell it. I also see *wee* and I know it's from Rasta. Bad man want to make Elton confuse so he can steal from them. Won't let him.

No one is in the hall. Everybody is inside their room. I listen to Vincent and Scott room because it's first on the corridor. It's quiet. I move to Elton room and I hear sounds. I don't know if they are fighting. They make loud noises. I don't know what to do. I try to open the door and spy but it's locked. But I hear

Elton say something like 'Best Sex' and my mouth become dry like the winds of harmattan. I want to vomit but I don't even know if I'm hearing right or not. My grandmother sometimes tell me that I like to hear what I want, not what has been spoken. Liar, liar, she always tell me. *Wonka nokware baako baako.*

I go home to my pastor's house, which is my house too. I tell him everything I hear when I was standing outside Elton room. He's annoyed like me that another man has entered Elton's life because I won't kiss him. Pastor ask me to find out what this man do for Elton to make him happy.

But nothing prepare me for what my pastor wanted me to see.

I should have known this was wrong. I should have known that following Elton and Rasta Ananse Kobby everywhere will not be good. When I walk into the Ambassadorial Hotel toilet and find out what exactly the devil do to make Elton happy— when I go into the other toilet, step on the toilet and look down to see what they are doing, I almost vomit on them if not for the white man that come into the bathroom with big camera on his neck like they have told him to come and take pictures of this abomination for *Ebony Graphic.*

Ahh, Jesus! My prayer is that you come down quick because there's lots of sin in this world! Man and Man doing things Man and Woman, and even animal and animal, will not even do. Oh Lord, Jesus Christ come down!

VIII

KOBBY
(Saturday routine; 7 days after the friends arrive)

1) The Pharmacist

Look who showed up today!" Arjun screams. His pharmacy is an addict's fishbowl. Cameras installed in all four corners of its mirrored edifice to spot whoever walks in to steal Ritalin or any other medication without prescription. It is also an establishment that prides itself on facilitating pharmaceutical distributions between India and Ghana. And also transmitting detailed reports about my wellbeing to my father. "We've missed you!" he says with his two assistants, who are best known for recommending (behind his back) local snake oils that can treat piles and a hundred types of cancer.

"You look good today, Kobby." He smiles, his diastemata embossing a residual innocence over his angular features. "What, you are not going to speak today? C'mon, you're usually nice to your doctor."

"Arjun, I've got tons of things to do today. Plus, a meeting with friends in under two hours."

"Well, you were supposed to be here two months ago. You're rationing your dosages and your dad is worried."

"Listen, all I'm getting from these drugs are side-effects. Which is really shit if you can't pinpoint what at all they do to help your body. Most of these things are supposed to treat schizophrenia. Honestly, those Pantang doctors took one look at me, without observing me for ample time, before arriving at depression. Do I look depressed?"

He points to a poster of Whitney Houston, Amy Wine-house and others, which says, *This Is What Depression Looks Like*, plastered next to a new one of an illustrated mother and child—*Postpartum Depression is Real*. The coincidence of these infographics, so synonymous to the thematic concerns of my past traumas, rattles me. My paranoia bounces off the mirrors and closes in on me. A hand slides over mine. I wrench my fingers from his hirsute own. I squint at him with suspicion. How much of a confidant has my dad made of him?

"Denial is a normal response after psychiatric diagnoses, that and thinking you know better than trained health professionals." He stacks on the counter each drug—lithium, amlodipine, Latuda, and metronidazole. A ziggurat of prescriptions growing with each visit, all of which will be held under my tongue until it's safe to spit out.

"You know, taking other substances like alcohol and marijuana reduces the efficacy of these medications," one assistant recites. I scowl at her.

"Kobby, it's too late in your diagnosis and we're still testing which meds work for you. That's not good. So maybe this time you'll stick to the dosage so we can have a breakthrough. And then you'll start taking less meds?" The pharmacist looks at me hopefully. "On to other matters," he says when I do not respond. "I've not read anything from you in a while, is work okay?"

"Work is fine."

"I'm telling you, this guy writes some of the best stuff I've ever read on any Ghanaian news outlet. He reports on crimes, murders, dark stuff happening in the city—"

"Do you know who the Sasabonsam Killer is?"

"He's got better things to write than sensationalised reports on a killer, who, according to the government, is just myth, and I too agree with that. I wouldn't rule out the possibility of those minuscule, gossip-mill papers disseminating photoshopped images for sales. And you all should read or listen to better things—"

"Oh boss, the other day did you not see me reading that book by the Kenyan writer who passes by to sell his books?"

"Did he also come here to ask for tramadol without a prescription?"

"Yes, but you know you told us not to give. Boss, his book is really good o." She places the paperback on the counter. *Ways to Know You Are a Born Leader.* The book cover drags me into a sinkhole of memories in which lies the putrid smell of Obroni Wawus that had haunted me months after its author had decided I was dead to him. I toss an Ahomka Ginger into my mouth to stop the sick.

"That guy's a junkie, why are you taking advice from him? When I say reading, I mean, quality stuff, novels, fiction—those are good for you, not that motivational trash by that Kenyan-Ghanaian person who's more Ghanaian than Kenyan and who, like his countrymen, all Ghanaians I know, hates reading quality stuff. The Kenyans I've met actually read, they love literature, and if you want a more stark example of which of the two nations are avid readers, I'll give you one: Whereas one Kenyan president is quoting Atticus Finch in his farewell speech, the Ghanaian president is plagiarising an inaugural speech from not one, but two American presidents! And look at that other one there too." He directs his tirade at another assistant. "She's always reading the Bible, has been stuck on Genesis three years since we hired her—"

"Oh boss Arjun—"

"Kobby, when are you going to write a novel—"

"Not my thing. I'm a journalist." I make a production out of rummaging in my pouch for money that should be in here somewhere, but, oh no it isn't, because I might be too poor to also take on monthly subscriptions for antipsychotics, or maybe it's true that I've got another pouch so identical to this one that has all my cash which I must have left at ho—

"Your dad's paid for these drugs already." Arjun dismisses my rambling and perseveres: "You know journalists also get their articles published in books and such. I read one the other day that I love, by one Eliane Brum, *Collector of Leftover Souls*, it's called, amazing articles on media-remote areas in Brazil—"

"Arjun, my mediums are newspapers and online journals—"

"I think the world would love to read some of your reports. You don't have to limit your readership to Ghanaians—"

"I work for a good newspaper that's attached to an equally brilliant and widespread online journal. If the world cares to read my stuff there's a website—"

"But books are—"

"Thanks, Arjun. I have somewhere else to be." I sweep the meds into my bag. And Arjun, in turn, reaches for my forehead. He yelps. His wrist is bent so far back his fingers might graze his forearm if I don't let go. But I'm too invested in testing the limits of his joints. Relenting only when his sales girls have made appreciable choruses to please, please stop.

"Kobby, really! I'm only just concerned about that scar on your forehead. Has your dad seen it?" His eyes have shrunk to tiny slits through which he observes new character manifestations that explain my medications. And I want to laugh, ask why it took him so long to get here.

"Please don't touch my face." I sound more apologetic than reproachful. "I've had it since I was a child. Tell my dad that I came here. Let him know that he should stop calling and that I'm fine."

"I guess you've always been covering that scar with your hair. I'll still ask him about it though."

2) *The Loctitian*

When I swing open the whingeing trap door, I do not waste time on perfunctory greetings, having long since adopted the coded mimes of seasoned customers to avoid those draining inquisitions reserved for newbies from my side of town. Those newbies whose Twi emerges with the consistency of constipated faeces bearing foul constructions and pronunciations that are scooped one after the other and paraded for workplace entertainment by the salon's self-appointed comma queen, who mocks these middle-class clients so as to incite in his colleagues exaggerated claims of dying along with raucous laughter, thigh-smacking, knee-hugging, floor-stamping hysteria—all of which are necessary reprieves from the oppressive heat of this tin-foiled salon. To signal for their boss, all I do is rake my nails through my hair, sending the youngest of the group dashing for an adjacent doorway. The rest turn their attention to the scalps where their needles are invested in an almost magical sword-fight against undergrowth, luring my gaze to follow their hands as they stab and withdraw. Stab and twirl their wands, strands coiling in the spaces between them and their subjects like the star-studded trajectory of a spell's slow substantiation. The synchronicity of these locticians' motions transforms their simple artisanship into a grandiose ensemble with metaphysical aspects. I turn doe-eyed—which for me is a common reaction whenever I'm in close proximity to all kinds of performing arts, from avant-garde exhibitions like that of the Crazinist Artist to the quotidian compositions of those Bonwire kente weavers.

Throughout this period of witnessing the locticians' dexterity, I am hypnotised to such an extent that, as if I were the subject of a time-lapse presentation, my features gradually sag, dragging with them my mood, which oscillates between windowsill nostalgia and doorpost melancholia.

"*Mr. English!*" The boss yells from their backroom. Their voice booms through the shop in a god-like manner. "*Ɔmɛnɛ* your hair is beautiful o! *Kwɛ mɔ styles. Ei, inyɛmi nɛɛ ofee nice o!*" They begin with the usual compliments. I smile widely even though I haven't yet seen them. "*Mmɛɛ mi, miiba!*" There are sounds of drawers being banged, the magnetic latch of cabinets unsticking and sticking. "*Mɛni sane po nɛ!* Where are the things?!"

"It's fine, I'll wait." I say.

"Sir, I've told you that when you come to my shop, no English. Over here, we only speak Ga and small Twi because those Ashantis have come here plenty and refuse to leave!" They finally walk in, their presence more domineering, their hair with wider bald patches than before. They lecture, "Do you know that after settling among us for years those bloody Ashantis have decided to call us Ants? Ants! What do you think the meaning of Nkran is? When those Ashantis get up they say they are going to Nkran, going to Nkran, when they should only say the English own 'Accra' which also mean ants but no one will know. Anyway, I wanted to charge you a lower price for these needles. But you know, your English is expensive-expensive. And you know how our needle is special-special. Sharp-sharp too, the way you like it. *Akɛjɛ* from Mali *tɔɔŋ*."

"In spite of their supposed durability, you never have any explanations as to why they keep breaking," I tease. They frown. "How much?" I ask.

They look at my hair then my espadrilles, and say, "*O shoe yɛ fɛo oo*. Can you give me how much you paid for the shoes so I can buy some for me and my Kojo Besia workers? Shoe *ekome-ekome* ten!" I chuckle, reaching into my pouch for any amount I can find out of kindness.

"Kuami Eugene o!" The hairdressers cheer at a disembodied radio, which fills the shop with Kuami Eugene's "Fadama Boy." All employees and their boss are now singing, wiggling their waists in a uniform dance. "Ei, Mr. English, over here we dance o! Don't bring your English-English self here." They snatch the money I extend and toss the needles at me. "You can't dance, you can't sing too. What a disgrace to your parents! Ah, *Costomer. Ɔmɛnɛ o shocki mi . . .*"

3) Passeggiatas as Adopted from an Old Italian Lover

I pass rows and rows of shops whose wares are spilled onto the streets of Jamestown. There's a duplicated Year of Return banner swinging from streetlight to streetlight. The sellers decide to smash their voices against the air and accost foreign-looking pedestrians with a jagged-edged chorus. *Adɛn na Aburokyirefoɔ ade tɔ yɛ mo ya sa ara, herh aha sei yɛ tɔ adeɛ o, monnim ara ma menka nkyerɛ mo, na sa ara mo nkwasiasɛm no mo ngyae!* These traders have worked out their buyer persona yet seek to convert those who fall outside these data sets with the viciousness of Lighthouse evangelists. No one with exotic features can walk by their stalls without being coerced into buying something they won't need.

On certain days, I encounter multiple men I've fucked as though I was flicking through the carousel of profiles on Man4Man. Not today. Today, a white man looks pleadingly at me, asking to be saved from a seller. I want to holler: *Hand in those reparations!* My prim upbringing admonishes these urges, so I hurriedly cross to the other pavement without a second glance.

I think of Brian, and how he'd have been the one hollering. On a typical Saturday, he and I would have a quick catch up in one of those white South African-owned coffee shops that are wary of Ghanaians who only walk in to charge their phones and use the Wi-Fi after purchasing a bottle of water. We would scroll through Man4Man as we speak to each other absent-mindedly, as if our meeting was but a drab meal, obvious that our attentions snooped into the other's phone, obsessing over who gets invited for a hook-up first. Brian always won these silent competitions, even when our profiles were blank. "Quick, let's take a bathroom selfie before I leave," he'd say, "for good luck." I would try my best to pout joyously in these selfies, ignoring the destructive jealousy that confused the enzymes in my stomach and made it turn on itself instead of on the slice of carrot cake I usually had during our meetings because we spent so damn long, I felt guilty about the bottled water I immaculately sipped. "What are friends for?" he'd ask as he dipped into his taxi, and I would respond as expected: "Just to destroy."

I watch a scuffle between two lorry drivers. I take out my phone to document the spectacle for my TikTok, but I get distracted by an Instagram notification. But it is not an IG DM. It is just one of those weird bookstagram photo tags that required everybody and their momma to invert a stack of fantasy books so they looked like they were glued to a finger. My Gmail app is next. No emails. Nothing waiting in my spam to cheer me up either. My phone is an emptied circus and I pocket it with displeasure.

Someone familiar crosses my path with books. "Not today," I inform him even as he holds my arm and scratches his fingers into my palm. "I'm on one of those book-buying bans that has become Bookstagram's most fashionable tool of performative literary activism," I shout as we separate. He looks at me as if I'm really insane. He becomes a reminder that I haven't posted anything on my IG in a while. So I hurry to the Tema Station newsstand. Once again, I scan the corpses on the newspapers with a delight which contradicts the horrified reactions from bystanders. I take out *My Sister, the Serial Killer* and snap, upload to my IG stories with the caption, *I'm late to the party, but so far it's living up to the hype.* An incoming Instagram call gets me excited. But it's only my boss.

"I'm so glad you are loving the book!" I move to a shaded area on the pavement and angle the phone over my face. She's screaming. "When I bought it at Heathrow, I honestly just wanted a quick flight read and found out too soon that it's a book you'd appreciate more than I. Also! You look well rested! Hey, listen, I know you're on leave, but we need to find news on the Sasabonsam Killer and find it quick—*ow!*" It's only now that I notice disembodied hands in her cornrows. I brighten the screen to find her in a salon.

"Your hair looks nice."

"It better be. I've got a date soon. At Santoku. Our second date actually. First time he's going to see me with my natural hair. Accra really is unreasonably hot to wear a wig on weekends too! By the way, he's okay, thanks for asking. But oh my God! Why do white people living in Africa love sitting with other Africans to discuss the entitlement of The Other White Person? The Other White Person is colonial. The Other White Person is rude to Africans. The Other White Person is rich and ignorant of their privilege. It's not enough to not be The Other White People. To live in Africa as a white person is to live with a reparative conscience. Every action, the simple ones such as breathing, walking, eating, analysed for its consequences on the African and observed in the light of its reparative merit or demerit. They need to stop talking about The Other White Person and start living that reparational life."

"Yaa, I've got to be somewhere soon."

"Is it work-related? Is it a morgue-visit? Again, I know you're on leave, but the Sasabonsam Killer, what are you doing about it? Do you want to come over and discuss? You could sleep over so you don't have to go home."

"I can't hear you over the sound of cars!" I disconnect the call, and frown when my IG Messenger tab has three new messages—none of them from followers I'm keen on messaging.

4) Perhaps a Date from Man4Man

My Man4Man phone pings. Someone, a local, wants to meet, and perhaps I would have risked getting my dick sucked in this congested area if Elton and I weren't meeting in under an hour at Osu's Thai place. This local doesn't take it nicely when I decline and blocks me.

Ahead of me, Accra High Street curves into the shanties of Osu. I bypass the ministries, the stadium, the Independence Square. The affluence and the carefully planned areas break off and fall away the moment I enter Osu through the 28th

February Road where Access Bank sits on the crest of these two social gaps. In inner-city Osu, contemporary Ga music blares from beer bars built with charcoaled clapboards and other low-cost material. Children and adults go about their daily business of hawking and cooking in the open while stealing moments to dance to Nii Adotey Tetor's "Oha Edɔ Mi." In this part of Osu, the sun lets up because the community is cocooned by trees that have been standing since first settlers planted them. The cool breeze carries the scent of frying fish and kelewele, the doughy banku bubbling on coal pots, the occasional piss and shit emanating from bushes and the foetor of a decaying roadkill. Fragrance and bad odour mingle and interact like the rival vendors who occasionally drop all pretence and take to the streets to quarrel. It's in these streets the real Osu shrugs off its jacket and unwinds, away from the gawking eyes of tourists on Oxford Street. Also the Osu that convenes, legs akimbo over gutters where tilapia grills are suspended, to voice its anger about the gentrification, which it has begun to realise happens when the ant in its own clothes bites it.

The loud music almost makes it impossible to hear my phone ringing. It's my dad. I decline his call with the preset text *Not coming home tonight* and continue to the Thai restaurant. On and on, out of rural Osu, back into more affluent areas, the 28th February Road leads into the renowned Oxford Street, where the faces and places are lighter and whiter. The sun revs up its anger. There are no trees to shade from its wrath. The people here have their sunscreen and their visors, their sunglasses and their sunny smiles. No amount of ultraviolet rays can get in the way of gentrifiers hell-bent on parading their elegance. I study a madman who closely watches a white family of four skip towards a high-rise. His eyes find mine and he offers a consolatory shake of the head as if I, and all those who haven't yet ripped off our clothes and walked the streets naked, are the ones who need comforting. There are also the Year of Returnee tourists browsing the kiosks along Oxford Street. Walking tall with their sky-high boots and their six-feet-plus heights, their sun-bleached locs and their revealing clothes, their open wonder at all things Ghanaian colours—red, yellow, green, the colours of Pan-Africanism, the colours of the ganja mesh bodycons sold by Rastafarians who refer to these foreigners as *brother-man*, and say *jah-bless* after every transaction.

I find the Thai restaurant right at the intersection between Osu and Nyaniba—a small gateless estate owned by richer Ghanaians who let shoe-box houses to volunteering personnel from Canadian and Dutch embassies who believe the apartment buildings on Oxford Street are rather pricey for the services they offer. Zayon Thai, as announced by the slanted signage, sits on the rooftop of a two-storey building sealed by bamboo roofing; a staircase extending onto the road snakes the property and connects the two floors. I'm about to ring Elton before crossing to the restaurant when a taxi screeches to a stop at the building. Out of it come Elton and Scott in their tees and shorts and their rubber slippers—only Vincent has donned a dashiki and a pair of Seano leather sandals—laughing at a comment from none other than Nana. The three rush up the staircase to the restaurant as Nana pays the driver with money obtained from Vincent. I hurriedly walk towards the building, wishing to meet Elton and the others before Nana joins them. But the taxi speeds away and Nana climbs the stairs before I can. At the top, he spots me lingering at the bottom. His disdain is expected. The sun burns through his purple forehead as his features slowly distort like an empty can throttled in a fist. It's as if he invites me into the mechanics of his hate and I can almost hear muscle after muscle crank as his face disfigures. His forehead turns darker, loses its purple hue. As if on cue, we both look up to see the sun vanishing, the clouds blackening. Pedestrians break into a shrill cry, running for cover before the rain inflicts its harm. Accra changes moods like this, unannounced, demanding the whereabouts of trees that existed before her residents became sellouts. The first drops of rain pelts over my scalp, then my batakari, continues through the lax elastic band of my Ankara trousers, finds my groin, cups my balls. Nana still won't let up his guard. He remains glowering, barring access to the others.

"Nana!" Elton's voice beckons him into the bamboo sheltering of the restaurant. He doesn't leave without sending a projectile of spit, which unfortunately doesn't miss. It lands right on my septum and trickles down my chin. I can't help but laugh as I let the rain wash away the scent of fish on my moustache. It's a laughter that comes out in spasms, in waves of segregated ha-has. I'm laughing even as I take the stairs in twos and threes into the restaurant that's empty except for Elton and his friends, who look up at me in wonder and assume that I'm in hysterics because the rain has left me soaking wet. Elton grips my wrist, asking if I'm okay. I drag my seat closer to his asking, "What are we ordering?" Scott wants to know if I have ever had Thai before. I shake my head no. "I'm happy to try new things," I add. "I'm sure you'll love it," Vincent says, "It has similar tastes to the stuff Nana makes for us." Nana looks up from his empty plate, and Elton shouts for the waiter. "I'll love Thai then I'm sure," I say jovially. Thunder reverberates through our table, making the cutlery clutter against the ceramic plates. "Ha ha," Scott is laughing, "how did you just say Thai?" Vincent throws him a look, but he misses it. "Oh, you Ghanaians always confuse us with your pronunciations. It's pronounced Tie not Thigh. Now I'm gonna find it hard to stop laughing, Lord Jesus. Ha ha." The skies emit a strobe of lightning which flashes over Nana's stony features. A little bit of spit-play may be nice if there exists an established consent along with a consensus that both parties must not miss the other's mouth; for disregarding these concerns, I just might kill Nana. "Ha ha," I join Scott laughing as I wipe off the spit's imprint on my lip with a napkin

Part Two

Sometimes, narrators cannot help their tempestuous nature. They, a roaring wind, might attempt to tip things over, tamper with the outcome of a story.

Good narrators know the best stories are those you do not interfere with. You let them happen organically. You watch. You let be.

I

Kobby
(8 *days after the friends arrive*)

Elton, do you ever wander into people's brains? A little Goldilocks meandering through the chambers of their dreams, sneaking under tiny bed spaces for their secrets, rifling through the drawers of their psyche, searching and fetching until you're left with nothing. Which, in essence, is being left with all that there is to them, knowing them intimately, as one would their own insecurities expressed through the appearance of fine lines and wrinkles, love handles, and Rawlings chains. My brain has got creaking wood boards for floors, door hinges that could use some oiling. I sense you. I see you invading. I notice you watching me when I'm not watching myself, when all that's within me runs across my features like the coffee-coloured stains of a leaking wall. I can't trust you, Elton. Your eyes pry too much.

Even now as you drive through these endless streets to our destination that seems elusive like dreams dying at the first break of consciousness, I see you spying through the rearview mirror. I'm squished between Nana and Vincent, holding my insides tight, trying hard not to let my skin graze Nana's. For when I do, when the car bumps into a pothole and he senses the tiniest traction between our thighs, his eyes turn on me, searing as the flick of a lighter against skin. Where Vincent and Scott have failed to notice these tugging tensions, you do not miss them. I pretend to focus elsewhere. On the back of my pale palm, on the V between my wobbly thighs, on my phone refreshing my Instagram for messages, refreshing my email, confusing the consistent vibrations from your phone as alerts from mine. Anything to stop the steam that rises up my throat anytime I find you looking. You wink at me. I turn away. Nana catches me staring at his tiddly hands covering his bulge, guarding his privates as if I'm a djinn that would spirit away with his cock. He glares at me. I turn away.

Outside the car, the dead, like sunbathing mermaids, are seated on the overturned automobiles rusting along the boundaries of the street. They wave at us—pabebe waves performed in unison, a visual of purgatory as endless pageantry. I should tell Elton and his friends this, but they all ignore the mangled and mashed vehicles, as if proximity to the deceased reminds them too much of their own mortality, too much of how, in a flash of twisted fate, they too could be victims to this country's infrastructural negligence.

I focus on Scott riding shotgun, his head shimmying like the Year of Return sign tied around the rearview mirror. He slaps Elton's hands away from the radio. "Give some respect to your elders, young man, LaBelle before Bailey Rae!" By wielding control over the car's tunes, Scott exercises his privileges for being the one to ring the dealership first thing in the morning when the rest of us were playing at being sleepy-eyed housemates; stealing surreptitious glances at one another over our phone (Elton), coffee (Vincent), worn *American Psycho* paperback (me), kitchen counter (Nana); languishing in this agonising silence which seemed preferable to summoning the courage for uttering the first, *whatchu doin?* In barged Scott: "Why on earth is it so much more expensive to rent a car in Accra than it is in Cape Town?" He looked to me for any wash-and-wear theories that might iron out his distress. "Stop using your year-of-return accent," I muttered. Vincent couldn't be bothered. He raised his mug towards Nana, "Mind making me another cup?" Scott turned on Nana, "Let me handle that! I'm tired of that instant coffee you've been making. I'll whip up some bomb sandwiches for the trip. I, for one, cannot wait to get road-tripping!"

Scott has carried his excitement better than the rest of us. I watch him dancing to the disco tunes wheezing through Atlantis Radio's static. "Oh, I miss the disco days!" he gushes. "How old are you, Kobby? Do you even know Patti LaBelle? What music do you listen to?"

"Um, I do love stuff from Florence Welch, Natasha Beddingfield—"

"Well, people like what they like."

A confused dragonfly manoeuvres into the car from Scott's window. It turns out he's terrified of insects. He screams at the top of his lungs, cowering from the pest's curlicue flight. Nana hurls himself at the insect, smashing it against the windshield with his bare hand. "Here you go." Scott is spritzing a mint-scented sanitiser into the Killer's hands.

"Damn, Nana," Elton says, "you go around killing bugs like that? You got skills!"

I turn to Vincent and see beads of sweat parade across the length of his forehead. "Are you okay?" I nudge his shoulders. He returns a weak smile, then gulps down his third and last bottle of water. His hands shake as the bottle rises to his lips. I notice, for the first time, the plaster-chapped skin of a backhand that has known too many hospital drip insertions. I sense his struggle to swallow his water from the laborious movements of his Adam's apple. "Hey." I take out an Ahomka Ginger from my pocket, packed to battle against my serious case of motion sickness, and toss it onto his lap.

"I hate ginger," he murmurs, reading the label.

"This is sweet," I urge. He pops the toffee into his mouth, placing his cheek against the window as he sucks on it resignedly, like a child does a nipple shoved into its mouth to quieten its wailing. No one else notices his discomfort. Even Nana, who's usually more attentive than the rest of us, keeps his gaze out the window.

I'd been against this trip the moment Vincent suggested it. "Kobby, it will be fun, we'll rent a car, go see those castles, do that canopy walk and be back in a few days—a week tops. C'mon, who turns down an all-expense-paid trip?" I scratched my eyebrow and stared at him blankly, a look that stained his excitement, made him screw his features in puzzled wonder. As I swirled my gin and allowed the clinking ice cubes to fill the dreary silence, I thumbed the scar on my forehead and let my memories spin on their reels, backtracking to a little boy on a school trip paid for by his mother who'd strapped him into the bus seat herself. With a smile that was an appendage of the threats she'd issued back home. Kissed him on his fore-head too, before disappearing into the bright sky. Soon, Vincent, like the rest, excused himself to bed, abandoning me with my drunken melancholy and the melted ice cubes. I've never toured the castles. Anytime I see a colonial building, I stiffen. My brain has begun ciphering the difficult stimulus every Black man of a certain awareness has to suffer, associating all things colonial with trauma.

"Elton, man, you gon' put your phone on silent?" Vincent implores.

"Yes, sir." Elton fixes the problem. "It's the Year of Return Facebook group, they stay posting all these boring events. I should probably block them."

That tiny window of hesitation before his utterance—marked by the quick glance in my direction—injures his credibility. How many travellers have confused or overestimated my interest in them just because we've fucked and delighted in the syrupy romance of a holiday fling with its false promises and mononormative parameters? To travel, in fact, is to indulge in the limitless buffet of treats a country has on offer. Hence, I wouldn't mind if Elton fucks others. What I do mind is losing this fiscal comfort, our convenient sex and its benefits, the bed and the breakfast; not necessarily the man who provides them. All I'm asking is to be recognised as the first of his escorts and accorded due assets should he decide to mess around for the rest of his stay.

"Oh shit," Elton speaks.

The entire car tips forward for the slamming of its brakes. There's a police barrier a few metres away. It looks like a deserted post, and for seconds we all heave the collective sighs of a band of criminals delighting in outsmarting law enforcement. But on the outer markings of the road we see them in the distance, a line of mean crows waiting. "How much do we have to pay?" Elton shoots his question to Nana.

"Don't worry, I'll talk to them," Nana says in that characteristic self-assured way of the Ashanti man, which makes me feel both at ease and irritated.

"Hey, officers," Nana calls out. We see a couple of policemen emerge from what seemed like the bushes to join the other two who swagger towards our car. "Officers, good afternoon," Nana repeats. The police dips his head into Elton's side, checking for all the particulars he'll begin asking for. He sniffs the car, and we are all screwed.

Elton smoked a joint alone minutes ago. *I've got nerves*; he shrugged us off when we all turned warning glances at him. To me, he passed a Tupperware of brownies. "You ever heard that song by Bill Withers and Washington Jr.?" he asked with a wink.

"What brings you to this side of town?" the police on Elton's side whose eyes we can barely see, his beret shielding them, asks. Elton is smart enough not to open his mouth.

"We're here to—"

"*Yɛkɔ hwɛ* Cape Coast Castle." Nana cuts me off.

"*Mo yɛ tourist anaa? Year of Return foɔ ni bi?*" Another policeman on Scott's side inquires, shoving his head into Scott's window and sniffing. He smells it too. He exchanges a look with the officer on Elton's side. Shit.

"*Aane, nso me yɛ Asante ni.*"

"*Asanteni na wabeduru ha!*" The other policemen laugh. Nana laughs with them. Elton and Scott join feebly.

"*Aha bɔn wee-wee.*" My heart falls when one of the two policemen states this, and as though he senses my trepidation, he asks me to empty my pockets. My locs and I have grown accustomed to our stigmatised parts singled out of public transport and frisked for weed or weaponry. A twenty-cedi note peeks out of my semi-emptied pockets. The policeman stares between me and the baiting cash, and huffs, suspects there's enough line to lure a bigger catch.

"*Officer, wee baako kraa nni car wei mu,*" Nana remarks, beating his chest in that manner that locals employ to swear. "*Me dɔ Nyame.*"

"Do they want money?" Scott asks, probably mistaking *Nyame* for "money." "We have cash, we can give you cash."

"We don't want your money!" one of the officers screams so loud all of us jump. "Everyone, out of this car." He commands. "Out!" He yanks open Vincent's door. As we're being emptied into the streets, Vincent deposits the contents of his stomach on the officer's pants. "*Jesus!*" The policeman yells, hopping around as if he's got hot coals on him.

"*Obi yare anaa?*" Officer No Eyes asks.

"*Aane,*" Nana answers.

"*Monkɔ, monkɔ, monkɔ!*" He yells us back into the car, "*Fa ne kɔ Hospital.*"

Elton steps on the gas. We're all so terrified it takes minutes of silence to recover. Relief kicks in when the policemen revert to crows. Vincent falls on my lap. I run my fingers across his back. "Are you okay, Vince?" Scott asks. He nods.

"Thank those awful sandwiches you made," he adds. Scott's laughter comes from a dead place and is short-lived. All of us laugh a little. Even Nana, whose thigh bumps against mine, chuckles and says sorry. The dragonfly unsticks from its spot on the windshield and makes a quick descent to the dashboard. Accra, with its moodiness and unresolved dilemmas, falls away. Despite the rocky start, Cape Coast greets us with its facile promises of relaxation, its salty air—

"Roll down the windows," Scott yelps. He sings: "*Respectfully, I say to thee, I'm aware that you're cheating . . .*"

THE FANTES

This is not Anansesɛm. Not a story. But a history. Our voices sing from the deep wealths of the sea. History repeats itself. The Sankofa comes again to visit its lost brothers and pays its respects to these Waters where we found home. We see the cars that drive past our shores. We see our brothers breathing us in. We as sirens sing the song of the sea, if they will listen. We will possess them and make them our vessels.

Our history begins not from our killers, not from the arrival of ships and pale skin. Our voices go back in time where Kwasi Broni never existed. Sad that every time our stories are told, we begin from bondage, from the dungeons and the ships that carried us away, leaving some of us here, here deep down down; the essence of our name, of our tribe, Fante, the half that left.

A brief history of our origins: we come from Takyiman in Bono State, from the Bono people who were pursued from Central Africa. The Moors, who could not succeed in foisting Islam on these Tshis, thought it wise to chase them out of the South Sahara into the Kpong Mountains and River Pra.

We began as brothers often do, thriving, hunting, raising food over the earth as one. But the land became so full with our children and wives, and what with the northern ethnic group waging war on our people, we needed space to breathe. *Yɛn mfantefo yɛmpɛ ako-ako asɛm.* We told our brothers, "You stay, we will leave and find lives elsewhere." Even before we moved, we dreamt of the sea. We the Fante, the ones who left.

We will take our Obunumankoma, Odapagyan, and Oson.
For every migration, we will need our leaders, these three who
can fight ahead as we move to possess the lands of others, and
our spiritual leader, Amona, who will be the eyes to our journeys ahead. We will march through kingdoms and receive hospitality and hostility in equal measure. We will fight wars to
walk through kingdoms. We will fight wars to rest in kingdoms.
We will die. We will carry our lost brothers and sisters over our
shoulders and cry. We will lose our eagle and our whale. We
will never stop until we reach the sea. We will eat herbs and
scrub with herbs and start fires in forests that have antelopes
and deer, luring, killing, and eating them to ease our weary bodies. *Yɛn mfantefo yɛpɛ dziban*. Our adversaries will take not only
the form of people but also harsh weather and diseases that will
cause fevers so contagious we will think it wise to not touch our
afflicted brothers. We will sing and bid them farewell as they
lie in death, the ones we won't be able to carry home with us.
Home is the sea. We will stop at nothing to get there.

Our story on land begins like this. We will settle near the
sea, Mankessim (after defeating the kingdoms of Amanfi and
Asabu not by military prowess but by intellectual manoeuvring,
infecting their best warriors with Guinea worm. Though other
ethnic groups are intent on labelling this reliance on our mental
strength "trickery."). We will have wives who'll give us sons and
daughters to replace all the people we lost on our journey here.
We will give them names of the dead. Piesie. Manu. Araba. All
through to Badu. The tenth child is where we stop with each
woman. We will live happily, own the land and the sea, make
merry with our Apatampa that can be heard over at Takyiman.
Our way of paying homage to our brothers left behind.

Our lives of simplicity and revelry ended when the ships began arriving.

This is another song of loss and defeat. Of betrayal we had
never known and of death we could only cease by laying down

our weapons and resorting to dialogue. The biggest mistake we ever made was to talk to the people who came with the pretence of trade. Our brothers inland would hate us for making treaties and agreements with the people who called themselves Dutch, Portuguese, English. Who looked like each other but hated each other and spoke strange languages. We mourn the bond we had with our brothers and sisters, replaced with the white man's Bond of 1844. In history, we will forever be known as the traitors because we offered little to no resistance to these strong people who learnt our language and took our women and gave birth to children who were as pale as them. We even looked like traitors. And when our women were unlucky enough to have been fancied by a governor or a high official and birthed more traitors who were only raised in the nicest parts of the castle, they became the subject of multi-generational novels, and everyone who read about them remembered this betrayal.

They did not only rape our women, they raped our culture and our language. So that when we sing—it is known that the Fantes' tongues sing even when they speak—we find their lexicons infiltrating our songs: *Mereko Church. Mereko Castle.* All words and cultures that never existed before their arrival.

The song of death.

We sang our dirges as we watched our brothers from inland march into the castles they built. They sang their dirges as they watched us march in single files into the churches the white man built. We told the stories of our heroes, but in schools our children learnt the stories of their heroes, coming home to us with names like Napoleon and Arthur and Don Diogo de Azambuja. During the day, we heard the names of their *akokɔsrade* children, and replaced our Piesies with Peterson, our Mansa with Mason. During night, to mock us, we heard the cries of our brothers, *obi mmra mmɛgye yɛn.* We heard the whips, *nnipa bɛyɛɛ deɛn.* We heard the cannons from their castles that placed a terror so deep we couldn't find the courage within to intervene.

We will never know what happened to the brothers and sisters that went into the castle. But we see them return in the brothers and sisters who followed the Sankofa sign centuries later—what they called the Year of Return, four hundred years since the first torture began. This one has the face of Obrunumankoma. Wasn't he his son? Can't be, he died centuries ago. This one looks like Odapagyan. He has flown from far lands and has come back here to protect us. The other one looks a bit like the child of the woman who fell in love with a common sailor who might have promised his return, but on the next ship everyone aboard was a clone of him and no one would step forward to claim responsibility. The worst of them you could sleep with was a Jimmy, foolish and innumerable.

We will sing to these returnees. We will call to them as they book into their hotels, throw pebbles at their windows like tragic lovers do. We will call onto their spirits, appeal to the brothers in them we knew. We will listen to their stories and histories, which will be ours as ours is theirs. They'll forever be Fante, the ones that left. We will possess them and make vessels of them. And should they refuse us, should they hear our pleas and refuse to do the bidding of our will, there will be consequences.

II

KOBBY

(8 days after the friends arrive)

Elmina, Central Region. A town sitting on the outskirts as a child at the back of a class, quiet because everyone has shunned it. A trip into this place feels like time-travel to old Ghana. Where the fever of a newly independent nation burns on the little red, gold, green flags appearing and disappearing, on vantage points around town, on discarded wooden lottery kiosks. Where colonial buildings repurposed into housing projects give the impression that their owners never left. A quaint town fastened to a sleepy ocean that constantly yawns, stretches, and races for the shore in breakneck speed ready to pounce at its bystanders with wet kisses.

Elmina, still complicit in the trade of humans (old habits die hard), trades its locals for foreigners. Among the Ghanaians walking along the shores of the sprawling beaches, and their little children dancing behind, and the straggle of dogs whom no one seems to own but disappear at night's approaching, are the white tourists who descend on this town and never leave. They, with their well-meaningness, cohabit with the townies, own a beachfront resort with an Afrocentric aesthetic. Much like the little resort Elton and his friends booked, having no knowledge that it is owned by a German couple.

"How could we not have known," Scott hisses in my ear as we are wheeling our luggage into our rooms. Elton, amused by the fact, considers owning property here. Vincent doesn't give a fuck, because, as Scott says, he went to private school and has more than a few white friends for a Black man in a very Black community in LA. Very fluent in white, this one—

"Shut it," Vincent growls at Scott.

The resort, like all the white-owned ones, is deceptively built in the design of a cluster of huts—the matrimonial setup of polygamist men—where each hut is named after some locally grown nut. Wind chimes have been suspended from the thatched roofs, seashells tossed across the moist clay compound. A big wooden arrow is etched with "*Akwaaba*" instead of the word's German equivalent. On the cobblestones that lead to the hut-styled quarters, we are stalled by Vincent, who drops his rucksack and gazes at the rising and falling waters. Entranced, we're each made to contemplate the vastness of the universe and our infinitesimal position in it, undressed of our worries, speeding towards the sea which meets us halfway, scattering seaside birds into the azure skies, frolicking. Nana breaks our thalassophilic reveries. He has piled all our effects into his arms to prompt us to keep moving.

"Welcome to Nkatie." Elton plays butler, swiping past the kente-draped doorway of our assigned room. I wince but do not bother to correct his pronunciation which translates to *Don't say "tie"* instead of—

"Groundnut." Nana translates. "*Nkatie*."

"Peanut. Americans say, peanut." I address Nana more than I do the friends. He huffs, says something that sounds like *Trumu-Trumu,* and carries the luggage in.

"They're running this place like a boarding school," Scott remarks, pointing at the neatly laid bunk beds resembling the layout of a prison cell. The room is painted the pale red of a crusted wound and bleeds the comforting camphoric smell peculiar to old women's ceremonial wrappers. A troubling possibility that the Germans are rummaging wardrobes in villages just so they could trap this fragrance to further accentuate their Afrocentric decor. Vincent and Elton pick up brochures placed on the bed like little treats.

"It's supposed to be eco-conscious," I inform them, "so the less energy used—"

"—the more money saved. I see what they're doing here," Elton interrupts, "Bloody whites!" After realising the horror of shared public bathrooms, the restaurant with the unexciting menu, and the tacky piece of formatted text—bold, italicised, and capitalised, instructing us that the resort has a **NO RE-FUND POLICY**, we all agree we are not going to like this place much. Except Nana, who leaves after dropping the luggage, his thoughts about the place guarded as every other thing about him. Elton, to my shock, offering me no chance to play dumb, announces to the others our sex schedule, asking them to steer clear of the room around noon.

"How did this place get TripAdvisor's approval?" Vincent wonders.

"There's your answer, in some tiny-ass font," Elton supplies, then begins reading the brochure: "*Half the proceeds of this place goes to the development of community projects to give back to Elmina what she's so generously given us.*"

"Ahh," Scott speaks, "so beneath all that soft White Saviour exterior lies a hard Robin Hood complex."

"Bloody white people," Elton cusses. "If only more Black Americans built resorts here . . ."

III

NANA
(8 days after the friends arrive)

They say we Ashantis always have a story to tell. So I will tell you one about fishing and hunting, from my grandmother, who know more than me, who raise me, who die in front of my eyes and in my hands, who tell me that I'll grow up to be evil and I laugh at her. This is one of her stories:

"Long time ago, there was a Hunter called Abompe, who wanted plenty, plenty meat. He was the best hunter in the whole of his village. When he went into the Bush, he came back with animals people couldn't even name, but would eat anyway. Every time he went into the Bush, everyone waited for him, singing hunting songs, as if they could smell the aromas of the soups they'd be making upon his return. In this village, when you have meat, you have wealth. Our elders also say: *Totobi tere nkwan*. The rotted skin of an animal enriches the soup. So one day—and there is always a "one day," there's always a time things change and they'll never remain the same—one day, he went to the forest and came back without an animal. He had killed all the animals in the forest, he told the people of the village. The villagers were so disappointed with him they threw their empty soups at him and wailed, what's a soup without meat? This village will be called Bosomtwi. That's another story you should find out. For a long time, people in the village had to replace meat with fish. They began eating fish so much the fish finish in the sea. The people began learning lessons on conservation and protecting nature. They made laws to prevent hunting and fishing on specific days. The fishes came back. The animals came back. And everyone was happy. Now go and bath. Today, we'll be eating yam with only kontomire stew, no fish no meat."

Fante people always laugh at we Ashantis for not having sea, for not eating plenty-plenty fish. They say that's why our stews are not nice, plenty Maggi-Maggi in our stews, *shito kraa wɔn-nim yɛ*. They lying every time. It's all they do, these Fantes. Tell lies and speak English in their Twi just to make our eyes *biri* us.

"When I was small, my grandmother used to take me to Bosomtwi," I tell the cooking woman who try to challenge me, try to challenge an Ashanti man like me, that we Ashanti don't have sea.

"*Bosomtwi na mo de yɛ too-known,*" she challenges, "Bosomtwi *no*, is it a sea or lake?" I smile at her. She's a nice woman wearing jeans and a t-shirt that let her breast fall forward plenty. They say Fanti women are blessed forward and backward, *ɔmo wɔ animuonyam ne akyinam*. I see that now. We are talking Ashanti versus Fante people like they are Asante Kotoko and Accra Hearts of Oak as I'm waiting for Elton and his friends and the Ananse to come out so we can eat together. This woman approach me in the restaurant that look like a hut for a chief, thinking I'm American like my friends. "What would you like to order?" she ask me. I look at her surprise, then say in Twi that I want fufu. "*Asantsefo* and fufu!" She shout, happy to find that I'm not one of them, that I'm Ghanaman. "*Mo ara moyɛ* predictable *tse dɛ Kwamina ara ɛtoa Ato so*. Fufu for breakfast, fufu for supper, fufu for lunch," she say in her very-very nice English. I tell her she should be English teacher. And she laugh and hit my shoulders, "*Asantsefo* your mouth can play song, you can sing a woman to marry you." I push forward my chest and hit it proudly, and tell her: "Look, they call me Nana, I am thirty years old, I come from a village in Mampong, but I live in Accra."

"Fufu is not there," she tell me, but I know she is playing with me. She take the chair in front of me, her back facing the sea, and that's how we start to talk about Ashanti foods and Fante foods.

You can see from the restaurant the fishermen boats that are far away and look like dot on the water. This place make me think of Bosomtwi and how happy I become any time my grandmother take me with her to buy fish to sell for her village. I wanted to become a fisherman when I was small. Because fish was so sweet and nice, especially the one they put in soup. Fresh and hot when my sister and I steal some when grandmother leave the cooking pot. "So you're a thief," this woman say to me when I tell her the story. "Don't come to the kitchen because there's plenty fish there to steal!" I smile at her. I want to tell her she's speaking the truth, and we Ashantis like meat a lot, and the only meat I will steal when I come to the kitchen is her. I never meet any woman who sit close and speak to me like I was Big Man. Maybe it's because she knows I'm from Accra. Does she want to marry me? Maybe I should tell her that they're looking for a wife in my village for me. An Ashanti like me.

"Nana finds a wife," I hear Scott, the *obroni* one, voice behind me.

"Wow, Nana. You a fast one, (ain't) you?" Elton voice. Without turning my face, I hear them come close from the way the boom-boom sound on the wooden floor get loud.

"Hi, I'm the waitress." The girl gets up and stretch her hand when the others come to the table. "Mina is my name." I want to tell her that she told me her name is Maame Araba, but I remember all Fante people do is tell lies and I don't want to disgrace her in front of my friends. I watch her shake Scott hand long, her smile stretch like her mouth is plantain. "What would you like to order?"

"We thought there was only one (dish) on the menu." I hear the Ananse's voice, and my chest rise, my hands fold.

"This is your first day, so we give you a treat."

"Sand witch, can I have a sand witch?" Vincent ask her, sitting on the chair she left. His face look sick still even after I ran out to get him *G* the moment we got here. Maybe I'll tell Maame Araba or Mina the liar to make him some sobolo. That will help him if he has fevers. Maybe he's having malaria. Mina keep her eyes on Scott, still smiling at him, not looking at us all even as she ask what we'll eat.

She leave to go bring our food and everyone sits. Ananse sits away from me on Vincent's end, but we're still so close and I don't let my eyes meet him else I'll vomit. Why would a man let another man put his pipi in his *botors* like he's a woman? Even at church service, pastor say man should never put his pipi in a woman's *botors* when they marry. Some old woman challenge pastor and tell him that *botors* eating is nice. Pastor continue preaching because everyone knows the old woman's sons and daughters leave her for abroad and she is now mad.

"Plans for today?" Elton ask everyone as we wait for our food. The air is nice and chill like we are in fridge and make the hair on my hands stand tall like grass. You can hear the birds doing kwaa-kwaa. If you smell hard, you can smell the scent of fish and when I close my eyes, I smile, as if I'm back in Bosomtwi where little boys like me play in the water, where my grandmother tell me it's taboo to wash yourself in the water, but people like to go against the gods and do it. At Bosomtwi, I remember, like all the little boys, I ran to the white people who come to see the lake asking them if they want to know the history of the place. It's how little boys there make money, telling stories of the lake; some true, some lies. So my grandmother taught me a song so that I can make money while she buy fish. Here's the song:

There was a Hunter,
who chase Antelope in the forest,
the antelope run away and away and fall inside a small river,

NO ONE DIES YET · 115

he went to stand at this river he has never seen before and
called the Antelope a god,
he call the river Bosomtwi,
which mean Antelope God,
he stop hunting and
live by the stream and
start fishing the fish,
selling the fish,
eating the fish,
fishing the fish, selling the fish, eating the fish.
The little boys of the village hated me. *You new forken boy getting so much money.* They caught me one day, ask me to teach them my song. I told them no, so they called me *nam*, and that's a big insult, and they put my head in the water till I couldn't breathe . . .

I open my eyes quickly and look around to see that I'm not in water. I see faces. I hear voices. To this day, I am afraid of water. I do not learn to swim. I do not become fisherman again.

"I'm thinking we should begin with the castles tomorrow." Scott say. "What do you think?" he ask Kobby.

"Not tomorrow." He answer too fast, shaking his head, scratching his forehead. Reminds me of when someone sees a snake. He is the snake, I want to shout at him, but my head is still slowly coming out of the water. "We can do Kakum National Park tomorrow. There's also (Hans Cottage), which I'd love you all to see."

Now when Elton and his friends are speaking, it's okay that I can't understand them, because they're from America. But I hate how this Ghanaman speaks, like he wants to be them, like he doesn't want me to understand one thing he's saying. Not like the English of the nice waiter girl. This English is very heavy like generator and only Elton and his friends understand him. I hate him. All this plenty school and you let another man put his *pipi* in your *duna*.

"The castle tomorrow." I speak too, all the others remain quiet as if forgetting that I'm here, like a group of chief elders who've forgotten a child or a woman sitting with them. Since Ananse became friends with them, that's how they treat me when he's around. Like I'm not important, like my grandma treat me, which make me annoyed. "We should go to castles tomorrow."

"I really don't care what we do, honestly." Vincent raise his shoulders. "Anything is fine, as long as we all agree that we're not doing any moving today, I need lots of rest—"

"On the beach, Vincent," Scott say to him, moving his hands up and down his shoulders. "Lots of fresh air will do you good. You're not going to stay (cooped up) under my watch." Scott is really good, good friend, I can tell. Elton has forgotten he has friends and only care about Ananse-Kobby, who is not agreeing with my plans.

"I don't think we should do the castles tomorrow."

"Why?" Elton turn to him. "I say we should do what Nana says." Elton has a big smile on his face. I know he's joking with me. "You don't have any reason why we shouldn't see the castles, all the other stuff are (secondary) reasons for being here. We came here to see the castles. Get through our Year of Return (programming). So we'll do that first." Kobby scratch his forehead, shake his head, his eyes open wide. I want to know what he's hiding, why he's afraid of castle.

"Well shit, Elton," Scott say. "Having two (tour guides) ain't such a good thing, huh?" Kobby frown at Scott. "I apologise, you're not a (tour guide). Exactly why we'll leave everything to Nana to decide."

"I say we do the Kakum Park tomorrow."

My head is still coming out of the water. It falls in, and it's pulled out so many times, the voices around me sound like little boy voices, then grown-up voices, then little boy voices again. Because I want it all to stop, I lift my hands and say, "Okay!"

The voices begin to stop if I sing the hunter song, so I sing in my head.

"Really?" Elton sound like something have shock him. "Okay! Kakum tomorrow."

I hear Scott begin to whistle with his mouth, looking down on the table, as if he is telling them something he don't want me to hear. All of them look behind me. I hear the boom-boom from the wooden floor. I turn my face to see who has come, thinking it's the waiter girl, and I worry why they are all acting like my classmates back in primary school when a nice girl is passing. Behind me is a fat white woman who has done Rasta. Her face look red like she is angry. She is with a tall macho-macho black man who I know isn't black American because he look very Ghanaian with the tribal marks from the Hausa people on his face. I turn my face to see the others, and I see that all of them are looking at each other and saying things only them can hear. I worry my head is still inside that water.

"Those (braids) sure do look as if they hurt." Scott laughs small in his hands. "He's (probably) her husband."

That's when I turn to the fat woman again. She sees me looking at her and wave nicely at me. Everyone who sit with me say hi to her too. I look at the black man and his hand is around the woman like they are husband and wife. I want to laugh. They look like children playing *maame ne paapa*. In Ghana, yes, fat women are nice and they can even win *Di Asa* and they even put them in Cargo and Adonko Bitters advert, and everybody call them *tokɛsɛɛ* and want to marry them, but when white woman be fat, she be fat with no shape like the circles our maths teacher make us draw in school with free hand.

"He wants the green light," Elton say very quietly, stretching "green" like he's singing a song. Scott laugh small in his hand again. Vincent look like he don't find what they're saying interesting. Kobby still look like someone throw shit in his face.

I try to understand what Elton say. Green light? I want to ask him what he mean, but I don't want to look stupid especially in front of Ananse. I just know like everyone on the table that the man wants to trick this white woman. And I'm not happy. I'm not happy at all-at all about his *sika anibere*. I look into Kobby face, and he turn to face me. We look at each other long, then he look away. Just like how the others sometimes talk to each other without opening their mouth and with only their eyes, I know Kobby know that I know he's met his brother-man. Another Ananse. I will call my pastor and ask if two man can marry in America, then I will know what Kobby really want with blind Elton who doesn't see him well-well. Green light.

KOBBY

Ignoring the others' poor attempts at subtlety, my gaze is unwavering, fixed on the interracial couple that just entered. Their affection for each other is displayed like a tacky performance by amateur actors in a warped reality TV experiment. "When you come to Africa," Vincent once told me on a night we'd all sat down to drink and watch reruns of Fresh Prince of Bel Air, "you're surprised, even angry to see white people. Not because it's not a normal sight, actually it's very normal for you to find whites scattered in the remotest places of the earth. There's just that part—fatherly, or call it protective—that part of you that spots a white person in Africa of all places, and thinks, not my people, stay the fuck away!" It's pretty obvious here who's being taken advantage of, and who needs Vincent's protection: not the tall African with ethnic scarification across his cheeks, who is possibly a Northerner. The sad white woman has no idea what's in store for her. Or maybe this is a temporary fling that ends the moment her holiday's over, a contracted romance. Not unlike my and Elton's relationship.

I find Nana squinting at me; his eyes hold mine longer than they ever have. A slanderous remark in an ethnic language is spat under his breath, something that aspires for the semantic sweet spot between gold-digger and piece of shit. At first, I am floored that he equates me with this opportunistic man, but my dismay is soon subverted by a slight heaving, the result of an interjectional chuckle. And then I can't stop the laughter. *Kikiki.* It is loud and audacious, just a tad facetious for the sake of dispelling Nana's suspicions. The white woman, who must surely think I'm mocking her, throws me a dirty look that comes across meaner because of her strained braids. She looks like an angry zit. Elton presses a foot on mine, but this just worsens my laughter.

"Food is here!" The waitress salvages the situation, teetering in with arms balancing trays of food. Nana is no longer interested in me: his attention shifts to the buxom woman who settles the dishes on the table, wishes us all "bon appetit" and runs a palm over Scott's arm.

NANA

I put my fingers deep inside the hot soup and I feel like I'm back home in my village, in my grandmother's house. Accra fufu is not nice like this, *kraa*. Fufu they cooked with Neat Fufu Powder can never be like fufu from pounding the cassava and plantain. I'm sure the others watch me eat with my fingers like they are surprised that I can eat this hot food without blowing air on it. I don't mind them and their American food that has no scent. Elton has raw eggs fried with the yellow side still on top, I want to tell him that looking at his food makes me sick and only fetish priest and traditionalists who want to curse people eat this. Vincent has that food he calls a sand witch which is just bread with something like sardine. Scott has a plate filled with plenty cabbage and carrot and other vegetables, looks like goat food. Ananse who is Kobby has groundnut soup which he calls "peanut-butter stew" and eats it with a spoon! A spoon! *Kurasinin bɛn na ɔkyem wei baa wiase!* Before eating, he take out his phone and a book from his bag, then he put the book by the food and take picture.

Scott say, "You (millennials) stay posting on the (gram)."

"I'm sure he's posting something along the lines of (Hashtag baecation)," Elton say. Under the table, I see him lift Kobby's leg and throw it on his lap. Kobby shake his head and laugh small, pressing-pressing his phone.

Elton take fast Kobby's phone from his hand and read what Kobby is writing, "On my billionth re-read of (Hashtag American Psycho), What keeps me coming back is the (violence), can you blame me? I love being a (voyeur) to those (scenes). From a (linguistic standpoint), these scenes are rendered (poetically). I know most of you will disagree. What do you think, (Bookstagram) fam?"

"Bookstagram? Is that Instagram for books?" Scott ask. "People really be doing the most these days. You've got a whole fucking account dedicated to books and shit. Can't stand y'all."

All Ghanaians who use Android like to take *salifu* of their face. Only this boy want to show the whole world that he know book. *Tweaaa! Ne ho ara ɛnyɛ hin.*

Kobby let Vincent and his friends taste the soup and the rice he has with it. He tells them it's a Ghanaian favourite food and I want to tell them all that he is lying, it is poor people food. The kind of food *tro-tro* drivers eat when they are waiting for their car to fill or what government give to children in village schools for the free school-feeding programme. Some time, a cat from nowhere come sit under the table and I want to sack it because it look like a witch with its black body and yellow eyes. But Elton move down and use his hands to touch it, give it food, let the cat lick and then use the same hand to go back to eating. "You's a good kitty-kitty," he say.

"What language do the people of Cape Coast speak?" Elton ask.

"They speak—"

"Fante." I say before Kobby say, again they all look at me as if they've forgotten I'm here. Now that I'm out of the water, I'm going to make myself present like it's maths teacher class.

"Yes, they speak Fante," Kobby continue.

"Cape Coast Fante different from Elmina Fante and not the same as Takoradi Fante."

"What Nana is trying to say is, just like English, they've got different (regional dialects)." Kobby try to talk for me.

"Which people speak Twi then?" Vincent ask, pronouncing the Twi like the sounds school children make with their mouth when they want to tease each other that one of them has *flatunate*: *tu-we*. I want to stop him immediately and teach him how to say it well: say tree, but say it fast. I don't like it when people say Ashanti things wrong. "I know the people in Accra speak Ga," he say.

"Lots of people speak Twi in Accra plenty. It's Ghana favourite language. Fante is Twi."

"So Fante is a (dialect) of Twi. Twi is spoken mainly by the Ashantis. Actually, there's so much (mutual intelligibility) between those languages that (linguists) want to consider Fante a (variety) of Twi instead of a (dialect). It's not as though Asante Twi is a much more (standardised), more superior (dialect) to be made a (variety at the expense) of Fante: they're both equal, Fante is (standardised) and taught as well . . ."

This boy really want to show that he know book. *Kwasia, paa.* So I speak: "Fante people used to be part of Ashanti people, but they leave to come to this place to do business with the white people."

"Actually, that's not the truth. (Oral) history has it that Fantes were already here before the (arrival) of the Europeans—"

"No." I stop putting fufu in my mouth and shake my head at the liar. I want to shout that I know better than him, I am Ashanti. These are our people, I know my history. Who is he to challenge an Ashanti man like me? Where is he from? Who is their chief? Which animal protects his people? What is his father's name? "The Fantes came here to give away people to the British for slave trade!"

This make everyone on the table quiet except for Elton phone, which keep doing *zzz*. They all look at the white woman behind me. I shout too much and the black witch cat run away, but I continue, "That's why you never trust a Fante. They sell all the people from the North to South to the British so that the British do not touch them and they lived here like kings. That is why they do Bond of 1844." I hear a chair scratch the floor and I know that the white woman and the Hausa man are leaving. The others look at them and Scott say something in his hands again and laugh. I want to tell him to stop that because he's a grown man with white in his goat beard.

Vincent do mm-hmm with his throat. "That was interesting, Nana. Thanks for the story. Kobby, what are you? What's your ethnic group? What do they speak?"

I turn my face sharp to Kobby. He take long to speak, a big smile fall on his face.

"I'm from the Ashanti Region."

"You are not Ashanti," I say angry, disgracing myself any-time I raise my voice, but I don't care. This Ananse is a liar! Calling himself an Ashanti makes me look bad, he's spoiling the Ashanti name! He eat soup with spoon! Spoon! *Kɔnkra kraa yɛmfa nnom kwan!*

"I'm from the Ashanti Region," he say again with that big smile. He does not look at my face as if I'm *saman*.

"What's your father's name? Who's your chief? Which animal protects your people?" To these people I know I sound like a fool, but if a real Ashanti old man is with me, he'll slap this boy.

"Nana." Elton puts his hand on my own, his voice deep and low. "You don't have to shout."

I go back to eating my food and keeping quiet. If I talk again, I will become more angry. He's not Ashanti. There are so many people in Ashanti Region that are not Ashanti. He won't even tell anyone what his father's name is. I'm sure his Twi smells like shit, like rat that have die from poison inside its hole. Who's this boy? Where did they find him? Why do you know so small about someone and still sleep with him? Does Elton not have brain? Does he not smell something like a rat here? I try to relax. My dead grandfather who was a hunter, who teach me to use his gun before we could even know ourselves, say, *Obi mfa aboa anim mmɔ homa.* You do not go in front of an animal to tie a rope. If you want to catch someone, stand behind them.

"Well, that (escalated) quickly," Scott say and, "I want to do some (yoga), do you want to join me?" he ask Vincent.

"Isn't it too hot for outdoor (yoga)? I'd rather be in bed."

"No, Vince, it's not hot, it's the perfect weather for—"

"It's almost noon," Elton say. "Go do yoga. Invite Nana to do yoga."

What at all is yoga? Is it like yoghurt but with their American voice they cannot say it well?

I look up from my food and I see Vincent and Scott opening their eyes wide, and I know that they are all doing that thing where they are saying something with their eyes, something they don't want me to hear. I'll tell my pastor that this Kobby has put something under their eyes, witchcraft, and these people have forgotten their first friend, me. Kobby's mobile phone ring and he takes it and put it down again. Work, he say and smile big at everyone. Now I know how his face become when he's saying lies. Maybe he's Akwapim, the ones who say please before insulting you. Those people can spit in your face and when you have cleaned the saliva you'll still find them standing there, smiling at you and still saying please. You don't trust

Akwapim people. When I get small chance to be in the room alone, I'll look again inside this Ananse's bag for that Sasab-onsam Killer shoemaker pin.

My phone ringtone, Daddy Lumba's "Mensei Da," begins playing, and I want to press "decline," but it's my pastor's number showing. I tell Elton that my pastor is calling me and can I please excuse myself for just few minutes, I won't keep long.

"*Wo wɔ hen?*" my pastor is screaming at me.

I joke, "*Pastor me pa wo kyɛw na meredi fufu ne mfante-mfante.*"

"*Kwasia.* I've sent you plenty WhatsApp messages but you're not reading! One of the friends is going to die!"

MID-DAY INTERLUDES

It's afternoon. And Elton and I are having sex. He's already double-checked that the door's bolt works. He's already kissed me against the door, kissed me on my forehead, the left corner of my lips, the lobe of my right ear. And that's foreplay enough. When we're laid out on the tiny rectangular bed, I hook my legs into the bars of the top bunk, puckering my asshole to clue him in on what I'd want next. I just wasn't expecting him to get carried away, eating me out like we have the room to ourselves all day. *Let me taste that, please.* His tongue swords in and out of what may be my prostate, a thorough oral vacuuming. When my excitement feels too good to contain, my body lets a fart loose. *Prrrr. Babe,* Elton breathes from the bush in my groin, *control yourself.* The sneer on his face encapsulates his joy at my weakness for his tongue. I fling the back of my palm at him, and it catches him on his temple. *Don't talk,* I instruct, wresting my dominance back. *Who you think you are?* He rises from my backside and moves onto his knees, his silver chain dipping into the ridge between his sweat-studded breasts. He spits into the cup of his palm and lubes my ass with more fingers than required. Then his dick follows. Since I had no chance to douche, there's a burning sensation in my anus which I suspect is my faeces and his dick knocking heads. The scent of poop rises in the air, nasty as a villain making a comeback. But Elton doesn't seem to give a shit; the occasional fuckups of copulating bodies mustn't get in the way of one's desire to nut. Unwittingly, our bodies have supplied us with lube. When I grunt too loud, he forces a finger in my mouth so that I can have something to gag on. *Shush.* I gnaw my molars into his thumb, grind into the soft flesh of cuticle. Irritated, he presses into my shoulders and fucks me with way more back than waist. I smirk through the pain, grab his necklace and wring it around his beard. *Fuck me like I'm riding you. Say please*, he barks. *No.*

IV

KOBBY
(9 days after the friends arrive)

Something is wrong with Vincent, Elton. You don't see it because you're occupied with me. I'd tell Scott, but I think he already knows. Or you perhaps know about it too but won't talk about it. A secret pact between friends I can't be let in on.

Vincent and I smile at each other as we both sit for breakfast: we are the only two who have chosen to prioritise fructose over fitness. I'm munching on your brownies, Elton, as I nervously refresh my Instagram for notifications. I push the Tupperware towards Vincent, but he declines and turns his attention towards the shore. We remain unspeaking as if being in each other's company is relaxing enough without needing vocal interaction. As if Vincent has suddenly decided to put a stop to his 101 lessons on racism he reserves for me.

Just last night I'd seen him, a shadow standing at the water's edge, wearing a black so dark it was impossible to catch the gleam of a human form swallowed into the deep-throat of the sky. "Ever heard of the water-walking Africans?" he'd spoken, almost making me think he was addressing the sea. He was deep in the kind of monastic meditative state that made one privy to the universe's furtive operations. The braying and smacking of thighs by waves in animated discourse. The flicker of torches from the distant canoes on a night's fishing expedition. The whispering of my bare feet against sand. "No," I'd responded, claiming my spot next to him. "Kobby." He smiled a thin smile that was a see-through to his disappointment, as if he'd been expecting someone else to have followed when he left the room stealthily and found himself at sea.

I should tell you about the AESMA episode occurring after minutes of tossing and turning over dead palm branches and pebbles, my surroundings unimaginatively assuming the set of *L'inconnu du Lac*. After a cruising scene during which we fuck, I watch Vincent getting dunked till he drowns, and Scott keeling over after being knifed. I'm pursued by a villain who morphs from Christophe Paou to Nana. From the woods where I spend hours hiding, I emerge, yelling, *J'ai besoin de toi, Nana! On va passer la nuit ensemble!* Before the credits roll, he slits my throat and I sleep. Should I tell you this, I'm certain you'd cast aside the obvious signs of my mania, dwelling instead on my obsession with Nana, who at the time of these fantasies was lost to a nightmare so violent his body succumbed to convulsions. The sight of which led me to believe I was better off sleeping next to Elmina's coastline than within reach of his demons.

"Vincent!" I spotted him as I headed back to the resort. Found him near the edge of the water. Unlike last night where he just seemed lost, now he looked like a man who'd failed to catch a bus, pacing impatiently for the next one.

"Vincent!" He turned toward my voice. He smiled a smile as joyous as his current background of little children cannonballing into the ocean, their pigtails and afros acting as parachutes as they flew, shrieking before drowning, then resurfacing and calling out to Ata and Ataa not to be wimps, to just leap like an *Alogo-springi*, like a *Tutulapatu*.

"Slept well?" I lay down my phone on the brownie crumbs littered over our breakfast table in order to engage Vincent in conversation. He offers no more than a nod to my question. With his head lifted to the skies, squinting into the depths of blue as if in pursuit of another realm unknown, he seems entirely different from the Vincent I encountered in Accra. The man before me appears to have wrung himself through some personality-disintegrating turnstile that has allowed into El-mina this vacuous shell of a human and detained all there is to him, his insufferable liveliness, in the other city.

I should make more of an effort with him and ignore my phone whose screen has erupted with a notification from a follower I couldn't care for. The brownies have lost all taste and I may be high on them, but I'm still anxious for more interactions with yesterday's story on *American Psycho*. If perhaps the weed's high and my anxiety are cancelling each other out, putting away these stale treats would be yet another disastrous action to add to my list of unreasonable decisions taken at the expense of my health. Out of frustration, I search my Google albums for a photo of *American Psycho* taken against the browning rot of my brother's obituary. In IG's caption box, I type: *It's like swishing some revolting spirit in your mouth, knowing that the longer you swish, the more your own saliva infuses with this spirit till you can no longer tell your spit from liquor. Reading* American Psycho *is swishing violence in the mouth until it becomes familiar.*

I hit "Post" and within seconds, my phone pings over and over again. Vincent seems like he's about to chastise me for setting the ring volume loud. I'm about to turn it down when a number pops up on my inbox tab. I tap it to find the follower whose attention I've been manifesting all week. **1 message from Aspecialkindofdouble**:

How're you, my friend?

People are always quick to point out my apparent lack of a social life. My colleagues, whose e-vites to their Friday-night *akonfem* parties I report as spam. My boss, who insists that anytime I walk into her office, I give off such a stench of being a loner that even she with her obsession for Gothic colours has to draw open her blinds to let out my bats. No one trusts someone without friends—their intrusive remarks about my life suggest—as if to live sans friendship is a resumé devoid of refer-ees. No one to vouch that your own life is worth living.

Aspecialkindofdouble and I clicked over reviewing books which weren't mainstream, mostly old and used books, forgot-ten backlists—the kind Bookstagram only posted for clout and rarely read, ditching them for overly hyped recent releases. She was a slave to her library. I had no source for literature apart from the book flea markets of Accra, reading only what I found accessible. About my very white Crime Fiction feed, which was the subject of many a shade-fest among the Black bookstagram community, she'd simply said, *No one needs to defend their reading tastes to anyone, Kobby. I love you just the way you are, never change for anyone.*

One night, a result of an extensive conviviality—the kind of online chat lasting throughout daily routines where participants could go on all day only realising the energies spent when one mentioned sleep—she asked the dreaded question. *You've got so many stories in you, Kobby, are you a writer?* I could have lied. I could have said no. After she'd hit send on that ques-tion, I imagined her shoving something into an oven, putting on a TV show, checking her phone for a response, shrugging when one wasn't coming, then getting up at the chiming of the oven, returning to a message from me saying, *yes.* An av-alanche of messages. I told her about the emails. I told her I had given up. I told her too much while tearing up under the blue-light of my Android screen. She replied, *Can I give you a call now? I could put this show on pause and let this chicken cool as we talk.* It wasn't the first time I'd heard her voice since she's usually uploading, on Black History Month, content dubbed WomenRaceNRhyme, where she reads, to the horror of those Toni-Zora-Angelou staple stackers, the works of unsung Black women poets. As expected, she directed on me this voice that held none of the lilt it reserved for Effie Waller Smith's "Apple Sauce and Chicken Fried," not as gravyish and sonorous. This was sharp with cautioning and advice, a discordant interlude on one of those soul albums whose haunting vocals made listeners feel seen, her warmth expressed not in tone but diction. "You listen to me, Kobby. Are you listening? 'Cause I'm about to tell you something I tell my students when it's college application season." Expecting a lecture, I waited, shrouded in the darkness of overlapping time zones. "Send them for fun, simply. Send them for fun. No expectations. That, in my book, is better than giving up."

How're you, my friend?

We'd become more than friends. This was a friendship that existed without having to pay that full emotional price of proximity yet was still valid and sure as any bond created in the flesh. A relationship that had been put through many issues in a relatively shorter time than an off-line one would allow.

I look up from my phone to Vincent, who has turned his attention from the skies to the water, who represents this disconnect between my physical world and the world I've built online. Neither aware of the other's existence, each with their own script and characters; and I, the orchestrator of both worlds, responsible for the marker slate deciding where one ends and the other begins. As I am thinking of a reply to Aspecialkindofdouble, I become more aware of the water dragging its nails across my cheeks, hands, legs, scolding all my parts that aren't covered up.

I turn to the right of Vincent. There's Scott on his yoga mat, stretching with Nana, who is finding it hard to imitate Scott's avian poses. There's an albino child wrapped in a fishing net and standing on the bow of a docked canoe with the words *Okyɛso Nyame Bɛkyɛ Ama Aso Me So.* They are the muse of a photographer who keeps cheering for more photos. Vincent and I see you, Elton, running back and forth across our view, shirtless, sweating, shoulders sagging as though you want to kiss the fine sand. You spot the photographer with the seemingly genderless kid, shake your head, and jog in the opposite direction. These routines are peaceful ways to start our mornings, I think. Unlike days woken up in Accra which begin with their usual unrest, moving as fast as commuter trains carrying sluggish passengers. Days in Cape Coast are undoubtedly the kind to open with Corinne Bailey Rae, a tranquillity as lulling as watching newborns sleep—so addictive there's a temptation to kick the cot and witness it all again. Over here, I am able to remove myself from the frustrations of the past days, and those ahead. Over here, I'm not a son whose dad texts him not to do anything stupid, or a man who ponders the mysterious killings in Accra and falls victim to an alluring delight that stretches his lips and steals the gravity of the subject. I'm not the man you fuck, Elton, or Nana hates, or Scott couldn't give a damn about, or Vincent lectures on life and Black History. I'm just a man, trapped in the vast world of the internet, still waiting on an email that might change my life. While spying the child model who speeds past Scott and Nana, screaming, *"Obroni ne Black Makuku,"* referring to Scott, and not the photographer who chases with his camera, I send Aspecialkindofdouble my reply: *still no positive response.*

"Can't wait for Kakum!" Elton snaps me out of my online world, implanting himself on the table. I look at you, and you're closer, Nana, seated with Scott too. And there's the waitress, screaming that our breakfast is ready, giggling coquettishly at Scott. I watch your jaw tense. There's only so much tension your jaw can hold, Nana. I almost hate how everything gets dull. Craving some lurid scenes, a bit of blood here, a twist of an arm there. How long until our perfect portrait of thalassic respite turns negative?

* * *

"Killer ants, watch your step!" the tour guide yells at the school kids leading our hike. I wonder if he's the same man that led the tour group—whose membership comprised students in a higher grade—that I'd been encouraged (forced) by my parents to join when I was only twelve to the others' fifteens and sixteens. A feat which would have made the list of most eventful occurrences, if that one student had chosen to die on another excursion.

"These children are slowing us down," Scott remarks, loud enough for the last kid on the line to look him up and down, up and frown. We're walking the centenarian steps to the canopy walk, traversing a brick path drowned in mud, brittle figs and leaves. Trees that surround us stick their branches out like crowds over the barricades of a race. The smell of grass and soil mixes with the odour of human activity circumventing our glistening bodies.

Elton, Vincent, and Nana are the last trio in the group. Scott and I converse about getting our daily cardio in with this exercise, and other random, unimportant topics flowing at the pace of a coughing faucet. Our exchange is depthless. Scott is always attempting something humorous coupled with a triviality that betrays his superciliousness. Anything otherwise would suggest an ability to fathom how a boy like me living in the Global South might understand the complexity of his American life with its American laughter-lines. So he forces himself into this restrictive social interaction, the kind of tolerable yet pitiful conversations between people on a cultural-exchange programme. Conversations about the weather, the flora, the fauna; which are *great, beautiful, interesting but God really likes showing off in these parts, doesn't he? Ha ha.*

He's my least favourite of the bunch and he knows. This makes us awkward in each other's company; not sure if we should change our feelings toward each other or maintain them. After all, he's probably thinking he's not going to be seeing me again after this trip, so why bother? I'm the negligible insect he shoos off his shoulder. Something that may even be interesting, he may be musing, but unimportant to him. Maybe he's stopped bothering with getting to know the men Elton fucks on these trips around the world, one of the million. He forgets my name sometimes, or pigeonholes me into a category that bears the name of the first man he met on these kinds of trips with Elton. Maybe it's the guy from South Africa, the first of Elton's African conquests, fucked and housed under the condition of helping the friends navigate the country's queer scene. This guy might be the one blasting Elton's phone with messages whose vibrations can be heard through the agitated murmurings of the kids and the crunching of dead leaves under foot.

Over the hubbub of twittering birds and buzzing bees, the woods also present a mystifying clangour which we'd all wondered about at the start of this hike. Stomping sounds that give the impression we're being pursued. Elton, in a bid to dismiss our fears, speculates, injudiciously, that we're listening to our own footwear echoing. Nana, under the influence of too many Nigerian dramas, thinks we're walking through an evil forest and insists that we mustn't look back. The tour guide has no answers to lessen our anxieties. It's the reemergence of this noise that makes Scott so terrified he flings himself into my arms, then apologises for being too much of a wimp when the sound fizzles out.

"I used to dance for Debbie Allen," Scott says, perhaps tired of my snippy responses to his jaundiced questions.

"Really?"

"Yeah, it's why I'm so fit." Wouldn't call him fit, just lean. "I'm surprised you know Debbie Allen, though."

I decide to indulge his condescension. "No, I don't know Debbie Allen."

"*Humph*. I suspected."

Elton and Vincent and Nana's trialogue crawls on behind us. Nana's teaching them the Twi names for things around us. *Ahaban*, he calls out the leaf. *Adua*, tree. When we encounter an army of dung beetles rolling faeces, he says *amankuo*, contra-dicting the generic *ntatee* my mind supplies beforehand. He's essentially a child who recently conquered the babbling stage and now enjoys the thrill of being understood, eagerly labelling everything in sight. I almost turn to let the others know that grasshopper isn't *akrantie* as he instructs.

Once again, the untraceable sound bustles past, louder than ever—hooves pounding the earth—and Scott reaches for my arm like one would a prized possession in the face of a robbery.

"Kobby, what do you do?" Scott sounds rather interested, surprising both himself and me. "It's odd I haven't asked sooner."

It really is strange that Elton and his friends haven't in-quired what I do. Everyone from the West who gets on these dating/hook-up apps has a million questions to ask locals be-fore agreeing to meet. Cock-blocking questions that horny Afri-cans refrain from asking one another to avoid getting their asses blocked instead of fucked.

Some Questions from Western Men Who Are Only Inter-ested in Fucking African Men: What do you do? How much do you make a month? What do your parents do? Have you ever travelled outside the country before? Europe? America? Any STIs? What's your highest level of education? Do you wanna meet up?

It's the ultimate unemployment office set-up.

How we get weary of these questions meant to decide whether we're people who won't rob them. "Must be hard be-ing a foreigner in an African country looking for a fuck," I told one French guy, a yellow-fever research scientist on a grant, who looked about twenty years older than his picture online. This I only realised when it was too late to run back into my taxi and leave; why I've stopped consenting to midday alfresco dates. "My friend," the scientist spoke, using the overdone, pa-tronising Ghanaian accent he'd picked up because he got tired of locals trying to swindle him, "you can't be sure who's honest and who won't blackmail you." I countered: "Then why don't you fuck the white men here?" He turned confrontational: "Have you seen them? I'm asking you, have you seen them?" He kissed his teeth and snapped his fingers. I was disgusted by these exaggerated Ghanaian antics. He added: "They are uglier and older here, and what sane traveller would want to fuck a white man in Africa? Isn't that a waste of travel, my love? We're going half-half on this bill, right? You pay half, I pay half." The experience would still have been insufferable had he chosen to reek of anything more pleasant than boiled cabbage.

Now Scott's asking, "I just assumed you were some sort of influencer, but you keep saying 'Work' anytime your phone rings and—"

A phone intercepts my vision. Instinctively I push it away, almost knocking it to the ground.

"Relax," Elton chuckles. "I already got too many pics of your booty. I just need a selfie."

"I'm not big on pictures."

"You have no choice, Kobby. We own your ass. We're fucking paying your way through this life." In the scuffle that follows, me ducking as he tries to get a good shot, Scott retreats to Vincent. I'm thankful and hasty to indulge in a sense of relief, until it's clear that I've fallen in line with Elton and Nana. I wince. Elton pinches my arm, requesting that I become a subservient student to Nana's tutelage. *Borla*. Rubbish. *Mpaboa*. Shoe.

For minutes, I suffer Nana while assessing his body—the tightening of muscles that form his quads, the large chunk of ankle that juts out with every step taken. It's a body whose contractions and relaxations strain against the fabric of its skin as if putting on a show for the world to glimpse its processes. I watch this sweet transparency of sininewiness, with eyes mimicking that greedy way the yellow-fever scientist's hands squeezed my parts as if feeling for the ligaments and tendons that make up my entire anatomy. The way he exclaimed, "Aah, you Africans are blessed!" and I winced, begging for morning to come so his leering appraisal would be over.

I find Scott moving in line with us three, having left Vincent on his own. Scott's blasé attitude isn't enough façade to conceal his obvious irritation, which provides unwitting proof that he and his husband must have separated because of a squabble. Theirs is a relationship that often feels like a paper boat braving real seas. How they've endured years with each other is baffling, makes me wonder what glues them.

I disentangle from the three, deliberately trailing behind.

"Hey," I flash Vincent a genuine smile which he misses. "It's beautiful here, isn't it?"

"Peaceful." He's not particularly studying the plants, just zoning off into the distance. When I make an effort to break the silence, comment on the scenery, or brush my skin against his, he seems flustered before noticing he's got company and submits a half-hearted response.

"Hey, are you okay?"

"Why the fuck does everyone keep asking me that?" He grunts, then registering it's me he's talking to, a stranger he rather likes, he replies equably, "I'm fine, yeah."

"You just seem a bit . . . off?"

"Did Scott send you to check on me?" We both look at the others ahead, who're struggling to keep up with Nana and his lectures.

"I think Nana's keeping him too busy to care about you."

The unknown sound rears its head again, but this time distinctly close. Vince and I spin toward the branches at our side. Through the leaves we see them: three white bodies tearing through the mangrove. They're brandishing cameras and wearing what look like bulldozer sneakers, platforms so huge they seem to be perforating the earth. Elton and Scott and Nana spot them too. So do the kids ahead who scream: *Obroni!*

Nature photography, the tour guide announces dismissively to keep us moving. The group is almost out of sight when it strikes me that one of them could be the photographer from this morning. Still, if he isn't among them, the moment presents itself as one of the many motifs of white noise and interference in all of Elmina and its environs. Even the nooks and crannies a local might withdraw into to take a shit or piss, only to be dispossessed of their privacy when a camera clicks.

"I could live here, you know," Vincent speaks, once the chaos dies and our hiking resumes.

"Vincent, if you get on your hotep shit, I'll scream."

His laughter splits through the quiet, reaches Scott who turns and frowns, then looks away. "You think I'm a hotep?" Something rustles under the leaves and Vincent barks "*Ɛwɔɔ!*"

Now I laugh. "Very hotep, yes."

"Hey, I'm just saying snake in Twi, isn't that it?"

"You just said honey, not snake. They're almost the same words."

"Oh?" He rests a finger on the chasm in his chin. "At least I tried. I'm going to stop now so you don't call me out on my," he draws air-quotes, "'hotep shit.'"

"I actually don't mind you going off on your . . . romanticism of Africa. It's actually nice that you like it here." And then I whisper, "I think Scott hates it here." My laughter peters out when he doesn't join in, then we're back to silence again. To stop him from retreating into the recesses of his mind, I say to him, "You know if something's bothering you, you can tell me, you know this, right?"

He peers at me, as if measuring my words. Then he leans into me, languidly, a dullness in his gaze. We're within kissing-distance, but I let my unease slide even when our foreheads touch. "I'll tell you something." There is an unsettling edge to his voice, a baritone that doesn't quite sound like his. "Promise you'll listen and do as I say—"

"We're nearing the canopy!" The tour guide jolts him. He becomes disconcerted by our nearness, looks apologetic of what was clearly a passionless proximity.

"This is huge!" we hear Scott squeal. Right ahead of us, we see the installation. The famous canopy walkway of Kakum Park, revealed through parted branches. "Looks like something from Indiana Jones," Elton says as he rotates his phone horizontally to take pictures.

The walkway is elevated five hundred feet above ground, zipping through stems of trees encircled by psychedelic butterflies flaunting their fluidity. It is an invincibly breathtaking scenery: dewy green the colour of basil, saturated with an odoriferous freshness that can only be associated with vegetal secretions. I sniff and savour the warmth; even now when I smell death lurking in the air. I remember it as clearly as I did years ago.

For my school's trip, some students had been wimps, refusing to get on the walkway. I still remember our old tour guide saying, as this current one shouts, "Are you kids not taught gravity in school, no one's died from walking on this—"

"—unless they obviously wanted to jump and die," Scott jokes. Which is what was reported in the papers that that one kid did. We listen to the recitations about the installation's stats and specs: "The walkway stretches about three hundred and fifty metres, connecting seven treetops. There's the short one that takes you right to the end, but I advise you to take the long one, it's fun."

"I'll take the short one," Vincent says, "I'm sorry I don't think I have the head for all that swinging." He points at a group of kids ahead who're screaming through the course. Scott insists that he'll follow Vincent, "But I'm gonna hold this against you for not letting us have all the fun," he adds.

"Do whatever you want, Scott," Vincent snaps.

Scott glances abashedly at me, then Elton. "I'll take the long one. Nana, go with Vincent." He walks to the installation, muttering things under his breath, shrieks on first footing, gets used to the swaying, manages a steady pace, then onwards.

I watch Nana carry one of the kids who won't quit wailing, a gesture I may have thought sweet if anyone else had done it. He leads the batch taking the short walkway. Vincent follows him. "Are you joining them or us?" the tour guide questions Elton and me.

The boardwalk creaks under Elton's feet, he jokes, "I don't think they made this kind of thing for people my weight." I laugh, and perhaps he catches my eye-roll even though I'm in front. He clasps his hands around my neck, a loose form of a chokehold, dragging my rear into him, swipes at the air and seizes a butterfly to force through my nostrils.

"Elton," I say, surprised, terrified, futilely fighting him off. "What's happening?" The walkway seems dangerous now that my hands can't grab onto the thick woven netting on its sides. I'm tormented by a flurry of images: the mashed mass of a teenager's body; joints having jagged-edged teeth that snarl through skin; blood, too much of it, flowing through orifices and crevices, fissures and cracks caused by twigs and branches, conical ends of snapped tree limbs.

"Was I a good top yesterday?"

"Elton, this is neither the time nor place for a conversation like this."

"Oh, the kids won't hear me, we cool, it's just you and me." He taunts again, in my ear, "Was I a good top last night?"

"Okay, on a scale of one-to-ten, five?"

"You're terrible." He pushes me off him lightly. "My exes loved me as a top."

"Elton, you cum too quick when I choke you."

"Nigga, you choke like you're squeezing the nut out of me. Plus, if I retained my cum to get through a few extra positions, I woulda crushed you, trust me." He catches up to me. "You know, Scott said something during our walk up here. When you and Vincent were behind, doing whatever you were doing—"

"Do I sense jealousy?" I whip my head around, and for a second I'm caught by his handsome brown face reddening against the scorching sun. Something warm stirs in me. A little erection in the most unusual place. Sins unfurling within God's strike.

"Scott is who you have to worry about," Elton jokes. "You and I have no commitment."

"Ouch."

"But listen, those two have been looking for a third for years now, maybe Vincent more than Scott, so I suggest you don't make things weirder than they already are." A pause. "Anyway, we know nothing about you, Kobby."

A beautiful white bird swoops in on the tour guide and the kids ahead, and they shriek, their agitated voices chopped into echoes that traverse the distance between the air and the forest below.

"Is that what Scott said?"

"He asked what you did for a living. I told him I didn't know."

"I've told you what I do, Elton." I haven't. "You just haven't been listening."

"Really?" I don't need to look at him to see his dubious expression. "Right now, tell me something about you, something you want to tell me, of course."

"You make it sound like I don't tell you anything."

"Tell me something now."

I flick through a chart of interesting things. My brother's obituaries. My mother's canine. The nightly rituals including AESMA I perform before sleep. The scar on my forehead which is a souvenir from the last time I attempted touring the region's colonial castles. Or must I tell him about the emails? Those seem like lighter baggage compared to the others. His pocketed phone vibrates, breaking the moment even when he ignores the alerts. I think of a myriad of South African men's names. Letlhogonolo. Mkhululi. Katlego. Reasons not to get too attached to Elton, in case he ignores my text messages too after he's left the country.

"Kobby?"

"I visit the hospital occasionally," I blurt out. I don't tell him I go to the morgues often, in the same manner people go to museums, for the opportunity to immerse myself in the stories of the dead. No one will find that charming.

"And?" He leans into me. "Are you, like, sick?"

"No. No! I'm not sick!" I feign a laugh. He laughs too, relieved. A thought occurs to me, opening up as a hole that promises escape. "But I do know when someone's sick . . . I think Vincent is running a fever."

"Oh." Elton isn't expecting this. "You think?"

"I touched his forehead," I say, briefly remembering the moments our foreheads kissed and how hot his skin felt against mine. "His temperature was a bit abnormal. Did you guys pack the malaria drugs?"

Elton freezes. "I don't think we did. Shit, shit, shit." He gets panicky, which isn't a good state to be in so high above ground. "You think he's going to die?"

"He's not going to die, Elton. Relax. If it is malaria, which I doubt it is, he's doing pretty well for someone who's never had it before."

"Whew, okay. I'll take your word for it, doc." And then he laughs, adds, "By the way, Nana told Scott and I this morning that his pastor says that one of us will die, 'cause of some evil spirits. Even encouraged us to pray about it. How ridiculous is that?!"

I frown. Could Nana's pastor be on to something? But Elton sounds so certain, so quick to disbelieve Nana's pastor's prophecy that it's no use aligning it with Vincent's odd behaviour lately.

"Wait. You believe in that shit?" Elton's eyes are gorging out of their sockets, his mouth agape. "With all your education and the books you read? Kobby, really? Listen, remember my friend—I'm talking about the older guy who lived here, the one who put me in touch with the dude who's got the good weed and those brownies you won't quit eating, he told me about weird experiences where strangers just stopped him on the street and told him that God had a message for him. The message? Unless he visited a certain prophet to revert a certain curse, he was going to die soon. He's still alive, mind you! Apparently it was a popular scam back in the day. Shit. They must have thought he was stupid enough to fall for it. But you. You can't tell me you believe in Nana's pastor—"

"Not quite. But I do believe sometimes we humans can create certain energies to invite dark spirits into our lives—"

"Honestly. Kobby. Let's just complete this course. Africans! The more you know! Talkin' bout some evil spirits. Ha! I ask for one interesting thing about you and this is what you choose to share? Well, it sure is interesting. And dumb. Ha ha! Can't say I'm surprised, Africa is where hoodoo originated after all."

Mid-day Interludes

It's afternoon. Elton and I should be having sex. Instead, we spend a precarious number of minutes plucking out the burrs from our clothes because Elton suddenly realises that he's got the weed stuck in many places on his baggy shorts, a situation he finds irritable given this is one of his favourite bottoms among his homogenous collection of shorts. He shrugs me off gently when I try to slip them off without partaking in his fuss for getting the seeds out. Concealing my displeasure at squandering the perfect opportunity for a gratifying post-hike fuck, I become consumed with the task of uprooting weeds, smoothing disturbed yarns, and occasionally soothing the prickly sensations on my fingers with my tongue. He watches my furrowing features for tackling an army of unrelenting burrs that has finagled itself into the ends of his crotch's flap. I find his swelling loins—what could be a reaction to my sudden servili- ty—a nuisance. "Why don't you whip it out," he finally speaks. I squint into his towering frame. From above I must look like a doting whore. "C'mon, closed mouths don't get fed." He un- zips himself and pulls out his bell-bottom dick. "See? None of that stuck in there." I pull down his shorts in one gruff move. He laughs. I bury my head in his groin. All of his hiking ex- ertions are soaked into the area, the smell of shea butter and sweat, talcum powder, and cotton. I fetch his balls slick with groin juice into my palms, give them a little tug and squeeze them over my tongue. "Taste it," he orders. But I have other ob- sessions. I'm trailing my nose against his fleshy quads, discov- ering the grassy scents of weeds. Around his shins are different flavourings, a distinct garlicky smell, another with the tanginess of oranges and a subtle whiff of onions. I unravel the scents of the tropics, a smoothie with clashing ingredients, at once sweet, then pungent, sometimes having an earthiness reminiscent of beetroot, not entirely pleasant but maddeningly enticing, a novel adventure into nasal eroticism. Elton looks down at me with hazy eyes, the expression worn for being mildly perplexed and turned on at watching someone's kink in motion. Enough foreplay for our time-bound fuck. I rip off a sheet on one of the bunk beds and he in turn yanks off my khaki shorts and my underwear all at once. He buries his face into my butt, and I wonder what smells he finds in there that make him burrow his head deep into the crack of my ass, perhaps a garden of tube- roses. There's nothing I'd rather imagine, just tuberoses. When the sheet is spread out on the floor, we both collapse onto it, expecting the other to take charge. We're both exhausted from the hike after all. "Come put your mouth on it." We've already dallied enough. I ignore his request and hop onto him, push his legs onto his chest. He stares through the V of his thighs questioningly, but does not object to my intent. I glide into his anus through the globule of saliva I've spat into it. With my toes acting as support and fuelling my thrusts into him, our faces become frozen portraits of pleasure, open mouths and widening eyes, flaring nostrils, and wrinkled foreheads trapping sweat. When I begin nodding erratically, he protests, "No, no." He grips my butt cheeks and chases his own orgasm, thrusting me into him as I'm overcome by spasms. "Don't go soft on me, don't." Despite his efforts, I flop out of his ass and collapse on top of him. "If you know you're going to leave me hanging, lemme top first," he complains. I rest my cheek on his chest and stare towards the walls of the room, my vision adjusting to a sheetless mattress belonging to Nana. "We fucked on Nana's sheets!" Elton finds this funny.

NANA

When Sarkodie and Efya sing "*Wo suban nyɛ nso mepɛ wo Sa ara,*" they were talking about girls like Mina who have a bad character, but boys can't stop liking them. Look at her now, *puu-ing* her buttocks in front of Scott when me and him are doing yoga. When Scott and I first come out, she follow us, and she say this time *dee* she is going to join us do yoga. I want to tell her that yoga is not for girls because it will break their hymen but Scott tell me to give her space so she stands in the middle of us. I don't even know what to say. I can't even complain because I know she is not a virgin. We're facing the sea that keep coming to touch our legs. Our hands are in front of us and we are squatting so our buttocks have stand up like Elton's pipi when he wake up in the morning and pull Kobby with him to the bathroom and I open my eyes small-small pretending I've not seen them. I am not a fool, I know right now that they're having sex that's why Scott want me to stay with him to do this yoga. I also know that Mina want to play *girlfriend-boyfriend* with Scott that is why she is doing *ahohyehyɛ*, sticking herself to us like bra on breasts. *Wo suban nyɛ nso mepɛ wo Sa ara.*

I thought Scott and I will be alone so that me and him can talk about what happened this morning, when I ask all of us to do morning devotion before we leave the room but he laugh and say, No Nana, we're not religious people. My pastor call me last night to repeat to me that there'll be something dangerous coming to one of the friends, and that I should encourage all of us to pray. I also told Elton because he's having sex with Satan himself so that he can beware of that Ananse. But he too laugh. One of them will die, pastor says, there are plenty evil spirits, plenty, plenty evil spirits. And the only way we can stop them is to pray. So even when I'm sleeping I pray. Even at Kakum, I pray on the rope. I wanted me and Scott to use this yoga time to say some few prayers. But now here is Mina doing all the things she's doing with Scott. I'm jealous about the way she laugh with Scott as if she can understand all the jokes he's saying. I don't even know why he's talking to her when he told me in yoga we don't make noise with our mouth just our nose and chest.

"This is too hard, Mr. Scott," Mina is saying, her voice like she's doing porno. I want to sack her now now now. "Where did you learn all this?"

"You know, I used to dance for Debbie Allen back in the day."

"Debbie who?"

"Never mind."

When the *ofridjato* from this morning who was taking pictures with the *obroni* man come to pass, he laugh and shout, "*Obroni!*" This make Scott shout back at him, "For the last time I'm not an *obroni!*" Mina is laughing.

"Maybe if we spend so much time under the sun and I get a (tan), everyone's going to see that I'm Black," Scott say to Mina.

"We'll call you whatever you want," she tell him: "We can even call you African man, or Kwasi Broni, or Kofi Ghana." I frown at the way she throw her hands and hit his shoulder.

"Mina, do you really think I'm white?" Scott ask her and his forehead squeeze with lines and I'm sure it's not because of the painful yoga position which is making my legs weak and shake small-small.

"Mina!" From the hotel we're staying at we hear a scream: "Are you looking after the food you put on the fire?"

"So something is burning and you did not hear it?" I shout at her but she's already running to the kitchen.

"Nana, do you think I'm white?" Scott ask me as he's moving into another position, one hand facing the sea, the other one facing the hotel and his legs bending small. I quickly copy him. "Nana?" He mention my name again when I do not answer. I don't know why he keeps worrying me with this question, why does he not want to be *obroni* when everyone likes *obroni* people? I am about to speak, but I remember how he play with Mina like he is her boyfriend. The *kaka* in my mouth begin to fill with blood.

"But Scott," I say, "you are the one who say in yoga we only talk with our nose and chest." That keep him quiet. I'll pray alone. I'll do all I can to make sure no bad thing happen to Elton and his friends. I'll protect them too, because we don't only fight with spirits, we fight with flesh and blood. "Where's Vincent?" I ask Scott.

"Probably wherever people with terrible attitudes go," Scott answer, "fuck do I care." I frown at him. I'll do what I can to keep my eyes on the three friends.

V

KOBBY
(9 days after the friends arrive)

T he fire is a chief priest. It sits. It stands. It springs up to touch the sky, or extends its finger-like flames in attempts to reach a prospective victim by their throat, dignified in its movements to cause harm or offer some ominous prescience through its incinerating temperatures.

I am trudging barefooted towards the colossus of flames, through moist sand and dislodged weeds caught in the crevices of my toes. I am hypnotised by the fire's enormity. Anytime I see a fire the size of a razing pyre, my nasal memories conjure the coppery smell of cauterising flesh, singeing hair, and congealing blood. The scent of a pig on roast.

Here's a morbid tale from one of my morgue visits, about a woman who was already a charred carcass when she was brought in; skin hanging off her body, her face a portrait of a flesh-eating disease—only visible were the crow-feet that clung to one eye like an elusive ceiling cobweb. News of her death had spread nationwide, splayed on the front page of all local papers. The dieners had told me she was lucky she hadn't reduced to ash, despite having already been devoured by flames when a hunter discovered her resting in his trap—her limbs extended as if she was only on the verge of advancing into the next strained move in a robotic dance when her killer pounced. To my boss's disappointment, even after she'd covered the trip to Kumasi by AWA, I couldn't whip up a substantial story for the lack of DNA records to help with her identity. There was also the sad case of the police not conducting any investigations, because in this country the police rarely bother with homicide unless someone, usually the grieving relative, pays them a hefty amount. So this burnt woman took all of her browning, overlapping lower teeth, her yellowed toenails, wisps of greying hair—and my chance at immortalising her—to the grave. The dieners, bathing themselves in incantations to ward off her spirit, had resumed what the killer couldn't finish. I inhaled her stench as they burned her in the morgue's haphazardly constructed crematorium—a pile of sticks in a backyard bush. I listened to the fire wolf her down, rather loudly, as though she were a bag of crisps.

I increase my pace to the distant bonfire when another human's shadow collides with mine. Nana. We're two moving objects taking parallel paths towards the sounds of revelry in the distance. Though his gaze is rooted to the destination, it's obvious my presence angers him—a certain harshness in his stare betrayed by the fire's glare which illuminates his puckered brows in russet tones.

NANA

Fire be like friend and enemy to me. I know fire from the food we cook in village farm, the firewood you place on top of the other, side by side, making a shape like star. Light the match and fire form fast. I learn to play with fire. I train it like a dog, keep my hands around it and blow it small-small until it become big, then the pot can be put on it. My grandmother say the only thing I do that she like is fire. That's the only time that in her eyes I become better than my sister. It's the only time that she look at me like I'm important, the way she look at my sister and say to her, "A girl has more use than a boy, someone will marry you and give us money for your bride price, but as for Nana—what use is a man to us?" In my language, we say fire like the way we say father. And I take fire as my father. Guide me, protect me, but also punish me when I do not take care playing with it; just like the song they teach us in school: *Fire is a good servant, fire is a good servant, but it can be a bad master too, master too.* When fire burns me, it burns me to say, You're a bad boy. So when I use fire to burn my sister, I tell her, "You're a bad girl, don't cry, tell grandma you took the meat and shared it." Till this day, if my sister husband open her thighs, I know he think of me, he think of how my grandmother step into the room when my sister was shouting. I use fire to kill.

I watch the Ananse as he close his eyes and walk to the fire. If the fire was close, and nobody was with us, just the two of us, I will push him into it. I've been waiting for the two of us to be alone for a long time, but Elton will not leave him alone. I've still not found the Sasabonsam shoemaker pin in his things, but I just know he's a bad man and one day I'll have my time with him alone. It's like what they say on Peace FM: *Amega ne Amega hyia ara ɛhɔ na yɛbehu amega hoho.* When two masters meet, we'll see which one of them is really the master. Right now, I make my prayer my sword. I don't stop praying in my mind because my pastor's voice become clearer and clearer in my mind. *One of the friends will die.* But with prayer, no evil spirit can win.

KOBBY

The fire performs a roll-call of those making merry at its feet. It highlights double-edged jaws—jaws sat within jaws, jutted-out cheekbones that are not unlike ethnic scarifications, noses with beak-like projections. At once, it seems like all of Eastern Europe with their glass-cutting Slavic features have docked on this little beach in Elmina, inviting us locals to gaze on the splendour of their all-white costume party.

It isn't hard to spot the only Black people—Elton, Vincent, and Scott: their presence is almost redemptive. The tension in my neck unlatches at the sound of Scott's laughter floating above the buzz like a palm cutting through a candlelit flame. Still, his joy manifests as a jab, a reminder that I am lacking the foreign blood that pulses through his veins, this key card that grants unwithheld hospitality at gatherings like this. Should Nana turn in my direction for a second, I might smile or nod, communicate our ethnic adjacency through a subtle gesture. Where I am reluctant, he quickens his stride and dissolves into the sea of white, oblivious to the attitudes his attendance inspires: purses tucked into armpits, wallets and phones felt for, eyes like store assistants following Black customers around shops.

Elton disengages from the ghostly congregation the moment his eyes find mine, the white jellabiya he'd hurriedly bought for the occasion dragging behind him like an overlapping self. He speaks over the wind as he nears, "When they said this was a Year of Return event, they missed out on telling the only Black people that it was going to be a bunch of white people at a bonfire." He takes in my orange t-shirt and blue jeans. I scratch my eyebrow. "How this hasn't turned into anything by Jordan Peele is a mystery to us all." He passes me one of two plastic cups he holds. "You never gon' catch me at a place like this back home. Scott almost ran, but Vincent, he kept walking like a man with no fucking sense of history." An image of Vincent plodding through the dunes to face a pack of white suprema-cists makes me smile.

I take a large gulp of the clear liquid with a slice of lemon, languishing in it like a body face-down in a pool. Regretting that I couldn't discern the liquor's proof from its stench, I try not to flinch from the burn spiralling down my throat. "But when you're in Africa," I wink at Elton and grab his hands, "tolerate what the Africans will." I pull him towards the crowd of about fifteen, to Scott and Vincent in the presence of an older white couple laughing at Scott's jokes. Everyone's faces darken at corners the fire can't find, an effect that makes us resemble figures in a courtroom sketch. The air smells of meat on skewers, prepared and fussed over by two men. I recognise one of them as the photographer from this morning. He smiles and waves. I turn away into the curious expressions of other white people.

"Oh hi, Kobby, meet the owners of our resort," Scott introduces in a high-pitched bonhomie tone, as if that could conceal his underlying message: The bastards finally show their faces.

I smile at the older white lady. She's got silvering blond hair and a pair of blue eyes that won't quit roving in their sockets like they are constantly on the prowl for opportunities. Eyes, which despite her age, remain sharp as a mouse missing the teeth of a trap. Her husband is a pitiful antithesis of what she represents. He is stick-thin with greying blonde hair, a man who comes across as a consenting pushover, his shoulders slumped, his movements dulled. He wears a t-shirt that has the resort's logo, with bold letters that scream CHARITY and an inscription in a language that could be German. The event's European attendance suddenly makes sense.

"You're together, right?" the woman asks Elton and me in her accented English. "Lots of gay men come to our place. We love gays. My husband and I," the man agrees with a slow nod, "were just recently thinking about hosting LGBT events to educate the village on sexuality. The people here like to deny it, but let's face it, gays are everywhere! We're looking forward to your donations to help organise this event."

"I have never heard of anyone asking for money to share their own knowledge on sexual orientations," Elton says.

I try to stifle a laugh, but little bits of it slip out of my mouth. The woman turns to me, her eyes narrowing in on my clothes, picking out details that seasoned white residents glean to differentiate between locals and other Black foreign nationals. She returns her attention to Elton. "We're eco-conscious, very eco-friendly. We're trying to minimise plastic. We're saving the baby turtles, oh have you seen them by the way? We are actually the first resort to actually begin such a campaign." She uses the word "actually" as often as a Ghanaian does. "And now all these local resorts are trying to copy us Germans. Who'd have known that sea turtles aren't actually meant to be kicked around if we hadn't arrived. You know, it's hard being ingenious in this country. No one has shame, stealing ideas that don't belong to them. Copy-copy, all of them—"

"It's called competition," Scott cuts in.

The woman hiccups as though punched in the throat. "Of course, look at me! Thinking I could leave the West and all its capitalism behind. Anyway, you guys are following the Year of Return's programming, right?"

"Not exactly," Elton responds, "we've just got some few plans here and there—"

"Oh, I mean the resort's Year of Return programme."

"The resort has a Year of Return programme?" Scott seems genuinely baffled. "Man, I was thinking the Ghanaians would be in charge of all that."

"You see, no one should ferment in their own juice. We've been here for a while. We're practically one of them." The old woman directs her auric smile at me. "We actually have a guide that would take you all around Elmina and Cape Coast. He's, of course, a local. Knows a lot about the town's history with the transatlantic slave trade and all that. I mean, you don't want to pick anyone off the streets," another look in my direction, "and make them show you around. We've also got a more organised tour. I mean, look online, it's all a mess of events, these Ghanaians—we love them by the way, have a knack of being disorganised about everything. I mean, you'd think the president who brought up the tourism initiative would make things more structured, they've just left it all up in the air—"

"And that's where y'all come in, right?" Elton says with folded arms, "The non-Ghanaians ready to put everything right."

The old woman hiccups again then looks to her spouse, who's still nodding. She narrows her eyes at him, perhaps urging him to speak. But he's slow to react; his actions lag like an internet call over a poor network. She resumes, "You know, it's all for the community. We are about the community. We only actually want to help out the community, I mean that's why we are getting the locals as guides, we could do it on our own, we've lived here for a while we practically sound like them!" She leans into me, and says, "*Chale.*" I blink and pull on a vacant expression. She switches her attention to her husband, "*Chale.*"

"You too *Chale* some," he shoots back at her with feigned seriousness.

"*Chale.*"

"You too *Chale* some."

"*Chale.*"

This asininity goes on for an offensive number of minutes. Elton and Scott look to me for some sort of explanation. All I do is stare, fascinated by a mosquito that has landed on the woman's arm. I want to stretch and bestow on her the kind malice Ghanaians are ready to offer in situations like these: slap hard at her arm and offer my bloodied palm as evidence of my thankless heroism à la Santo. I shrug, wish her malaria, and turn to Vincent, whom I expect to be staring this woman down with all the incredulity one could lobby into a gaze. But it's the fire he focuses on. He looks hypnotised. A blankness that's calming to watch, riveting as observing sediments descending to the bottom of a suspension. I listen for the crackling embers through the revelry that surrounds us, hoping to zone off like he has and tune out the white woman's babbling. But I catch sight of someone Black. Nana? Only taller and wearing white. In the dark, this person's tribal marks appear masked.

The Northerner we met on the first day stands with his fat braided woman who distracts him with a piece of skewered meat, force-feeding him as he engages with the white photographer. He even has his fingers locked on the white man's elbow, an act whose interpretation could be double-edged. A plea for one's attention or a demonstration of affection. Whichever meaning the gesture attempts I'm determined to brush aside for my conviction that Northerners are friends of whites who in turn are Friends of the Earth. Whites run lots of charity schemes up North whereas in Accra they steal our land, steal our jobs, and steal the good seats at cultural exhibitions so they can be the first to grab the microphone to voice their observations on African culture when the programme line-up clearly stated "Question Time." My eyes find Nana, who's standing at the outskirts of the event. For a change, I realise I'm not the target of his ballistic glares.

Nana's eyes like flames burn into the Northerner, who now dances to the floating notes of "Bambi" by Jidenna. The man possesses a fluidity that's baffling given his astronomical build. He's an entrancing sight. The white people start following his steps, grotesque shadows puppeting behind him. The ugliness of their coordination, like the few seconds of unbalanced momentum one suffers before giving in and smacking face-down on a slippery linoleum floor, confounds me. The only move they perform without fault is one that I wish Africans weren't so susceptible to when dancing: sticking out their tongues. The Northerner sprightly jumps in front of his white woman who happens to be the only one not dancing, gets on one knee at exactly the moment Jidenna tells Bambi that he's got the wedding invitation. The Northerner holds a spectral ring before her.

The couple's witnesses swoon and cheer: "Love's in the air!" When in fact this isn't love, just an exaggerated performance to renounce his Ghanaian-ness for whatever nationality this white woman holds.

Poof!

The fire begins puffing thick black smoke into the air. Elton grabs my wrist and forces me back. *Poof! Poof!* A succession of blasts erupts with the chemical smell of burning tyres and a showering of soot. While everyone's retreating, someone hurls himself at the explosions.

"Nana!" Elton shouts.

Nana seems deaf to the surrounding sounds. With something resembling expertise and familiarity with fires behaving wild, he dips a stick into the furnace: this stick is so small the flames trick us into believing they've swallowed his entire arm. He draws a thick, melting lace from the fire, rescuing it like a bedraggled animal in a storm. There's silence as Nana kicks sprays of beach sand onto the liquefying fabric.

"Now how can you compete with that?" Scott jeers in my ear.

It's only a matter of minutes before everyone resumes their usual chatter and dancing. No one thanks him for what they assume was a task expected of him.

"He's one of the workers, isn't he . . ."

"I hope he's being paid well . . ."

"We'll send him home with the leftover barbecue—that should feed his family the entire month . . ."

"I doubt it, have you seen the way those Africans eat?"

Nana remains alone, eyes trained on the fire, finding purpose in a place where these white people cast stares like stones at him.

"So I take it everyone here owns a resort on the beach?" Vincent is back from the fire.

VI

NANA
(9 days after the friends arrive)

The first time I touch fire and fire burn me, my grand-mother teach me pain. She took small hot wood from the fire and press it on my back. I shout. I cry. But she will not leave me alone. I was crying and she was talking: Our elders say, *Abɔfra se ɔbɛsɔ gya mu a, ma ɔnsɔ mu, na ɛhye no a, ɔbɛto atwene.* Then she slap my back, again and again until I stop crying. She ask me to say what she say to me again, pulling my ear. I shout, "If a child wants to touch fire, let him touch it. If he burns, he'll throw it away." She shout in my face: "Did you burn?" I answer her as tears fall from my eyes.

Now tears fall from my eyes as I look into the fire. The fire take me back, back home. To happy times, when I learnt how to jump over it and jump over it again in my own game. To sad times, when it burns me and I learn my lesson not to play with it. I sit quiet. Looking at the fire look at me. No one talk to me at this party. Everyone laughing and having drinks. I watch Elton and his friends and the Ananse who look like one of the white people laughing with them and speaking into Elton's ear. I watch the tall man from the North with the white woman talk to some other white people, laughing with them and drinking, drinking. My heart pains me. I want to leave. But if I go away, who'll look after Elton and his friends? Who'll protect innocent people from the plenty Ananses in the world? So I talk to my old friend, fire, and I don't leave.

Krekete Soya

Krekete Soya
Krekete Soya.

I hear singing from far away. A song I know. I look around sharp, thinking I'm back in my village and surrounding me is plenty children who gather around my grandmother and the fire to listen to her stories. But I still see *obroni* people.

Krekete Soya
Krekete Soya
Krekete Soya.

The singers are girls in a long line, like ten of them walking to me. *Krekete Soya.* They look like *maame wata* that come out of the sea. I think I'm going crazy. Are these the plenty evil spirit that pastor warn me will kill one of the friends? I blink one-two and they're still there, coming for me, singing. I jump from the sand, afraid. I turn around and see all the white people and Elton and his friends sit down quiet. They too can see the girls. *Krekete Soya.* I slowly sit down like everyone, covering my mouth to cover my shock. I see Mina, leading the girls in Adowa, screaming *oooh-aaah* as the girls continue singing *Krekete Soya.* She looks like a Queen Mother, cloth tied around her breast and waist. She comes to stand in front of the fire and she and her girls surround us. My eyes *biri* me watching her. She look so beautiful with white marks drawn around her eyes like they are stars shining near her eyes. Her dark skin becomes gold like the fire and every time she jumps you'll think the fire obey her and—*woof*—jumps too. Mina, or Maame Araba or whatever your name is, you make my heart do *boom-boom-chay*.

She land on the floor one more time after a jump that make dust fly into my eyes. She raise her hand and the *Krekete Soya* girls stop singing. She throw sand into the fire and the fire does *shhhh* as if telling us all to keep quiet.

"Long time ago, the people of our village sat under the full moon to tell stories by the fireside!" Her voice sound like a fighter voice, Yaa Asantewaa, or like the girls on *Ghana's Most*

Beautiful. I watch her smile a lot to the *obroni* Scott as if he's one of the judges.

"An old woman will come to the centre near the fire and begin telling us stories to entertain us and teach us valuable lessons." Her eyes fall on me, she sees my smile, but does not smile some. "Today, I'm your old woman." There's a small laugh from Ananse and other people laugh with him too. I frown. "Today, I'm your old woman and it's night and there's a fire, so there'll be a story. Are you going to clap?" Everyone quickly claps happily and I clap too. She's doing a good job like my own grandmother who sat by the fire and become a different woman whenever she's telling us stories. Mina throw sand on the fire and again, we all hear *shhhh*. "Here's the story of why the hawk takes the hen's chicks. You'll listen and then you'll learn."

I know this story. I know it from start to finish. Something about her voice make me listen and I stop looking at her beautiful face and the water from the sea jumping up and down behind her, the fire making her face burn bright.

"Long time ago, the Hen and the Hawk lived side by side. Like all the animals in the forest. Snake was friends with Sheep who was friends with Wolf who was friends with Bear. No hate for other animals. Just one common enemy. Do you know who that enemy is?" She throw the question at us like a piece of meat they've throw for cat. I want to raise my hand and answer, but the Northerner who sits in front of me, even blocking my view small-small, talk: "Man."

"Man!" She scream his answer, and then in a deep voice, she begin: "*Many men, many many men, wish death 'pon me now I don't cry no more . . .*" The white people laugh, some of them sing with her. Elton's hand go up and he use his fingers to make a gun shape as he sings with the girls this song I don't know. *Shhhh.* The fire speak. We all become silent. "Man kills the animals so occasionally the animals will have to work together to run away from him. But that's not the story today. Today's story is about Hen and Hawk. I'll tell you how Man divide the other animals some other time. How Bear begin hating Wolf, how Wolf begin hating Sheep, how Snake begin biting everyone. So that he, Man, can hunt them down. But not today. Today's story is how Hen and Hawk wanted to make a drum, but sly Hen didn't want to help. And that's how the hatred begins." She pause and look at everyone, just like my grandmother do, checking if everyone's quiet and listening, then she continue again, "Long time ago, Hen and Hawk lived in huts closer to each other. They did everything together. One day, Hawk told Hen, Let's make a drum so that when we get tired from all the work on the farm we'll play together. Hen said, Oh, I wish I could help but I'm always tired from the farm. How can we come back and do another work again? Hawk said, Okay, then give me your cutlass so I'll go cut trees and use it for the drum. Hen said, My cutlass, like yours, is tired from the farm. How can you put them to work? Okay, Hawk said, then give me some of your . . ." She stop and look at me, I don't know if she's forget what Hen ask for next, I try to tell her with my mouth opening without talking, but she look away. "Give me your matches." Matches? I frown. There's no matches in this story. How can animals use matches? Hen ask for axe: axe, not matches. "You know, my box of matches is tired, said Hen. Hawk asked for so many things but Hen would say no." I look around to the white people, and I worry if they can tell she's lying. Matches? Matches? I look at Ananse, he's Ghanaman, maybe he'll know, but the Ananse has that big smile he put on when he's telling big lie, and I see him talk into Elton's ears. Elton say something to Scott who say something to Vincent who's the only one not looking at Mina's face but at the fire that does *shhh* when Mina throws sand into its eyes. "So Hawk went ahead to make the drum. A very big drum, and when he plays the drum, there's one song Hen hears in her room. *Krekete Soya. Krekete Soya.* Girls, sing with me. *Krekete Soya.* Audience, sing with me, *Krekete Soya*." I'm the only one who looks like he's not having fun. Mina look at me again, but instead of looking away like she does every time, she squeeze her face at me for being quiet and then the fire does *shhh*. "Hen was so jealous of Hawk. So jealous when Hawk was playing she wouldn't even sing because she was ashamed. So one day, and listen to me, in all stories there's always a one day. There's always one day that things change and they'll never be the same." I see the fat white woman smile at the Northerner. He kiss the top of her head, blocking my view. Something in me burns like the fire when it does *poof*. I am angry. I am angry at all the liars and the tricksters of the world. I want to tell all the people here who the liars are. There with Elton. There with the White Woman. There standing in front of us, throwing dust in our eyes.

"One day Hen told Hawk that she's very sick and can't go to the farm with him. Hawk asked those questions, can I have your cutlass, can I have your matches . . ." I bite my tongue. ". . . Hen said they're all sick. So Hawk went to the farm with his tools. And Hen, seeing that Hawk had left, ran to the drum, playing it, playing it and singing, *Krekete Soya*—" This time everyone joins her before she ask them to, "*Krekete Soya. Krekete Soya*." *Shhh*. "Now Hen has a beautiful voice, and when she sings, she can make all the animals in the forest stop whatever they're doing and listen. She sings about how she tells Hawk she's sick—" The girls around her sing, *Krekete Soya*, dancing Adowa this way and dancing Adowa that way in circles and hooting and beating their chests. They're joined together like the human beings we cut-cut from paper at school. "She sings about how Hawk asked for her cutlass and matches—" She pause and make sign for everyone to join the girls sing: *Krekete Soya*—"She sings about how she heard Hawk play the drum—*Krekete Soya*—She sings about how she got jealous—*Krekete Soya*—She sings about how she want to sing and sing and sing—*Krekete Soya, Krekete Soya, Krekete Soya*—Now all the animals heard her, including Hawk who was at the farm. He stopped working, and like all the animals, he followed Hen's beautiful voice which keeps singing—*Krekete Soya*— Then Hawk pounced on her—*Krekete Soya*—He collected his drum—*Krekete Soya*—He played his drum—*Krekete Soya*— And he also begins singing—*Krekete Soya*—He tells Hen that for lying to him—*Krekete Soya*—Man will always catch her and eat her—*Krekete Soya*—The animals shouted because that was the biggest curse in the forest—*Krekete Soya*—They begged for Hen—*Krekete Soya*—Hen was crying too—*Krekete Soya*— Asking for forgiveness—*Krekete Soya*." *Shhh.* Everyone keep quiet. Some people laughing because others say *Krekete Soya* after Mina throw sand into the fire. All of them like stupid children who believe Mina's lies, who don't know that Hawk didn't catch Hen playing the drum until three days. "So," Mina continue slowly, cleaning the white marks on her face, "so, Hawk told Hen that he was going to take her children every day and there's nothing Hen could do about it. Till this day, Hawk still catches Hen's children. And that's the end of the story."

Everyone begin clapping loud. Mina bows. Some old white woman gets up with her and claps, "Wasn't that a beautiful story, everyone?" The people clap harder. Then the old woman throws sand into the fire, it doesn't do *shhh,* she throws sand again, it doesn't make a sound. She turn to Mina. Mina throws the sand. *Shhh,* the fire speaks. "Okay." Everyone laughs, the old woman eyes die small, then she smile big like the Ananse does. "This is one of our Year of Return programmes. We hold this every Monday night to raise funds for projects we're (embarking) on in Elmina." She look back at Mina, "The beautiful Mina, who did a beautiful job, will now go round and actually collect everyone's donations. If you don't have the money, you can give us your numbers and the resorts you're living in. We'll actually find you and take whatever you give. This village still needs more toilets. I mean, if they continue (defecating) outside—and they do that with (impunity), we're all going to suffer. So give . . ."

At this point I get up and leave. Everyone here's lying and it looks as if this white woman is *hyɛ-ing* Mina *nkuran* to lie so she can get money from these white people. I do not take the *asaana* drinks Mina and the girls are serving everyone. I watch Mina who smile with *feree* at Scott as she serve his drink, I hear him move closer to her and shout in her ear, "You did well." Mina laugh with him as if he is using *takra* to tickle her ear. So she likes white man more than black man, not surprised. I'm angry and I don't even tell Elton and his friends that I'm leaving. I don't think they will know I have gone. To everyone here I'm like the little dust the wind blows away which no one sees until it enters their eyes. I want to walk back to the hotel, to even see if I can go and find the Sasabonsam shoemaker pin in the Ananse's bags, but it feel like I'm not in the mood. Not sure I can even sleep tonight, *kraa*. *Ahh Mina, w'ayɛ adeɛ ma ahye me.* So I keep walking and walking and walking until I turn back and I can only see the light from the fire and not the people sitting around it. I find a coconut tree and sit under it. I watch the sea fall and jump, fall and jump, fall and jump and then I'm sleeping . . .

She come to me in dream. She touch my shoulder. I frown at her. Mina or Maame Araba, what's your name? She tell me I can call her whatever I want. I jump up and turn to her. I call her liar. She look surprised. You are liar. I say again, *Nkontomponin.* I'll never lie to you, she say in that condense milk voice that used to make my mind sweet me but now it make something in my stomach burn me. She make as if to touch me, I slap her hand and step back. You don't like me anymore? She ask, sad-face. *Maame Wata*, I call her. Maybe she is the evil spirit that Pastor say will kill my friends, I think. I catch the hand she want to use to touch me again. You're a witch, I say to her. She spit in my face. She try to pull her hand from mine. She use her other hand to slap me. It feels so good. I push her on the floor. I go down with her. *Wo yε barima ara . . .?* She say, looking at me as if she's challenging me. I begin to tear her dress. I turn her around. And then I begin to fork her. I fork her buttocks. I slap her buttocks and I fork it. I hear her laugh like a witch and I cover her mouth. It feel like I'm in another world. It feel good. It feel so sweet. I don't last for long. I remove *pipi* from her and I spray my future children on her back to carry. My body shake when I'm done. I think I'll wake up, shouting *Jesus, Jesus*. But I don't. I'm still sleeping. She's still lying down. Light from some hotel shine on her. I touch her, she's real. I begin to get afraid. Hey, I say to her, hey, I shake her. She turn around slowly to face me. *W'awie?* I frown at her question. This is no porno dream. I've sin. I fall on the floor and begin to beg her. She laugh. I squeeze my face as the *kaka* in my mouth begin to fill my mouth with blood.

KOBBY

"*Gahss,* this was *fun*," Scott says, woozy, speaking in that languorous way Elton has teased as "drunk yet still clinging to the bougie." An accent which, Elton adds, reminds him of the white South African couple that had taken the friends wine-tasting in Stellenbosch, their speeches pretentiously sensationalised so both stressed and unstressed sounds fought for equal attention. Scott had spent the entire tour snickering behind his wine glass at the couple's airs.

"To be *honest*, I thought this *was* going to be *laark*, a reenactment of *some* Ku Klux Klan or *that bullshit* MAGA. You *ever* heard of them?" Scott stares at me questioningly, swirling a finger around his plastic cup as though it were a prized chalice. "*Whiiite* people, *hunting* down *Blaaack* people, you *know* that history, don't you? *Ayynyway*, I love the *whiiite* people *here*. So European chill. Very *niiice*. What do you think, hon?" He taps Vincent's shoulder.

"When are we leaving?" Vincent asks, bored. He switches his gaze to the heavens.

It's a beautiful night sky, pitch-black as a panther's coat, even bearing a similar tactile invitation. Perhaps a little stroking might release a colony of stars hidden under its fur. It presents a more beguiling subject than the mute socialising I've endured with clusters of white people who only talked to Scott and Elton. All these whites situating the story of the Hen and Hawk into some postmodernist, postcolonial literary discourse—that way white people here love to talk about slavery and colonisation as though they might offer new insights to people who were enslaved and colonised. Vincent's question has been on my mind since the clock struck twelve half an hour ago. I'd have asked if Elton hadn't broken away with the owners of our resort. Those three are engaged in a conversation that feels urgent, leaning into each other as a matter of conspiracy. An unspoken rule, I'm guessing, is we can't call it a night without Elton.

"C'mon, Vince," Scott speaks. "What's up? You've been out of it lately. What's going on? You can talk to me, right? We're supposed to be married . . ." He's overcome by a bout of drowsiness, tosses his plastic cup along with the Asaana drink Mina and her girls dispensed. "Hey!" Annoyed he's lost Vincent to the skies again, he retreats, attempting to walk off, but knocks into someone. "What the . . ."

The woman's frown evaporates even as Scott, unjustly, decides she's at fault. "You guys are in my resort!" she exclaims, as if we'd ever forget her Caucasian rendition of box braids and the beautiful man by her side. "I'm Milly, he's Faisal."

The Northerner offers his hand to shake all three of ours. A strong, impressionable handshake. A handshake meant to prove one's worth but that belies it, betrays an overcompensation for some deficit.

"Indeed, I'm Faisal." I crane my neck at his accent, which is as Northern as it can sound with its Arabic influences but also British in the way a second, subjectively more important language seeks to erase the first. "I'm her husband also. We're married." Milly rolls her eyes at this addition. He throws his arm over her shoulder and draws her tightly into him, kisses a piece of exposed scalp.

"Didn't know you two were married!" Unlike me, Scott doesn't bother containing his shock.

"We met at uni. Cambridge." She pauses with a knowing smile. "We were in a study group together: International Relations. We hit it off, married too soon. Two years later, here we are."

"All braided up and shit. Crazy!"

"Indeed! Crazy. And beautiful!"

Milly laughs, basking in her husband's compliment as she palm-rolls the ends of an untangled braid. Once again, he finds a braidless spot and nourishes it.

I feel a brief sense of shame for equating these romantic exchanges they are keen on exhibiting publicly with the stuff of reality dating shows starring a foreigner and a local who conveniently aspires to a visa. I'm now intrigued by the couple's story, though I pretend nothing interests me as much as the white photographer beyond their shoulders—he's picked a Kpoo Keke liquor sachet from the sand and now smiles at an unknown distance, as if the litter had only been couriering a message to him. He catches my eye and grins.

"I'm sorry, I didn't catch your name." Milly's broad hand is stretched to me. I gingerly take it. Her palm is as warm and sticky as a snout, oddly soothing.

"I'm Kobby—"

"He's Vincent." Scott steps in for Vincent—something he's been doing a lot tonight.

"I'm Abena!" the white woman yips and lunges at me, enfolds me in one of those rocking hugs. The fire makes an odd sound behind us, as a dog would growl to indicate its forgotten presence. I immediately check for Nana and frown when he appears missing. "We're practically siblings!" she beams as she pulls back.

"You're siblings," Scott snorts.

"Yeah, Tuesday-borns in this country go by Kwabena—the longer form of Kobby, and Abena," Faisal explains.

"So that's a lot of hugs given to a lot of people then."

"Oh, you!" Milly goes for Scott's shoulder playfully, a gesture that takes Vincent's focus off the sea. She turns to me, unmindful of the reactions her poke elicited, her tongue sliding out, long as a cassette's tape, her breathing audible, streaming out of her mouth in steady pants. Such puppyish enthusiasm. And even before she speaks, I know what's coming—

Ways White Women Accost Ghanaians Whom They Are Eager to Befriend: My day name is Ama; You can call me Ama Ghana; Oh my god, are you gay? You're so brave; I met this Ghanaian guy that I'm into, can you tell if he's interested in me or a foreign passport? I'd like to practice my Twi with you, I know a few words; Your English is really good, you don't sound like you're from here; My favourite Ghanaian food is Red-Red—

"Which part of Ghana are you from?" Milly asks. "The Ashanti region, I'm guessing. *Me pɛ fufuo paa. Fufuo ne light soup.*"

"He only speaks English." Scott appears offended on my behalf.

"Milly's working on her Twi," Faisal, who pre-chews his wife's absurdities, says. "It's ridiculous. She speaks Twi to everyone who's Ashanti and tries to impress them. Yeah, it's getting tiring, honestly."

Milly sends one of her playful jabs his way. Scott lets out a strangled interjection.

"Anyway, how did I do?"

"Pretty well," I answer, equably. I quite like her, I think.

She's made me feel present in a way I've not felt during our time with the whites.

"We should have dinner—lunch, whatever—sometime: I could do with some Twi lessons. Faisal here, like everybody from the North, sees no reason why he should learn Twi even though it's obviously Ghana's most spoken language."

"I haven't heard Kobby speak much Twi," Scott says before I have a chance to reply. "But we know the perfect person who can help—"

"I'm going to rest," Vincent announces. Scott shrugs. Vincent leaves, though not in the direction of the resort. The fire makes a mild popping sound.

"Has he always been like this? Silent? Brooding?" Milly inquires.

"I have to go after him," I announce apologetically.

"Yeah, you go get him." Scott rolls his eyes at me.

I turn to Milly, "I would love to help you with your Twi."

"Nana speaks better Twi!" Scott shouts after me.

Vincent appears to have gotten far in the little time he left. I speed past resorts lit across the beach. I use their dim lights to avoid stepping on buried bottles, shreds of discarded fishing nets, and one abandoned crab trap. Yet, despite my cautiousness, I step on a furred coat. A dog. It scurries off, yowling.

"Vincent."

Vincent is a shining lighthouse rooted in the ocean, the white of his jellabiya luminous against the dark. His arms are parted, his eyes scouring the heavens as he wades through the sea with an ease that looks messianic. I succumb to the urge to sit crosslegged on the viscid parts of the shore to watch him . . . frolic? *Or does he think he is one of the water-walking Africans he mentioned this morning?* He doesn't back down even in the face of onrushing waves. He's now soaked to the torso, swaying, dancing to the roaring wind, the entire choreography coming across as a ritual—almost as if some invisible puppeteer is responsible for his motions. He lingers where swimmable waters end and life-threatening currents begin, where his form contracts and the ocean's dark ink rushes to scrub him out. I'm entranced.

"Vincent?"

I have to concede that Death, by this hand, by Vincent's execution, unlike anything I have read or imagined, looks so serene, like a Renaissance oil painting: a tiny trunk surrounded by vast waters projected onto canvas, devoid of any violence, a mere stroll into the afterlife.

I probably shouldn't call out to him like I did this morning.

"Vincent!" A voice like a bark shoots through me.

I come out of my trance to find none other than Nana, rushing for the drowning man. For a moment, I think he's going to toss himself into the ocean, but he only kneels at its edge and hollers.

It's too late now. A wave, shaped as a ship's bow, advances towards the man who's now completely submerged except for a halved skull.

"*Boa me!*" Nana shouts despairingly, "*Obi mmoa me! Help!*" The wave covers Vincent and smooths out the waters.

I exhale into the accompanied silence before rising to brush grains from my soaked jeans. Although a life has wrapped up, there's something vaguely unsatisfactory about the incident, the entire experience as pointless as turning the final page of an allegorical novel without grasping its underlying message. Vincent thought he was a water-walking African, so he died? If this isn't mythical ambition gone wrong, what really were his intentions? Had he been suicidal all along?

Eli, Eli lama sabachthani!

Nana's visceral scream makes me recall his pastor's words: *One of us will die.* One of us has died. And Elton would forever have to live with his flippant laughter destabilising the gravity of this preacher's prophetic foreboding.

I slowly approach Nana, to express whatever trite condolence

I can manage. But something, a rock, pierces my foot. I bend to caress the aching toe and end up freeing it from a fish bone. When I look up, I see him, Vincent, ghosting towards earth. His shoulders slumped, his eyes cast downward—what must be the disposition of one whose suicidal intentions have been thwarted, whom death itself wants nothing to do with.

I slowly withdraw from the scene, back-pedalling to the fire. The only proof that I had been here and did nothing to help will be spotted by morning, lone footprints tampered by children who for some rudimentary self-assessment insert their feet into mammoth prints to gauge how many more years until they can join their fathers at sea. Nana's cries pursue me, relentless as a child grappling with school-gate abandonment. I'm left to speculate on his reasons for choosing to remain useless at the water's edge, when he could have relied on the foolhardiness he exhibited before the roiling flames.

Nana can't swim.

I sprint into the night. A smile spreading as my arms, wide as a wing. No one dies yet, but I see how Nana might.

VII

KOBBY
(10 days after the friends arrive)

All four of us wake up around noon, the sun hanging so low in the sky its heat feels like a searing. We sit for an overdue breakfast, each in a cogitative silence filtered through the sounds of wind chimes invested in their sword-fight. On any other day, we'd have been aware of her lushness, taken a dip in her waters, twirled until our visions have balled her shapes into all that we know and can see of the earth. Today, we are blind to Elmina's charms.

Nana seems focused on the distance, where the herons and seagulls shriek and take off because of the black cat hell-bent on clubbing them with its paws. Vincent sits facing the direction he careered off to last night. He taps the table in slow, irregular pulses, distracting Scott who sighs intermittently as if catching himself contemplating things he really shouldn't. Elton, you may be the only one who could be attentive to Elmina's charms, but your probing gaze hounds my every move. You notice my tense grip around the brownie's Tupperware. Your eyes follow my hands anytime I attempt to console the itching scar above my eyebrow, which has always camouflaged into my skin, but today chooses to swell with memory and spectral blood. I've smiled tightly to your telepathic "You good?" and quickly averted my eyes so you do not glimpse the fault lines from which my past traumas push against at the mentioning of:

Castle.

I turn sharply to Scott, who repeats his question of which Castle we should tour first.

I've been thinking up and pitching whatever itinerary comes to mind, even if there's little to do in Elmina and Cape Coast that, for a group of Black Americans, holds more relevance than the castles.

"Are we going to the castles . . ."

"*No, I'm not going.*" It's 2003 and I'm standing before my parents.

"*You'll go,*" my mum insists.

"*It's compulsory, you need to know your history. It'll be fun.*" My dad doesn't understand that I've always been a little empathetic sponge, soaking up trauma wherever I find it, and generational trauma is something I fear I won't be able to wring out. Pain that doesn't die away, pain that won't cross over. That scares me. Still, he holds this trip over me as if it were a rite of passage. His dad went; in fact, far more dads than he will ever imagine, a lineage of men witnessing history or playing a part in it, went.

"*And for that reason, you too have to see it too. You cannot opt out of history.*"

"*No, I'm not going.*"

"*I'll drop you and your brother off at the bus's meeting point myself,*" my mother says. "*Don't be chicken: if you get scared hold your brother's hand*"—

"Guys." Scott's steady banging of the table brings me back to the present. "Why's everyone silent? We have Elmina and Cape Coast Castles to choose from."

"We do both."

I turn to Elton, who may have sensed the reason behind my fear and avoids my eyes. His own selfish need to explore the castles presses down on his will to save me. He lets go.

Someone screams. Nana pounds at the table with a ferality that twists one of its legs. Scott takes out his sanitiser and squirts it into Nana's hands. I watch the tiny spider with spindly legs hobble off the edge of the table after Nana's assault.

There's the sound of slippers slapping against the wooden floors of the restaurant. A scrawny girl we've not seen before brings in a tray. She's dull-faced, not as bright as Mina, and perhaps too young. Her Bantu knots give away her age. She should probably be in school. She's clumsy as she methodically sets the eggs before Elton, bread before Vincent; Nana gets the instant coffees and teas packed in little wrappers; to Scott she leaves the flask of hot water. To me she curtsies, spins, and almost runs back.

Scott giggles. "At least Mina says hi."

Before Vincent can take hold of the flask, Nana seizes it and begins topping everyone's mugs with water. Though it's windy, sweat cleaves to his skin and creates a darker neckline on his red shirt. He picks up the Nescafé and begins wriggling it open. There are flakes of crimson discernible in the nail that wrestles with the wrapper. Whereas at home his movements are quick and even malicious, ripping things open so effortlessly, here, we all watch him struggle like a new cub on its first solid meal. Elton looks at me, then Nana, looks at me again, and I know he's feeling for tension between Nana and me. He takes the Nescafé from Nana and does each tearing.

"*Me ma wo akye!*"

We turn from Nana's jitteriness to see Milly and her husband, Faisal, heading for our table. Milly's smile is less a window to her perfect dentition than an exhibition of her teeth as objects capable of harm—it's that way her upper lip disappears into her gum, giving her the look of a deranged rabbit. Today, she exudes an apparent glow, the outcome of her milky complexion restored since her braids—stretched to a ponytail—no longer pinch her pores to draw out blood. She's bursting with colour, an embroidered rose blooming in the fabric of our dourness. Every artefact of her clothing—bracelets and waist beads, which might as well be jiggling tambourines, a buoyant batik bubu arousing semblance to the local fishmongers, whom I'm oddly certain are the original sources behind her appropriations—operates on this sole premise to enliven our gathering.

"Oh Lord," Scott says under his breath.

"What's she wearing?" Vincent wants to know, a worried look on his face.

"You're friends with her now?" Elton mocks.

"Oh hi, everyone!" Milly signals Faisal to bring her a seat to our table. She touches my shoulder in a show of affection and says, "Did I get it right? The greeting. Did I say it right?"

I scratch my eyebrow. "It's afternoon. Though you said what you said right, during midday that's not what we say as greeting."

"What do you say?"

"Just 'Good afternoon' will do, Milly," Scott says.

"*Me ma wo aha*," Nana supplies. Milly turns to him as if considering who he might be, then planks down on the chair Faisal brings. "Anyway, what are your plans for today? I was hoping we'd begin those Twi lessons."

"We've decided we're going to see the castles, right?" Scott responds.

"Exactly what Faisal and I are doing today!" She looks up at her husband standing above her like a guard who smiles the way a parent would to try placating others for their overbearing child.

"Which castle are we going to?" Elton asks.

"Cape Coast Castle, then. That's the one furthest away?" Scott asks me.

"Yes," Milly answers instead. "Right?" She looks up at her husband who nods, running an arm along her shoulders. She grabs his ring (which is plain brass with the markings of a cannelure) to stop the hand's movement. "It's going to be fun."

"It's not." Vincent's tone is brutal, shuts Milly up. He adds, "I'm driving." Elton and Scott share a look.

"We'll be right behind you all in a taxi, of course. Unless you happen to have two free spots in your car?" Milly looks to Nana and me, the Ghanaians who've probably been to the castles so many times they would want out of this trip.

"Nah, we all going." Elton's response is more to me than anyone else. I keep sipping my instant coffee, shifting my focus from him to the sea. There's a group of men pulling in a net, shouting, "*Chow-boyi, chow-boyi.*" The spectacle lures the little kids who'd have otherwise been diving off reefs but are now tugging on a phantom rope behind the older men. The women surround the fishermen with their pans, ready to out-buy one another. Invading the excitement of a big catch is a woman in nothing but a brassiere and a wrapper, shouting as she waves a phone in the air, yelling, "*Ei, ei, Mese MoMo naa ba oo, Momo naa ba!*" She draws in a small crowd, everyone fascinated by her discovery. At the outskirts of this scene is the white photographer, snapping away, almost tarnishing this idyllic scenery. This simplicity of lives and roles and the general ecstasy in the air kneads at my temples, mitigating the carnage concealed in the piece of dead skin above my eyebrow.

"Now if everything's settled." Vincent drags his chair back.

"Oh, is it that new girl again?" Milly remarks irritably. We stare at the new waitress heading for us with a tray and dish cloth tossed over her shoulder. She unnecessarily bows at Vincent, whom she almost collides into as he walks out of the restaurant's hut. "She's just so timid, it's sad to watch." Milly says this as the girl wipes down Vincent's side of the table. "Excuse me," she catches the girl's hands and gives it a squeeze, "where's Mina?"

The girl makes eye contact for the first time. We spot the resemblance between her and Mina now—which may only be because of the brown waitressing uniform. The mole stuck underneath her chin diminishes the length of her neck, which is retracted to make her timidity a lot more imposing. She parts her lips in an attempt to answer Milly—*Please-Please Madame-Madame*—and fails, even though her hands do not cease wiping Vincent's vacated spot. Her fingers graze Nana's arm, and his mug slides from his grip, falls on the ground. The mug gives a little shimmy, then it plays possum, despite not suffering the slightest chip. We watch the girl break into a frantic mess of apologies, her actions like her speech, toppling over the other, as she picks up the mug and sets it on the table, snatches it back before Milly's order to please get the gentleman another cup has ended. Elton seizes the mug from her, asks that more Nescafé be brought instead. "See?" He pours some hot water into it and raises it up to demonstrate. "No leaks." There's a tiny crack—an almost invisible line beginning midway and eating into its base. It will take many cracks, many more fault lines, till a mug like this crumbles.

VIII

KOBBY
(10 days after the friends arrive)

When we were young, we were susceptible to a certain riotous curiosity about the world. A trait adults were wont to brand mischievous, since the only way we uncovered knowledge was to fuck things up and observe the causality of our disruptions. My mates, bar I, would stick their fingers into their pubic regions or asses, scrape odours into a nail and serve it up the nearest kid's nose. A journey into Cape Coast's carnage is exactly like this—a foul-smelling finger driven up one's nostril, twisted and churned, until tears and breakfast or lunch or whatever snack gorged in between mealtimes is vomited.

I plaster my face against the partly yawning window, immediately recoiling at the sabre-toothed scents which encircle the vehicle. The Cape Coast we drive into knows no deviation from the Cape Coast I saw as a kid dreading the horrors of imperialism. I soon feel claustrophobic.

The city, once an old British administrative capital, presents its interior as an artistic installation. It flaunts the pulchritudinous colonial architecture, and the sun-scorched locals hibernating on their concrete walls, for the band of white tourists keen on archiving the relics and ruins of colonialism. Thus, the city takes on the shrewd character of those who built the interior's ancient churches and schools—imperialist deceit camouflaging, in sprawling columns draping gargoyle-like shadows over the steep roads, in perforated screens and balustrades which were a front for concealing colonialists spying on indigenes. Tourists are encouraged to look on these structures, to document these attestations to the coloniser's kindness, and to do so quickly. Before the city's viscera splits and colonial embellishments surrender to the torture sites lurking on the coastal periphery.

Despite the city's proximity to the Atlantic Ocean, Presbyterian pennants do not sway on power lines, clothes are not boogieing on drying lines. There are no percussive whispers of soothing winds like there are in coastal cities. Just still air charged with the whiny hum of wraithlike flies. In spite of these visuals, nothing summons a chill through my spine as the hordes of school buses—with tires sucked into fenders—crawling towards the castle. Among the uniformed children cheering whenever their vehicles hurtle past ours is a familiar face reflected in every passing bus, my twelve-year-old self poised against a window. His face is translucent matter, the framework of his emotions—fear, irritation, disbelief at the passionate *gyama* of his mates—can be spied on through the constriction of a pore or the thinning of muscles over his eyelids. One bus lurches and all its kids lean in toward its screeching wheels. When he reappears, he's looking directly at me, with a smeared wolfish grin, blood secreting out of the gush above his eye and dripping into the white paintwork of the bus.

I'm riding shotgun, next to Vincent, who's the reason all the German hand-me-down commercial buses are zipping past, blasts of smoke puffed into our car as a parting shot. Vincent's torso trembles as he leans further into the steering wheel and peers at the road. Elton, Scott, and Nana strive to preserve their masks of inscrutability, their lips sealed tight against any rebellion to Vincent's authoritarian grasp over the wheels. He'll let no one take over even if he's spent most of the journey driving in circles. I've been grateful for these moments of delay, while praying he'll turn around and decide against this trip. But soon, the car halts, its engine dies. I feel the vehicle rise an inch as the others dismount. The dashboard looks even more irresistible, calling out to my itching scar. I could be twelve again; I could slam my forehead against any available surface.

"Kobby." Elton's voice. "Are you coming?"

Welcome, old friend, the castle whispers to me. It appears derelict save for the sunken-cheeked, sepulchral faces peering through the tiny openings cosplaying as windows. I frown, at the balustrades on each of its three floors and the shadowy figures perched over them, at the pink roofing pouring onto certain balconies like an expectant tongue looking to trap a bug.

"KOBBY!"

The castle's white walls are cracked in certain areas, and though their rust has been concealed by a coat of paint here and there, the edifice's general appearance mimics the inconsistency of bleached skin. A white which looks like all of humanity has dragged up against it; the little boys who scrape the walls with their initials, the wardens who chase them away and rub their spat-on fingers over these letters; the enslaved who leaned on these walls to catch their breath, the captors that kicked them off. Each stain tells a story. History is a pattern we live in, a stencil of fate we perpetually inhabit. The enslaved being coerced to their doom, my mum strapping me into the bus and telling my brother that he must force me into the castle, or the voice of Elton encouraging me to get out of the car and join their tour. Everything replays, nothing's new.

"Kobby, are you okay?" Milly's voice.

"Kobby?" Scott's voice.

Elton slides into the car. I'm already giggling when he says, "You don't have to come if you don't want to."

"Then why are you still here?" I palm my face. Embarrassment. Relief. A feeling akin to these. After all these years, there's still no guarantee that I wouldn't regress into my infantile mischief, that I wouldn't injure myself for a convenient excuse to

opt out of the tour. "Run along, Elton. I'm not leaving this car."
I say this even as I laugh, else I might just add that he and his
friends are not as wise as they—Vincent more than the others—
have led me to believe. Who in their right minds would allow
themselves to suffer this ordeal? This is not a statue to ponder
how close its portrayal is to the original. Neither is it a plaque
whose words could make onlookers believe they were privy to
secrets of a distant time. Not a history lesson, a textbook you
could flick through to find parodic illustrations. All of those
hold you back while giving you the impression you're being let
in. This is a door.

Elton clasps my thighs for what could have been a minute
but feels like longer. Then he leaves to join Vincent, Scott, and
Nana, Milly, and Faisal, who walk through the castle's gates,
which seem to shut themselves, swallowing up the group. I'm
left with the maudlin chorus of the castle's humming flies.

Old friend, why so distant?
I never thought you'd be back.
To come all this way
and still stay far away.
Come, come, you all,
I'll let this one off just this once.
He'll be back. It's equally your story as it is his.
He'll return again.

The Enslaved

Were the voices in your head. The voices of the dead. We are the brothers who never left. The brothers who were thrown overboard. Welcome.

This was our last home on land, living on borrowed time, on shackled time that still stretched, and stretched, until space became smell became hell, before we were taken to sea. Take off your shoes and step into our footprints that have mangled the floors, shifted its form until the bottom has worn so thin you can feel the fires of hell underneath. There is no ground in this dungeon that is not an imprint of a thousand overlapping footprints. By adding your feet to ours, you are adding your stories to ours, the way our mothers did as they placed our hands in theirs when we were little and prayed for us. We pray for you.

Feel the walls. You don't even need to touch them to feel their rotten texture, the sounds of death ricocheted off these cement bricks. See the mould that wants to cover up the prints of our hands, the metal chains that sing against the paint, against the floors, dirges heralding the dead.

Over here, each room has its voices. Each room kept two hundred of us in tiny spaces that rival the little stores dotted on the streets that you saw on your way here. The voices cry, until the sound of their tears becomes one harmonious din. Listen for the sound of air nowhere, the sounds of here laid bare.

You listen to this tour guide whose sensationalised descriptions are rehearsed and performed for years until, like us, he passes on, and someone takes over his narrative. Nothing these men and women say can paint an apt picture of what we went through. Listen to us. *Agyei*. Listen to our voices. *Miigbo oo ei!* Feel, see, smell us. Don't imagine. We are all around you.

Awieyε yi yεn mu hwan na wo de maa no?

Hwan na wo do too wɔn nsam?

Yε mu hwan?

Awieyε yi yεn ara na wo de ahyε yεn nso?

Hey, you with the broad back. You who has to stoop when you walk through our chambers. Can you for a second stop to think about what brothers of your height went through? You, with that skin, that cursed skin from the blood that raped us and sold us. Your kind did not even make the domestic slaves here. You were trained and given the best of language from your mothers and your white fathers in order to act as a bridge between two cultures, so you could push your people down the slippery slope. Not unlike the ground you tread on, enhancing trade lines between two cultures, selling death in exchange for our lives. You, who listens to us often, you who looks like one of those who journeyed all the way from Benin, you fat Bantu, someone like you would have been pushed into us, pasted into us, squashed into us until the room was able to take its quota of two hundred. You all look like us. The corn-skinned men among you, whom we see lurking around the doorways, they look like those who pushed us out and dumped us into the boats. No face here is new. No voice here is new. No new here is new.

Do you see the little heads sculptured on the floors? The tour guide tells you they mirror the facial expressions of those here. He shows you the one bandaged. He shows everyone the head sculpted with a bandage, it's one of the repetitive lines in his script. He tries to make you imagine this man as the one who rebelled yet still couldn't escape, was crushed and thrown in here. Can you see the here and the then? Over there he shows you the other man whose mouth remains open. That man's mouth stunk by the ninth day they kept us here. A welcoming smell, we'll have to admit. Urine, faeces, blood, dead, and decaying bodies a foot high choked us, more times to death. The heat from the stench is regulated by a stream of water thrown from the little spy-holes above to keep those who can survive alive. So when one of us opens his mouth by the nineteenth day, and you can still smell the fresh breath of stinking body processes, you're thankful he's not part of the mess dragging us to hell or offering respite by death. Maybe he'll be part of us when we're out of here on the ninetieth day. Maybe he'll be dipped through the Door of No Return into the ships. Or, unlucky or lucky, be passed through the door of the captives who are too weak to survive, so are stored in another room until life, like their cries, exits their lips.

Aaah, my favourite part comes. The part where the tour guide turns off the lights and allows you to imagine our situation. Stupid local man with that Ashanti face blinds you all with the flashes from his phone camera, so you missed the moment. The moment of standing in the dark with us, tied up too, your destinies tied up with ours too. We reveal ourselves to the one who listens, the hefty one from Benin. He's in another world. His darkness began longer ago than yours. We eat up his silence, knead his brain with our little voices. We need him, he needs us; even if he's refused to hear our pleas for help. *Mba ye! Maa!* So in that ten seconds, when all's dark except for the camera flashes, this Vincent sees a bloodied, bartered face, breathing into his own. This slave's chains are lifted up so that he can see his own privilege, remember his history, so he never forgets that before he became, he stood in our spots. The lights come back on. We disappear.

"Vincent, Vincent, are you okay?" Someone draws his eyes open into the present. "You're warm. You need water. Here, take, sip." The tour continues. We move around, hoisting up our chains like the skirts of the white women who party in the governor's quarters above so we don't disturb the tour or steal the guide's shine. There's someone drawing everyone's attention. A fat white woman wearing our clothes, wearing our hair, she is whimpering. The tour guide asks if she's okay. She rests her head on a man's shoulders. This man looks like one of the men from the North. He is even taller than the fat, bald one. Centuries ago, men like him would have been stripped naked and put in the town square, their genitals ogled at and prodded by women like the one he enfolds. He's a beauty of a man, the marks on his face. He would be branded as a JSS slave. JSS always had the best of us. The voices of our brothers sent beyond the sea came back to us in little prayers, ancestors now, we lot, informing us men like him, men from the North, mistaken as Ashanti, were kept as breeders to keep the supply of enslaved constant even when trade was outlawed. He's too wrapped up with his white woman to hear us speak to him. We walk past these two lovers as the others move along to the female dungeons. Compared to ours, these were palaces, housing fifty people less. If you listen to the voices, you'll hear screams so shrill we wonder why they couldn't pierce through these thick walls and reach our holes beneath. The half-caste supports his broken frame against the walls, doesn't mind the mould. He watches through the fingers covering his face. The white woman falls on the ground. So theatrical, this one. Muttering something that sounds like, Oh heavens. She's yanked from the floor by her tall man. Heaven cannot be seen from here, but the church can. If you look through the spy-holes, like the tall, bald one does, not needing to bend like he did in the men's dungeons, you'll see the first SPG church. Back to the voices, back to the suffering, in here if there's a God, we can't hear Him amidst the wails and cries of the women. *Dzi nyɛ. Mɛ ku.*

Nyɛ mate nu agbɔ o
Kpɛdɛ nunyɛ nɛ magbɔ

IX

KOBBY
(10 days after the friends arrive)

I n the car, there's only so much one can do, so many brownies one can eat, to divert one's attention away from the image of the colonial figure ahead. Nothing in my phone—not my dad's texts, not the missed calls from my boss—distracts from the twitching above my eyebrow. To let what was once my sleeping scar lie, I take out my pill box. I shake it. Confirming there are no medicines throwing themselves against the walls of their cages begging to be free, which is a sign that I've subjected all ten olanzapines, ten lithiums, ten amytriptilines to my tongue's torture, sucking until their hard ridges turned soft. I tease out a deformed tablet. I allow it the luxury of bleeding onto my tongue for a second too brief to be regarded as such, before spitting it onto the brown earth and sticking out my stained tongue at the side-view mirror for a proper laugh. But these histrionics can only keep me entertained for so long. I contemplate sending Aspecialkindofdouble one of those "just checking in" messages, but I google St. Louis's time and decide it's too early to message, so I let my phone slide into the V between my thighs and gradually, resign my gaze to the castle.

A memory unfolds. In it, an altercation with Vincent in Accra about the castles during one of his drunken lectures. Vincent, who's read *Lose Your Mother* and believes that's enough preparation to see the castles. Vincent, who stares at me with fascination anytime I pull out a book written by a white man, and laughs a little to himself. What had begun as a mild after-supper dialogue had quickly regressed into a fulminous headlock, an encounter we both chose to discount like newly-weds after an awry attempt at intercourse. Given his tendency to grouch, Elton and Scott excuse themselves the moment he begins fixing himself a drink. *Where y'all kids running to?* he hollers when the others disband, then faces me with the broadest gin smile and sigh, *You listen to me, Kobby*, and launches into his disputable monologues. That night, he'd gone on and on about the importance of Black Americans joining the Year of Return train, to "go back home" and see the castles. From his botched argument, he'd somehow arrived at the awareness that the castles, enveloped with their traumatising history, could be metaphorised as the missing rib of every Black American, and that to forgo this experience was to deny oneself of knowledge on what he referred to as "the Genesis of the Black race." The way he spoke about Ghana with the lips of an idealist, he could have been a CNN ad on luxurious travel that comes on right after reports on the devastation of yet another Middle Eastern country by America itself, the way he spoke about Ghana with the lips of an idealist, rising above all the decadence of her people, ignoring all my rebuttals about the year's financial havoc on the working-class Ghanaian. For someone drowning in G and T's, he still held his head above the liquor, rounding his lips, hot with disquisition, to prevent incoherent slurring. Always quoting some author or race scholar to earn his arguments shreds of validity my ignorant self couldn't take apart. Whenever I dared to counter his quotes from Nkrumah and Kwame Ture, even our current president's insistence on diaspora's return, which he brandished at me like the proverbial final nail in the coffin before hammering away, I couldn't have been vocal enough. Despite his intellect, he was the kind who couldn't hold an argument without swelling with seething ire, becoming a grotesque, bulbous thing, like a grossly magnified shadow, of sweat sealed off and discharged as spittle, growing louder as he grew rounder. "Don't you think that the Year of Return and all the prompts to visit these castles is an avenue for a country like this to profit off of Black Pain?" I'd asked. He fell back on the couch, deflating. "Maybe that sounded harsh," I rushed to placate. "Don't you feel like you're being . . . what's the word? Maybe exploited isn't the exact word." He smacked my thigh, "Kobby!" staring for an unnerving amount of seconds before resuming resignedly, "I don't think you understand the significance of this tour for people like me, I don't think talking to you about these issues helps either of us, you'll never understand." He left for his and Scott's room, the living area punctuated with the mime of the almost muted television. *Pum, pum.* Elton, seated out on the patio, had tapped at the glass partition and slid it open. "Kobby, get your ass right here this second, it's now my turn to chew your ear off."

Someone raps on the car window, a man asking that I check out his wares. I stare at the necklaces, bracelets, and keychains with pendants fashioned in the image of the castle. Who wants to move around carrying the baggage of colonisation on their neck, the shackles of enslavement ringed on their fingers? Maybe Vincent would. Maybe it's one of those things I will never understand.

I get my answer when all three friends walk out of the black gates. Hobbling as though roughened up and then let out. They look changed. Different. Almost like they've been wrung through a blender, emerging with their parts in disarray. I shake my head at the souvenir man, who then directs his peddling pizazz to the group of white tourists rushing out of the gates. I step out of the car. The coolness of the air-conditioning surrenders to the hot wind.

"Hey," Faisal says when they're closer. He and Nana, dictating the group's pace, seem like the only ones that have made it out unscarred. In his arms is Milly, who looks like a kid that went tumbling in the mud during playtime. Her braids, as well as her bubu, are caked with dirt, she's sniffling in tissues, hand-fanning cool air into her eyes. "Are you okay?" her husband asks me without purpose.

When I answer yes, it's not to Faisal. I want to reach out to Elton, to extend something more useful than my pained smile. My motor skills become a dismembered lizard's tail, twitching and twisting yet unable to connect with its torso. This ineptitude is an extension of my failures as a son, a friend, a person. This paralysing wariness concerning matters of somatic consolation, urging someone to crumble in the certitude of my strength, does not come without dreading the bartering of emotions between our bodies. It's moments like these that make me certain that I'm indeed a product of my mother's womb. She'd passed down her nutrients along with her innermost sentiments to me. I have imbibed her inadequacies, and despite having convinced myself at an early age that I'd only been an enclave within her body, these years of maturational epiphanies have coerced me into the concession that, though I hadn't emerged as hers, I did in fact emerge as her. And perhaps Elton has sensed this deficit in my person.

Where Vincent and Scott are visibly wounded, both with red-rimmed eyes and slumped shoulders, Elton holds himself together, his torso folding into itself, casually, as if withholding chilly temperatures. Though his feelings are hooded, were it to be ever intimated that he made an outcry to be held and loved, it would be in this minute he's tasked himself with drilling a hole into the sand with his sneakers. Often, I've encountered men like him sheltering under the curtained awning of torso-only profiles on Man4Man. Men so skilled in the art of the aloof and cropping gym-mirror selfies, yet their need for affection easily discerned even if conveyed only through passing gestures such as a momentary hesitance to twist their door knobs and see you out, an awry hug that separates on the assumption that things might get too intense if it isn't cut short with a curt fist-bump, pre-hook-up small-talk segueing into existential topics segueing into neverminds when responses graze the seal of their carefully bottled emotions, a post-coital averting of eyes after unveiling too much of themselves by being way too endearing when given a poop-dick. Elton and I are only just engaging in convenient fucking after all, a simulative relationship which mustn't emulate the intensity of those with the promise of time. Still, I want to avoid coming across as the guy who stuffs his hands into his pockets where others would offer them in a fussy show of concern. With effort, my arms rise towards the three friends, and coil, the empty imprint of a hug nesting in them. Whoever wants this lacklustre excuse of an embrace can have it.

Milly lurches at me. She grabs me hard and closes her body around mine. Faisal tries to remove, her but she shrugs him off.

"I'm so, so sorry," she cries. Vincent catches my eyes; what could have been an oncoming fit moulds into a fist. He turns his back to Milly and me.

"Okay, guys, what happens next?"

"Home?" Elton replies to Scott, voice sounding like it's been cornered and battered. He clears his throat. "I think we should leave now."

"We're going to Elmina Castle," Vincent announces, his back still facing us.

"Vince, we can't do that after—"

"Fine, I'm going on my own then."

I try to push Milly off so I can talk Vincent out of this. But she yowls. I make do with shouting over her head, "Vince, you just went through a lot—"

"How the fuck would you know?" And he's right. Nana steps towards him and tries holding his hands. "Don't." Vincent wriggles away, walks to the car. The engine is reluctant, cranks, then roars; two blasts of a horn becomes Scott's cue to leave. He pats my shoulders, moves around me, and takes my seat in the car.

"You can join them," Elton says to Nana. "I'm going to the resort."

Nana's eyes dart between Elton and the rented car, a pendulum unsure of where its loyalty should swing. But Vincent drives off, leaving us with the reproachful sound of screeching tires and the wails of Milly reminding us over and over again that she's sorry. On the outskirts of this scene is the white photographer snapping away, as if this were an important gathering worthy of dissection by future historians.

Nana gets us three a taxi, and we abandon Milly crying against the crumpled shirt of her husband, who wards off the souvenir peddlers screaming, "*Madam, Madam,*" suggesting her woes be alleviated with retail therapy. Elton rides shotgun and doesn't adjust the rearview mirror to suit his customary inquiry into Nana's and my backseat relations. Nana whistles, an old gospel song which used to be my mother's favourite, something about heaven being home and life being just a journey. The taxi driver picks up this tune, bolstering Nana's tentative pitch, and in doing so, he fosters an esoteric bond with Nana. The melody is a heavy thing; reminiscent of the squealing tires of a gurney, it trundles into the car, bringing with it an uncanny resonance whenever its harmonisers pause for an intake of breath. Unnerved by the sudden funereal atmosphere, I roll down my window, take deep breaths, and knead the growing irritation above my eyebrow with my wrist. Nana cups my knee, digs his fingers into my thigh. Whether this is done in solace or abuse, or a mix of both, I decide not to dwell on its intent if it eases the itch of my past.

Why do you run?
We are your brothers.
Come feel our wrath.

The castle plays the role of the torturer and the tortured, the result of colonial ghosts and dead enslaved embroiled in a turf war. Nana's fervent whispers coax me into a world which assumes the blood-red of my drooping lids. Images of the castle are replaced with little schoolboys cracking devilish grins through the open wound of their angelic faces.

* * *

Elton tells Nana to leave the room the minute we arrive. Nana looks between me and him and turns for the door. It bangs on his way out. Elton grabs my underarms, forking me off my top bed and dumping me onto his. He asks that I take off my clothes. I oblige without hesitation, and in seconds we're both naked, sprawled over the narrow bed, looking into the constellation of the woodwork above. The quiescence is a third feature in the room, uncomfortable as the presence of a disinterested voyeur. Although lives beyond these walls have demanded that I take advantage of situations like this, let my hands glide over body parts and cover others with my mouth, this is neither the string of awkward minutes preluding a hook-up, nor is it a time to devalue with sex or thoughts of it. Still, my body is egressive with its urges, even a dog simping for a belly rub possesses a certain coyness missing in my curled toes and my fingers twiddling my pointy nipples. Even more maddening is the taste of horny in my mouth—a ravenous overdrive of my salivary glands flooding my tongue. Sex has always been my body's combative measure against its stressors. Perhaps what's more gratifying is the opportunity to scrub clean the dregs of cum and bodily fluids afterwards, my body bleached of its agitations, emerging pristine and renewed. If only I could convince Elton that this is what he needs too: sex not just for sex's sake, but sex as an overture to a total body-cleanse of life's horrors.

"You know what hurts me most? What I can't quit thinking about?" he begins, "That other Africans sold their own brothers and mothers and fathers into that castle. They fucking sold their own blood into that." I rub his head, noticing the specks of stubble surrounding an otherwise smooth patch to his scalp. It occurs to me that I could deflect this touchy story of the castle with something else, something lighter, perhaps ask him what age he began balding, but the burden to switch subjects doesn't weigh heavy enough. I choose to become the sieve he filters his emotions through for clarity.

"Why didn't you want to come?"

The sounds of the birds chirping near his window fill the room. I play the role of the therapist who refuses to be the patient. Our vice-versa relationship ends with our sex. There'll be no reversal of roles here, no switching of positions.

"Shit, if I knew what had been waiting there, I probably wouldn't have gone in." He pauses. "I don't know. Maybe I'd have been more cautious." He takes my suddenly stiff hand and spreads soft, sedative kisses on it. "It's okay not to see it, really. Hell, I don't know why Vincent and Scott would want to see the other ones. I understand they want closure. Do you not want closure?"

I watch a bed bug graze his arm, its mouth forging its way across his bicep in a zigzagging pattern. I should flick it off.

"So there's a tour guide, of course. He's got all these words to paint a vivid picture of what happened. But somehow you can't help the thought that all this is some rehearsed shit. I wonder how often he tells the story in a day. At least three times, maybe. In a year, he'd have told this about a thousand times. There's Vincent and Scott and I, quiet, you know; even though we went into this castle together, we all feel separated by our own pain. I've never felt so alone and afraid like that. Anyway, all my friends who came to the motherland came back with stories that it was going to hurt, but I never believed them. I'm tough, you see? The moment I entered, I knew it was gon' be like everything I've heard and more. I heard lots of voices, like the people, my ancestors were speaking to me. I could see their faces. I will never forget the smell of the place. It smelt like . . . old blood. It's kinda like knowing so little about your-self all your life, and in a few hours all the mysteries about your existence is revealed to you. Who's going to save you now? Not the history white America teaches in schools. None of that shit. The scales have fallen off your eyes and you start seeing yourself for all that you've been made to be." He pauses. Perhaps sur-prised as I am by his perceptive rant. "Anyway, all I'm saying is, I now understand why you stayed behind."

That baiting unnerving silence.

"Nana was taking pictures the whole time," Elton laughs. "Shit was annoying. But you can't tell a brother how to act when he sees the place his ancestors were killed. He even let the tour guide take a pic of him near the Door of No Return—now the Door of Return. My man even did a deuces in a couple of them pics." Another laugh. "There was the fat, white lady. Who couldn't shut the fuck up. Crying as loud as those damn roosters in this resort. She behaved like it was her history, like her people were the ones who were killed instead of the other way round. It felt dirty for her to be doing that, like she was playing us, teach-ing us what grief should look like if we all claimed to be real hurt. She threw herself at Vincent when we were out the castle. You know, the same way she did you. Man, that was weird. But my man wasn't having it. He pushed her off. Her coon almost got an ass-kicking when he tried stepping in. Vincent is my boy, I know him. He'd have given that tall-ass white-loving nigga a story to take home to his mama. Whipped his ass good."

"Yeah, Milly was weird, but there's no memo on how to act in times like that—"

"But what you don't do is try to minimise our pain by mak-ing yours obvious. Too obvious. That shit is very white. I don't know. I don't know. There must have been a way for her to recognise that she was out of line. At some point, just fucking stop. But she was just 'bout starting, she began rolling on the floor—"

"Really?"

"That bitch deserves an award. Anything for the Best White Tears of the year." He laughs too. "She was worse than Nana and that husband of hers." The sound of our laughter, like the sporadic slamming of trap-doors outside the room, feels cathartic.

"Thanks for waiting for us, though. You're a good guy."

It's a compliment that throws me off. "I waited because I thought I'd have the balls to walk in."

His breathing slows. I sense he's expecting me to say more. When I do not, he heaves a sigh and slides up so our heads share the same height, wraps his doughy arms around me. "For real though, you've got the biggest balls I've ever seen." He gives my scrotum a squeeze, and I shriek, throwing an elbow toward his loins but catching him in the ribs instead.

"You're special." He kisses the back of my ear. Our bodies naturally assemble into foetal positions, a performance drawn out for an unintended cinematic effect. We remain in each other's lungs, heartbeats, each other's warmth, a kind of parasitic relationship that, to my surprise, brings comfort. I do not want to disengage just yet. Like I do whenever anyone's big-spooning me, silently counting to fifty before muttering some excuse—about the weather and inconvenient temperatures. Against my predilection to persist in this position, I'm too aware of his semi-hard penis casually resting—pressing—against my butt, suggestive as a key buried into an enclosed palm. I slide my hands down his groin and take his dick in my hands. I prod it until it's firm and then I guide it into my ass. There's a sharp intake of breath when all of him pushes into me. It's the second time I've allowed him to penetrate without lube. As if I'm unconscionably asking for the same pain he offered the first time around; *Slice through me Elton, hurt me, fuck me, make me forget.* But this time he's gentle and sweet. He does not so much thrust as swell inside of me, like an unleashing of worms into my arsehole—that time I sat on the toilet and had to wait for minutes even after the shit was over, for the clew of roundworms to wriggle out of my ass and plop onto the layer of porridge-poop in the bowl. It's the first time we have sex with emotions resembling love or something similar. Slow and sensual. As though we've each realised what delicate beings we are.

When our limbs are nestled in each other's, and our breathing resumes normalcy, we're in that place of post-coital high, between heaven and earth, dreams and reality, the dozing off and the waking, the kisses and the cuddles and the sweet intermittent murmurings (*You know . . . I could teach you something that could give you intense pleasure, mm-hmm?, I call it AESMA, okay?, you think of all the bad things that could happen to you and then you imagine them happening to you but you stop before it gets too real like edging but this time you don't go over the point-of-no-return for a shattering orgasm, okay that's some outta pocket white-people shit don't do that, you're no fun, sounds like you could get yourself real hurt . . . like you could die, Elton too many things can kill me but my imagination isn't one of them, shh let's sleep.*) Nothing can penetrate this bliss: not even his phone buzzing—with messages from the Xhosa, the Zulu, the Tswana men—could interrupt the moment. But something succeeds. Something crashes the moment. The Germans.

"What the . . ." Elton's voice tapers, the sounds of the repeated banging cutting him off. With a hesitant groan, he jumps off the bed. I watch a gecko race into oblivion, terrified by the thundering door.

"Elton, Vincent, Scott!"

Elton signals that I stay put, and hobbles while pulling up his shorts en route to the door.

"Elton!" The German old lady bellows as the door sings for its rusty hinges.

"Is anything wrong?"

"Are Scott and Vincent in there with you?" The husband wants to know. "Scott in particular, is he with you?"

"No, he isn't, he just . . ." Elton's speech falters. I hear the door slam. "These motherfuckers just barged in here with questions and ran off without waiting for answers."

"Why Scott?" I ask, rising off the mattress. "Why would they care about Scott?"

"It's probably unimportant, which is why they ran off." He walks to me and pushes me down on the bed, wraps his mass around mine, and begins kissing my back. "Ready for round two?"

One of the friends will die. Nana's pastor's words have me triggered. "I think it's best if we checked on Scott."

"Fine!" he concedes. I watch him make an attempt for his phone in his baggy shorts on the floor. Mine rings on top of his bed. He grunts, launches himself up, and palms for it without getting off our mattress. One look at my phone's screen and he's frowning. "Why's Vincent calling you?"

X

NANA

I have done myself small like the wall lizard who my grandmother say are witches sent to look at our cooking and go gossip to the other witches in the spiritual world. I'm watching through the window and hearing them. They are having sex. They use the window curtains to cover the window, but I hear them. I know what sex sound like. First it sound like the bed is hitting the wall. *Pa Pa Pa*. Then it sounds like one of them is shouting. *Yesssss, yesss*. They're enjoying it.

All of a sudden I hear someone come behind me. I think it's Mina, but it's the other one who look like her. She's holding a pan of water to throw in the bush behind me. But she stops and looks at me standing by the window. I look like thief. She look away from me and go pour the water in the bush.

I walk away from the window and follow her, looking at her buttocks, not big like Mina own. But I become hard again.

"*Wo din de sɛn?*" I ask her.

"Patience," she say, walking fast to the kitchen.

"Patience, *wo nim baabia Mina wɔ?*"

She shake her head. I nod. I ask her if Mina vanishes sometimes like this. She says yes. Where does Mina go to? I ask her. She raise her shoulders. This girl nice, *paa*, but I don't know if she has voice. Not like Mina who didn't stop talking. If they bring me wife from the village, I want her to be like this one. Patience. Even look at her name. I smile at her. Pastor will like her.

"Do you have chicken in the kitchen?" I ask when she's going inside the kitchen which is an *apata*, with smoke coming out from the top.

She nod.

"I want live chicken."

She look at me funny.

"Do you have?"

"Plenty, plenty chicken, bra." She finally use her voice. Her English not good like Mina own. But English is only useful when you can talk.

"Okay, I'm going to the boss quarters. I'm going to ask where Mina is and come back. When I return, I'll come for one. I'll pay."

On the way to the boss quarters, I see the white woman they call Milo *o sɛ* Million *o* standing outside her room. She looks like she's waiting for someone. Looking at her watch, frowning. I try to greet her—*Me ma wo adwo*—but she doesn't see me. She turn and walk back into her room. You shouldn't be called a woman if you don't have buttocks. Straightforward on the beach, I see the white photo-man with his camera trying to take picture of something on the sand. If Ghana is nice, and if he won't stop taking plenty-plenty pictures, they must ask him to pay money every time he take picture. Imagine how that can bring money into Ghana pockets. One day, he try to take pic of me when I was doing that yoga thing with Scott. The way I look at him. He almost throw his camera away. I don't know if white people have their juju, but over here you don't let black person take picture of you like that. Else they're going to sell your soul.

I'm about to knock on the door of the boss quarters when I hear them talk quick-quick in that their *aburokyire* voices, mentioning Mina's name. Do they know where she is? I don't understand half of what they're saying because their English sound different-different coming from their mouth, not like the Americans that you hear on TV, and being with Elton and his friends has make me come to understand small-small. And they also talk in some other language which sound like they are saying the word *akesha* over and over again.

("You'd think by now she's going to stop running with every guest here.") Then the woman add, *akesha*.

("Yeah, these locals always wanting to secure a foreigner as a husband. It's so sad." *akesha*)

("She's pursued every Tom, Dick, and Harry." *akesha*)

("Every Peter and Paul." *akesha*)

They keep quiet for a few minutes. ("Are you seeing a pattern here?")

The old woman laugh hard. ("Do you think she's going in for men with cliché names? Ha ha, Bernd. That's funny!")

I hear the sound of a book opening fast-fast. ("Don't you realise something odd is happening here? That every time she runs off with a man she returns without them, only to check them out?") Quiet. ("Like that Harry guy she went with whose company came here to ask of his whereabouts.")

("Are you saying we should start taking cards instead of cash? I've already told you that the government would find out how much we're really making and up their taxes.")

("Oh stop this, Paula! Is it all about money to you? Do you not find it odd that white male guests are disappearing from your resort?—Paula! Mina is making these white men disappear!")

("Of course she isn't. You think Mina's killing them? Now that sounds funny. She's only bringing back the money they abscond with.")

("Whatever's happening I won't trust these locals—")

("The only thing they're capable of is the bit of witchcraft they accuse each other of. You know, over here they say witch instead of bitch. And honey, witches are harmless. Besides, if she's missing, it doesn't support your theory that she makes the white men disappear. There's been no white man in the resort lately.")

Quiet.

"Scott!" The man shouts as if an answer has come to him like they taught us that Albert Einstein had a Eucharia moment.

("What about that mulatto?")

("The locals, they think Scott or anyone who's from the Middle East is white. Do you know if he's in the resort?")

I hear footsteps coming towards the door and I run. I run to the kitchen which is near. I see Patience cooking and she and the mouse that is chewing a yam on a table don't see me when I enter.

"Vincent! Elton! Scott!" I hear the *obronis* knock hard on our door. I want them to enter so they'll catch the two of them having buttocks sex. Maybe they'll not do anything, because wasn't it the *obroni* people who brought gay-gay things to Ghana? That's what Pastor say.

I think of all the things I hear these German *obronis* say about Mina, most of it I did not understand but I hear "kill." Mina, a killer? Sounds so funny I laugh *kikiki* in my hands, but I shake so hard that the shelf of silver and aluminium cooking utensil move small and one fall down. The girl turn behind but doesn't come and check. She goes on stirring the shito she's cooking, which make my throat choke so hard I want to cough. These Fante people like too much pepper. They tear shito like it's sea water. I want to tell her to stop making the shito hot. But I hear the sound of something doing *kukukuku*. I look above me and I see, next to a box of rat medicine, that they've tie three chickens with shoe lace and pack them on the top shelf tight like the man who calls himself a tour guide say they do to the slaves in the castle. *Kukukuku*, they say, looking at me. I raise my hand and tell them to shush. I'm about to catch one of them when I hear the kitchen door bang close. From where I stand I see the two *obronis* walk in. The yam mouse ran away.

"Mina (asked you to cover for her as she goes about her crimes didn't she?)"

The woman is the first one to shout as she walk into the kitchen and grab Patience by the back, looking to push her head into the big pot of hot shito. But her husband stop her. Even though I can't understand what they're are saying to her, Patience understand it and she's already crying as the woman is shaking her from her shoulders. I want to step in and *pataa*, but I need the chicken so I keep quiet and make steady.

("What does she do with the men?") The man ask her as his wife shake her. ("Where's she now? What's she up to?")

"I don't know madam, sah." Patience talks as she's crying loud like a small baby. "She don't tell me anything. She just leave always and she tell me to do her job until she comes back."

("You stupid bitch, witch! I'm going to put your head into this hot sauce and you're never going to have it back again. Do you know what you're going to cause us? They would shut this place down, we would lose our resort!")

("Paula calm down!")

("We're going to lose our only lifeline, Bernd! We have nothing, nothing. We can't return to Germany. There's nothing for us there besides knitting and nude beaches!")

"Shut up," the man says to his wife. ("Look, girl," he turn to Patience, "do you know if she's said anything about a man named Scott? Or Harry? Or any other white man she's run off with?")

"No, sah, all she says is that she's going to come and she'll come back with plenty money." She pause as she blow her nose. "This time she say that she like the new *obroni* that live here. I don't know his name. Last night after the Anansesɛm I didn't see her. This morning too it look like she didn't sleep in the house. I just think that she has run away again and I came to work for her."

("You fucking bitch, witch! Does she tell you what she does with the men? Does she kill them?")

That talk they are having is so funny, I want to laugh! Mina, a killer! I know if I stay here long I will laugh and make noise.

So I put my hands up and take one chicken. It make a lot of noise as I untie the lace, but the people are shouting at the girl to help them find Mina so they don't hear. If they only know. I go outside through a back door I find. Happy to leave the kitchen and its hot pepper smell. And that's when I see the Ananse running out of the room in the direction of the sea. The fool is so busy he doesn't see me. He run quick-quick like in his head they're singing *run-run-run there's a fire on the mountain*. I make *gidigidi* and run with my stolen hen into the public bathroom.

My pipi is paining me from all the hardness it's becoming anytime I see a woman buttocks. So I think I'll try to urinate. Maybe I'm being cursed for my sins. Or maybe Mina give me gono.

In the bathroom, I hear the sound of toilet flushing. I want to do quick and hide the chicken, but it's making so much noise. A man walks out of the toilet. Sees me standing at the door and say, "Oh, it's you," then he looks at the chicken with one eyebrow raised.

He's naked, his buttocks is hard but looks big. *Agyina gyina hɔ*. Buttocks that have stand-stand there, like we say in my village. The *kaka* in my mouth begins to fill with blood. I remember how much I hate him. He's a crook. Another Ananse.

("Could you tell Kobby Milly is waiting for him to teach her?")

I let the chicken fall from my hands. It does *kukuku* so loud I think the world can hear that I'm breaking all of the Ten Commandments. Thou shalt not steal. Thou shalt not kill.

KOBBY

"Hey," I call out, halting. She's seated under a coconut tree, her legs like tentacles looped around her loins. With a fist, she pounds the stem, causing the plant to shudder. Above her is a bundle of brawny nuts, assembled as footballers huddling and scheming over a strategic win. Should they disperse, her skull will be hammered into her clavicle, flattened like inquisitive nails caught peeking out of their panelling. I'd like to see the poetry in this death, to hold up a fallen drupe coated with the sand her blood adheres onto the fleshy epicarp. Hence, in place of a cautioning against her suicidal naiveté is a grin. "Milly!"

"You're late." Her braids are bunned to conceal their slow unravelling. Her neck hides under a green t-shirt that complements her grey eyes. On the t-shirt is written, *Emancipate Yourself from Mental Slavery*. There's a set of turquoise *ahwennee* lying above the waistline of her jeans. Rarely have I taken notice of these features I'm now attentive to. Could I be getting sentimental that this may be the last time we see each other before I bid the resort and Cape Coast goodbye? Or maybe my boss was spot-on about her postulation on fatphobia—*If you want to confirm you're fatphobic, watch how you treat the added layers of fat on your own body. Do you ever see a fat person and see them for things other than their size? When your gaze holds their added layers, do you not treat them the way you treat your own fat, which is to stare and stare until your entire being is reduced to the pound of flesh you hold against your judgement?*

To appease her vexation, I employ a tired wisecrack, "If I wasn't late, I wouldn't be Ghanaian, would I?"

"True." She aims her fist at my knee. I am quick to duck. "Faisal's never early for anything. I'm the woman, yet he takes longer showers. He uses gels and splashes I would never use. He shows up late for everything."

"He smells like he takes his time too." This, I do not say. Instead, I say, "So! I brought brownies!" I take out the polythene from my pocket. At this point of their staleness, they look more like *poloo* than brownies.

"Oh yum." Milly wants one. But she hesitates. "Are these spiked?"

"With marijuana, yes."

"No, thank you. I don't do anything I can't test. The only place I've ever done drugs is Amsterdam. Over there, you can test what exactly is in what. Even in the UK, you can't be certain about the stuff people pass off as recreational drugs. How much more Ghana where you've got failed systems? No, not taking that risk. They look nice though, even if poorly made."

"Our first Twi lesson!" Lowering myself onto the sand, I inject some cheer into my tone. It's a propitious coincidence that we're seated in the same area where Vincent attempted drowning. At late afternoon, the entire scene looks serene; the sea is soothing, the winds caress instead of slapping and clawing at eyes till tears run down cheeks. There's even a sweet smell in the air, almost sickly, something I can't help but associate with shito made from rotten shrimp. Luckily, it's not too overbearing. Whatever convinced her to pick this spot, I'm grateful.

"So what will be our first lesson?" She takes out her phone, which becomes her notepad. "I'm sorry, are digital devices not allowed in this class?" She notices the distance in my gaze which appears fixated on her iPhone. I immediately fetch my own phone and, for a while since visiting Cape Coast, turn on its data. The screen erupts with notifications. New messages from my boss. New messages from my dad. New messages from Aspecialkindofdouble which I'm spoiling to read.

"Hello?" Milly snaps her fingers in my face.

"Of course." I say, glibly. "Today we're going to learn . . . common phrases in everyday Twi and their meaning."

"Oooh, I got a book for that. They sell that on the roadside. Hey, did you take your lesson notes from those?" She hits my shoulder.

With every swipe, it's a genuine wonder how she remains purblind to the racist undertones of her actions. I decide to change the topic. "Let's explore death in today's Twi lesson."

"Ooh. Spooky."

"In Akan, death is *oh-wu-oh*."

She imitates my pronunciation, and I'm not surprised she's perfect at it. She even flicks back the phantom loc around her face, pleased with herself. "I like that a lot. There's a hint of surprise in the word itself, an interjection, oh! Confirms the language's syntheticness." My brows pucker in response to her deductions. "You know Faisal once told me Ghanaians consider suicide a sin by God, the Christian God. I wonder what Akans think? I mean, the Akans before colonisation? Do they have language for suicide?"

I blink. Odd question. I want to go off-script and tell her the Akans treat suicide as they do all taboo topics: shut up about it until they have to deal with it. If it happens that someone takes their own life, they're treated as if they didn't exist; no one to wash their body, no funeral wake, buried without a fuss, a grave shallow enough for dogs to dig up. "I'll take your questions later. But to learn a people's language, you have to understand the psychology behind it—"

"Linguistics 101, I see." She nods appreciatively. Again, she flicks that loc out of habit. "I have a language degree."

I imagine grabbing her by her bun and breathing against her ear, Are you going to let me teach you or not? The vision feels so lustrous—seeing that blood rush back into her face. A half-baked smile lingers on my lips. I allow myself a larger bite of the imagery: *I am yanking out her braids, forcibly detaching hair from scalp. There's blood spattering on my face like raindrops on a sunny day. I am frolicking in her blood; every pull is easy as tugging* kontomire *by its roots. I am yelling at her to give us back our culture, our heritage, our pride. Hand it back, bitch. I'm emancipating you from mental domination, bitch.*

"Kobby!"

Fingers snap in my face. Hers. "Focus," she yells. And laughs at me. "What were you thinking of, Kobby? You looked like you had a cotton bud up your ear."

"Okay. So to understand Twi, you have to get the concept of death and what it means to Akans. Akans love funerals. It's one of those opportunities to look good—fashion-wise, I mean. They celebrate the dead. They even take loans from banks to bury their dead. The size of one's funeral is usually an indication of the life he lived. If someone's got Big Funeral Energy written all over them, you've got to become close to him while he's alive: that way you get an administrative role in the organisation of his funeral. So you can have some of the drinks and food to take back home." Milly's cackling, anything to ease her mind before the blow. "For the Akans, dying means you're en route to some-place better. When someone dies, they become, ɔsaman, which is ghost—" she imitates again, then transcribes it the best way she can on her phone. "For Akans, ghosts are not necessarily a good thing. When someone dies, they must cross over, they must not stay with the living. So rituals are done on the day of the fu-neral to ensure the person's safe trip into the afterlife. Everyone who dies becomes an ancestor, which in Twi is nananom nsam-anfoɔ, which loosely translates as Ghost Elders." Throughout my lecture I steal moments to check the time on my phone as Milly makes notes. The skies are the colour of washed-out jeans. The sun has disappeared. There's no one around. All we have for company are the waves that wash up to our sand-crusted feet and the lulling sound of the wind, the strange arthropods that climb up our bodies seeking refuge from the water. I wonder how long until this is all over. "When someone dies, here are some wishes you can give the person: da yie, which means sleep well, me ma wo due, and wo ne nyame nkɔ, which means you and God should go. You can also say that to someone leaving for a trip. The Akans think dying is a trip into the afterlife—"

"Do you think all those castle slaves crossed over?"

Silence.

When I finally speak, I'm addressing the distance. "They ha-ven't crossed over. How do you cross over after dying that way?

No justice in life. No justice in death. I see no reason why they should cross over."

"It was the most painful thing I've ever witnessed. You should never see it, Kobby." I find her shivering, trying hard to hold herself together. Elton's words about her behaviour in the castle loop in my head. "I said good luck to them. In Twi," she whimpers. "*Me ma wo tiri nkwa.*" I nod. She adds: "Which loosely translates as, I give your head life." I stare at her with scepticism now more than ever, taking apart her actions. Is she trying to impress me with her Twi or does she care about telling her story? She sniffles. A lone tear falls from her eyes and soaks into the neckline on the t-shirt. She fans air into her eyes. She's such a good actress, I almost do not see through her bullshit.

"I don't know how to stop these tears. I keep thinking of how justice can be served. The UK government is thinking of giving reparations. Back home, I used to be in support of the idea of reparations. But now that I've seen . . ." She points in the direction of what would have been the castle if the trees along the shore didn't protectively seal the horizon to prevent her from using it as prop. "I wonder how much you can give to repay this loss." She howls, then falls onto my shoulder. For minutes, we both sit in a silence punctuated by her snuffling, looking at the sea in case we might be gifted answers to the world's mysteries.

"Look at me," Milly laughs half-heartedly at her lot. "I came to Africa to build a well; now I want to build a wall around this country, keep away all its oppressors." Just like that, the White Saviour jumps out of her.

My phone wriggles in my hand. All my attention and spite at Milly is sucked into the device. Sitting intrusively in my notification bar is an icon shaped as an envelope. Gmail. I draw down the bar for a preview.

Hi Kobby, I did enjoy your writing!

"Kobby? Hello?" Milly snatches the phone just as my heart lurches.

"Can I have my phone back?" I bite my lip to rein in my growing irritation.

"No," she shakes her head. "We are having a lesson; let's finish it and then you can go back to whatever it is that's taking your focus. Is it Elton? Is that a booty call?"

My anger pulls at my throat, ejects into my mouth, has the bitterness of Artefan on my tongue. I touch her jean-clad thigh. "What if I told you there's a way to pay it back?" I squeeze gently. "Pay back all the past harm."

"What? How?" she asks, doubtful. Then she notices. My gentle transformation into a distorted version of myself. She catches my retreating orbs. The slow retraction of my Adam's apple, then my trembling fingers against her thigh. Perhaps this is the time she considers taking off. When my mask falls off. The reality of my curtained self revealed. But for her, it'll be too late. A darkness shelters us, a presence shadowing our bodies. She twitches, a flailing attempt to turn.

Thump. Her head is whacked into its medial position.

Thump.

Milly has fallen head-first on the ground, a genuflecting supplicant, unconscious. Behind me, Vincent mutters his thanks, the zipper of the body bag he clutches whining. He looks to Scott—in whose hands the assaulting shovel shudders—and says, "Now we kill her."

SUBJECT: RE: QUERY, 1000 WAYS TO DIE IN GHANA
FROM: agentkate@cbnwhyliterary.com
TO: kobbymanu@gmail.com

Hi Kobby,

Thank you for the opportunity to look at sample pages of your work *1000 Ways to Die in Ghana*. While I did enjoy your writing, I feel I'm not the best agent to champion your work. However, this is just an opinion from one reader in a business that's highly subjective. I may turn it down, but I am sure someone may well come to a different decision.
All the best.

Kind regards,
Agent Kate

PS: As I said, I loved your writing. It's very Aronofsky meets Tarantino. (I always hate comparing the works of ethnic artists to Western ones, as I'm sure you have better, African comp titles/film, so forgive me for my Caucasian limitations.) So here's something high up my MSWL. I recently finished *Homegoing* by Yaa Gyasi. I'm sure you've already read it, given she's Ghanaian. Why did it take so long for me to get to it?? Anyway, if you've got anything about Ghana's colonial history or the transatlantic slave trade, please send my way.

XI

KOBBY

(10 days after the friends arrive)

For years since its post-independence publication, the book *Amansan Asantefo Twi*, tracing the origins and evolution of the Akan language, has suffered the pillaging of its contents—whole sentences with perplexing structures as seen in pompous doctoral dissertations—by newspaper articles, textbooks, and the sermons of radio mallams who are quick to prove themselves lettered to an audience bloated with Christian scepticism of necromantic divinations. Given plagiarism in Ghana can neither be checked—any attempt would leave one with a year's worth of weevilled beans to sift through—nor contested, since the idea of intellectual property—particularly one based on anthropological research—is almost farcical, in the dawn of the new millennium and the arrival of gluttonous portable printers excreting sheet after sheet, this cyclopean, vine-smothered work languishing in the private archives of the Balme Library, curtailing access to students even after they've powered through the bureaucratic hurdles required for its visitation, would lament the injustice of all its material repackaged as a bite-sized edition, retitled *Anuanom Yensua Twi: A Guide to Speaking Akan Like an Ashanti* and sold to clueless tourists needing flimsy flight literature in VIP buses undertaking the six-hour transit from Accra to Kumasi. Since Milly once belonged to the category of "clueless tourist aching for Twi lessons," I'm certain she purchased the watered-down version of the original; thus, hers will be denied the entire chapter that details Akan rituals performed during the burial of victims of homicide.

Vincent and Scott ignore my prompts on the funeral rites to send Milly away with, and though I babble out my experience visiting *Amansan Asantefo Twi* for the purposes of enlightenment—presenting my readings as fun pop-culture listicles like those on Buzzfeed—rather than obligatory praxis, in order to slash the inflating silence that has ballooned into our bond as accomplices, they refuse to recognise my efforts to lighten the heavy air that surrounds us. Too tone-deaf to pick up on my humour, rejecting my offerings with harsh, even disparaging remarks. In their minds, or more precisely, that of the dead enslaved who've chosen Vincent as their conduit—and he executes his duties with a light-handedness that ushers their words out of his lips like tentative whispers, poetically rendered, having the quality of the gentle glide of a hydrofoil merely grazing the water's surface—my reading on old customs is "irrelevant as these defunct traditions themselves, to be dissolved and forgotten as the ocean eats up flailing hands that can't survive its currents." Scott is a blunt translator of Vincent's sibyllic messages; his rendition, carnal and Germanic, is so divorced from the original's subliminal effect: *No, Kobby, you don't get a living hen and slit its throat just to sprinkle its blood over her body. You don't burst eggs. You don't bury money where the spirit dies so the troubled soul can be appeased. And if you don't shut the fuck up . . .*

From the dead enslaved, here are the rituals that matter: Vincent pulls out a razor, one meant for facial hair, shaves her skull bald; with a hot iron whose glowing elements are nearly dimming, he brands a fairly legible A.S. on her back; rusting shackles are clamped around her ankles and wrists; he ablutes her body, splashes pails of brine at her as if hacking away her very existence. Scott helps place her into the body bag in a supine position, her hands resting on her crotch in an odd manner that makes me briefly recall Nana. To be sure no one other than a mating dog duo and the jaw-slacked fishes drying on an amoebic reef is spying on our dealings in these waist-length shrubs, I look around, dutiful as a third party whose mechanical effort has rarely been required owing to an unspoken convention that he possesses the tendency to fuck things up without trying. *Her pulse is weak*, Vincent announces. *Perfect.* I watch the others shovel tonnes of sand as well as errant crabs on top of Milly, only stopping when the bag is filled to the brim. Then, as if it were a charitable offering of a last slice, they confer on me the privilege of stomping the entire load down. Together, we carry Milly into a canoe rented earlier by the two, pushed into the ocean by Scott who's either living through these moments with spikes of adrenaline or has been masking all along, this scapulae-strength under a shawl of effeminacy.

We set to paddling.

"You guys sure we're doing the right thing?" I ask. I'm seated in the middle, charged with securing Milly's torso in case she rises and has it in her to exert a force capable of capsizing the canoe. Not that she's got any luck against the tonnes of sand and the shackles, but an unwilling captive would always want to escape, and in our current situation, it would just not be feasible sending the dogs after her.

Scott sucks his teeth in a manner that's very Ashanti. He must have picked that up from Nana during their yoga sessions. "Funny you've got morals now when you didn't a while ago. Brian told us a lot, you know? He didn't just tell us what you do for a living."

Brian. He's partly the reason I've been a co-conspirator to murder. I exhale audibly, looking to my rowing arm—my triceps bulging to make iridescent the serrated wounds that spiral along them, these physical indentations of Scott's malice when he'd ambushed me after I'd turned away from Vincent's lecture on the dead enslaved without giving a definite answer on whether I'd help with snuffing Milly out. My gaze roams the azure expanse surrounding us, turns out ours is the only canoe ascending towards the elusive horizon. Almost an hour at sea, and we're either slow or still haven't reached the ancestral graveyard Vincent promises. The sea is oddly calm, none of the roaring and moaning that has characterised our seaside respite, nothing but the slight rippling we send out to the universe with our paddling, corroborative with Vincent's claim that the "dead enslaved have willed the sea to still like okra soup after its surface has crusted." Incidentally, my misgivings on Vincent's validity—his communication with otherworldly spirits—and his general levelheadedness abates, perhaps owing to a proclivity to believe in the existence of a world beyond the borders of science, something to thank my Africanness for. Although this tendency to dwell on the superstitious does nothing to quell my worries, these nibbling concerns gnawing into the silence that shrouds us, not per Scott's convictions about a haunting conscience, but a hunger to uncover the theory that underlies Milly's death. Ignoring Scott's abrasive remarks, I voice these questions: "How is killing Milly this way going to solve the centuries of injustice? Will this make up for the millions of deaths?"

But, "Kobby, trust me, this was the only way. The voices wouldn't stop. They tried to make me take my own life because I wouldn't help," is the sole answer Vincent has for me, offering it brashly over his shoulder to shush my interruptions. For all his learning, entwined with his irritating penchant to summon deceased race activists by the ouija board, grafting their theories with his problematic rants, it's a wonder he fails to recognise just how irresponsibly moronic this response is; that he could not be bothered to run these murderous ideas through the pestle and mortar of his philosophic dialectics before implementing them; that he decides to take a life without instituting measures to tackle any consequences, any obnoxious voice of conscience to heckle with for the rest of his life; no earthly motivations whatsoever beyond the dictations of the dead enslaved. He remains relaxed, seated at the helm of the boat, with his hands up high, presenting sibilant prayers to the skies, oblivious to the tangible manifestations of my irritations, my fingers clenching the paddle tight, intent on swinging the wood at his tilted head, knocking him off the boat, swatting at Scott too, bashing their heads repeatedly—I imagine they'll put up some fight, scramble for my paddle to yank me off the boat too, but I won't stop—until they drown. Until the ocean eats up their flailing hands that can't survive its currents.

"Besides, you're too late, Kobby," Scott's lips are close to my ear. "You're equally guilty. You should have voiced your reservations when we talked you into this. You're an accomplice now." There's a shaky edge to his voice. If for Vincent this death is to free him from the voices, for Scott these accusations are to free him of the guilt for having done this.

"There's a joke among the ethnic groups here," I begin, an attempt to make Vincent aware of the ramifications that lay ahead. "Actually, there's a comedian . . . DKB? He's got initials for a stage-name, not sure if those are the right initials. Anyway, he told this joke which has become popular with Ghanaians because it's too true." The sound of the waters swishing against the paddle trickles into the suspenseful gaps of my story. "The joke goes like this: If you want to beat up an Ashanti man, he'll tell you all of the properties he's to inherit from his uncle. He wishes that hearing all he's worth will make you quit. If you want to beat up a Ga man, the Ga man will tell you all that he'll do to you. He's hoping his vocal display of his abilities would scare you into thinking you've picked the wrong person for a fight." Vincent holds up his hand. Scott and I stop rowing. Our boat though, oblivious to the memo, keeps drifting. Vincent whispers something orphic into the air and then fires three successive claps. I watch the two place the body bag on the ocean top, and feeling purposeless again, I look around to be sure no one can see us here even though the shore has evaporated into myth. My attention is stolen by a sudden movement in the bag as it sinks beneath. The bag takes the form of Milly wriggling. This is what they've wanted all along, the dead enslaved, according to Vincent, need her in a state below the conscious, almost alive, yet nearly dead. Her strength is futile against the water, which eagerly gulps her down. The sea remains a calm accomplice, swirling in concentrics, playing back our reflections as if shifting all blame on us. Scott rubs Vincent's back softly. We wait for minutes, for the bag to hit what we perceive is the ocean floor. Vincent snaps his fingers.

"Let's head back now."

With effort, which Vincent provides now as much as Scott does after the former has lost all clergic pretence, we turn the boat and paddle back in silence, united by a resolve to put Milly and the sea behind us, striking the water's surface with swift strokes.

"What happens in your story?" Vincent wants to know as the shore springs back into view.

I turn to his sweat-steamed face. "There's the Hausa man. He doesn't mind how many times you beat him up, he'll knock on your door the next morning for a rematch. He's going to keep coming until he makes you pay. Then he'll stop."

"This ain't the time to be talking shit," Scott snaps at us, his voice strained with his single-handed efforts to keep the boat at its usual pace.

Vincent ignores him. "But what's the point of this fable, allegory, anecdote? I'm just not getting the ethical fuss here?"

I smile wanly. "The Hausas constitute a larger part of Northern Ghana." Dramatic pause. "And Faisal is a Northerner."

The xylophonic tunes of "Yen Ara Y'Asaase Ni" shrill in the distance. It's so faint each of us could have mistaken it for an object of our imagination. We all turn to one another worriedly. Could that be a witness? Flashbacks of Milly pulling out an iPhone during our lesson. Could it be Milly's? Scott begins paddling faster. But it's no use. It doesn't ring long enough. This sound, a poltergeist, erupts again when we're docking onto shore. We all cast rummaging glances into the vast emptiness of shoreline and sky, where a flock of shorebirds circles above us, shrieking.

* * *

The last sunset I spend in Elmina is going to be—as scheduled—with Elton, to the exclusion of everyone else, "a little romantic getaway in a romantic getaway." He said this while cracking the shell of a peanut with his teeth. "You will love this place, it's this secluded oceanfront tavern, with minimalist decor, the perfect setup for a dreamy bromance between us two." Somehow he'd omitted that this rendezvous too kicks off at an hour regulated under the vast liberties of BPT; as a result, I've shown up on time to be accosted with another date featuring the infamous white photographer and his damp-wall smell. I've been attempting to abandon this alfresco afterthought of a ramshackle beer shack lacking the romantic ambience Elton had so hyped. But the endless provision of Kpoo Keke sachets (from this stranger who had simply swatted away my gratitude with an unamusing "just doing my part in supporting Black businesses") makes it difficult to leave.

Six single-shot sachets are all it takes to forgive Elton's tardiness. Ten of these, and Elton's elusive appearance is but an expected outcome of a never-ending hunt, a Sasquatch stakeout. Sixteen single-shot spirits, and I'm ensnared in the luxuriant sensations of near-intoxication, tingly and warm and softening. And swaying. Fading in and out of the white photographer's oration on *Ghana this, Ghana that.* My attention drifting; to the sound of waves splashing the rocks of a distant reef; to the reggae ("One Love" by Marley) streaming from the ghetto blaster inside the beer shack; to the loud-mouthed Rastafarian starring in his one-man bacchanalia under the watchful eyes of his purring black cat.

The presence of something decaying—the smell of rotten meat—occasionally flits through the tiny breathing space separating the white photographer and me. This isn't enough to disrupt his monologues, even if responsible for the slight disturbance of his features.

He's nondescript. His is a head I've glimpsed on so many white necks—from its oblong bone structure, its nose shaped as a marquee over wafer-thin lips, to the side crop and gelled top of his hair. A carbon-copied semblance transforming only when he barks into self-congratulatory laughter for his barely risible sense of humour, his blandness fluttering to reveal the calicoed aspect of a thoroughly inhabited face.

"I was called out by a market woman for wanting to take a picture of her without her permission. She screamed—right after grabbing my camera—'Pictures only tell half the story!'" He laughs.

"I was once accosted by a market woman who wouldn't let me go until I bought something from her. No one would help free me. One guy actually crossed over to the other sidewalk like he found me threatening or something." He laughs.

He's an American, capturing moments during Ghana's Year of Return for an online journal which "wasn't well-paying!" A declaration he thought I was stupid enough to believe, even after I discovered said publication bore the initials of the state where it operated alongside "Times." Even when I gave him that *boy-please* askance look I'd perfected in the days of the yellow-fever research scientist for white expats toting empty wallets to scare off locals who—as that old Frenchman reeking of boiled cabbage had put it—were mercenaries of companionship, seeking *de l'argent*, money for *compagnie*.

"You've got to trust me on this," Damp-wall Smell implores, "the pay's actually shit."

This isn't his first time in Ghana. Having lived in Osu too many times during each visit, he decided—convinced his editor—that to produce outstanding photos, he ought to be ensconced far out of the capital, closer to the symbols of enslavement and colonial exploitation that dominated the itinerary of diasporan tourists. "Besides," he adds, "I got bored with Osu. Accra really has hidden pockets she only empties for her expats, and after a while you sense a pattern to these events with—if they'd forgive me for saying—annoying white people, who, despite living in an African city, still crave a western lifestyle; as seen in the way they pretend Polo Heights' rather stodgy pool could be anything compared to a lido; creating countless WhatsApp groups to organise and split bills for the same five-course Asian-fusion fine-dining experience at XO; always driving out to Big Milly's every other weekend, and somewhere in Busua for the long weekend; illegally acquiring marijuana for someone else's going-away party held inside a jacuzzi-studded loft in a Clifton Home or some other place in Cantonments. And those going-away parties, lots of those, everyone's leaving always, but the city never purges all its white people. Soon though, all your friends—the fun ones like you, as in me, who have taken a liking to some local heartthrob for whom they're always in need of a shoulder to cry over—leave, and then somewhere along the line you too leave when your contract or assignment is over. But you'll return, to this city that has made you feel at home, this peaceful paradise in Africa where your American dollars mean a lot more than they do elsewhere. And finally, when the opportunity to return is near, you decide, before the plane glides onto a runway, that you'll do Africa differently." By differently, he means listening to Stonebwoy and Shatta Wale, regurgitating opinions on Ghanaian pop-culture thieved right out of the mouths of locals, a transactional gregarious existence thriving on adopting another's culture in exchange for goodwill and creating a false sense of solidarity, which will eventually lead to a separatist life, a severing of an umbilical cord from his white flock, so he can feel immersed in "the real Ghana," otherwise known, according to him, as the *Shatta Movement* experience. He laughs.

I smile.

We might have killed the wrong white person.

We dumped her into the depths of the ocean, a distance I find my gaze wandering to, as if perchance I'll be able to make out exactly where she is dead—or, if Vincent is to be believed, dying: an ongoing process that'll stretch throughout centuries, the implications of which would mirror the perpetuity of Harm Inflicted on the Black Body.

We killed the wrong white person.

Maybe if Vincent hadn't been possessed, maybe if Milly wasn't in close proximity to suffer his madness, if I hadn't chosen to help for the sheer joy of witnessing the violence, watching Milly's appropriations slide off her scalp and feeling some sort of satisfaction, watching Scott strike her, watching her watch me in the few scurrying seconds she realised that her life was at stake. If Vincent hadn't returned from Elmina Castle, requesting my presence so he could walk me through all the apparatus he'd acquired for Milly's murder, doing this with an unsettling ease as if he was merely unpacking purchases after grocery-shopping. "Where's Scott?" was all I could say. "In the bathroom," Vincent replied, "probably shitting out all his anxieties. Anyway, what do you think of this blade? Would it do the job?" Scott materialised as a third shadow hulking over the car's boot where Vincent was itemising his acquisitions and bombarding me with questions on this or that tool even if I was too dumbstruck to form an opinion. "If you don't help we will do it ourselves: just don't get in the way," Scott gripped my tricep and dug his nails into it. Vincent seized my arm from Scott's, filling up the emptiness in the latter's clawed fingers with the branding elements. "Go get this heated," Vincent instructed. "Secure the canoe that will be needed to transport her." We stared as Scott hauled the body bag of instruments on his shoulders, and headed towards the cobblestones leading to the lodge. Where or how he was going to accomplish these tasks, he didn't share. "You know," Vincent spoke, minutes after eyeing me in some form of assessment. "Scott told me you went after me in those moments I almost killed myself, but I have no recollection of seeing you, just Nana. Also, in the car back from Elmina I was trying to find truth in what Brian told us, that you had a weird obsession with reporting deaths . . . maybe you never intended to do anything but watch as I attempted to drown, so you could report it?" I kissed my teeth. I put my hands on his shoulders as well, so that we were linked not just by our bodies but, as he'd soon discover, by our intent. "Why me?" I asked. To which he responded with: "Scott is the one who brought the idea that you could distract her with those Twi lessons." I shook my head. "No, Vincent, why do you think I won't go report you all to the authorities?" He turned erratic; all the veins erect over his features made him look satanic, then he began sermonising: "Because the gods have chosen you, Kobby, don't you see? You are about to write history. You are at the fucking right place at the right time—be grateful, very few people will come this close to doing the bidding of the ancestors—" He seemed so enraged that if I hadn't shushed him right away, he might have exploded. "Vincent, what do you want me to say? That I've got no conscience? That I wouldn't mind seeing Milly die? I only need you to be entirely sure this needs to be done." He grinned and said, "Weird, I thought you'd be worried that I'd tell Elton and Scott you watched me almost take my life and did nothing to stop me." He traced his fingers over my tightening brows as if forming a unibrow. "I'm not manipulating you into doing this. Why must I, given you've already expressed interest? Trust me," he added, "this is best, there's no other way. You should think of Milly as a symbol, not human; that way the violence we unleash on her will be more bearable."

"What does she represent?"

"Huh?"

"If she's a symbol, what does she represent?"

The only answer he could give was a befuddled expression. Then blinking profusely, as if snatching his wits from another realm of consciousness, he replied, "I'm not sure what the purpose of all this talk is. Anyway, we intend to take her from behind, with ether, so lure her away from that man of hers, and then we'll find you. You really don't have to do much, just watch."

Watch the wrong white person get killed.

The perfect white person sits so close I can make out the wispy, yarn-like hairs arranged over his lips in even sparsity, twitching around, like microbial activity as viewed under a microscope, due to the blasts of air heaved out of his flaring nostrils.

"You don't talk much, do you?" he asks.

So I lean in. Too.

In this country with only a handful of locals who can host, you need a back-up white expat. When all the apps only cough up men whose nudes are cast against the backgrounds of cracked walls, charcoal-graffiti walls, smoked walls, eroded walls, walls so shady you can barely picture having any fun within them without the interruptions of a raging mob, there's when your back-up white expat comes in handy. He'll be the one to call when in need of brass doors with secure locks, wallpapered sound-proof walls, fluffy towels laid over layered sheets. There is a certain comfort to be had from fucking men in enclaves where a country's repressive laws are impenetrable.

After all the dramatic fuss of leaning in real slow, it's a dry, spitless kiss. With no tongue, no embellishments, bare as an ashy elbow. We both pull away to find the Rastafarian hovering over us, his locs carried by the wind and floating in the moon's halo. Without the locs, he wouldn't look this exotic; the many slashes across his cheeks and his misshapen teeth bring to mind

King Ayisoba. Up close, he reeks of the deodorised scent of *obroni wawu* sold on the streets, making me recall an old lover, who I immediately blink out of memory.

"Bosses," he says more to the white guy than to me, in a mix of LAFA patois and pidgin, "me love you two, and me nuh tink no bad mind for you. But you see the people here are backward and have plenty bad mind for the things you do, so if you nuh want bad man come hussle you two, make you for take this . . . to your room." He looks at us with a definite pause to see if we got his message. "Yah mahn, yah mahn, me I'm from Jamaica, so me tink you can do whatever you want fi no problem with me. Those Germans tink they can sack me from this land, what my *nananom* lef give me. But I go stay because this is my home away from Kingston. Everybody come inna me place for my good sativa, me will stay here till Jah come down—"

"I unnastand, I unnastand. Bless you," the white photographer responds, and to get rid of him, asks, "Could you get us more drinks?"

"Yas, yas, I like you. You are my paddyman. You have understanding. Ras Boniface guh make some drink for yuh. Kpoo Keke . . ." And as if to enforce his rules, his cat slides in between us as he leaves.

The white photographer and I succumb to the chagrined silence of the apprehended, smiling wryly at each other whenever our gazes meet. Then he laughs, "Do you think he's really from Jamaica?" I shake my head, deciding against telling him Rasta's got the gap-toothed smile of an Akuapem native. I watch him fiddle with the zip of a Nikon bag that's slung across his torso, covering the slight impression of a distended belly and the hornlike projection of his flap. When he pulls out his equipment, the bright screen of this camera scorches my eyesight, withering my orbs into needle eyes. He shows me his work and asks what I think. I'm not really in the mood to speak, and thankfully he senses this and keeps flicking through the images: men at sea, women with pans, children arms wide over the bow of a canoe. Nothing exactly spectacular, far too much exposure in many of them. I suspect he's going to edit these photos for a dramatic effect; grainy details of sunken-in cheeks, tactile sun-battered skin, dark emaciated arms cast over pale blue skies. He stops on a photograph of me running across the shore, bleary but still cinematic in the way blurred photos depict an action frozen in time. "You have such beautiful black skin, I wish you were my muse." I peer at him. He returns my gaze. I weigh his face for suggestiveness, any sign that he might know more about the image in question than he's letting on. But his face soon regroups into its bland formations, like a solved Rubik's cube, devoid of any mysteries whatsoever. The picture is so expertly cropped within the rectangular frames of the screen, it's difficult deciphering at which time-frame it was captured. I can't tell if it's from the moment I was rushing to offer Milly Twi lessons or when I was returning to the crime scene with the hen I'd pilfered from the resort. At the risk of sounding suspicious, I do not ask any questions about the image, questions my twitching eyes may have already betrayed. Then our drinks arrive, and they reinforce my near-drunkenness. I watch the photographer stroke the cat to establish a sense of camaraderie with the Rastafarian now dubious of our closeness. "*Chale!*" He fist-bumps the dallying man who beams and says, "You too are my *Chale* man, yah, yah, Jah bless." He doesn't stop cooing incoherent languages into the cat's fur even after its owner has walked off. Occasionally he turns to me with one of his disarming smiles in an effort not to lose my attention. But I'm already lost,

within the confines of the camera's LV screen,

running towards Milly who's either dead or soon to die;

in one scene with the plastic bag securing the hen, and in another I'm empty-handed;

sometimes seated with the white photographer, who replaces Milly, as I wait for Vincent and Scott; sometimes spreading the hen's blood over Milly's final place on earth, in case she returns and demands why I didn't give her the burial rites promised to femicide victims like her, who are so delusional they believe they can wear our braids and beads, and win over our men.

I see Vincent and Scott strike the white photographer with the shovel as I burst eggs over Milly's dying place and bury the dead hen,

I'm about to the leave the ritual grounds when I smell hints of it lingering in the air—the decay of an open wound left untreated,

I begin hounding the scent through the bushes,

stopping when I spot something like a black-furred mammal race towards me,

Nana springs up on both feet. "*Ɛdeɛn na wo yɛ wɔ ha?*" he asks,

avoiding his eyes, I squint at the silver necklace curled over his sheeny collarbone,

he's not tall enough to obstruct the carnage of swirling feathers and blood dripping from the blades of marrams, the gooey jaundiced colour of what happens to be a crate of eggs smashed over a mound. "*Wo pɛ deɛn?*" he bellows, gripping my wrists with fingers that leave a bloody imprint on my skin,

I run.

"Kwabena!" the white man screams in my ear. He laughs. "Do you often zone out like this?"

"Do you want to learn Twi?"

"No!" He guffaws at my question. "I just really only want to get to know you. I don't find enough gay men off Man4Man."

I smile at him, feebly. "I'm sorry. I kinda have an ongoing theme this year."

He pinches his brows together, such thick elevens etched between them that I'm almost tempted to draw a unibrow over his hurt. "It's the big guy, right?" I nod unnecessarily. "You like him?" I do not answer. "You and I, I can tell we'd have been great. A nice interracial couple . . . Such lost potential. You know one thing I'm hating about this Year of Return? Men like you who'd have otherwise been interested in me like me have diverted your affections to these other foreigners."

XII

KOBBY

(11 days after the friends arrive)

There's a faint crack running across the centre where the charging port aligns with the front camera, only visible when the sun's rays skid against the tempered glass of the screen protector. Elton tells me to watch my phone before flicking off the grains of sand with puffs of air, kissing its screen and handing it back to me. "Why so jumpy," he shouts over our juddering luggage dragged along the paving stones. He hasn't noticed Nana, whose lengthened shadow overlaps mine, trailing us moments after we emerged buttoning shirts and zipping up crotches, swiping sweat over backhands and snorting the leftovers of our manic pleasure balled in our nostrils. After hurrying Vincent, Scott, and Nana out of the room with promises of joining them at the reception soon, we'll step out to discover the latter hovering, like the bees serenading the bordering thymes of the stony pathway. *Jesus, Nana!* Elton isn't too pleased to find we're being hounded. Nana seizes the fallen suitcase and wheels past without a word, shelling spit ahead of him as if he were performing an asperges.

We've come to Elmina, lived our lives and taken others'. We've packed our bags, settled the bills, and said our byes. "We'd love to have you back here again," the German couple says, "you're family to us now. Thanks for that donation. Although little, we appreciate it."

"Hope it goes to the community," Vincent yells back with a cutting laugh whose sheer volume rivals that of the moaning exhaust. Vincent is in high spirits for someone whose hands are stained with the last breath of a soul. He's seized Scott's shotgun position, shimmying to a tune only he can hear. Scott fishes a cigarette and a chrome lighter out of his purse. "Oh Lord, Scott only smokes when he's anxious," Elton jokes, rolling down the halfway windows. Nana's an odd sight to glimpse: he's got one hand thumbing the thin silver necklace I'd spotted him wearing in the bushes—an accessory I never noticed he owned until last eve; his other hand is pressed against his pelvic region, and although his eyes are closed, his left eyelid twitches—a door opened slightly with the pretence of being shut so as to check if I'll spy on his crotch. I cringe at the novel ugliness in his misanthropic mien. At some point, I'd have to bring myself to admit that my unsavoury attraction to a homophobe could have benefitted a hastier demise.

"One more stop before we head to Accra?" Vincent asks.

Elton's particularly excited for our last stop. We're headed to meet an association of African Americans living around the borders of Elmina. Brothers and Sisters of the Returned, they call themselves. An event he'd gleaned off the Facebook Year of Return page.

"Plus, there's food. Hot, spicy southern fried chicken like they do back home," Elton informs us. "The host of this event left Alabama fifty years ago—she was only forty back then."

"Man, that's wild," Vincent says, "fifty years in Africa! Africa is great, but the States will always be home. If I ever retire elsewhere it'll be to the South of France."

"We'll have a good time," Elton's saying as he turns on the radio. "We better watch out for the homophobia though. You can never be sure with those old Black spiritualists."

"Hopefully we'll just get the anti-voters," Vincent says.

"Dude, why you always gotta play this UK chick?" Corrine Bailey Rae, whose "Put Your Records On" plays, is Vincent's next topic of concern.

"Even though I'm from the Eastside, I've still got a soft heart," Elton retorts in a tone that contradicts his words. "Keep your stuff, so I can have my stuff too."

"What you talkin' 'bout with this soft heart nonsense? Everybody know that ain't true. You think we don't hear your phone ringing every second." Vincent sucks his teeth. "Some player."

I pretend to be gnawing at my cuticles when Elton looks my way before answering, sotto voce, "Can't a nigga be a player and still have a soft heart?"

Vincent laughs. "Hard to take the Detroit out a nigga. But for real though, this shit is tight. I was living in New York when it came out. Hot 97 played this every day. You would be in the bodega getting cigarettes, standing by the counter singing it as your stuff gets bagged. Scott, they played this in South Carolina too?" Scott doesn't respond, sucks his cigarette with the delicate cautiousness of someone siphoning fuel through a hose. Vincent launches into the Corinne Bailey Rae song, becoming increasingly aggravating.

The two men begin belting out the lyrics with no intention to melodise these words, let alone harmonise their voices.

I turn away from the two's persisting mirth and look through Scott's window to watch the thick smoke from his lips atomise in the direction of the gunmetal grey sea flanking the thoroughfare. This sea snakes all the way to Côte d'Ivoire, a part of the Atlantic through which Elmina's enslaved were transported to the Americas, which to most descendants of the enslaved could only mean another graveyard for more ancestors. Lining the outskirts of this road are wooden stalls piled with that Fante kenkey sold as souvenirs for travellers wont to return to the capital with gifts. Far from being an ordinary souvenir, this kenkey refuses introduction without the fuss of its accompanying legend. In an ancient time, when history hadn't yet wised up to document itself, the Ewutus, a sub-Fante tribe, warred with an enemy whose conquests became the stuff of lore recounted to spread terror throughout Fanteland. Having little iron for spears and even less expertise for warfare, these Fantes enlisted the one skill they were good at, preparing kenkey so hefty that when eaten, it took hours to digest. Kenkey became an ingenious improvisation for the lack of artillery, swung at fast speed like balls from cannons. Their enemies were torn between fleeing and eating. *Yɛrebɛba ha dabiara abɛ dzidzi.* In another version of this legend, their foes had laughed as they ate the kenkey that flew at them. Realising too late that the dough used had fermented beyond recovery, they fell into a deep sleep, which the Fantes weaponised and made corpses out of their dormant bodies, thrusting spears into them while singing, *Baby dze ɔmpɛ su sɛ osu a ɛkɔm na ɔdze no wɔn mma no kooko wɔn mma no nufu wɔn saw kɛtɛ mman ne da aba w'ada!* There are few stories of heroism and war conquest in Fanteland. And the Fante, a perpetual braggart with her penchant for superfluous language, may never quit sharing this tale to both willing and unwilling audiences. One vendor screams in fine Fanglish, reminding people that Fante kenkey is a meal for warriors, nurses, doctors, security men on night-shifts: Come, come and buy my kenkey for me o! *Fa dzi fante-fante ne nkyefua, ah adziban! Dzi dzi!*

The images that drift past us turn sharper as the car decelerates.

"Alright, kids, let's be on our best behaviour," Vincent says good-humouredly as he unbuckles his seat belt. I dip my head below the window's frames for a complete view of the expansive fortress, which is built with shiny sandstone and walled with the red clay used by the villagers to make huts. The entire ensemble brings to mind a dirt stain on a white page. A clash of modern and traditional architecture, inspiring more confoundment than praise.

"Impressive," Elton says without a hint of sarcasm, and leads the gravelled path to the property.

"Reservation?" Two large men at the see-through bamboo

gates intercept us. Stereotypical bouncers with bodies enhanced by fitting shirts, narrow waistlines accentuated with
belted trousers.

"Oh no, they're with me!"

Brian's arms are stretched wide, his tunic noctilionine, his
popped collar so high up it swallows his entire neck and ren-
ders his outfit more costume-y than fashion. "If it isn't the Black
Americans!"

"Oh, dear," Scott mutters.

"Thanks, Brian, but we've made reservations," Vincent shouts.

"You guys remember his name?" Elton says as he gives our
names to the human blockade that's parting anyway upon Brian's instructions.

"It would be wrong to see y'all stand outside and not claim
acquaintance. What are friends for?" Brian bounces to us as
though he's wearing pointy heels instead of boots with huge platforms. He's so tall he makes us, even Elton, look Lilliputian. "I
should have known I'd be seeing you guys here. There happens
to be a meeting of Black Americans and you niggas just show up
in town! Vincent, Scott, and Elton?" He totally ignores me.

"I didn't expect an upturned collar to be your style," Vincent comments as we follow him. We can barely catch a glimpse
of his skull from behind.

"I have a right to show my *collar*, darling. I'm beautiful and
I know I'm beautiful!"

Vincent cackles. Scott frowns and mutters: "He's so wrong
for fitting his stupid pun into that."

"You're not one of the Black Americans, right?" Vincent
mocks. "What are you doing here?"

"Oh, I'm shagging one of them niggas here," he says, waving
his arms dismissively. "But that ain't the story you boust to tell,
he's DL and old. Man's got too much ED, he'd rather fold into
his foreskin than come out to play. Not what I'd be messing
with if I ain't gots me some bills to pay."

"He's just so predictable," I catch Scott whispering to no one in particular. And if he's referring to Brian's sourcing of expressions from the collective pool of pop gay culture phraseology, I have to concede that, indeed, Brian sounds cliché, mimicking the Atlanta gays I come across in Facebook vids who stay hollering on couches at brunch. I refuse to blame him for emulating language that has been accorded enough freedoms to allow flexibility. It would be interesting to witness the consolidation of queerness and modern Ghanaian languages, the lexical liberties that would be forged between these identities. I would like to gaze on the flair of this language's speakers, who might possess the beautiful fluency I once espied in a group of gasconading South African gays at Alley Bar. Queer men who switched and mixed, and fashioned linguistic cocktails that made everyone pause, lean in, and drink in their lavish compositions.

Brian ushers us through lanes of trees that have boards with their assigned scientific names hammered into their ancient barks. As we draw nearer, we hear the crashing waves, pounding drums, and frenetic ululations. The ground vibrates with the energy of dance and revelry, the air tinctured with an adrenaline-spiking, limb-softening magnetism that I find peculiar to Asa Baako season. That time of the year when my boss's generosity in booking festival tickets and rooms in ocean-front resorts arouses a suspicion which is later drowned in fancy cocktails and the haunting vibrancy of Juju music.

"Oh, by the way, these guys are a group of hoteps. They just performed some ritual to appease the ancestors, watered some trees which they've labelled by the days of the week. Simple right? Not like the belongings y'all buried yesterday."

"Belongings?"

"Scott and I buried some . . . valuables after Elmina Castle." Vincent quickly explains to an Elton who's hardly listening, focused on the banquet ahead.

"I was touring the castles with this DL man when I spotted

these two at the shops getting a shovel and a huge bag," Brian rambles on. "Anyway, did you guys find the ether y'all were searching for?"

"Ether?"

"Ethanol. For libations. That stuff," Vincent fills in. Elton's now staring at Scott and Vincent with amusement. He turns to look at me.

"No one told me this?"

"You didn't want to come to Elmina with us." Vincent throws his arm over Scott as he says this; the latter is fixated on kicking an unfortunate pebble crossing his path every few metres.

"You hoteps are really inventive. You've got more ingenuity than our chief priests," Brian says.

"I'm not a hotep." Elton keeps his tone level, even if reproachful.

"Then why are you here?" Brian almost walks off. He spins, adds as an afterthought, "You are due a retwist." The only acknowledgement he pays me.

"I hate your friend." Elton addresses me, and leaves for the buffet. I gaze on a huge banner slithering around the stem of a baobab tree, coiling the letters Y-E-A-R-of-R-E-T-U-R-N. On a platform is Wiyaala in her signature mohawk performing her famed single, "Tinambanyi," thrashing about the stage to the charged beats of her song. She's almost nebulous, attired in a green jumpsuit that blends in with the surrounding verdancy, contrasting the stark brown costumes of her background dancers. The audience of this cultural procession is a crowd of about fifty dressed up in traditional African regalia. An elaborate exhibition of batakaris, ahenemas, kanzus, agbadas, confers on them all a regality that casts the rest of us—sporting t-shirts and jeans, baggy shorts and lofty sneakers—into the roles of mangled, molten candles assigned with lighting up a medieval soirée. A plethora of African American accents are kneaded into the ongoing revue, voicing commentary and drawing comparisons with known mutations to these dances.

"So it should be," a woman donning an agrarian hat screams into her filming phone, "the Black diaspora taking from the motherland and vice versa. When Beyoncé and Solange show up in the country in a few weeks, they better be at events like this so they might learn a few moves. *Ooh, watch them whip, whip, watch them nae nae.*" Scott avoids a duo of younger light-skinned women who try to initiate conversation with him, departs to an empty chair in a deserted part of the venue, and sits facing the sea. Vincent is next to abandon Nana and me. He imitates the dancers' legwork as he crosses the grass-patched ground. Nana snorts at the dancers flapping their arms like a bird about to take flight

"*Dagombafɔɔ bɛn na ɔmo sa agbadza.*"

Despite his palpable animosity—squaring his shoulders high and crossing his arms over his torso, I giggle in response to his remark. He glances at me, then quickly averts his gaze to avoid registering our forged kinship. I take out my phone for lack of activity, go through my IG feed with mild interest, halting on a coincidental video review by Aspecialkindofdouble on *All God's Children Need Traveling Shoes.* A pity I cannot hear the assuring warmth of her voice; I settle for the auto-generated captions and the animations of her contoured heart-shaped face. *This might be my all-time fave of Mama Angelou's. This serves as a reminder of the spiritual significance of Black storytelling. You can't just get up and conjure a masterpiece like this, our authors be coming undone just so they can put books on our tables. You can't read this book without feeling things. Now it's time for me to start booking that flight to Ghana . . .* A tap on my shoulder. Nana points at Elton, who's beckoning me to join him at the buffet.

I manoeuvre past a stream of conversations—

"Seems like everyone here's either from Chicago or NYC . . ."

and, *"I took that DNA ancestry thingy . . ."* and, "Oh I found out my ancestors were from the area of Guinea . . ." and, "Y'all that thing isn't for me, it changes its lying ass every single time. If you did any anthropology y'all will know we all look Bantu and that's enough"—as I beeline to a grinning Elton. His face twinkles with such boyish mischief I sense I've stumbled on a teenage version of him. This makes me feel a slight twinge of something akin to love but not quite, something like a roughly sketched cupid heart. After he reprimands that I'm with him and must go wherever he goes, we experience a reversal of roles when he instructs that I, in some silly rendition of nuptial vows, *take this plate* of chicken he proffers, *to carry and to hold, in good times and bad, in diabetes and heart disease . . .*

"You like it?" he asks. I nod vigorously, chewing into the piece of meat, savouring its creamy, garlicky notes. He becomes the guide who watches me experience his culture. And as I take another larger bite of the chicken, I become the tourist. Almost as if we've stumbled on a piece of America in Ghana, one whose rhythms and cultures and culinary undertakings are foreign to me.

"You won't get this anywhere but in America. On a holiday. Or anytime you drive to grandma's place down in Detroit for brunch." He chuckles as I load my plate. "Ha ha! Welcome to Black America. It's this shit that gives us all diabetes by the way, so you be careful."

"Hey, none of that diabetes in my sweet chicken." We turn to see an old woman on the other side of the table. "You done lost your mind talking 'bout diabetes. I'm ninety, and ain't no diabetes in this body." She pats her breasts emphatically.

"Seestah Lovelace Grace." Elton makes an attempt to curtsy while balancing his plate; a piece of chicken rolls off and plops into a scavenging army of red ants. "This chicken is good. Reminds me of holidays with my gran."

"I don't know you, young man." The woman's ancient. She's

wrapped in Ankara cloth and wears big hoop earrings. "What's your name? And what part of Alabama you from?"

"I'm Elton. I'm from L.A. but I was raised in Detroit."

"You Northern folk can't cook," the old woman says with a frown that accentuates the wrinkles on her velvety skin. "You want good chicken, you come to Ghana. That's where your Aunt Seestah Lovelace is. And I brought some of Alabama with me to these Africans. None a them make good chicken."

Elton shares a look with me and laughs.

"What's your friend's name?"

"I'm Kobby."

My accent is the giveaway. She turns back to Elton. I focus on my chicken. It turns sour in my mouth.

"Elton, you need a good West African name, none of that colonisers' bullshit. How long you been here?"

"I'm on vacation, just for the Year of Return."

"You thinking of living in the motherland, right? Fifty years I lived here and not once have I missed America. Maybe I miss how festive Christmas is over there, or Thanksgiving, with all the fuss over getting the biggest turkey. But I don't miss it. I don't miss it. I won't miss it. I'm so close to nature here listening to my Nina, Aretha, and this African music these folk got. When you get the opportunity, pack your bags and leave the States. Leave and don't look back. Our fathers, our ancestors, this is what they wanted. We were born here, we need to return and take back what's ours. The motherland is ours, all of it! You know the story of the Igbo Landing? When I took the trip back and did all the rituals, blessed the land, fed my ancestors, got crowned Queen of the Efutus, I knew I was living my ancestors' dream when they drowned theyselves on their journey to Africa. Come join us over here and meet your sisters and brothers. Follow me." Elton, with all his forty years of living, permits himself the opportunity of being a child once more as he takes her hand and allows her to lead him away. He shoots me one last apologetic look before he trots off with her.

My pained smile finds Vincent who's busily flapping his arms with the dance crew. He's doing terribly, of course, but the dancers urge him on with vigorous nods and cajoling uh-huh's. He catches my gaze and moves over to the buffet. "Lord, I don't have the knees or the elbows for the dances you guys have got here."

"But you love them anyway," I say to him. He pauses.

"Kobby, I know you think me hotep or whatever. And I've resisted the urge to tell you that's horrible and insulting because all you've been to us is kind, giving us your time and showing us around. I just think for someone who reads and knows a bit about the Black American experience you'd be a lot more sensitive when you're putting labels on people who're just trying to connect with their lost heritage. I think it's rather insensitive of you, an African, who's got all his history about him, to poke fun at people like me who are trying to learn."

"Wow."

"You know, it's fine if you don't get it. That's just my two cents. I still love you. But all I'm asking is you be a sensitive brother."

I experience the beginnings of a silent fury at his audacity for making a molehill out of what had only been a humoured tease. He has the privilege of mocking me for reading books by white authors—pursuing reading for reasons outside the parochial function of self-preservation becomes a cause for hilarity, yet I cannot poke fun at his eagerness to romanticise our culture and put on weird airs so as to draw closer to us locals?

"You might want to go keep him company." He levels his gaze over my shoulder. I turn to find Scott with his head in his hands.

"Sure, Vince." I opt for leaving despite my urge to bring my own sentiments to the table.

"Why are we here?" Scott sounds despondent, tossing his question at the wind than at me.

"To eat sweet old Alabama chicken."

He doesn't laugh at my weak joke. "I just want to sleep."

"Now you're acting like . . . Vincent days ago." Mentioning his name makes my throat twist despite my efforts at getting this rage to dissipate. I, like Scott, could use some uplifting. "Relax, have fun. You're with your . . . long-lost brothers in the motherland."

"I hate hoteps."

"Not only you, hotep!" Brian's behind us.

"What are you doing here, really?" Scott spins in his seat, irate.

"I've had too much to drink, I keep going into the bushes to pee." When he realises he's not wanted with us, he totters off elsewhere. There's a part of me that wants to reach out to him as I watch him go, to keep him company in a place that all but acknowledges Ghanaians like us.

"This place has got a nice view," I say. The sun lights up the water, spreading on its surface bejewelled crystals. The tiny fishing boats seem as stagnant as antiques in a living area. Flamingos on the reefs are pecking at each other's feathers. It's a bird's-eye view of the coastal seas that I've never glimpsed until here, and I marvel, sampling a bit of the peace awarded owners of this scenery. I wonder, also, how much money it takes to lay claim to something this good, which chiefs had to be consulted and moneyed, which locals had to be vacated. "You can see the castles from up here," I point.

"Don't get me started on the castles."

"You don't have to feel guilty for Milly's death."

Silence.

"Listen, I must apologise for getting you into this—"

"No need."

"No need? Kobby, you took someone's fucking life. No need?"

"I didn't take anyone's life. I only watched. And besides, in my line of work I've seen too many dead bodies to know, by a long shot, that you two are the kindest killers. So just stop this . . . whatever it is that's causing you to act up."

He's gobsmacked, stares at me for seconds. "If you had a baritone, I'd have thought it was Vincent speaking. He put these words in your mouth, huh? Told you to come tell me to snap out of it, didn't he?"

We both watch Vincent and Elton with the old woman tipping a jerry can of water over a mound.

"Well, at least you've found out how convincing Vincent can be, and now he's added murder to the list of things he can get others to help with . . ." I sigh. Indeed, if I've let Vincent convince me so easily that a woman who was nice to me could be processed for fish feed, maybe I really deserve all the drugs both Pharmacist Arjun and my father force-feed me.

"Hello." A middle-aged man approaches us. He wears a green lace bubu that clouds his skinny frame. "My name's Brada Kilimanjaro Kofi. Seestah Lovelace Grace's secretary. I'm going around for donations in managing the upkeep of the place."

"We're Ghanaian," I tell him. "We're with the dance troupe. In fact, we arranged the chairs and took care of the catering." Scott nods. He walks away.

"Kilimanjaro Kofi? Who gives them these names? I'll probably be fucking Table Mountain Vince tonight."

"You forgot the Brada." I watch Scott laugh—covering his face to stop the mirth from spilling out into the world. Scott must learn to live with the death of Milly. It will take a lot more listless days and sleepless nights to get comfortable with the new godlike function he's discovered about his humanness, the ability to take one's life, easy as giving life, constricting the flow of oxygen in one and nurturing that flow in another. What other likeness to God have we not tapped into yet? What more forbidden fruits are there to chance on?

"Brownies?" I offer the same polythene that I'd offered Milly yesterday.

"Can't trust the shit y'all got here but . . ." He inspects the snack and takes a bite, "Dry as hell," he pronounces, "If there was any marijuana in this thing, it's long gone. Gone with the fucking wind that made them stale." He peers at me when I chuckle. "Wait. You know *Gone with the Wind*?"

"Scott, I've read the book," I say, my stuffed mouth cushioning my irritation.

"Who knew? Well, I read the subtitles. And picked up the book much later, even when I knew I wouldn't have much success with a thousand-page novel—especially when it was forced down our throats in high school. But, I love, love Margaret Mitchell."

"Did you used to dance for her as well?"

"Fuck off." Our rippling laughter propels us forward, and we grab on to our chairs' handles to keep from flying off. It takes us minutes to recover from our slanted ribs, after which we struggle to right ourselves to our initial posture.

"It honestly feels freeing," Scott says, as if he's probed into my thoughts. "To have ki—handed Milly over, I mean. I feel like we've paid a colonial debt. You know?" I frown. "Seriously though, I don't know about you Africans, but sometimes I always feel like we're eternally indebted to our ancestors, whether we choose to be or not. But I'm not sure you get my drift since you don't even want to tour the castles; you can't go through that experience without wanting to pay back your ancestors for all their sacrifice. You cannot even see the first fifteen minutes of *Roots*, *Twelve Years A Slave*, or any of the thousands of Middle Passage/slavery movies/shows/Broadway productions, you-name-it, and not feel eternally indebted . . ."

All at once, Scott's words shrivel until they are replaced with a buzzing sound like what may arise from the clash between FM signals and cellular waves. I experience vertigo, which creates the sensation that I'm gravitating to the castle in the distance. Our surroundings are next to dissolve: the whites of the skies become the blank space on which an email is projected, the castle a faded watermark. *Hi Kobby, I did enjoy your writing!* I've somehow spammed the rejection letter, ineffectively, it turns out, convinced myself so much excitement and blood was flowing in and out of my body and others' to contemplate the possibility of my life in shambles, dreams snatched away because of a stupid offer for representation that refuses to materialise. In the end, it's the details of the email that break my resolve to steer clear of it, that shimmer of opportunity dangling below its salutation: *PS: I did love your writing. But anything colonial is high up my MSWL. I would love to know more about Ghana's colonial history.*

I've always found backstories an unnecessary supplement to a plot on the verge of resolution. But here's a special request from an agent to a young African writer looking to break in. A backstory tied to this country's past. You want a colonial narrative, Madam Agent? Here you go:

Long ago, when I couldn't dream of a life with a nine-to-five and thought I would become an author before twenty-five, I frequented a beta-writing group whose alias, Quirky Writers of Ghana, sounded like the right advertisement for the eccentricity I'd hoped for. This funnel diagram enlightens best the core (and what would later become obsolete) objective of this group:

To support ourselves as artists. Creatively. Emotionally. We're
all like liquid in a funnel, waiting to be filtered out by the
industry. The ones near the bottom of the funnel possibly
have what it takes to break out, yet we're all
equally gifted writers. When one breaks
out of the funnel, they cause others to
follow, they pull others with them.
Remember your brothers
when you make it
so we all can
break
out.

The first meeting was staged like a support group, members introducing themselves by their WIPs: *I am working on a story of effigies that realised they were robotic inventions of their African ancestors*; *My novel's about a man who uses black magic to con a set of greedy European investors.* Another shared her dark poetry about the rise of dinosaurs—with a twist: *They spoke African languages and were pets to Africans.* I spoke: *Hi everyone, I am Kobby and I write crime novels about how to murder people in Ghana and get away with it.* Our leader stared at me for far too long. *Interesting*, he said. Everyone else chorused his praise.

I find myself wading in a deep black hole of pain. Sorting which stories need to be heard and which need to be silenced; the gift of the writer to highlight the paramount also becomes his curse to obliterate other voices. You want colonial, Madam Agent? Well, here you go. As readers, we noticed there wasn't much diversity in African fiction, only stories staged around wars and political unrest. We were optimistic that the world would want fresh voices like ours, why wouldn't they? Yet, we returned to each meeting reading out rejection after rejection. Soon, our gatherings deteriorated into comfort-eating sessions to fuel our charged rants at the entire publishing machine. *Why's it that all the literary agents of most African authors don't accept queries, just recommendations? Why do most African writers need to be residing in the UK or the US to get publishing deals? Really, why's it easier to sign on white writers who write about Africa than it is to sign on Africans writing about Africa?* Some of these rants were true. Others were said out of spite. **In history, you'll find there isn't a single truth. Because history is a story memorialised, and all things from memory can be botched and blotted out. Rooms and rooms of stories whose switches were turned on and off, on and off. Eventually, history becomes the rooms we choose to illuminate, the rooms we choose to lie in and weep.**

History is pain for the African. Who therapises the authors once you've put them through the pain of history? Forgive us, Madame Agent, we are young writers, who speak without hedging our words. We are fraught with the emotions your rejections pile up in us. Our queries were coins tossed into wishing fountains, never materialising into the fortunes we hoped. It's 2012. It's 2019. Still, you want to only publish those stories about our castles and those enslaved. When will Africa get a break? Our group disintegrated, people leaving, people staying for misery companionship, ending up in each other's beds, overlooking boundaries such as gender—all of us belonging to the category of failed creatives. For twenty-two-year-old me, this venturing into libidinal polyphagia, eating whoever was available without customary preoccupations with rinds and labels, was the stuff of Bildungsromans—a word whose accentuation had me screaming and spasming into our leader's greasy palms, and only after I mastered its pronunciation did he jack me off all the way. Right in his hands, I came of age. He was a Ghanaian Kenyan, fancied himself an outstanding poet, had a penchant for psychoanalysing his members, reminded me almost hourly that his nilotic genes made him, and all East African marathoners superior to Ghanaians who were quick to cum, and who direly needed the services of his gifted hands—a book he'd often rave about with his heavy Ghanaian accent that compelled us into doubting he'd ever been to Kenya (even if his WhatsApp boasted the standard safari selfie of himself and a giraffe being intimate), for he'd been abandoned by his dad who'd snuck him into Lafaze Community Hospital's nursery and disappeared, a time in his life he evoked in his poetry as often as he did in casual post-coital conversation.

He would read my work after we fucked. *This is exactly why you're not published, too many clauses here, the grammar's all wonky, you're not a good-enough writer.* His poems were drab, on UFOs subjugating the human mind and making us restore the planet, some sort of metaphor about climate change and its effects. *You guys don't get it, you don't get it,* he'd yell at us during readings, *I've even made illustrations to go with this poetry. Look at them in the printed sheet before you. Look at the aliens!* The sex was great, so I kept up the pretence that his poems were also, made him feel like a god amongst men. Physically, he was indeed a demigod, a lean body that I would always remember for its sheen of sweat whenever he answered his door naked except for a flimsy piece of underwear, his thick penis curving downwards into the base of the fabric like an eagle's beak. Among other things that I was forbidden to share with the rest of the group were his sub desires, an antithesis to his domineering persona outside the bedroom. *Harder, Kobby. Harder.* **My past is hard, the walls of these castles are hard, the enslaved that survived in them were hardened.**

If you want a bit of my colonial history, I would have to soften it with my own personal stories. Do my stories not qualify as post-colonial, do they not happen after the colonial? You want a war? Here's a war between creatives in Ghana. Out of bed, I made this god feel like my centre. I praised him and raised him. Until he did the one thing we all dreaded: he published himself. Who's this guy? Self-publishing? Wow, what a god! His obsession over the success of his book was the last burial rite to usher our group into the final stages of its demise. He hosted public readings and made sure we were all present to double the attendance, a bunch of chain marketers moving around clueless readers vouching for his book like the sycophants we were. I will never forget the night before his book launch when he called me over, already screaming about his *obroni wawus* before I could fully step through his door. *I cannot wash that smell out of these secondhand clothes. I cannot wash the whiteness out of them. Please help else my book will never sell if I'm to show up to my launch stinking like Western hand-me-downs.* He got angrier each passing day as the woes of self-publishing ate him up. *You have a book blog, why haven't you reviewed my book yet?* he asked during the one time he invited me over and wasn't in the mood for sex. It would be the end of us. I told him that I couldn't review his book. Said rather plainly. Resignedly. *Why? You don't think my book is good enough? You love my poetry!* His laughter was maniacal, stretching thin his features that had grown even more gaunt as self-publishing sucked the self-promotion out of him. I told him that poetry wasn't my brand and that I'm not sure my audience would buy his book even if I reviewed it. He countered: *I could write the review for you, you could post it on your blog!* I kneaded my temples for his relentlessness. *I don't think I've got the right influence to push your book. Secretly, I'm scared that my followers do not give a shit about my content. I'm scared that my only audience is the two or three friends I've got out of my two thousand followers.* He bellowed: *Excuses! Excuses!* His anger charged through the tiny chamber and hall he'd rented, putting the emptiness of the place in scope. He no longer looked like the artist whose looks and presence had me bewitched. He'd shrivelled into this tiny insignificant thing—looked like his own walls were closing in on him, his own failure was catching up with him. Since we began fucking he thought I was under his control, a mentee who lapped up his every word. It's my hand in the publishing industry that I employed to make him suffer. Key players, us bloggers. As powerful as all the critics of big publications, and maybe even as you, Madam Agent. One bad review is all it takes to smoke out comments such as: *I almost bought this book the other day, thank you for putting me off this book.* In his eyes I had become all the gatekeepers who'd prevented him from breaking into the industry. He lashed at me with his vitriol: *Are you even not trying to deny that you're jealous that I crossed over to self-publishing? That I could be the next E.L. James because I took the leap you all are afraid of? I fucking published myself: none of you have the balls to! It's why I am the leader of you stupid writers who are never going to break into the industry because you think people give a fuck about the stories you tell. I will succeed with or without you all. Get out! Get out of this room, my life! The earth doesn't claim you to be one of its creators! Your art holds no morals for this world. You are just a piece of shit lying in a slushpile somewhere forgotten. Tell this to the others too. Tell them I'm no more going to be their shepherd. You're all a waste!*

To think that the entire world cared about stories that mattered to us. We all needed to pay our colonial and post-colonial debts to be taken seriously, it seemed. To get a leg in the door we needed to write sensationalised realities, expressing pain, despondency, depicting cities ravaged by soldiers under a coup. World building an Africa that couldn't run contrary to the jaundiced cinematography of Western perceptions. All of us like goats tethered to our histories, waiting to be milked for our stories. A farm churning out post-colonial products on a mass scale. The world wouldn't want us to escape. Not yet—

"Kobby . . ." Scott's face hovers into view. I want to tell him that he mustn't feel indebted to his ancestors, that it's the world that has created these narratives, bombarded us with stories of enslavement to make us think that we, the living descendants of the enslaved, need to atone for their sacrifices. But Nana's fingers are clawing into my thigh, wrapped with a quilt that smells like Seestah Lovelace Grace. And there's Vincent and Elton, asking,

"How was the castle?"

The castle?

My surroundings begin to solidify. I look out of what I realise is our car's window to find we are in front of the monstrous colonial symbol. Cape Coast Castle. I stiffen for the pain that shoots through my forehead's scar.

"How did you find the tour?"

I find myself wading in a deep black hole of pain. The voice of the warden becomes my fire torch into Cape Coast Castle's carnage. *This is the route where slaves were ushered to their prisons, watch your step!* I have to dig my heels into the steep floors to slow my pace. Even so, it feels like I'm free-falling into a kind of hell. Into the dungeons. Rooms and rooms of stories whose switches are turned on and off, on and off. The voices. I smell the blood of their owners before I hear their screams. I have to press into the walls for support. *Feel the walls. You don't even need to touch them to feel their rotten texture, the sounds of death ricocheted off these cement bricks.* History becomes the rooms we choose to illuminate, the rooms we choose to lie in and weep.

"Thanks, guys," I say with a tight smile, snuggling into the blanket of the returnee old lady. "Thanks for letting me face my fears."

"You couldn't see it through," Vincent's saying. "All you had to do was walk through the Door of Return and you didn't." A pause. "You don't remember anything, do you?" He guffaws, before delivering the blow. "You were possessed by the ghosts of the dead captives—"

"One minute, you and Scott were sitting facing the sea," Elton adds. "The next you were running to me whispering, *the voices are after me*—"

"That's how I knew you were possessed." Vincent chuckles. "But before we could calm you down, you took off running."

I reach over my back to palm my damp shirt that has left cold patches on the seat's upholstery. The movement is tasking on my shoulder, and a quick survey of my arm reveals tender spots. Nana. I turn to him. Suddenly recalling him pinning me down over a patch of grass, the feet of Seestah Lovelace and her guests lined up before me. As I hollered: *The voices! They're coming after me!*

"Right before our eyes, our ancestors were leading you to them—"

"Vincent is bullshitting," Elton says.

"This ain't no joke!" Vincent is upset. "Why would I joke about something serious like that?!"

"Scott and I both agree it's MP." Scott looks both shell-shocked and confused even as he nods to Elton's claim.

"MP?" I ask.

"Marijuana Paranoia."

"The brownies . . ." My voice trails off as I'm taken back to the moment I was stuffing my face—

"So y'all think I'm stupid, huh?" demands Vincent.

More photosensitive flashbacks featuring myself and the last two brownies crusting at the bottom of the Tupperware, and Scott—whose face is a split between disbelief and happiness, the kind you're granted when high, when you've got an ear-to-ear grin and a sweat-stained upper lip and you don't give a fuck if your heart stops right this minute because this is true happiness—Scott is screaming, *This is true happiness from the motherland!* Then he whirls with the Tupperware in hand and all at once he looks so beautiful and so blue—as in, his skin is fucking blue and by the time he's completed a 360 his happiness is replaced with a look of horror. *Kobby!* He's screaming, a voice that isn't his own: *Old friend, to come all this way and still stay far away.*

"It's not the fucking brownies!" Vincent is banging his hand against the dashboard, snapping me out of my hallucinations. "I'm telling you guys, but you're not listening, y'all can't know what you've never experienced!"

"Vincent!" Scott screams. "God, you can be so impenetrable sometimes. Things do not always have one fucking explanation. There's always the logical reason, which is that the weed got to him, and I would know this because I was standing right next to him when it happened. And there's . . . whatever your reason is. None's false! So now can we fucking go back to Accra, I'm tired of this damned town!"

At this, Elton turns the key in the ignition.

"I'm still so proud of you, Kobby . . ." Vincent is saying. "I told them we should take you to the castle and see how that cured you of the mania these two fuckers insist it is."

There's still a residue of Scott's shock from when the hysteria set in. He keeps spying on me through the rearview mirror in case I might relapse. I catch him and Elton rolling their eyes at something Vincent is saying to me in the backseat. *Now you know what they put our ancestors through. Now you know what Black Americans go through their entire lives . . . So proud of you.*

Whenever I force my memory back in time, I can't seem to remember where Scott and my conversations ceased and what resolutions were made. Feels like I've slept through a movie and woken up to find that life itself has fast-forwarded. *You sound like a fucking conspiracy theorist*—Scott did tell me, and this seems to be my brain's landmark before the weed took over, right before he'd waxed on about the ubiquity of slave narratives in American media—*Something is wrong with you, Kobby. You need to go back to your roots and retwist that shit, or is it the brownies?*

Now that I've come out of whatever voodoo I had slipped into, maybe I should re-emphasise my stance on the matter. *Scott, you mustn't feel indebted to your ancestors, it's the world that has created these narratives. Bombarded us with stories of enslavement to make us think that we, the living descendants of the enslaved, need to atone for their sacrifices. Our ancestors were more than their chains, so we too can be more than descendants of the enslaved. We too can tell other stories.*

Yet I can't bring myself to utter this. It's the kind of thought that you stumble on after a smoke. And that which when voiced vapourises into the sophist nonsense that consumes its syntax—its tendency to draw attention to itself without serving any semantic purpose. The kind of thought that's easier to voice when the speaker himself is a writer who's worked it over and

over again until it sounds no more practical than beautiful—
guaranteed to elicit a finger-snapping applause from an equally
pretentious audience who might also just bullshit about how
"deep" a quote it is, along with prompts to "preach" or "speak
it, brother."

The castle remains a dominating figure even as we abandon
it. I wonder how much I remember of its rooms and stories.
Mostly just a blank film of time and the voice of the guide leading me down a black, gaping hole, into rooms so dark sight
becomes engorged with tears. And I know, having been forced
through this experience, that I am going to be writing that en-
slavement-cum-colonial narrative. I know I'm going to free myself from the chains of the African artist by subjecting my art to
the preliminary penitentiary penmanship of the West's obliga-
tions for the African Novel. Anything to feed white liberal guilt
for their ancestors' actions. Another literary undertaking that
might further entrap readers like Scott who believe they're the
primary target audiences for the West's African Novel.

Nana's fingers are biting into my thighs as he whispers
words whose concrete syllables are for his hearing alone. I close
my eyes and begin composing the first sentences of this novel,
words which come to me either through spiritual influence or
the machinations of my own wit:

*Independence came and left. Colonisation left and came. Milly
came and left.*

THE DEAD ENSLAVED

We're the voices that have lived on even when our bodies, bruised and broken, have absented. We're the ones that left but never left. Who considers us? Who listens to us? You, perhaps? You who crosses the ocean and finds the places your ancestors lost their lives. Do you consider us? Do you think us your relatives too as you think of those who survived and from whom your parents' parents were born? Where we're from, which is where you're from, we had no designations as cousins and uncles; all of us brothers, all of us husbands to the other's wives, all of us fathers and mothers to all sons and daughters. All of us brothers.

Revenge is all we seek. Bring those bodies. Let's break their lineages as we break their bodies. Let's make them watch us separate mother from child, fathers from brothers. Let's break their language. Let's trample on it and infuse our own languages into their mouths so they lose their tongue. As our living descendants say to one another *Hello* and think that's a Fante word, forgetting the old way of greeting each other, let's rob them of their expressions so when they go back in time, they won't be able to fathom why *Me kyea wo oo* isn't English. Imagine that! The English with all their superiority, who think no other language is more important than theirs, as prideful as our very own Ashanti brothers—imagine the English speaking our Fanglish.

We laugh underwater as we hear them talking to each other in chains, languages that don't sit well on their tongue. We've been assigning them to pick marine debris, cleaning up the oceans they've destroyed with their plastic waste and harmful fishing chemicals. A little oppression and their knees hurt, their backs bend, their mouths plead for sunscreen. Bring out the whips and watch them going off about their rights. Ha-ha. *Nkwasiafo.*

Let's create an alternate reality under water, where the evildoers get punished, and we get the justice we deserve.

You from the Americas, you who knock on our doors *agoo*, you whom we ask, *mo ne hwan? Yɛyɛ mfantsefo, wɔ fa yɛn firi Takyiman dze yɛn kɔɔ Cape Coast, dze yɛn kɔsii ɛpo bi so, dze yɛn pɛ Jamestown, ɔnyɛ yɛn Jamestown oo, Jamestown a ɔwɔ aburokyire man do.*

You from the Caribbean, you who look ethnically diverse with the blood of the Kalinagos and Taíno. Even the dark-skinned ones among you look different, look like a cross between an Igbo person and someone from Ashanti Kingdom. *Akyiwadeɛ*, you don't know the Akans don't like to mix, but times have changed so we accept you anyway when you knock on our doors. We ask, *Ɛ le nwane?*

Yɛ le Nzemama, you answer, how did you come into enslavement? We were hiding out in our forests in the western belt of Ghana, until a century before Ghanaian independence they picked up our King Kaku Aka, who tried to unite all the southern chiefs to fight the enslavers; one by one they took us after him, though these *Anglesifo* didn't take us into exile like they did our chief, they sent us back-back, they almost wiped out our lineages like they did the Guans, but here we are, back after four hundred years.

You from the Europes, from Bristol, from Liverpool, from Glasgow, you come knocking on our doors; we ask, *Ame kae nényɛ?* You say, *Me nye vɛgbe to o*, we're people from British Togoland where we were captured some three centuries ago, to boost the industrial revolution in England, just so white people could eat their sugar and have their tarts. We have come back bringing you fifty white men and women, all who work with Nestlé, take them, use them, they're yours now.

You from the Australias, you come to us knocking; we ask, *Wun lei nyɛ a? Ti nyɛla Dagbana.* How did you come to leave for Australia? We took the plane like everyone else and left, Ghana was hard so we wanted to see if Melbourne would be kind to us. To you, we respond jokily, *Enti mo fulanifoɔ mompɛ fa koro ntena?*

We wave at you as you drive by after bringing us gifts. We don't care for the wreaths, thanks for those bodies. Thanks for hearing our cries under water. Thanks for doing the bidding of our will. We send rain against your windshield so you can hear our million thank yous. Now go, and tell all your brothers to come visit us, each with their sacrifice. When you cross the border that seals Cape Coast from Accra, when you look out the window and do not see the sea, know we've left your heads, but you'll forever be in our hearts.

Mo ne Nyame nkɔ.

Nyunmo kɛ bo aya.

Mi i a dogo, yikplɛ Mawu.

PART THREE

For a good ending, the narrator must exit leaving questions unanswered. Over here, think of a hurricane, barging in, barrelling through things. Defying order. Defying science. Overturning reasoning. Everything left open, left hollow. Silent as the aftermath of a wreckage. For if readers can find their own answers, tie solutions to the open ends, who would ever be right? The beauty of interpretation is that it leaves room for possibilities.

I

KOBBY
(12 days after the friends arrive)

Elton, there are too many ways a journey to Accra could meet its end; somewhere in Winneba to have an international driver's license confiscated by the police; a flat tyre in Gomoa with the occasional good Samaritan offering the contact of a towing service whose own landlines are craving an urgent pickup; a bathroom break in Buduburam where we dismount to reward our bladders' restraint in some bandit-infested bushes. These events being suppositional, relatively safer scenarios that your friends and I, had we not flown over pothole and ramp in our haste to return, could have survived. Any stroke of bad luck to stall our trip would have had life-saving consequences. When we finally made it into the city, each one of us with our heads lolling to one side, some of us drooling, some of us snoring, we all woke with a start. Not because of the air that had now become fumy, or the chaotic noise slithering into the car like stage smoke, but the presence of death descending as a premonition, which we all glimpsed in the alerted puzzlement that had taken over our once calm features. We turned to one another agitatedly, as if making an inventory of lives that existed before Cape Coast and after. Accra would kill us.

Accra. Accra. Accra, says the conductor of the Yutong Bus plying Market Street. It's unlike any part of the city the friends have been to. It's the crowds. It's Makola. Everyone is screaming. A fellow takes Elton's hand and asks that he check out the jeans strewn over an arm. "Man," Elton responds, "that's no original. Look there, it says Abercrombie and Fish." The abo-ki's nasal voice takes on a pleading tone: "My brother, I no go lie to you, you're my brother from another mother how say I go lie to you, this be quality, original, no *synthe*." He turns to Vincent as if to ask for the latter's confirmation, but Vincent growls: "Nigga, if you don't back the fuck up." The people here are experienced in smelling tourists a mile away: one whiff of foreign blood and they pounce, dragging one limb, nibbling on the other.

"This is intense," says Vincent, wiping his forehead with a handkerchief that used to be white.

The plan was to nip in and out, find suitcases for the friends to transport all their souvenirs back to America. But we found shea butter, cheaper than the fancy ones in the high-end stores at Labone; dashikis, which made Vincent recall an Uncle Shawn back home had requested one in green, red, yellow colours, to attend Juneteenth cookouts. Soon, the suitcase hunt was aban-doned for the trail of cheap products in Tudu. Seano slippers. Year of Return Ankara prints. Wire-mesh bodycons in Pan-Af-rican colours.

Until now, when we're trapped in the swarming human traffic at Makola, do we remember we've bought all these extra souve-nirs and no suitcase to pack the old ones in. Here, the sun pun-ishes us for our terrible choices; frying us like fat-soluble treats, sweat sinking into our shirts, into our shorts, into our shoes.

"Why did you bring us here, anyway?" Scott's question finds me amidst the chaos.

Yes, why?

NANA

I've been following them long time. I've been eating their backs with every step they take. I've been watching them buy unnecessary, useless things. Why are they here? Why do they let the Ananse take them around? After all I've done for them.

Who collect-back-collect better prices for them? Does the Ananse go low enough? Can he even speak the Twi in twists and turns like the people here do as if they're your friend but they're not your friend but you still have to play with them like you know them from Adam? These sellers are cheats. They're the same as the people around who throw ludo dice for *chacha* and get people to bet with their money. They'll sell you this China-made things at big, big price. That cloth Vincent buy which has Year of Return sign in Ghana flag colours is cheap and made from China. Everything China-China and when you buy it and take it home and you come back the next day say-ing the thing is not working you'll be speaking to the air. Your money will go with the air.

This place is too many people. *Ntoose, Amane*, Chicken, Turkey. The sellers on the roadside shout. Sometimes Vincent get missing on my eyes and then I see Elton's head and then I see him holding the Ananse hand and then I feel like they've betrayed me all over again. But I still follow-follow them. Like a *Togbɛɛ*.

KOBBY

"'What a shock!'" Vincent reads from a hoisted banner that is an obituary, the image of the deceased disproportionally horizontal so that even in death he is being ripped in halves by his mourners who scream, *agoo-excuse*, into the pedestrian shoppers.

"Who died?" Elton is the only one interested when a coffin moves into view, carried by five men in dashing black suits and matching gloves. These pallbearers dance forwards and back-wards, stalling the pace of the mourning troupe. Elton, with the advantage of his height, announces that there are about a million of them—an expanse of black-red crowds sandwiched into the shoppers and hawkers.

"Watch out for your gadgets!" an Asian man bellows at us.

Pans, baskets, carts of produce fly into the air. Toes are stepped on, torsos double over. Someone claws their fingers along my arm. My face is buried into Elton's collarbone. It takes a while to register that in the rising hysteria he has scooped me into his arms.

"Vincent, Elton!" Scott's scrambling attempts not to lose us. His voice is a dismembered participant in the pandemonium to draw out missing parts from this Pandora's box of conjoined bodies. When push comes to shove and we've triumphed in the minor combat it takes to reunite, Scott is cussing, Elton is laughing, in spite of the augmenting chaos. Vincent is too silent, almost unresponsive, his eyes glued to the horde of motorcycles and commercial buses—adorned with strips of red and black cloth—driving recklessly and engaging in merry-mourning.

"What the fuck is going on?" Scott asks.

"The dead guy was a popular *troski* driver," the Asian American man answers.

"*Troski?*"

"*Tro-tro.* Commercial bus driver," I supply, staring at the new guy.

"My uncle's got business here so I occasionally visit— from Canada—no one should live through winter in Winnipeg . . . uncle's got a phone store right here in Tudu. Huawei, Itel importers since 2005," he says, as if to answer my speculative gaze which scans his sparsely-bearded face and rests on the suggestion of a pierced nipple in his soaked tank. "We knew this guy, the dead one. The people called him Book Man. Apparently, he was killed by the Sasabonsam Killer."

"Who?" It's the friends' first introduction to the villain headlining local papers.

"Oh you guys haven't been here long. Lemme guess, Year of

Return? In a couple of days you'll be gone? Nothing to worry about then. He's only targeted locals so far. And if the government is to be believed, he's just lore made up by the people. He doesn't exist." The stranger disappears into the throng, who are resuming their quotidian activities now that the mourners have trickled into a thin line of wailing women.

"What do you have in your bag?" Elton's pushing his thumb in my face, showing me the bubble of blood ballooning from it. "I think something in your bag pricked me."

"Sorry, it's probably the safety pins for when my jeans' zipper gets ruined."

"Mm-hmm. Thickums." He winks at me, clasping my hands.

* * *

From the cantankerous sun, we seek reprieve under the marquee of a shop that has metal matchstick mannequins dressed to the nines, with hats and jewellery and coats whose furs are animated by the breeze from a dust-frosted ceiling fan.

"Where are we getting the bags?" Scott's umbrage is directed at me.

"On the next street, perhaps," Elton answers.

"Kobby, do you have any idea where we are headed to?" Scott turns to Vincent. "I told you we should have let Nana join us."

"Are we really going to survive this, and still go to the Festival of Ancestors?" Vincent asks.

Given my cynicism about the intent of the Year of Return, due to the capitalism that has infiltrated its celebrations, I would never have considered attending an event such as the Festival of Ancestors (otherwise known as Nananom Nyiayɛ) if my boss hadn't sent a screenshot of the pricey e-tickets she'd purchased. In the time it took to come up with a plausible excuse to refuse her invitation, I smelt Vincent's morning coffee before I found him hovering over me. "Oh, you're also going to the Festival of

Ancestors." I never got around to declining my boss's offer with Vincent's ongoing lecture: "Didn't think you'd understand the significance of a ceremony like this, but glad you're coming!" I did not grant him the satisfaction of validating his prejudiced notions, so I held my tongue, as I do now, sticking it onto my palate—pressed so tight it becomes clear that I'm penalising my own inability to utter dissent.

"Hello." We hear a voice from the shop's interior. Its owner weaves through the railings of clothes to ask if we're buying anything.

"Suitcase, do you have suitcases?" Scott demands.

"No suitcase. What I have is shoes, bags, tank-tops, abortion belts." She's not bothered we're not women. "You don' have girlfriends and wives?" She asks matter-of-factly. "Then if you not buy from me, leave my store! You're blocking my market. Leave, leave, leave!" She causes a spectacle.

NANA

What at all do they want to buy? Why do they keep walking around with no aim like *kubolors*? Do they not know that they've been going round in circles, doing places they've already pass? Everyone here knows that if you want something there's a street of people who sell shoes. There's another street of people who sell bags. There's a bigger street of people selling tomatoes. You have to go to Makola inside which is arranged to what people sell. Does the Ananse not know this?

I watch the woman sack them. I hide myself in the people who look at them and point. I look at them go away. As if I care about this woman, I go ask her what this people want. "*Ɔmo nenam nenam, ɔmo ntɔ hwee. Sɛ ɔmo yɛ criminals aa mennim. Wo wɔ hɔ saa na ɔmo aba b'awia wo.*" I want to laugh. I love Kwahu people, but they're too greedy and think everyone who don't buy from them are suspect. I shake my head, doing like I'm sad with her and walk *shabo-shabo* to where Vincent and his friends and the Ananse pass.

KOBBY

On a street dealing in variegated forms of unkosher meat, some reddened with food colour, some whitened with crusts of rock salt, others browned by the scorching sun, Scott bursts out, "Really, Kobby? What do we need all this meat for?" To which Elton replies, "We could get the hide and make the bags ourselves." One man raises a skewered alligator to Vincent. He barks at the seller, "Get it away from me!"

The buyers bargaining while sticking fingers into these moistened animal parts, the knives sawing flesh or slamming it over logs, the skins draped over shoulders in the manner of a shawl. I observe this production, whose exaggerated roles of third-world commerce I find comical enough to ooh and ahh and interact with these vendors in a way that should demonstrate to these foreigners the ways in which they could appreciate the effort that went into this elaborate exhibition of the nation's varied dietary preferences.

"Vincent, are you okay?"

Elton and I spin to Scott, then to Vincent who's resting against a dwarfish signboard of Nana Addo with the words "4 More Years."

"I'm okay. I'm fi—" His next words emerge as a series of croaks; he clutches his chest. He collapses.

NANA

I see Vincent with his body bending. His friends are holding him. The Ananse stands behind useless. He doesn't see

when a man in madman clothes moves so close to Scott and
then begins running away. Ah!
Elton tries to chase the man who has stolen Scott's bag. But
plenty people have already begin chasing him too and it looks
like Elton is chasing the people instead of the thief.

KOBBY

It happens too quickly for me to process: Vincent falls on
the floor in a dead heap, wisps of dust are bullied for their resting place as he thuds against the ground. Silence blankets this
portion of the market for a second that stretches like a voters'
line. Scott yells at Elton to return from chasing the thieves. Too
soon, the market has morphed into an Emergency Ward. All
voices erupt into a single chorus for help. I watch Vincent, now
writhing on the floor, spittle dribbling from his mouth. I am
blind to the panic that has engulfed everyone, market women
moaning as though they've already been contracted as criers for
his funeral. Vincent is all I see. A dying Vincent.

"*Fre taxi!*"

Someone yells too close to my ear. Nana. I watch him jump
in the way of a vehicle that refuses to stop. The taxi driver has
no choice but to let a trembling Vincent into his car. Nana,
Elton, and Scott arrange Vincent on their laps like he's a flimsy
napkin at a formal dinner. "Are you coming!" Elton barks. I
jump into the taxi and ride shotgun. "He needs air, drive fast,"
Scott instructs the driver. But the street is crowded. Nana
sticks his head out of the car and shouts, "*Obi wu!*" The market women yell at the *tro-tro* drivers ahead. The road clears
in five minutes. Air fills the vehicle. "Vincent, Vincent," Scott
barks. I look at the rearview mirror and see Vincent motion-
less. Dead.

"I'm fine, guys."

There's a collective sigh of relief.

"Great, great." Scott is on the verge of tears. "We're going to the hospital."

"No, we're not. I'm fine. I'm fine," he insists, resting his head calmly against Scott's leg, unbothered about the fuss he's worked everyone into. "Don't take me to the hospital."

"Vincent, we need to go to the hospital."

"Bosses, hospital or what?" the driver asks with a temper.

"Kobby, give him directions to the Airbnb," Vincent commands. "I just need to rest."

It's the first time I'm called on to take action. I tell the driver the hotel's at Ridge.

"Nana," Elton calls out, stupefied.

"Nana's here?"

"*He*—" Scott's tone is caustic, "—got the taxi to stop,"

"Really?" Vincent chuckles.

"Your purse, what are we going to do about that?" Elton asks Scott. "Do we report to the police?"

Nana's laugh is large and warm, a hot towel on a feverish head. "Don't call police." How often does he laugh with the others when I'm away?

"It only has my sanitiser and . . ." Scott adds with horror, "My phone! You sure we can't report this to the police?"

"Don't call police." Vincent mimics Nana.

Over the chatter about the antics of the market women and how Vincent had worked up the entire Accra—*Even a goat on the verge of slaughter began crying,* Elton's saying, I scroll through the notifications on my phone; the usual ones from my dad asking if he should lock the gate and asking about my meds; an unusual video from my boss seated in her office, her nails in her cornrows, scratching and tapping at her scalp, as she threatens that I'm not to miss the Festival of Ancestors.

The taxi reaches the apartment building. Everyone but me

steps out. I'm about to let them know I'm leaving to meet my boss at work.

"Bro, your charge be fifty Ghana cedis," the taxi driver says.

I frown. "Fifty Ghana cedis for less than half an hour?"

"Fifty Ghana cedis."

Until now I've not paid him much attention. He's burly and short. His face is the surface of a worn basketball—whomever he owes his conception to connived with another's terrible genes to painstakingly pointillise him into being. His large hands, also dotted with eczema, grip the steering wheel. He stares straight ahead. Unmoving.

"I'll give you twenty." I take the note from my pocket and drop it on the dashboard. I attempt to leave, but he grabs my wrist. Something metallic coats my tongue.

"Is everything okay?" Elton sticks his head in the window, sees the man's hands covering my wrist.

"Everything's fine," I respond, my voice more irate than intended. "You guys go, I will handle this."

"Sir, is anything wrong?" Elton directs his question to the driver.

"Fifty Ghana cedis. Don't speak your big, big English to me my man, just give me my fifty Ghana cedis."

Elton spots the money on the dashboard. "Oh, you ain't got fifty?" He reaches into his pocket. The man loosens his grip.

I get out of the vehicle. I place my hand on Elton's, light but still carrying all the warning I intend to convey. "He's not getting fifty. He'll take twenty."

"Boss, I'm not taking twenty o." The driver slams his car door shut and barrels towards us.

"What's going on?" Vincent and Scott ask in unison.

"I'm not taking twenty. I'm not taking twenty." He grabs my wrist again.

I butt him in the head. He staggers yet refuses to let go. I yank him towards his car and toss him into it; he stumbles head-first into the front seating.

Bam!

I will not stop slamming the door into his waist until I've made sense of the indecipherable pleas mingled with his theatrical hollering; neither will I stop if I've not fully investigated the impact metal has on bone when swung at varying levels of intensity, testing how much blunt force can cause a spine's rupture. I'm only doing diligent research for the writing fodder: nothing here's done for pleasure—listening to a grown man cry for his mother does not excite me. It'll only take a few minutes to record the crunching sound of metal against tailbone, if only he's patient with me and fucksake stop moving away from the door—doing that just shifts my focus to another body part.

"Kobby." Elton's voice.

The door attempts one last half-hearted swing.

"*Wo yɛ okay?*" Now I have to act like I care about him. The man nods with effort. "Okay, I'll wait for you to leave." He hauls himself into his driver's seat. I close the door for him and thank him for accepting the twenty. "Guys, please refrain from using your Year of Return accent where unnecessary," I say without turning to them, waving even after the car has turned a corner.

II

KOBBY
(12 days after the friends arrive)

I sleep like the dead. When I slowly come to, I'm bombarded with the loud banging of cabinets, the popping sound of agitated oil, the smell of fish and flour and spice. I hoist my stiff body out of the swathing sheets, stepping into the ruin of books and broken interlocking needles. My leather rucksack is turned inside out, its strap ripped on one side and twisted over the tiled floor, the entire set-up connoting a lethal fall following a failed harness. Quickly, with the help of the zebroid rays diffused through the blinds, I sweep everything into the bag and slide it under the bed. Although this conceal-ment is undertaken retroactively, serving little purpose, like a prayer recited while writhing from the after-effects of a poi-soned meal, my devotion to the ritual promises redemption, as if I've gone back in time to correct an error whose conse-quences were life-threatening.

In the bathroom, I rinse my mouth with Elton's mouthwash, almost use his toothbrush, almost replace the dead taste of my mouth with the liveliness of his. Frankly, I've been using his every-thing these days, including his poopourri, which is still an inven-tion that baffles my mind even as it stifles the havoc of my intestinal gasses. I pat my face with a tissue held over the chlorinated trickle from the tap. There are those lines of sleep that stretch across my skin like healing knife scars. I survey, with my index finger, the ser-rations scarving my neck, tiny embellishing sores that I connect to the other with a gentleness akin to a lover's caress. I smile.

The vibrations of my phone lead me to it. I trace it as one follows blood drops at a crime scene, and find it swimming in the whites of Elton's sheets. One new message from Aspecialkindofdouble. *Where are you? Bookstagram is wildin'. It's about Akwaeke Emezi's new book, the American pubs won't send proofs to accounts with less than 3,000 followers, that's all Black people, lmfao.* I quickly type a response: *Hey, I received one odd rejection recently, this agent who'd just read* Homegoing—*white, of course, said she loved my writing and wanted more stories on Ghana's colonial history, aka another slave narrative. I do think I'll write one and send to her. Love you.* I hit send before I can rethink the "love you."

Whatever's pitter-pattering over the stove invades the living area with its spiciness; *hwentia*, Maggi, and *kpakpo shito* are fighting with the diffuser's sandalwood. Nana avoids my eyes, staring, with a mixture of puzzlement and resignation, at Vincent and Scott cuddled up on the couch.

"Kobby!" Vincent shouts. "We're waiting to get defence lessons in case our wallets get stolen again."

I respond with a wan smile. I'd almost forgotten my incident with the taxi driver.

"Use your voice sparingly, Vince," Scott admonishes, kissing him on the cheek. I look to Nana, who chops his vegetables slowly, his eyes still glued to the couple, stewing in his hate.

"Did someone call out the Kung-Fu Panda?"

Elton draws open the patio doors, sticks his head into the living area, and motions me over, hastily repositioning the joint tilted oddly in his lips before it falls. I set a half-empty Voltic on the counter, next to Nana. Only then does he switch focus to me, or rather my fingers, looking away quickly before his gaze finds my other hand skimming over those neck wounds.

"Careful, Elton," Vincent mock-cautions. "Call for help if you need us."

"Really?" I feign Vince a stern look before ducking into the patio.

"You should see Nana now," I say to Elton who pulls me into his lap and places little kisses on my back.

"What's up with Nana?" He passes me his blunt. He's so stoned, I could get a contact high off his breath. His eyes are red holes enshrouded in the thickets of brow and lash.

"Nana's dying now. He's just realised that Vincent and Scott are gay!" I drag smoke into my lungs. And then I laugh. Elton remains silent, gazing at me. "What?"

"You're so beautiful when you're sucking on things."

I wriggle off his lap and take the seat next to him. "Flattery will get you no head, sir." He steals the weed from me before I take another drag. "Seriously, most Ghanaians haven't seen this many gay people in their lives. Here's the funny thing: Ghanaians attach effeminacy to being gay. They'll call a fem boy gay not because he sleeps with men, but because he is girlie. And then they become annoyed when they find out this fem guy sleeps with men. Being gay here doesn't equate to sleeping with men. Sleeping with men is an abomination, which you could get lynched for. Not being *gay*." I draw air-quotes over the word and giggle. Elton is distracted, clearly has no room in his head for my theorising. He looks at the cluster of apartment complexes that make up the skyline of Ridge and all of Accra. It's an evening not unlike the first of our meeting—receding clouds and purplish skies, a temporary sombreness lifting when nocturnal city-dwellers start surveying the night's opportunities. Perhaps Elton experiences this déjà vu too, squinting into the skies for a fraction too long, during which I attempt smoking the roach without singeing my lips.

"I've loved it here," Elton speaks, "I'd never have imagined being able to buy a ticket and getting on a plane to leave America. I never dreamt of this growing up. I thought I'd live a simple life."

"Is this not simple?" I say teasingly, and laugh.

"Yeah, call it whatever you want. But where I grew up, find niggas who could get themselves flight time instead of jail time, and you'd be looking for—what's the expression? Haystack? Needle?" I nod to urge him on. "I didn't live the easiest of lives. And now look at me. Living the dream?"

"How was your childhood?" In the past, I'd refrain from quizzing my flings about incidents beyond the present. So, to juxtapose this misdemeanour against standard Man4Man etiquette, here are questions African men ask users whose profiles are labelled "visiting:" *Sup? HUD? Can you host?*

"Why are you asking about my childhood? 'Twas cool. Nothing special. I got bored and ran away from home when young—too young. Your friend's right though, you're due—overdue a retwist."

"Why?"

"Why do you need to retwist?"

"Elton, why did you run?"

He sighs. "I am not close to my family. I left home when I was thirteen. At home, my step-dad was an alcoholic and he beat my mother and my brothers. He especially didn't like me because I was smarter . . . it was frustrating for him. He also sensed that I was gay—although I was still figuring it out—which added to the complexity. I realised I couldn't survive there so I asked my mother if I could move in with my grandmother. I lived there for about two years then moved to New Orleans to live with family. I alienated myself from my uncles because I got credit cards in my grandmother's name and accumulated some debt that made my grandmother file for bankruptcy. I was smart enough to understand what was happening, but too young to fully realise it. I returned to Detroit to live with my grandmother again at sixteen. By then I knew I was gay and began meeting other gay friends. I met a gay couple and they allowed me to live with them until I finished high school. I went on to college and never looked back. My friends have become my family. Vincent and Scott are like family to me . . . the family I chose. You never say anything about yourself."

I smile coyly. "Maybe."

"No, you don't. Scott told me what you do for a living. Man, I was shocked. We looked up some of your work online because I wasn't going to believe him. You. Are. Grim. Those were unsettling."

I wince. "Or you could just say I do my job well."

"But who comes up with a job like that?"

"I work for a newspaper-slash-online magazine. There was a murder. I covered the story. I got told that I should stick to grim. So I was given my own column, where I cover violence."

"Maybe my question is, how does it come so easy to you?"

"Hey, is this an interrogation? I only write about the crimes, I don't commit them."

"Maybe." He jokes. "We saw you in action today. You were . . . fierce. Plus, you're being intrusive about my life, so I'm only throwing back the questions like you throw it back in bed."

"This is why I don't go around telling everyone. They think I'm some killer."

"Are you not?"

I punch him in the ribs.

"Hey, I'll call for help if you try anything funny."

I let myself fall on his lap. This weed's effect. One moment I'm funny, soft and light, in another I'm winged and trapped in endless flight. High. Higher. Suns and Sons. Scrambling in the air and grabbing onto clouds that promise not to slip through my fingers. Like cartoon characters realising too late they're mid-air with no ground. I guffaw.

Elton cups my rocking chin in his hands. "For real, though, you never say anything about yourself."

"Why should I? This is just a fling! It's nothing serious! The question you should be asking yourself is, did I have great sex? Not, did I get to know him well enough!"

"Well, maybe it's not just a fling for me. I don't know. But I want to get to know you."

"You're leaving in like tomorrow!"

"Not tomorrow, but who cares? I could be back sooner than any of us think. I like you."

"Okay! What would you like to know? My family got broken right when I was born! I had a brother fascinated by our neighbour! They were in proper love. But my dad wouldn't allow it. She was a girl, yes. Ha ha! It was the story of Romeo and Juliet. Two rival families, two children who loved each other. My father used to call them filthy cats, always sneaking around to have sex. I would stalk them and watch them have sex. Ha ha! Anyway, he told my brother he'd die before he allowed him to marry that girl. Our people do not marry Fantes. According to him, Fantes would empty your entire life into theirs and run away with everything you own. Ha ha. Some tribalism idiocy, yes, but he's from a generation that had nothing better to do than form stereotypes about other ethnic groups. Anyway, so they, my brother and his girlfriend, had a Romeo and Juliet death. Simple. So death pretty much haunted my days. A brother who committed suicide, a mother who was so distraught that she killed herself, then my dad followed. I'm alone. I'm all alone." Saying this makes me believe it. It's a lie I've told no one but have spent a lot of time fleshing out so it could have a functioning heart, legs to walk on its own, a mouth to nullify silences so others could seal its omissions with assumptions. A lie which in itself is art, designed to imitate life.

"That's fucked."

His grip around me tightens as though he's scared I might slip away. He stares at me unblinkingly, his forehead lined, his mouth rounded—what I realise is a reflection of my own features against his. Empath that he is, he's mirroring the facade

I've painted on. If life were a performance, I'd like a quick aside to laugh my head off.

In a fortuitous turn of events, our inseparability is severed the moment coruscated beams flash into our lateral vision. Elton and I converge at the railing of the balcony to spy the thousands of sky-lanterns swimming in the ink-blue night. The swishing of the patio doors notifies us of Vincent and Scott's intentions to join this incorporeal viewing of the Festival of Ancestors. The scene imitating a swarming of fireflies has us in its captivity, each one of us dead to our surroundings and poised against the cliff-ends of our emotions. It takes a while to recognise the sweaty warmth of Elton's fingers clasped around my own, which brings my trembling to attention. If at first I'd allowed Vincent, and my own scepticism, to diminish my adulation for the ancestors of the Middle Passage, I realise now how insular I've been in my criticism of the Year of Return and its ceremonies, which is to admit that—far from my concerns of the year's limited outreach to locals—the Year of Return isn't only for encouraging Africans and Black people beyond the pond to visit, but to gather with those already on the continent in commemorating this history of pain and celebrating the resilience of our forefathers. I ignore Vincent's efforts to sully the integrity of my sorrowful mien, distinctly aware of his wary stares anytime I snivel or dab at my eyes. To solely credit these soaring sky-lanterns for displacing my cynicism to the sentiments supporting the Year of Return would be reductionist and dismissive of the power of vigils to arouse in bystanders an influx of sensations that hack at all resolve to remain noncommittal.

"To the ancestors," the others recite with Vincent. I do too. Inaudibly. Elton's mouth swoops towards my own, lips plastered on mine—with the impact of a bird smashing into a windowpane—in case I'd forgotten where we left off before this distraction. My initial hesitation notwithstanding, his quest to taste my marijuana-infused emotions feels honest—even if not appropriate—for a moment like this.

Ako Balm. N'akyi yɛ ne ya. Ako Balm. Ne nan yɛ ne ya. Ako Balm. Ne nan yɛ—

"Herh!" The seller on the street below makes out two men kissing and exclaims, "*Jack mo yɛ deɛn!*"

"*Yɛ tie Peace!*" I shout back.

Not long after our chuckles and sighs and our muted meditations to the skies, Elton, in stoned jocosity, howls the chorus of "Like A Star" by Corinne Bailey Rae for the vanishing sky-lanterns. Vincent begs him to quit being silly. There's a rapping on the patio's glass in whose direction we spin to find a segregated Nana who mouths something Scott translates to "Food's ready."

"Guys, I'm really sorry that I let us miss the event." Vincent offers his apologies as we step into the bright fluorescents of the apartment. Nana flits between the kitchen and the living area, bringing in plates of fried fish, jollof, beans, avoiding my eyes even when he sets the dishes at my end of the table. We begin tucking into the meal, after the others have watched me—whether in fascination or exasperation—snap pictures of the food in differing angles.

"No white fiction today?" Vincent asks.

My phone chimes. I expect another furiously composed message from my boss.

"Brian's sent me a text message," I read out loud. "'Are the Black Americans with you? Tell them there's something happening tonight they want to see.' Then he leaves an address."

"Do you think it's a queer event?" Scott wonders with a tonal suggestion of disinterest, all his attention saved for tackling fish with fork.

"We should go," Elton decides. "We've got a few nights left in Accra; we might as well check out one of the main reasons we flew here."

Vincent says, "Where's the place? How far is it? What time?"

At the mention of the address, Scott takes out a phone from the breast-pocket of his faded maroon long-sleeved shirt.

"You've got a new phone so quick?" I ask, squinting at the device.

"Nana gave it to me. It's what he was unlocking at the market when we were, you know . . . Anyway, it's temporary."

"Hey." Elton scoots closer, points his cutlery at me. "What are those marks on your neck?"

Even if I do have an answer to appease his concern, I'm late to voice it. Nana beats me to this, a non-verbal admission of guilt manifesting in the crashing sound of ceramic. The three friends turn to him. He looks so mortified, he makes a dive below the partitioning counter to pick up the fallen pieces.

"*Agyei!*" Nana yelps.

Since I'm the closest to the kitchen, I rise out of the couch and head for him.

"Are you okay, Nana?"

Vincent's voice reaches him before I do. On the tiled floors are drops of blood raining from his palm onto the crescent pieces of plate. Stealthily, I advance towards him, enticed not so much by his blood—which in another world, or a different crime scene, I would have gravitated to like a forensic analyst on the verge of piecing together a valid hypothesis—but by the possibility of witnessing a man who holds himself together in such a stony, self-assured ostentation of strength wound himself in a manner so recklessly banal.

"*Gyae saa!*" He retracts his arm when I grab it.

"*Wonso gyae saa no bi,*" I reproach, rescuing his stiff palm and letting it bleed into mine. "*Nnipa paa na wa yɛ wo ho denden saa no wode kɔ hen?*"

My Twi leaves him nonplussed. I turn on the tap and run the water over his hand until the bleeding subsides by the third immersion. I'm not gentle as I wrap on the bandage I fished out of a cabinet housing Ziplocs of weed. Even so, he expresses nary an emotion to acknowledge the pain I suppose I'm inflicting. Rather, his eyes are sealed to my neck, marvelling at the wounds. I permit myself a slow sinister smile, an understated malice rendered buffoonish by the glow from the overhead lamps. Only then does his face contort like it did hours ago, repulsion rippling his brows and nose and lips; even his gagged Adam's apple communicates a portion of his hate. He's trembling, his torso shrunk backwards in a manner that suggests an intent to sever the rest of his body from the arm I tend. So easy it is for us to swap roles. No longer on top of me, he becomes the victim. He yanks back his arm and darts towards the bathroom.

* * *

The others are attiring themselves as fit for their first queer event in Ghana. They do this while avoiding Nana's gaze following them on their trips to the ironing board—an improvised portion of the kitchen counter—and back. Scott alone has embarked on these trips many times, annoyed that he's got nothing suited for the experience but a pair of leotards he reserves for his Saturday jazzercises back home. He quizzes me on varying shirts swinging sluggishly on hangers plastered over his torso; this, or that, and do I really think he might fit into that after weeks of stomaching Nana's high-carb rice and beans regimen? Elton yanks me into the bedroom and shuts the door on Scott. Douched and sexed (on the precipice of Elton's final, penny-pinched PrEP), I emerge to Nana hunched over the kitchen counter, festering past his best-by date with a scowl which pursues me to the balcony where I'll be idly double-tapping Bookstagram posts and littering comment sections with complimentary "nice stacks" and unnecessary "thank you for your honest reviews."

Elton's iPhone accosts me even before I close the patio doors, whirring with abandon on the plastic chair its owner reserves for smoking. Unsurprisingly, the phone's not password-protected. Elton carries himself like a man who's got nothing to hide. I would have been disappointed if he didn't apply the same standard with all his devices. I see WhatsApp notifications from one Viwe, tiered messages asking the same *Hi* or variations of it: *How are you, just checking on you.* Despite Elton's double-ticked silences, Viwe's far from realising they were just a temporary shag for a tourist. How many times have they fallen for these short layover trysts from conferencing Bretton Woods volunteers, Emirates flight attendants, and December Diasporans who, without rewording their Man4Man bios to reflect the duration of their visits, have led hopeful locals to believe they're just LTR-Oriented Dog Dads seeking a special someone to be the Bonnies to their Clydes, Queens to their Slims?

Elton! A new message arrives. *You're online, please respond, are you okay???* I'm figuring out a way to evade these gunpoint inquisitions when I hear the patio doors slide open.

"Mosquitoes," Vincent says. And begins rubbing a viscous substance over my arms. The perfumed lotion scratches out traces of exhaust emanating from the hibernating road below. I am dumbfounded by his actions, which he has undertaken without consulting first my fragrance allergies. Nonetheless, my skin tingles whenever his palms detect an erogenous spot.

"Lemon basil oil," he says without disrupting his performance. "The old lady at Elmina gave me a few bottles. Apparently, our forefathers used this and orange peels to drive away mosquitoes. Kept it a secret and watched the malaria epidemic wash out missionaries and colonisers. More than a repellent, I'd like to think of this as an amulet, maybe even an ectoplasm from our ancestors' survival of colonial plunderage."

By these cantillations, his care takes on a ritualistic intent— nothing of the romantic sort that had been a cause for concern and introspective debate. Although, confined within his conniving kindness is an ulterior motive he has no idea I'm privy to. Since our return to Accra, I've noticed his shadowy presence, immeshing as a Faraday cage: in all those instances, I've retreated into the digital haven that is Bookstagram.

His hands finally attack my own, suctioning my phalanges into his oiled palm, wanking each finger diligently. He executes his finishing touches with his lips, brushing a kiss over each deltoid. "Elton did well choosing you," he speaks. "You really are a sight at night. You glow in the dark." He grins, rivalling the whites of his t-shirt. "I probably wouldn't have messaged you had I seen you on the app, my type's a lot more . . . flamboyant."

Clueless to his intended route of conversation, but sensing an incoming monologue, I turn off the backlight of Elton's phone and pocket it. I lobby all of my insouciance into a drawn-out sigh and wait.

"Tell me," he covers the space between us. "You and Elton were high a while ago, weren't you? You, crying over the sky-lanterns, and him, singing." He snorts. "Y'all are nuts." A pause. "You know," he says after clearing his throat, which has no effect on the charged air between us, "I've loved Accra. But I honestly cannot wait to leave. I miss home, dearly. Everything here is slow, the transport system, no trains, all those potholes we've had to deal with, not to mention the chaos from this early morning. Accra is terrible for my health. For some reason, the old lady at Elmina thinks I'll return, spoke to me lengthily about getting a name change—impossible, I like your names here, but Vincent suits me well. She says I could be crowned king of a small village." He cackles. "Now that was appealing. But I can't imagine a life here. What do you do in a place like this?" He casts his arms into the air, in a show of despondence. "Really, what do you do, Kobby? Tell me. I need a good reason to move, I need to find some light here. You're oddly silent today."

I shrug. "You could own a nice little house by the beach. Clean air, right? You could maybe have a road named by you or something, they did that for Dubois, but I mean, he is Dubois and you are Vincent." He grunts. "Oh here's an idea! You could fight against the anti-LGBT laws."

"Nah, activism is for the young."

"Yeah, you probably shouldn't move then if you'll be okay seeing queer people oppressed and killed." Even I wince at how disingenuous I sound.

"You want to talk to me about oppression? Really? When you and Elton were kissing out here! Really? There's no fucking oppression here, Kobby. Don't guilt me into caring about shit. People die everywhere for being gay. Why don't *you* be an activist, Kobby? Yet everybody expects us Black Americans to ride into affairs that aren't ours like we're fucking knights. Like we've generated some formula for protest."

An odd turn of the conversation, for which I'm too perplexed to manage any response. His face—this sweaty thing it's become, no longer oozing the charm that I'd once wanted to fuck—fragments into a memory that references my boss's concerns about BLM, a rhetoric she'd propagated in the heat of a drunken diatribe and trellised with her usual penchant for (conceited) metaphors. She'd criticised the movement as "a defeat-device, popularised after proving, in the anti-racism lab that is leftist America, that Black lives must matter, possessing a deficit evidentiary in its failure to fight racist emissions on the world stage and secure Black lungs outside its laboratory. And that's a fact!" She'd finalised this with a bang of her glass against the psychedelic bar, unwittingly signalling the West Asian bartender for a top-up. As if operating on telepathic waves, my phone shrills the ringtone I'd assigned for her. In the other pocket also, there's Elton's lovelorn Viwe begging for my attention. Vincent moves to the far end of the balcony, granting an illusive assumption of privacy. Now's a good time to slip out of this situation, the outcome of which I'd intended to be an appetising conversation peppered with non-escalating digs. I did not expect to pick up the tab and be ambushed by Vincent's sad politics. My boss might find a little mercy in my case of abscondment if I use Vince as an excuse; my first in-person encounter with the "Baldwin-Coates American"—the subject of her elaborate lectures on Blackness, whose non-inclusive, anti-internationalist IGTV Hot Takes she decides are "the shortcoming of popular anti-racist culture." And yet, for a certain conscientious twitch, I flinch at the idea of tarnishing Vincent in this manner, especially after partaking in my boss's own cunning psychoanalytic tactic of spawning covert feelers in casual conversation to unmask others' flaws. So I let the phone ring on until it quiets, followed by an insincere calm which brings with it the city's faraway noises. I flick a nail against the railing. The resulting sound mimics the beep-beep of a heart monitor. To kill this conversation or to keep it alive. "Vincent, no one's asking for your help. Here too you'll be queer. Here too you'll be oppressed."

He tuts. "If you think I'll leave America just to get oppressed elsewhere—"

"South of France. France. Fucking France. Another farce!"

He stutters, screws his eyes at me in confusion. "As I've said, if I do move, I wouldn't give a fuck about what happens to anyone here, will live in my own space, retire peacefully, that's it."

Who's this man I've been seeking knowledge from? Who's this man who isn't a god of his dogma? "Be not borne by the author, but by the words which he's written." This I address to the night rather than the man beside me.

A sirening vehicle drives by, illuminating Vincent's face with its blue-red light. Acting as luminol. Revealing the splotchy pattern of his malice, which he has masked with the dark.

"Who said that?" His voice is the only indicator of his spite.

By some epiphanic discernment, occurring in these seconds of observing a throbbing vein in his jaw, I watch his face morph into Scott's and back, their similarities betrayed, their condescensions merging in certain ridges and overlapping in others. In one's appearance is an unimpeachable gnosis enforced to a superlative degree, whereas the other, Vincent's, for the line splitting his chin into halves, delights in the bipartisan battles fought within the comparative to shame an opponent. If in those early days I'd noted his insidious curiosity for what it was, a blackened yolk scrambled together with a pond of healthy-looking eggs, I'd have avoided these traps to engage in the verbal scuffling he relishes. Now, just like he would if our roles were reversed, I enjoy giving him a taste of his own snobbery, delaying his enlightenment to puncture his inflated worth.

"That was said by an activist you're always referencing. Henceforth aligning your ideals with his will be a bit delusionary, don't you think?"

"So just because you've done a little reading on race you think *you're* some expert now, huh? You can't know what you've never experienced. You'll never understand."

This sets me off. "Vincent, I fucking understand. I understand it all! I understand the reasons behind the Year of Return. I understand all the things you somehow think I shouldn't because I'm African and 'can't get it.' Even Milly's death, which you let happen with no viable explanations or motive, is understood. Is her death not a symbol for reparations—"

"What?" He looks confused.

"You said she was a symbol. You said this to me, Vincent. That she's a symbol. So wouldn't she represent reparations to the ancestors? And to you, wouldn't her death be retributional?"

"Not everything needs an earthly meaning."

"But it does, we're human, we deal with tangible, scientific interpretations—"

"Milly's death means nothing." He grips both my shoulders. For a second I fear he's going to tug me over the railing. "At first, I thought the ancestors didn't reveal themselves to you because they're not your history. But maybe they didn't because you're so invested in the physical world you can't transcend into the portal where their voices are clear—listen, please hear me out: few things require a neatly tied theory to be understood; the rest is God and we've got to accept that. End of. It's best we forget Milly, forever. Hope you've not told Elton?" He doesn't wait for a response. "I'm going to check on the others and then we'll go meet Brian." He kisses me on the lips.

When Vincent leaves, I take care of the Viwe Problem, with one simple message: *Hi Viwe, I'm in Ghana. I don't think I'll return to SA soon, take care :)* I trash all evidence of this correspondence, and hit the block button with an exasperated sigh. What I've done to them, I hope that in the future, if I'm stuck on Elton or any other tourist without the balls to end things via text, someone else—another stranger in a foreign land, if not a boyfriend—will administer the same kindness that I've shown Viwe and euthanise an unrequited connection to save whatever shred of dignity I'd have left.

III

KOBBY
(12 days after the friends arrive)

The problem with East Legon—if ever its pompous residents admitted that their paradisal vicinity isn't exceptional to the issues plaguing Accra's affluent neighbourhoods—is that it spends too much of its time trying to market itself as middle-class relatable, the silver bullet to Accra's land guard era when, for its shell-corporation Airbnbs, V8 four-wheel rides, and flagrant subjugation to real estate companies, very few Ghanaians—for whom falling for the allure of giant sign boards advertising grinning, key-swirling Black homeowners isn't just an exercise in wishful thinking—can live in its gyms and suites, ignore the price-tags of Maxmart's imported produce, and contemplate between DNR and Honeysuckle for dinner. Needless to say, its residents entail a posse of Ghana's (recently elected, new-money) politicians, European expats, and a scattering of unsuspecting regular middle-class folk who made *de minimis* settlements for land when it was but endless miles of red dirt interspersed with beanstalk bushes.

My mother so much desired to be the latter type of East Legon denizen. It was from her my disdain towards the neighbourhood was inherited. She was a woman who loved few things and staged protests of insurmountable outrage peculiar to labour strikes for those she hated. Thus, before we were old enough to manufacture our own opinions, hers became the carnauba-waxing stage of our thought-processes. For her failed intuition—demanding Father purchase land elsewhere, she always spat, under her breath, spittle and curses whenever we reached Shiashie on our Sabbath pilgrimages to East Legon Presbyterian Church, as if it were the neighbourhood's fault that Mom's dream neighbours had chosen to live within the airport's reach rather than the hilly areas of our remote home.

"So how far is this East Legon?" Vincent asks as he slides into the Uber. He turns to the rest of us in the backseat, ignoring the driver's attempt at answering him. "So listen, I've got a feeling Nana's been following us."

Scott nods to Elton and me, suggesting this is something he and his husband have pre-discussed.

"Um, yeah, he tends to get overly protective of me. Nothing to be worried about," Elton says.

"So I changed the code to the apartment. And . . . he's locked in."

"It works that way?"

"You can put in a code for the entry and exit. Anyway, this is just to protect the people we're going to meet tonight. We don't want the homophobes on them." Vincent turns to the driver. "Boss, how far is East Legon?"

"My brother, the location wey this Google Map dey talk say e be East Legon dey funny me. I live at Santeo side and this place far from my place and Adjiringanor saff. E no be East Legon o! E check like say e be East Legon Hills. What price Uber sef give you?"

All three friends turn to me.

"Okay, so in Ghana if anyone attaches Hills to any place, ETA will probably be over an hour. Two hours tops."

"For the gays we'll travel a thousand—"

"The queers," I snap at Scott, casting a look in the driver's direction. He's already cocking a brow at Scott through the rearview mirror. "For the queers, we'll do anything."

At night, Accra amps up its scant charm, displaying light where possible, darkness where Condemn Dealers have hacked into street lights and stolen all armoured cables, sound where roadside pastors have taken over pavements with their speakers and ask passers-by to make an offering of proper one-cedi, smell where street-food caterers douse their stir-fries with an unlimited supply of spice to draw in pedestrians. Elton speaks to the others: "There's little difference between Accra and the food truck sites in Crenshaw," while I shut my eyes on the city's sights, my head bobbing to the rhythm of the vehicle's mileage.

If ever I made any happy memories as a child, they'd be found in the backseat of my dad's car during night time. Looking out the window as Accra softened and sharpened, zoning out of my brother's and father's voices, jerked at the force of a pothole bump or the lurch from screeching brakes. I'd pray for all the delays that could lengthen the time we took to get to Mother from school, maybe a police checkpoint, maybe a faulty truck causing a jam. Even then, nothing could prepare me for the tightening in my sternum when face-to-face with the red of our prison-bar gates. Only when I had grown up, and the harm had slunk away like a hand against a steamy window—in its wake a trail of unfogged vision, would I realise I was captivated not by the night's sights or the ride itself but simply by the idea of perpetual flight, the possibility of a haven existing not in a destination but in the evanescence of blurred motion, wherein I transform into one of many streaks in a bokeh, and my brother, happiest when we're home, wouldn't find me upon turning to the back seat, grinning ear-to-ear, with his youthful portraiture of Mother's face.

The Uber comes to a stop in the middle of a dead road, no lights, just a row of bushes as far as the eyes can see. As we dismount, the driver unleashes his tirade after holding it in the entire drive.

"So I drive all this bad road and you guys no go fi give me anything small say, big boss make you put am for your pocket inside. The whole day I no job. This be my first ride and after doing all this long drive you sani go make the trip a card trip."

"Kobby, I think someone wants you to blow their back out," Elton jokes. All three friends look to me for some translation, if not redemption.

Vincent takes a five-cedi note from his pocket. The driver tuts, even though he looks mollified, refuses the money and revs the engine. "I hope say you go give me five stars." He speaks to me only. "*Kwasia* boy, you think say I no understand what queer dey mean. *Me wie school na y'awo wo? Trumudifoɔ nkoa na y'asesa mo afiri America aba ha. Aboa mma.*" He steps on the gas pedal and sprays dust all over us.

The guards with hands clasping their crotch—a stance that makes me briefly recall and commiserate with Nana, who at this moment must be suffering from crate anxiety—would look a lot more menacing if they didn't have the physique of porters at Abossey Okai who made a living hauling spare parts into customers' cars, or had they any clue what other duties came with their roles besides fixing their gazes straight like guardsmen.

"Y'all not gonna ask for the password?" Scott asks the guards.

"Them talk say some Black Americans go come," one answers, showing us through the parted dwarfish gates—an odd installation for a house this huge.

Over a brick-laid path, we tiptoe on the ingrown grass to avoid crushing any of the snails for whom it seems the pathway was built. Elton makes a crunch sound. Scott jumps in fright only to find the former sniggering, holding a bar of Snickers. Vincent, eager to discover what's waiting on the other side of the blood-red mahogany door, is in no mood for the others' squabbling. He jaywalks over the brake-averse creatures and pushes through the door—whose knob is designed as a shell—without reading the banner above it which indicates he's entering the premises of a Satanist worship centre.

Wafting through the crowded living area is an absurd re-
cital chant possibly procured from Kanayo O. Kanayo's *Blood
Money*, which may still dupe an ignorant law enforcement officer or a wandering local into believing they've trespassed the
realm of an occultist gathering. The only necromantic detail
Brian has deployed for the safety of the venue, and for this he's
pleased. He hugs the friends and asks, "Do you think if we got
raided tonight we would all avoid jail?" To me, he thrusts a
stop-sign and says, "You smell like a hotep."

He steers the friends ahead, briefing them on how he got the
place (some guy he's fucking) and what plans he has for tonight
(drinks and drag).

"You know, Kobby, that's the problem." Vincent steps back,
visibly irritated. "You guys have semantically satiated the word
'hotep' to mean every Black American doing the bare minimum
to go back to their roots. That's wrong and I can't help feeling
offended. Do y'all even know who a hotep actually is, or you
choose to be ignorant?"

Mahogany, oak-panelled surfaces, one bamboo erected in
a pot of loam. Rugs, everywhere. Golden frames bordering
mirrors, one chalice seated on the mantle of a logless fireplace.
Candles competing with the moody lighting. A POP ceiling
with escargot patterns. A pleasant smell of tobacco lingering in
the air. Who's Brian sleeping with this time? Everything in this
living area paints a wealthy hoarder who walks around with a
staff (bearing a golden snail), looks down over his belly as he's
being sucked—a passive observer to his own pleasures, and an
active legislator in parliament, where he makes up for his idleness in the bedroom by doubling down on anti-LGBT laws.

The lack of aspiration towards any form of debauchery in-
tensifies my concerns for the minimal security the venue is operating on. These guests, whose eyes I've been avoiding, stealing
furtive glances through my locs which I've brushed onto my
face in a sad attempt at preserving anonymity, demonstrate an

aloofness to the order of the day. Some of them isolating into their phones, others huddled in groups and on their phones— no inclination to interact beyond splintered glimpses, all of them angling towards the entrance as if this were the preliminary event for which they were biding time to ditch. Their resolve at unsociability seems impenetrable, until Elton winks at a light-skinned, 5'7" fellow. This guy looks away to adjust the mould of his belly over his trousers' waistline, and, like an infectious yawn triggering several others, this action betrays all manifestations of self-consciousness scattered across the hall; fingers raking through scalps, balances twitching from shoe to shoe, palms swiping noses. A domino effect exposing their years too: twenty-fours, twenties, nineteens possessing unlined skin altered, under the glare of blue screens, to resemble thirty-somethings with demanding lives. Their ages, however, should not take the fall for their timidity . . .

"Ghanaianness comes with a conditioning to be indirect about one's intimate or romantic intentions"; these words were trotted out at a party—pretty much like this one in agenda but with a lot more ambition in performance—flaunting, in the age of "Shake body" and Falz's "Soft Work," a city's obviously Londoned and moneyed queer folk, spinning and swaying then sinking into the white expanse of that Ikoyi apartment. A comment, whose authorship I'm not entirely sure should be attributed to my boss, who was prancing about with an uncorked bubbly in one hand, and who until then had never let on she was bi. Or, as she shared upon refilling my glass with just the right amount of focus to drink in the svelte owner of that penthouse slammed onto her hip, "an eschewer of all labels. You throw labels at me, I rip them with my teeth"—And just like that we've got new meaning to eschew, her partner chimed in, after which she, my boss, farcically broke into Beauvoirian outrage: "Oh sure, we kiss on the lips, we hug, we touch each other's breasts, but we don't do anything down there, so you can't call us lesbians!"

"Make una think about am for one second, how often do Ghanaians make the first move for anything?" inquired the by-the-way-I'm-6'3" bald man, a strong contender for the ownership of the mystery quote, who'd never once left my side since I touched down in this hetero-suppressed Lagosian enclave. "The only reason you and I are talking is because of my Nigerian side. We'd have not spoken if I were Ghanaian-Ghanaian. I lie?" To which I replied: *Ha ha, maybe!* "Every time I go to Accra—Bloom Bar or Sandbox, guys stare at me till I leave. Or even if they approach, their pick-up line will always be, You look familiar." *Accurate! Ha ha!* "By the way, I'm Ewe on my mum's side and Igbo on my dad's." *That's a double-wahala if ever I heard one.* "My prick, you mean? Na joke a dey joke, abeg, it's manageable. But I know what you mean. My Igbo name is Chibueze, given by my dad's family, but my mother's side won't let my Igbo people be great, they insisted they'd already chosen for me Mawunyefie, which translates as God Is King. So for this Lagos, na only me dey waka with two names wey get the same meaning—" *Ah, na wa o,* I replied mockingly. His phone buzzed. He retrieved it out of the back pocket of his jeans, inspected the notification and thrust the screen at me. "Can you read?" *What am I looking at?* "Just in: 'Ghana refuses to grant gays' rights despite aid threat.' Not Tony Blair, not David Cameron can save us now. Sigh."

Sigh indeed.

"Everyone's a bit of a snob, right?" Scott, snapping me out of my momentary detachment with the present, asks.

"They're young, Scott, give them time."

"No, honestly in my time the gay clubs were a lot more fun than this. I went to a few until I found out most of them were still an opportunity for white gays to grab Black men's dicks. Over here, no one's even making advances. All on their phones. Must be the generation—"

"And the location." Brian whirls to face us, ditching his conversation with Elton and Vincent. "Everyone knows to lie low for a while till it's safe to touch. Even in meetings where the only physical interactions are the distribution of pamphlets on safe-sex, people are still carted off to jail. Plus, this isn't a gay club . . ." Brian trails off on hearing the bells at the entrance announce the arrival of someone new, then, "Okay, guys," he screams, "in thirty minutes, the doors boust to be locked, so you better call your friends who've not made it yet and let 'em know we boust to get things started." He swaggers towards the mini-bar.

"I just wish he'd stop the cringe slang." Scott says.

"I don't know 'bout y'all, but I'm this close to dipping." Elton announces. "I understand the whole fear of not touching. But no drinks? No weed?"

"Calm down," Vincent prompts. "He says it'll get better." Then directs his attention to me, "Yo, Kobby, is this your first gay club . . . gathering, whatever you'd call this experience?"

"In Ghana, yes."

"Wow, I wonder why."

I ignore his sarcasm.

"He probably never gets an invite, you know, given his issues with 'the Queen.'" Elton supplies. "What are your thoughts, though?"

"I don't think this is the crowd Brian hangs out with. The people here are what you get when you open Man4Man on Legon campus. In my uni days, I'd always date off-campus—"

"Probably explains why the men here wouldn't speak to each other: everyone wants a daddy—"

"Bro," we all turn to the voice that interrupts Elton, "guy, you remember me?" His sharp-ended starter locs, his lankiness, and that accent bring up a memory of the first meeting with Elton and friends at Republic.

"You're the waiter at Republic," Vincent says in my stead.

"Yeah, how far na?" he says to the others, but his eyes rest on me. "You fine o. Everything cool?"

"Yeah, sure," I answer curtly and turn to the others to find they've scooted a few metres away. Elton winks at me. Only then do I realise this Nigerian is interested in a lot more than saying hi. "Are you good, also?"

"A dey." He smiles. "The programme don' start?"

I chuckle at his choice of words. "Not yet. So I'm guessing you've not been here long?"

"True. I just dey reach. Na ten my shift finish."

"Lots of white men being a pain in the arse?"

"Pain? You say white men dey pain?" He leans in closer to clear his incomprehension. "Not just white men. Arabs. Chinese. Ghanaians. All of you. Boss, you sabi pidgin? I be Warri boy o. I no dey unnastand wetin you dey talk. Come down, come down, make we yarn broken. My English no sweet, na Jenifa English me I fit yarn, o."

"I see." I let my gaze wander around the party that looks like it's finally picking up, the music swapped for something by Todrick Hall, Brian handing out drinks in plastic cups, Elton making smoke signs to the light-skinned 5'7" guy who still hasn't paid him mind. Scott and Vincent conversing as they eye the people in attendance.

"You sabi dance?"

I sigh resignedly, "I do. But I can't."

"Make I teach you." He begins voguing to Todrick Hall . . .

"I see."

"Do you dance?" Chibuze asked. In the many moments he raised his glass for a sip, he spied me over the rim, intently, as if he'd reasoned that to him, I was his tunnel vision, a light he kept edging towards.

All around us, everyone had suspended all pretence of decency, engaging in an orgiastic dance that resulted in un-moored spaghetti straps, a floating detritus of underwear tangled in the hook of heels, wet patches on flaps. (After a while, I got comfortable seeing my boss in a state of libidinal undoing, her head lolling against the shoulder of her partner, who feasted on her jugular.) If the Nigerian Ghanaian had wanted to join in on the debauchery, he did nothing to communicate this, not with his hands firmly clasping his liquor, nor his body maintaining a distance that—however small—was considered chaste by the standards everyone else had set. His question, then, it seemed, was an attempt at kindling conversation rather than an invitation to emulate the others.

"Like, honestly, Ghanaians have the best nyash-sets, a known fact across the continent and even in diaspora communities: even South Africans will concede to this. Such a shame that none of you can dance." *Yes, we're horrible, really, we leave the dancing to our Ivorian counterparts.* "I went to a queer house-party in Dzorwulu one December, was the dullest I'd ever been to. Also, too many white people—which is really just a fact about the entire Accra, but it was also in that part of Dzorwulu where all the expats live. Anyway, no one danced, except for the foreigners. Everyone was just checking the other out, like it was a Bloom Bar annexe. Surprised we didn't meet, you and I, but I doubt regular Ghanaians were even there." *Regular?* "I find in our countries, there's two communities, and limited opportunities for both to mix, because the diaspora gays go out of their way to avoid the local ones more than they would an STI infection." He gestured at two vascular men tucked next to a shoji that parted to the balcony, unclothed and making the most of what partial privacy two silver-grey curtains offered. "I'm going to the bathroom. Help me get another drink, *abeg*."

I stared at his leisured swagger until he turned a corner. I roamed the apartment on a liquor hunt. Everyone I moved to insisted their bottles were off-limits, leaving me with no option but to interrupt my boss and her partner. "Come with me," As we weaved through the guests, I was instructed to call her, my boss' partner, Dalia, an anglicised version of her name. "Not my government name, you know? There's still way too many people here that I don't trust enough to disclose who I am. So how are you liking Nigeria? Yaa tells me it's your first visit." *I love your apartment? It's frankly the only place I've been.* "Ha! Funny! Maybe after the meeting with the investors, you two might have more time to explore Lagos. You'll love it." In the shoe-box foyer, we found a deserted rosé seated next to a giant floor-length mirror surrounded by the footwear of all those present. "At least you're having fun here with Chibu. He's got chat, hasn't he? He likes you, it seems. A correct guy. Unlike most of us, his parents' wealth isn't tied to a political appointment. They did care work when they first got to the UK, got rich, and now own multiple care homes. They've even got a huge seven-bedroom house in London's own Ajah—Essex. Anyways, he's well-travelled. Well-mannered. He's in Ghana almost every other week." She said all of this with a probing gaze, sussing out my interest. *Yeah, Chibuze is nice,* I responded, extending the glass towards the bottle she held. "Chi-bu-eze. You think he's nice? Well, take the whole bottle." She pressed it onto my chest and leant into me, my face inches away from the sweat-soaked bust of her strapless jumpsuit. "I'd rather you guys do things here than anywhere else in Lagos; it's safer here." *Do things?* "Bathroom was just code for something else, you need to go find him." She cackled and shoved me out of the foyer. "He's so subtle. And you're so slow."

The party has come out of its shell. Under the heat of Brian's saccharine invectives, more bodies have coalesced, everyone's regurgitating what small-talk comes to mind, voicing whichever platitudes are readily available on the tongue. All of it looks staged. Yet, like a brilliantly written production, there's a natural flow to the motions. None of it contrived, no ebbing loquacity, and in not too rare cases, there's rippling laughter spurred by shared grievances suffered aboard the treacherous voyages of collegiate lives; in-jokes about the shenanigans of fraternity-style halls (the usual fracas between Commonwealth Hall and the boys of Legon Hall), GPA-drowning courses, notorious and preda-tory lecturers. Of all the couples, the only one wrongly paired is me and the Waiter Guy, whom I'm enduring for the glimmer in his eyes as he sums up his life's memoir, from the streets of Warri to Madina Zongo—half of which I've zoned out of.

"Bros, the needle you gave me dey do wonders o."

"Really?" I take a step towards him. "Have you . . . used it for . . ."

"When you put small oil for your head inside, it go smooth. But it go wound you well-well, if you no take your time use am." My interest deflates. I spot Elton in conversation with the light-skinned guy, whose attention he has finally secured, even though the latter backs against a wall as if intimidated by Elton's hulking frame. Elton's smile reflects against the tiny framed mirrors above the boy's head. Across the hall, my eyes meet Scott's: he's made it his mission to observe my reaction to Elton's behaviour. For him, this is more profitable a pastime than listening in on Vincent and Brian's conversation—even if our host has swept all of his locs to one shoulder and fixes a leering gaze at his chatterbox companion. Scott winks at me and chugs down his drink.

A phone is waved in my face. "Give me your WhatsApp number? Maybe we can meet somewhere nice. Maybe Accra Mall. Get to know ourselves."

"Hmm. I see."

I had been seated on a liquor-saturated couch for minutes, playing voyeur to the scenes of men without the context of gendered clothing. All of them touching, cupping, tonguing, engaging in a hedonistic performance, which is the boiling point of parties like this one organised on the premise of un-inhibiting fun. *Everybody's free to do whatever they want,* was the cajoling line my boss had used to lure me out of the Banana Island Airbnb in whose rooms I'd planned on squandering away the entirety of my first international trip. *Body no be firewood. We cannot come and kill ourselves,* were other lines bandied around by guests upon arrival, whose shoes and socks and shirts came off once they became comfortable enough to shed their decorum. I watched all of this with an indifferent softness that earned me dirty looks from some other attendees puzzled about the Ghanaian drinking himself into an idle stupor in defiance of the night's agenda.

"Hey." My boss emerged from the bodies just as her partner, Dalia, in lace panties, walked past to the foyer. I was hauled off the couch with a single pull. "You're good?" *I am.* She sighed, flung an arm over my shoulder. "You want to head back?" *No, it's peaceful here.* She nodded, and we shared a camaraderie silence where she joined in observing the party from my viewpoint, turning away almost immediately upon discovering how invasive this perspective felt. "I was having fun until Dalia wanted . . . a break." Through the door of the lobby, there was Dalia inspecting her thigh for a vein, a syringe looming in her hand. My boss spun me away from her partner's vices. "Maybe we stay with those we love because they make us happy. If they stopped making us happy, we'd leave, wouldn't we?" *We should.* "Hey, you know Chibueze is still waiting for you?" *I know.* "And you'd rather be here?" *He's a nice guy but—*"He's almost a local? Is that his flaw? That he comes to Ghana often?

Ha ha. Kobby, since we were little you've always told these elaborate stories about your life. When will it be time to accept

bottom-shaming culture, and how tops aren't it?" The audience's response is loud and positive. "You know, there's another nuance to bottom-shaming that's cropping up in my years—among friends of my age—although some of you young ones have experienced it too: tops complaining that we're not tight enough." Dramatic pause. Few nods around the room. "There's no such thing as loose hole, only too many penises without the appropriate girth." Uproarious laughter. "You probably know this already if you've had dicks that poke your asshole instead of filling you up." More laughter. "Be safe, guys. Love one another. None of that animosity shit with other bottoms. Make money, not shade. Money trees is the perfect place to throw shade. That's a reference from a Kendrick Lamar song—do they play Kendrick here? Listen, when you are my age, you're going to realise little things like this, like community, like togetherness matter—also, when you reach your forties, and new research shows that you need to jerk off at least twenty-one times to be cancer-free, please pay your debts. I thought taking student loans would be the peak of my life's regrets; now I realise that I should have attended more orgies in college. I've cleared my student loans and now I've got a backlog of ejaculations to settle." Few people are unaffected by this joke. I'm one of those laughing into the surrounding air misted with liquor from unguarded lips. "This advice may not be useful now, but when you're my age, please get your prostate screened. Also, keep in mind that bottoming is only a phase you will grow out of when you're thirty; then you'll become a vers bottom who never tops. A vers bottom whose titles were obtained through honorary degree from his gym, after arching with flying colours for his dumbbell rows, and then later in the locker-room showers—"

"We asked for advice, not a Netflix comedy special."

"Fair," Scott concedes, raising his hands in surrender. "I should probably only tell these jokes to people whom I'm certain will get green cards. Perhaps I should use the rest of my set to houdini y'all the fuck out of here. Y'all ever heard of Houdini?"

"How do we be gay in societies where there's consistent, continuous oppression?" one of the younglings hibernating on a couch asks. Everyone turns to him. "You know it's horrible here. We're always being abused. On campus, people are getting set up to be beaten. One minute you think you're going to suck dick, the next you're kneeling in a viral TikTok and being yelled at."

"Hmm . . ." Scott sighs. "You know what? I'll be honest. Being gay is shit everywhere in the world. And don't let the American gays on Instagram fool you . . ." His voice tapers off as he stares at the POP ceiling. "You know, in cases like this no one talks about how lying low helps. I know it sounds contrary to all what you guys have these days. All that pride to parade around without fear of being harmed, making people aware you're gay and here to stay? But, as my good friend always says," he fixes Elton a stare, "'I'm gay-gay but I'm also not gonna die because I want to flaunt my gay at a bunch of homophobes.'"

"What if we're fem, what if we can't hide our gay?" another asks, inspiring murmurs around the room.

"If drag queens can tuck their dicks perfectly, you can also do the same for your fem-ness."

There's a collective gasp as everyone turns to the owner of the offending remark, who happens to be Elton's light-skinned guy.

"You need to leave!"

"Guys," Scott interrupts the oncoming pandemonium. "We can turn this into a forum, I want to learn something here. Anyone's got suggestions that are . . . helpful?" He stretches an invisible mike into the audience.

"You know what I think?" Vincent leans into Brian as Scott solicits opinions. "You can start a real foundation out of this. Create a Crowdfund or GoFundMe. This could be real activism stuff."

"I'm not an activist," Brian says.

"But you did say you organise these meetings monthly to check if everyone's practicing safe sex and routinely testing for STIs. That's activ—"

"I'm not an activist," Brian snaps. Turns to Elton. "You should ask your boyfriend what they do to activists here. Ask him. If these media houses are not inviting them on air to make fun of them, they're blasting their faces everywhere to encourage targeted killings. I asked that he report on us, even went out of my way and put together an event for him so he could meet us all, but he disappeared."

"Brian, I was in Lagos," I say.

"And when you got back, you never checked on me when you knew we'd been raided by a mob." He's shouting now.

"Brian, I was lying low. Everyone was lying low during that November of 2015."

He takes a step towards me. "We needed you. But you were never going to help, were you? You never did want to be a part of us in the first place. And now look at you, inviting all these foreigners to tour our spaces—" he spins to Elton. "—which by the way, I must say it's the first fucking time I've seen him with someone who isn't short, rotund, and with a nose fashioned out of a carrot. He refused to date anyone in the community because he was scared any association with us would lead to him being outed. So he only went with white people whom he asked—and this became so known we felt embarrassed—to buy books for him. How fucking pretentious is that? Books! Books! Lots of money-boys are out there trying to survive! Get on Man4Man and people are begging to be MoMo'd twenty cedis for food. And now white folks don't patronise them because there's a new guy on the market who receives books as payment. Books!"

"Brian—"

"Kobbyyyy!" he hollers, spittle and rage tossed onto my face. *"Wo nenam nenam na w'ane abɔ wo ho no, wodwen sɛ yɛntee yɛ!* We are all ashamed for you!" He brushes past me for an adjoining door.

The entire hall lies captive to a silence that segues into cleared throats and jesting coughs.

"Honestly," Scott speaks. "You guys have redeemed yourselves. This is the best gay party I've attended in Africa. And I've been to South Africa."

Elton and Vincent turn their backs on me, a performance drawn out to suggest their irresolution, although their towering posteriors make clear their decision to lay a brick wall before me. I smile, a guise worn over my imminent discomfiture, wherein I envision my wits tossed back and forth in a torrent of fury and decadence, blood and tears razing this closeted sanctuary of snails and mirrors. I rush for the exit, my phone in hand.

He answers on the first ring. "Daa, don't lock the gate."

IV

NANA
(12–13 days after the friends arrive)

M' *aḥyɛda na m'anoa* jollof *ama ɔmo*. I've fried the tin tomatoes well and fried the fish too. Just a little ginger and garlic in the food. Even put my secret ingredients *hwentea, kpakpo shito* and bay leaf in it. Jollof with no Maggi. Who will waste their time and cook jollof where the rice have remove one-one, which if you don't take care the jollof can become hard like *dade sapɔ*, and when you have finish all the food and leave the chef the *kanzo*, you don't even treat them nice or even say thank you? All this plenty work I've done for them: taking my time to take them out to see Ghana, to let them get things to buy cheap-cheap because no one can cheat them when I'm with them. Still they don't respect me. Still they lock me inside the house like I am *efie kraman*, an animal. Today we'll see who's who.

I sit at the place Elton and the Ananse smoke and wait. 11:00 P.M., no one has come. 12:00 A.M., I find some of Vincent's mosquito cream and pomade my body with it. Vincent, who I've done plenty thing for, agreed with his friends so they all lock me inside. After all I've done for him.

After that night in Elmina he came to me crying like a baby, telling me that he know why my pastor say he's going to die, telling me about Milly the white woman and what he has done to her because of the voices he hear in his sleep, the voices that made him want to kill himself. Do you remember, Nana? Do you remember? He hold my hand on the beach, shaking so much I want to hold him and put him on my chest. Vincent, yes, I remember that you walked into the sea and almost didn't come back. But why did you go kill a white woman? What has the white woman done to you? In Ghana, white people just help us here a lot—No, Nana! He shout for my top to shut up and say, the problem here is that Faisal will kill me now that I've kill his wife. Your pastor was right all along. He squeeze my hands and say, if only someone can help me out of this situation. Vincent, I don't understand what you're saying, I said to him, which was a lie, because I think I know what he was saying, I know it so well I begin to cry too. I tell him no, I tell him that I've already killed people in my life, I've burn my grandmother and in Elmina I've kill—Nana, listen to me, it's already getting to seven and Milly hasn't come back, I'll die soon if Faisal finds out, prayers won't help keep me alive, I'm not a murderer, I didn't kill Milly, I just went to give her to my ancestors, *your* ancestors, help me else I'll die, if you love me you'll listen to my words and do as I say. Do you love me? Am I your friend? I can get you a visa, you could leave Ghana, start a new life in America. I cry and cry, because Vincent will be fulfilling the prophecy my pastor has already given me, that someone will come and take me to America. But why me, Vincent? Why me? *I chose you, Nana, because you told me how much you hate Faisal, that he's Ananse the spider and he's only tricking the white woman for her money, look, he's already a bad man, so you're not sinning when you kill bad men.* I lie to myself that this is the reason Vincent give me even though I was saying it to myself. I repeated my reason as I dug his hole to bury him, after I've poisoned him with rat medicine from the kitchen when he was in his room worrying because his wife was keeping long and I told him to calm down and drink this Sobolo. I still said this to myself— *Faisal, you Ananse, you deserve to die*—as I cut the hen neck and spread the blood over his grave, break some eggs too so his ghost doesn't come back and find me.

After all I've done for Vincent!

It's 4:00 A.M. by the time Vincent and Elton and Scott come home. I'm crying where Elton smoke and do gay-gay things. I've become a small boy again, crying *dendenden* when my grandmother lock me in the room to teach me a lesson. I swear to God that if she let me out I will kill her. And that's what I do. I'll kill them today, I swear to God.

The thing that is paining me the most is they forget I'm here. I look at them come in with the Ananse. They all drink water. Vincent goes to the door, and I hear him press the code that make the door open and close. Is he the one who change it? I'll make sure he suffer. After all I do for him in Elmina this is how he pay me.

"Guys, the code is back to the old one."

They all go into their room and I plan that I'll kill all of them in their sleep. I will cut-cut their throats. I will ask them why they're bad to me when all I have done is be good to them. Especially Vincent. Especially Vincent. I will wait for them to sleep deep. Not like my grandmother who doesn't take long before she sleep, I know these men will keep long before they sleep so I sit outside and wait patiently.

The Ananse come out to the kitchen after some time. He drink water before he goes to the door and leave. I will start with him. I go to the kitchen and take the butcher knife. I follow him, quickly run down the stairs as he use the room they call elevator. He's standing outside when I get out, looking at his phone, waiting for his Uber. I don't even check to see if anyone's outside. I run for him. I'll kill him and push him inside the bush where they're doing new building. He doesn't see me coming fast from his back. Then a car comes to park in front of him, he turn and I see it's not the Ananse, it's the tall one who wear long shoes and long coat. He open the car door but his bag fall. He sees me as he bends down to pick it. On the road is some of the shoemaker pin I see in the Ananse bag this afternoon when I try to choke him. I go closer because I don't believe what I'm seeing. But I touch some on the ground. The boy thinking I'm helping him take the pins, say:

"Thank you! What are friends for?"

"Just to destroy," I say because I heard it in some Nigerian movie before.

"Oh wow, you catch on so fast. And you gots yourself some manly-manly hands too. Yum. Why don't you come on up and fuck me in the ass sometime." He close his bag and say, "Tell Elton that I had fun. It's his loss that he didn't want to join in . . ."

In my mind I'm thinking of that one time that I see the Ananse use his shoemaker pin to kill a man in some dark corner. But this time, I don't see the Ananse's face, his face keep vanishing so that this man's face is what I see. The car drive away, leaving me with the Rasta's laughter. I don't know what to think again. Is the Ananse not the Sasabonsam Killer? Or do they work together? I am running back to the elevator. My brain, my chest, all of them are beating faster. The *kaka* in my mouth has fill my mouth with plenty blood, I spit some in the elevator. I still have Elton and his friends to kill. Vincent. Especially Vincent. 1, 2, 3, and 4. Bell. I run out. I go to their room and press the code.

The door does not open.

V

KOBBY
(12 nights after the friends arrive)

11:59 P.M. He's been waiting for this next date for as long as Elton's been in Ghana, so he kicks the door behind me shut and bathes the room in an ashen light that contours all objects with a soft blur, setting the ambience for what is going to be a long night. First, the curtains sway, in a ghoulish breeze whose chill shrouds me like a jacket offered in a rainstorm. This breeze is innocent till it turns turbulent: proceeds to knock a book off my shelf, kicks open my wardrobe, yanks down the wall clock, a glass cracks against the concrete floor, all my Ordinary's clamour—swept off their resting place, along with my lube, shampoos, conditioners, oils. He's so meticulous about these preparations that the effort comes off more chivalrous than he'd have ever bothered with were he alive. Finally the bed creaks from the pressing weight of his spectral presence. I smile at the outline of the patinated headboard. "Not yet," I murmur, slipping out of my shoes, dropping my bag to the ground, and stripping to my briefs. Just like he'd have instructed were he alive. Since the concept of a haunted house is only a procession of funereal energies trapped into a building, I am responsible for imprisoning his spirit in this room. I have created the conditions that have invited his soul to linger. For instance, the walls (an unimaginable brown) are buried under a collage of all the newspapers that published the news of his death together with his gruesome remains, which, as the years have gone by, have browned and moulded with the text of his biographies and obituaries, leaving just the headlines: *Boy Dies From Kakum Fall*, *Teenager Jumps off Kakum Canopy Walk and Dies*, *Kakum Canopy Walk Kills Boy of Fifteen*. The shrine that has become my room, which is his casket, stinks of wet socks and damp sneakers, musty shirts, Rexona roll-on deodorants, all of which condense to create the fragrance of his adolescence that I have gone lengths to replicate even if it means hunting for products (Sivoderm Powder, Eversheen Cocoa Butter, Kurl-Out Pomade, that Ginseng toffee only Mother and him loved) slowly dying out of commerce.

12:05 P.M. I'm too tired to bother uprighting his upended mess, an activity that I could always fall back on to postpone sleep for a little more than an hour. Instead, I find my phone and check for messages from Elton (there is none), messages from Aspecialkindofdouble (there's been none since the last I sent her about the agent). I consider sending her something but—for the guilt of prioritising what flimsy tryst I have with Elton and his friends over our timeless bond—I change my mind before hitting send. Idly, I scroll through Bookstagram until the UI becomes a blur of blue and white lines and I'm almost dozing off . . . My lids rupture!

12:36 A.M. Hungry, I exit my room. I'm uncertain if my heavy footfalls or maybe the earlier ruckus is responsible for waking my dad—I hear him slap his cover cloth over his body. Or was he awake even before I arrived? The corridor, which marks the entry to all the bedrooms in the house, is home to a darkness that has characterised my father's life and mine since our losses. Everything outside the lived-in rooms is pitch-black, no ounce of light except for the glint of keys nailed onto the door panels of those emptied chambers. It's a wonder how I can navigate this dark to the kitchen, whose impressive white refrigerator is a shadow of its former glory now that it has no basketball magnets (from my brother) or notes (from my mum) or even electricity (out of my dad's utility budget) to power it. It's one of the few possessions that hasn't suffered a polypropylene cover (unlike the cars, the couches, and most of the cutlery secured in bubble wraps) in the emotional downturn that has plagued the residents of this house. In its spider-leased compartments I occasionally find leftovers from my dad's take-away life. A glimpse into his diet since I stopped performing mother's culinary duties once I found life outside this gloom. Today, the rancid smell of the fridge encases a glass jar of an unknown opaque sauce which I sample with a finger to find shito—tangy on the tongue, and soon to mould. This will do. I locate a tissue-wrapped disposable spoon that can only manage dollop-sizes, dip it into the jar and head back to my room.

12:45 A.M. I begin shooting Instagram content over my brother's obituaries. Using my boss's DSLR, the books—as many of them as possible, since I'm never certain when next I'll be back to this house—are set on a table, and *flash, flash,* the pictures turn out brilliant, matching the sinister vibe of my current IG grid; books splayed over newsprint backgrounds highlighting words like *Shocking, Dead, Suicide.*

12:58 A.M. My phone beeps. Not Elton. A blank profile on Man4Man asking, one: *where you dey,* two: *are you top,* three: *can you host?* I sigh, prostrate over the concrete floor, my fingers hovering over the touch keyboard. From these few messages I've already gleaned that, one: he's a local, two: he's a bottom repulsed by the idea of fucking vers men, three: can you host comes as a cry for help; scratching noises along walls, begging to be let in like the girl from that Akan fable returning home to parents who've locked her out, a cautionary tale about monsters in the dark. Only this time, those we must fear are the humans living inside, and "can you host" is a squeak in an airtight room after scrambling efforts to break out. *Ɛnkye wo, Dora. Ɛnkye wo, Dora. Me maame ei buei me.* But the mother turns a blind eye, keeps the door locked despite the abuse happening on the other side.

2:30 A.M. In the days I ransacked the internet for solutions to remedy my sleep of past traumas—anything but taking my prescribed meds—I found edging; masturbating until I became so exhausted I fell into a deep sleep. Chamomile seemed like a better substitute for the many nights my dick was too sore to be put through another wanking ordeal. But I'd spend less time in bed than I did on the toilet; peeing and watching Dr. Alan Mandell's YouTube for more sleep remedies that only seem to work for those who subscribe, like, and comment; peeing and scrolling through r/sleep for more remedies by anonymous Redditors who begin every contribution with their time in Iraq. Truly, there's been nothing as efficient, nothing as remarkably powerful as devising and taking years to perfect AESMA. I have no scientific reasoning to prove why it works. I'm only certain its success relies not on all the effort I put into it, but the incentive for all this effort: the obvious premise that death is an antecedent to uninterrupted sleep. In my last AESMA episode, in Elton's Airbnb, Nana had taken the place of Louise in *Lullaby* by Slimani. Since I'm no longer afraid of Nana, the idea of replaying those scenes does not inspire the terror that would later grant the orgasmic fulfilment I'm used to. So, as it happens whenever I'm in this house, I stick to my usual AESMA fantasy, "death by accidental suicide" as one newspaper put it (pairing their article with a cartoon of a boy foolish enough to believe he could survive jumping off a treetop walkway). It is also the first of fantasies that led to the birth of AESMA.

Almost 3 A.M. Three hours until I'm woken up by my body's premeditated sleep-wake cycle. *I believe it's time we begin the rituals, don't you think?* The bed moans, its dashboard pounds the wall. *Let's climax now, shall we?*

3:00 A.M. I perceive an uncanny presence as soon as I pull open the drawer to withdraw the discoloured canine I salvaged from my mother's mouth. Mother's efforts to harm me are futile, though she pants over my shoulder, all of her six feet angled into observing the ceremony I retrieve her tooth with, swishing it in the evening's silvery light to spy its evil glint where the enamel suffers a serrated chip. I only extracted this tooth to improvise for the missed opportunity in acquiring one of a similar kind from my brother's carcass, or just about any of his parts—wasn't too picky, anything as simple as a piece of skin sustained from his fall—to lure his soul from the afterlife. Given the circumstances under which I sourced this canine (slamming a crowbar into my mother's lifeless profile), I've had to live with the frequent dental abscesses that often result in tie-dyed patterns of blood resting in the cusps of my molars. I crawl under the bed and fish out the musty jersey and smelly socks, place the tooth on the pile and lie supine, breathing in, breathing out, listening as my body dissolves into the cold concrete, sinking so my brain steers ship.

3:05. *I let my imagination run wild, through thickets of trees, animal noises, children's voices, until I'm on the canopy walk. My gaze is bent over the distance beyond the rope netting, where there are branches and leaves sprouting as afros, snatches of light crevicing through the array of vegetation—these luminous spaces I will soon tumble through.* Deep breaths. *I hear my name shouted and whirl to find my brother's face. He grins.* And

I see that discoloured canine that I took from mom,

having returned home,

from that Cape Coast excursion of 2003,

to a house whose smells had been silenced with bleach,

a bucket of red the colour of diluted Sobolo seated in the stead of the *Akwaaba* doormat outside my parent's matrimonial room,

from which my dad emerged looking strained and panicky,

yet still forcing a smile despite himself and asking,

Where's your brother? And what's that bandage you have on your forehead?

Mr. Manu! cried out the voices of a teacher and the tour

guide from the porch. My dad shot me one last panicked look before heading out to his visitors, who bore bad news. I stepped into his room and found Mother splayed over the bed—a pose strikingly similar to that of the Vitruvian Man, but instead of the ceiling she had her face tilted to the door. Many of my memories of 2003, the year of visiting Cape Coast, begin with the blood—

oozing out my forehead,

and closes with the minutes spent rooted at the entrance of my parents' room,

watching my mother's slow exsanguination, the syrupy red of her blood pooling over the faded rose-patterned Ashfoam mattress.

It's 2019 and spasms are exploding through my entire form for the duration of this AESMA exercise, my scalp is slammed against the concrete floors of my room, I take deep inhalations and long exhalations as my throat slowly constricts, I blink back my present surroundings and allow my imagination to overwrite memories of 2003:

Brother's not alone on the canopy walk. They have the look of a couple on the verge of eloping, walking hand-in-hand, mischief dancing in their eyes, unfazed even when the wooden boards dip treacherously at the impact of their summed weights. Her usual cornrows are stretched so far back that her forehead becomes a papery sheen reflecting the sun's rays. I pretend that I have no idea what they're up to. I stick to my script: Hi brother, hi Yaa, why are you two falling behind? *As they close in on me, I sense their sinister disposition—this moment is when I truly begin fearing for my life.* You hurt us both, *she says. I switch my gaze between the two, my countenance a genuine offering of puzzlement.* What are you two talking about? See, let's catch up with the others before—*She shoves me. Death by this hand looks so serene, a painting of nails pushing a torso over a bridge. Everyone but me fails to recognise the poetry in this death—limbs snapping, skin*

shredding as if compressed into a mincer, head enduring way too
many cracks, blood, too much blood filling the accruing distance
between my killers and me . . .

"Kobby!" Back to the present. "Kobby!"

My dad's banging on my door as I'm dry-retching over the
concrete, my body convulsed in a puddle of mucus and spit in
which I'm entangled like a web.

"Kobby!"

Whatever the reason for his banging, I'm sure rescuing me
has little to do with it. He's too concerned about the state of this
building, which he's been slowly selling out to vulturous Condemn Dealers feasting on the corpse this home has become.
And on the numerous occasions he's spied me through my window tossing books at the shutters, breaking another wall clock
he's replaced, sending a foot through the wardrobe, crashing
yet another bed-stand water glass, sweeping all my Ordinary's
to the floor, he asks that I stop behaving possessed, pleading
to desist from ruining the house he's put up on Tonaton. I'll
wake up to my anti-depressants assembled next to my door, a
reminder that he's evolved into this healthcare provider whose
relationship with me is only professional, having severed the
biological after losing both sons; one to abuse, the other to suicide that could have been homicide—not because there's reason to prove this, but in this country, everyone assumes foul
play until the dead speak for themselves.

With effort, I stretch for the paperback on the floor and hurl
it at the door. This silences his supposed concern. I hear his
retreating footsteps. My throat feels parched from the combi-
nation of my dry retching and the shito, and I'm sure this will
later result in an infection whose antidote lies somewhere in
my antibiotics/painkiller drawer. Yet the allure of death is so
strong this minute, I feel it would be unwise to fan its flames
by presenting it with ammunition. Among all the methods of
dying, an overdose seems too lazy an attempt. Always pictured

my own death among the pages of *Iliad*, which is to say that I want a death deserving of documentation, perhaps plastered in newsprint too, something worth deconstruction. I lug my leaden body onto the bed's rail, struggle past the mosquito net, and collapse into the thin sheets.

I die.

Not exactly. Not today.

Even on days of good sail, the weather makes a swift turn, the currents kick in, a shark's fin appears, rowing is made difficult, tossing and turning, waters turn greasy. And right out of the chaos, Scylla and Charybdis show up, in between mother and son, their voices the lighthouse of my distant past guiding the way my limbs find land: *Son, you need to walk like a man! Brother, stop swinging your waist! Oh shut up, he's only teaching you how to be a man. Get inside the room, brother. Do you want to be a weakling like your father? I can only raise strong men. Don't shout. Shh shhh, men don't cry . . . help! Daa!* Daa!

Banging! I jump out of bed, panting, my ears are ringing, the contours of my past's ghosts sharp on my vision. "Kobby!" my dad's shouting, "hey, I'm here!" Too late. Always late from work. I stretch out in the chalk outline of my spit and mucus, the smell of my entrails more comforting to lie in than my sheets. Ringing. My phone, Elton. Is he rescuing me? Not Elton.

"Kobby, you've been avoiding my calls—"

"I'm home."

"Why? Listen, you can come to mine now. What do you need? I can send an Uber over right now."

"I just want to sleep."

On the other end, a sigh. "Well, you know you can't do that over there. Hey, I'm always here for you. I just need to know if you still want to work for me. All this hide-and-seek in the past few days has me worried. You'll always have me, but you might not have a job for long if you keep this up."

"I'll send something this minute. Been working on a story."

"I hope so. I'll be expecting it. But I need you to be here. That's all I'm asking. I need you to be present." Line dies.

I stare at my phone's blank word-processor until my dad's knocking subsidies.

5:37 A.M. *How do you begin a murder story starring a curious foreigner and an opportunistic local without giving away the entire plot—who died and why? You start with the obvious villain.*

VI

KOBBY

(13 days after the friends arrive)

My younger self walks through the church doors, and our eyes find each other's. This experience is nothing of the hypothetical sort expressed in the captions of millennial influencers, online posts, and blogs titles such as: "A Letter To My Younger Self, or If You Were To Go Back In Time . . . What Would You Say To Your Younger Self?" ("This generation of adults with our abrasive upbringings," my boss says, "the reason all of us—in spite of Boomer derision—are writing memoirs at *such wee ages*.") I know it's him, not for the coincidental scar on his forehead or the familiar route by which his attention circumvents the fan-clustered ceiling before slipping into mine, but for our shared mannerisms: the saucer-shaped curve of his shoulders, the way he glances at girls his age and imitates that feminine postural discipline. I know it's him when a hefty Bible is thwacked on his head for crossing one knee over the other. And for those seconds his mother berates him *sotto voce*, her lips balled into a narrow slit through which the dark alley of her diastema can be spied, blood from my abscessed tooth spills onto my tongue. Dear Younger Self, it gets easier after you've slammed a crowbar into your mother's cheekbones.

"Heavens to Kobby." Elton waves a hand across my thoughts and directs my gaze to the pastor on the podium hyperventilating into the mike, his sermon ballooning in him before it's vomited at the congregation. And there's Nana, waiting beside the pastor, or racing before him, a surfer twisting through a wave, or a translator, a face-wiper, a collar-fixer, unsure what action to take next. Eventually he performs all his duties simultaneously, tackling English and sweat and crooked ties, smoothing his pastor's delivery for a reverential applause from the members of Santa Maria Jesus Loves Me Church.

"Not gonna lie, Nana's fierce up there," Scott remarks, clapping as well.

"He's in his element," Vincent says. "When he's not cooking beans and fish, he's feeding multitudes with the living word, praise Jesus!"

My hands are secured into my underarms, obstinate about lauding Nana's efforts, his periphrastic translation in which images and symbols his audience might find more useful are invoked for interpretation—sometimes at the expense of the message's intent. It's an almost competitive stance between translator and pastor, where the former's one foot ahead, relying on humour—the way a Peace FM broadcaster might—to oust his master, making the sermon a lot more exciting than it is. Basking in everyone's praise, Nana's wiping his own face and shiny skull, aligning his bow tie; his smile widens until his jaw refuses to accommodate it anymore. He turns toward me. He watches me run my palms over my neck, suggestively. This makes him white as his suit.

NANA

I don't know why Vincent and friends bring the devil to church. In the invitation envelope that I gave them, I did not tell them to bring the Ananse too. Scott told me not to worry and that Kobby will not come even when I didn't say that I don't want him here. Maybe he was lying when he said Elton didn't want to see Kobby again because they find out that he's not a good person. But maybe the Ananse has use his evil spirit to fool Elton too much that Elton can't stay away. This is a fundraising programme, not deliverance; that's why we invite new pastor to come preach and make people donate more. I keep my eyes from the Ananse as I do the Lord's work. But sometimes, when my eyes move from church pastor to his wife, to the deacon and the elders who are sitting front row and who have to make sure that I am ready for the promotion of Chief Translator in the church, my eyes will fall on him and I'll remember how he makes me sick *ankasa*. But to God be the glory, no one will be harmed by God's own in God's church, just like the visiting pastor say.

When I clean the visiting pastor's face, I say in his ears that time is not on our hands so he should begin with the blessings because that is what make church members give plenty. More "you're blessed in your family" like Pastor Chris say is what works for this people, and maybe it will work for Vincent and his friends too. Because if they don't give big, plenty money, all the work I've done for them will be *kwasiasem*, like Kaly-bos say.

"Cain did not give and God didn't give."

"Cain de ne nsa to ne tiri etiemu sɛ, Awurade m'adi kwasiasem."

KOBBY

The sermon has reached its crux, judging by the breathlessness of the pastor. He punches the air, aims his words with his hands to the ceiling, calls forth the blessings of God in pseudo-poetic couplets that usher his audience into a passionate ovation for the God they serve, or for this man whose messages bear the gravity of empty promises delivered by politicians campaigning in working-class communities. With their peeling faux-gold earrings and scarves hiding unravelling braids, their yellowed armpits, and pages flying off their Bibles—all elements of self-denial to afford bountiful sacrifices, who's to say the men and women of this Santa Maria parish aren't deserving of a miracle? Though the members of this church are of a different social calibre than the ones I grew up with in mother's hoity-toity East Legon Presby, there's a uniformity in church culture which brings to mind hours of enduring parents screaming for the Lord in such arousing sentiments that might cause any bystander to be swayed by this veil of repentance.

I find my younger self again, now resting his head against the pew as he forlornly watches his mother toss herself into the air for yet another *Yesu ose yee/Yɛ De De Yɛ De De* chant. Dear Younger Self, in times that I become susceptible to what I've come to realise is a trick of the light on the depictions of a mother's love—triggered by scenes of a breastfeeding woman in a *troski*, a mother-toddler duo crossing a street hand-in-hand, even the mournful mien of a mother wilting over the loss of a child—I have to stop myself before these portrayals inspire a longing for a mother that never once was. Mothers don't owe us this proverbial love; life is enough. Now move on from romanticising this image of your mother demonstrating utmost love to a deity, who also looks the other way when you're being harmed . . . so you don't hesitate when the crowbar's pointing to the ceiling and there's nowhere it could land than down on your mother's head at whatever intensity you choose.

"Aaamen!" Vincent screams, swinging his hands like windscreen wipers.

"If you don't shout your Amen for your blessings, God will take them away from you!"

"So Black church is the same everywhere," Scott remarks disappointingly to another wave of Amens.

"So you come to church, you praise God, and He raises you!"

"Aaamen!"

"So you bless God with your treasures, He makes sure you worry less!"

"Aaamen!" Elton's laughing at Vincent's antics.

"I'm not joking, man. Y'all need to get your ass up and stop blocking your blessings—Aaamen!" Vincent is waving a handkerchief that has Pride colours.

"Does Vincent really think this is the best place to out us?" Scott's asking.

"Rainbows are a religious symbol too, Scott. Relax," Elton says.

"You're right," Scott concedes. "I could literally go all drag and catwalk to the pastor but no one will know. Everyone in this country has a shit gaydar. Even Mina, the Elmina waitress, whom I thought might know I like my coffee like I like my sex—with cream, kept sending me messages to meet her at the beach at midnight. Whatever it is she wanted, I knew I wasn't going to give her dick."

"Hey, are you okay?" Elton's asking me, giving my hand a squeeze. "You seem . . ."

I'm not sure what he's trying to communicate with these deliberate, intermittent acts of chivalry. Why can't we just fuck without these random displays of his interest? "Why do you like me? Why do you bother, Elton?"

"You don't like me back, why do you care?"

He stares at the pastor who has launched into a long monologue on sinful spirits. *The shpirit of adultery, the shpirit of forgetting to tithe, the shpirit of putting folded red notes in the offering bowl.* Subject to my scrutiny, Elton's bodily fluids go into overdrive—temples glistening, lips enduring an abnormal amount of tongue-smacking, fingers loosening their grip and turning moist in my palms. Yet I am too dehydrated, too greedy for a dose of affection, especially now when I'm chock-full with olanzapine and a psychedelic array of antipsychotics, when I'm surrounded by people who are at a loss on how to love their abused gay children, and whose only concern for me is that I swallow my meds. What's that ingredient that keeps drawing him to me, some redeeming quality that I'm not aware of which adds a sprinkling of light to my darkness?

"You possess a silent strength that I enjoy," Elton speaks. "I like that you're mysterious. I could watch you all day and never figure you out—"

"The *shpirit* of gayism!" This makes Elton jump. Scott is giggling.

"Gayism? Is that even a word?" Vincent turns to me. But the pastor has transgressed to other sins:

"The *shpirit* of premarital sex!"

"Some of you men are horrible in bed!" screams an old woman with a gele on a simple lace outfit that looks like a night-gown. The pastor continues unperturbed, and so does she, re-fusing to be bulldozed into silence. "You think we will let you trick us into marrying our daughters like the way you married us and told us that God doesn't want divorce." A group of ush-ers accost her. "If He doesn't want divorce, He should allow a test-ride!" They drag her out, her profanities building up resis-tance to the ensuing distance.

"Intense," Elton finishes. "Our sex is intense." As the church recovers from the spectacle, as the murmurs die down and the laughter fades, Elton turns to me, a move so swift and deter-mined I have to duck into the pew given his tendency to get frisky in the most homophobic spaces. What he does instead is less favourable than a kiss:

"What do you like about me?" he asks.

"The devil is a liar!" the pastor hollers.

"Aaaamen!"

Elton's searching for wilted roses on a gravestone.

"Hey, I'll be coming back," he tells me, urgently. "This ain't just a fling for me. It could be so much more." He pokes me in the rib. "Give in. Give *in.*"

If he's really listening, he should hear that my eyes are begging that he never comes back, that things are just good when they're fleeting. I've already begun vetting his replacements: other Year of Returnees who'll show up with their stories and their need for ephemeral affection as they ponder their history and heritage, relationships fuelled by hedonism and existing by the dates on return tickets.

"Oh, one more thing I like about you," he adds; I can smell the joke on his breath before he delivers it: "You talk to yourself a lot. Like every time I turn to you, I see your lips moving."

"You're lying!"

"Ha ha! No. Why do you think you always find me staring when you look my way?"

"Somehow, this is worse than I expected, it's not even something embarrassingly adorable as, 'Kobby, you snore in bed'—"

"No, I snore in bed, you talk to the air. See how we make a very unlikely but compatible pair." He pokes me again in the rib. "What do you like about me?"

I smile placidly as his face turns sour with each passing second of my silence. *I like it when your face breaks like it's a heart,* I refrain from saying.

"Now it's time for your donations," the pastor announces, saving Elton from my unwavering reticence in the face of his growing shame.

NANA

"It's time to show God the love God has shown you." The pastor say, walking around the offering bowl like he's a prayer warrior that can't stand at one place. He begins calling from

2,000 Ghana cedis. "Those with 2,000 Ghana cedis should come and put their money into the offering bowl." I don't need to do translation here because the Ghanaians understand the money he mentioned. Nobody come forward to give to the Lord. "Pastor say *dee w'amma no, ɔbosam gyam retwɛn no. Ebi mo wɔ asɔre ha, mo tutu obroni wawu firi container akɛse akɛse. Mo 2,000 cedis, old currency no twenty million, ɛwɔ hen? Mo di nyinaa asan akotu Obroni w'awu bio? Ei!*"

"I hear some Year of Return people are in the house, all of them should rise for me," pastor say. Everybody in the church turn to Vincent and his friends, they all look shy, Scott has put his hands on his face. "If you're not going to rise up for me, rise for the Lord." Vincent get up first and the whole church clap. Scott and Elton join, Elton wave at the church, *Medaase, medaase*, he say.

"Nana here tells me that none of you are married." I see the Ananse put his hand on his mouth trying not to laugh. "*Hwɛ, mmaa n'a mo wɔ asɔre yi, moanyere mo ho ara, Year of Return foɔ bɛ baa bɛ san mo akɔ ooo! Ɛsɛ sɛ mo kyekye ɔmo. Herh! Youth ministry, choiristers mo wɔ hen?*"

Vincent and his friends look so confused and the church laugh. So I decide to translate to English, "Pastor wants the young girls in this church, those who want to marry Year of Return people, to get up and come and choose!"

The pastor raise his hands to keep the church silent. "So if you want God to open marriage doors for you, come and bring the Lord 3,000 Ghana cedis." The whole church become quiet and they wait for the three friends. Vincent and his friends are whispering and shaking their head. General overseer and head pastor of Jesus Loves Me Church look at me from his chair in the front, he look at me like I have disappoint him and my face begin to die. Vincent and his friends are quiet for more than a minute.

KOBBY

Dear Younger Self, with your head over your mother's bosom seeking armistice where she's burning with fury, existing by coping measures until it becomes impossible to navigate the incendiary traumas swallowing your life whole. Where do you begin putting out the fires? Will you begin at church, where your mother tucks you into her loins the moment a certain evangelist—with a penchant for shouting *Holy Ghost Fire*—sees in you a gift that could be used in the Lord's service? Has she already heard the wildfire rumours of boys and girls singled out for their "gifts" and never returning the same? Will you begin at home, where Mother, in spite of *dumsor*, lights up a candle to hunt for the dolls, the *nkuro* cans improvised as cooking utensils, the toffee wrapper you use as lipstick? Has she yelled at your dad for being too soft on you, demanded he uses the ginger enema to burn up your anus so you remember to correct that Kojo Besia sway? When all fails, does she blame herself for marrying him, blame his Akan bloodline sullied with Ivorian gene pool (that scintilla colonial degenerative supplementation of French flair)—grounds for which paedos like Holy Ghost Fire Evangelist will target her boy? Will you begin in school, enrolled in Taekwondo and cadet? Does she alert your brother to keep an eye on you, your brother who takes after the strong men in her family? Unlike the halfway man your father is, this your brother is a fireball of a teen. He's got all the schoolgirls coming home with him. He even manages to *ron* the neighbour's mysterious daughter, who, after hours of bonding, braiding, and burning the ends of her wig extensions, confesses she's always yearned for a younger sibling—just as your mother, curious about the foul relaxer smell, walks in on her assisting with your first Jheri curl. Does Mother douse your hair with Omo? Does she attack your curls, scrubbing and sniffing, screaming and scrubbing, battling this indelible smell with a horror you won't exploit until university for your one-person production of *Macbeth*'s Act 5, Scene 1, a performance that will provoke an entire auditorium to unending pyrotechnic applause?

"Hey, Mr. Man!" A hand grasps my shoulders from behind, tilting my head to face the podium. "I'm the pastor talking, but you're looking at someone else." The entire church briefly turns to me after the preacher's admonishment. How long did I zone out for? Why are Elton and the others unseated, standing with their hands tucked behind them, mimicking the morose disposition of pallbearers before a coffin?

"Three thousand Ghana cedis so that the Lord will bless you all with a wife. In fact, you can pick one from this congregation after making this donation."

I snicker at the pastor's words. Over at the dais, Nana's sweating into the long-sleeved shirt donned under his suit, growing ashamed with each passing second the friends spend whispering to one another.

I find it irritating that after all Nana's chaperoning and cooking—services uncalled-for yet received without complaint, these three are unmoved by his unspoken pleas to show gratitude for his unremitting friendship. I slam my thighs on Elton's shin for his attention. "That's just a few hundred dollars when split amongst you three!" I whisper.

"Isn't that a lot?

"Nana deserves this!"

"I see he's consulting his treasurer, Mr. Man," the pastor comments, although Nana believing otherwise, serves a glare my way.

"Pastor, here's a hundred bucks each, that's all." Elton with his friends retrieves the notes.

"Dolllarrrrrs!!!" The pastor hollers into his mike. "Dollars!" The congregation replicates his frenzy, jumping about, screaming, others fighting to hug the friends. "Someone check the exchange rate for me." The pastor begins chanting, the instrumentalists offer the accompaniment to bolster his song, "Check the exchange rate for me! Check the exchange rate for me . . ."

"Two thousand and fifty Ghana cedis," Nana supplies, looking visibly relieved.

"That's not 3,000 Ghana cedis." The pastor cuts the excitement short. "Brothers of the Lord, I know you'll do anything to meet the Lord's demands."

Vincent puts up his hands in surrender, shaking his head, until I tap him and whisper, "An iPhone costs a lot more than the remainder—"

"So you want me to drop my phone into the bowl? Don't be silly, Kobby."

"Vince, Scott's using Milly's iPhone—"

"Well, I assure you the last thing Faisal will be doing right now is tracking his dead wife."

He ignores the concern he's inspired, and turns to Scott.

"Consulted his treasurer again. Let's see what he gives next." The pastor's expectant. He grasps Nana's shoulder blade and asks the latter to sing as the friends take their time. The whole church falls into the gravitational silence drawing subjects towards a singular event. This blanketing quiescence echoes Accra's ambiance during the 2010 FIFA World Cup semi-final penalty session, for which Asamoah Gyan missed his shot and caused nation-wide heartbreak, even if doing so had saved the lives of those who'd have gone joyriding had we advanced to the finals. But what good is a life lived with a heart that has upped and left? Gyan had driven lots to drink anyway, cursing their lot for being Ghanaian, this dual atrocity of suffering a failing economy and a national team that always qualified for tournaments only to publicise their shortcomings on a world stage. So when Scott pulls out Milly's iPhone and waves it in the air, he transports the congregation back to 2010, to an awards ceremony where Gyan and his teammates, victorious, had secured the World Cup. Plastic chairs begin clamouring. Tambourines clashing. Everyone's putting aside their differences and hugging whoever gossiped about them, whoever wore a popular print best, whoever snatched the lead part to cover a Sinach tune. I rise from my seat, journeying through this fog of revelry, to my Younger Self jumping on his pew. I'm extending an embrace metres away when his mother wags a finger at him, and complains, "When it comes to fooling you get so happy, *nso yɛ ka Bible asɛm deɛ* you'll be sleeping when the pastor is preaching, even if they use Yesu Bible to slap-slap your face you don't get up, *gyimie-hene*." I halt. Have I had it all wrong? Were you real? Have I, for my meds, been victimised by the materialisation of unresolved excruciations superimposing present circumstances?

"That was fun," admits Scott, the last to slide into the waiting Uber after exhausting the celebratory fuss showered on him.

"You felt like a king, huh? Like an *Ashantihene*," Vincent says, referencing the moments Scott had been mounted on the shoulders of the pastor and paraded around the church.

"Pure ecstasy!" Scott breathes into my ear. "Although I'm pissed we had to hand over that phone."

"Where to, bosses?" the driver demands, tracing his fingers over Google Maps' UI.

"Ridge," Elton offers.

"Not what the map's saying, bosses."

"Kaneshie." Everyone turns to me. "I got something I need y'all to see."

"Y'all?" Scott shrills, "Y'all? Brian's rubbing off on you, and soon you might be dating too many Black people."

"Scott," Elton hisses.

Any indication that we're in motion is evinced from the car's constant ascension and plunging. Otherwise, the windows present a repetitive reel of uncompleted buildings, wooden kiosks, gutters suffocating with plastic, wounded roads plied by dusty cars and little boys lugging jerry cans. Vincent, seated in front, has opinions about the unequal levels of development in Accra. *As do NY and LA,* Elton counters. *No one has said those cities do not have their faults . . .* I tune out of the conversation, a comforting blankness slowly tugs over my head, makes my eyelids droop, expunges the brown preset of the shanty communities we pass, until all that's left is darkness . . .

"Kobby." When I come to, we've arrived at our destination. The friends are already out of the car and are eyeing me suspiciously as I dismount from the Uber Mantis. We're in a junkyard staring at a shack made of corrugated tin and other car parts salvaged from the surrounding ruins.

"Are you sure we're at the right place?" Vincent sounds doubtful. Yet, behind me, I hear their fricative padding against the gluey silt.

"I'm your tour guide, am I not?"

We enter the shack and the whole salon stands erect like an impala investigating a potential threat. Early Sunday, and judging by the condition of the place—no hair in sight, every inch spruced with care, spotless but for the corruscating dots shining through the leaks in the roof—it's possible we're the first batch of intruders. The hairdressers, upon recognising me, quickly direct their puzzled expressions to the three friends of dubious origins and unknown intentions. When the kinetics haven't kicked in yet, and Vincent isn't rotating his wrist while speaking, and Scott's not pouting to the actions of others he considers absurd, and Elton hasn't donned his leering gaze that remains anywhere but the faces of men he interacts with, one might encounter some frustration in pinpointing the orientation of these strangers. The three strategically avoid the curious gazes of our unsuspecting hosts as they wait on me for some form of introduction. The friends glance around the shack with such wide-eyed wonder that I experience a momentary jealousy for their fresh pairs of eyes in viewing: the walls with galactic arrays of showbizzy photos chronicling (visibly queer) patrons and their loc histories; the hairdressers, these translunary men without whom a place like this might feel uninspiring as a barren night sky. Whatever mystery I'd teased into the airs with which I'd unveiled the location has elapsed, and soon, the hairdressers, for Scott's knowing winks to his friends, have inserted the last piece of the puzzle which would reveal that these outsiders, with their heterosexual composures and fashions, are homos, or to put it crudely as one of them does: *trumu-trumu foɔ no bi*. The persisting silence bulges in the shed until it becomes clear that there's been some disruption in energies, causing the diminutive manager at the backroom to holler and enter, resembling a paternal character in a Black sitcom having fuck all to do backstage yet emerging with a prop that implied otherwise, primed to deliver their lines:

"*Mɛni sane po nɛ.* Mr. English, you know this place is a loc'ing salon, why have you bring to me three men who have no hair? *Obroni no ferɛ ne sɛn . . .*" They turn to their workers: "*Bold*, why have you bring me three *bold* men?"

It would be wrong to let my meds take the fall for what I, with my own free will, under the pretext of presenting a heterogeneity to the city's scene, had decided was a great idea: bringing the friends to the occupational premises of these queer men for matters unrelated to monetary resolutions. As though this is some stint in poverty tourism, an exhibition where guests can ruminate on their privilege while being thankful for not ending up in this double-whammy of queer quandary: to be both a victim of a country's laws and its endemic impoverishment. My conscience takes on Brian's voice, and I bristle at his acerbic critique, but the old manager, upon glimpsing the concerns scripted over my features, grins and says:

"Year of Return *foɔ no bi*?" They approach Vincent. "Mr. English, next time you're bringing friends over, call *ansa*! *Ofee lucky akɛ ŋmɛnɛ* Sunday." They clasp Vincent's hand. "Do you want us to do bonding?" Said mimicking a British accent, "We have nice wig locs that'll cover your *bold* hair."

Vincent's laughter is hammy. "I'm Vincent, these are my . . . friends, Scott and Elton."

"You two want wigs?" They rush to Elton and Scott, shaking them vigorously. Scott curtsies, his humility a new component of his condescending parts I've never witnessed until now. "Friends, they came all the way from America just to look at us? Switch on the radio. Put it on Peace FM. *Twaa* Abeiku Santana *oha mi, ebaa tswa wɔ lalaa.* If these people want a—*obroni no fɛrɛ no*—circus we'll give it to them. *Aloo?*"

"It's fine," says Vincent, apologetic, "we can leave, we meant no harm."

"Sire, leave for where? You came to see me, the Queen. You have never heard of me, huh? They call me Mama Di Mama. You can't just come to my salon and leave without paying respects. Properly." They turn to their employees, speaking with a sense of urgency, "Abeiku Santana, where's he? *Tswaa lɛ ohami.*" One of the workers runs over and hands the phone. "Abeiku, Mama Di Mama is who's speaking, *ofainɛ, isaloonɛ efee dull, mini kɛ gospel?* Sunday so we can't be—*obroni no fɛrɛ no sɛn*—secular? *Tswaa wɔ lala* so we can make things go sharp-sharp?" Elton and his friends keep their eyes on me for the entire duration of the call, their faces a gallery of pained and fascinated expressions.

Hmm . . . Sugar Daddy

"This be KaySo from Tema!" The hairdressers shout as the song booms from the radio.

And so begins the expression of energies restrained in bodies. We don't just dance, we're in transcendence, numinous and free—for this I am certain, proven by my boss's words, *If you want to know someone who's free, watch how they dance.* Under the perforated ceiling all of our parts are awashed with spots, those which we've spent years hiding. We're animals and diseased, a community cast far and wide, but for our dots, we will forever be connected. According to the manager, who mounts themselves onto a table, "This is church! And let the sinners praise the Lord!" *Hallelujah*, the workers ululate, triumphant over some victory unknown. Vincent browses the images on the walls with an enlisted attendant who barely listens to the former's interrogations, torn between duty and dance. Scott is cornered next to a shelf of oils, the perimeters of his face patrolled by bristles wielded by a clique under the supervision of one strikingly made-up employee who also records the ordeal for a disembodied audience: *Y'ahyase ankasa, makeups wei me ara na me yɛɛ ye.*

Nothing escapes digital documentation, which is why Elton is subjected to speaking engagements as a Hollywood big shot: *Yo what's up it's your boy, producer, label executive, Elton from the West Coast chilling with my friends in Accra, Ghana, Africa*—"Tell them you're coming to share green cards," a staff member embodying a makeshift teleprompter dictates—*We giving out tons of green cards, visas, short-term, long-term, you wanna come to New York you gotta come through me.* It's no surprise he exceeds expectations, sending the members of his camera crew running elsewhere and assaulting their keypads with giddy mischief. I'm making the most of my wakefulness, swaying, before my drugs enforce their curfew on the little sunshine pulsing through my veins—this little light of mine that won't shine because of the self-centred radio presenter desperate to be heard over his music. This little light of mine that can't shine thanks to Elton. Who, in spite of his commitments, always finds time to grind against me or simply entrap my waist in a grip that defies secession. The only respite I'm allowed for his intrusions occurs when I think of his imminent departure. It excites me. Soon I won't have to deal with his habit of seizing my attention into his fingers, a flaw making him human in a manner I find most unbearable, a desperation to inveigle oneself into another's affections, another's skin. A parasitism of dystopian disposition wherein others are reduced to hosts, persons for whom volitional independence—even for momentary escapism—is outlawed.

My phone rings too loud. Elton agrees to a separation so I can answer it. Not a call. Just another email whose *Hello Kobby, Thanks for submitting to us but* . . . is truncated in the notification panel. Do rejections ever lose their sting? Whatever the occasion, they can never be well-timed. Whichever format—personal or prototype, there's still an afflictive "but" around which all other text crumbles. I try to dress up the ache with a laugh, a little pirouette that catches Elton by surprise. Ha! Elton has me in a dip, dangling a hair's breadth from this slough of despond, of drugs and pasts and dashed publishing dreams.

"Hey, are you okay?" Elton is concerned.

"Yeah, I'm fine." He props me up. "I just need to pee. Is there a bathroom somewhere here?"

"Owula," the manager instructs, "don't do number two, go straight. Take the door on your left hand when you go inside my office . . ."

Hey, I'm already texting Aspecialkindofdouble as I head for the manager's backroom, *another rejection just came in, I don't know, maybe I'll write that colonial/slavery novel after all.* The little kiss emoji doesn't survive the bleak backroom, it's backspaced before the message is sent, in case it betrays my current state enough to warrant a call. Today I do not possess the restraint that keeps one from coming undone in a public toilet.

I almost miss it, if not for the stream of light gushing through the rusting wire mesh windows, which illuminates the crisp-white toilet, the bucket of water seated near the exposed tank, the off-white floor tiles, my dust-drenched feet, and brushes past me into the backroom. Even then, I have to succumb to the curiosity aroused by the fumy essence lurking in the air, the glimmering shavings littering the floor, the row of slender silvery bars arranged over the working desk. The bars' edges are barely sharp when I run my thumb across their shapes, possibly about to be worked into needles soon. My gaze fetches the outline of the mallet, and another which should be a tool sharpener concealed with a blackened work-cloth. I'm more interested in the exercise book labelled "Jotter/Inventory," which takes me back to my school days with its illustration of Lady *GEStice* in all her graduation/matriculation garb.

"Toilet paper *na wo hwe-hwe anaa*?"

After what's transpired during these seconds of unmasking the secrecy of the backroom, a novel harshness has invaded their voice. And as they close the distance between us, the eclipsing light behind them becomes dimmer, sharpening their form and diminishing the mystery that enshrouds them.

"So you make these needles yourself, yet somehow they come from Mali?"

"If I *kra* them from Mali, can you buy?" They slap my hand away from the book and flick open the pages. "You see how many of you come for my needles?" Their fingers trace the rows and columns of their tabulations containing tallying strokes, an expansive documentation of names represented by abbreviations of unreasonable lengths.

"All these people are part of the community?"

"What do you think? The whole of Africa, we are number five for people going to internet cafe to look at gay porn . . ." They pull out a drawer, fishing, from underneath the tray of finished needles, a foolscap bearing similar records as that of the jotter but with pictures and what appears to be names . . .

I chuckle. "The boy selling foes at Accra Central—"

"The first person who came for the needles. Met him ten years plus. Now has one wife and one child. He invited me to the wedding just one month after the first and only person he killed." They don't linger over the last word as though it's of negligible concern. "What name do you think I gave to you?"

"I don't know, the boy in a *tro-tro*?"

"*Wonnim* how many people I see in a *tro-tro* . . . but you're *costomer* so I should find you fast."

"So what's up with the other names that no longer bear tallying strokes?"

"Some of them travelled and some of them don't want to do this gay thing anymore. I don't blame them. Men are hard to love. Men in this Ghana are too hard to love. *Kanzo sɔɔ. Kanzo* can even be chewed. I've seen you." They stop at a page. "The shy boy in the Kasoa-to-Accra 207 *tro-tro.*"

There's a picture of me just when my locs were in their budding stage, taken here at the shop without my knowledge. All the years of my visits detailed on the single page dedicated to me. There's a fastidiousness about the entire documentation—bearing scribblings commenting on my mood during every encounter, the recurring letters Q-U-I-E-T standing out among all the other text—which leaves me impressed and iffy at the same time.

"See these." They flip through several pages that have been crossed with giant X's. One glimpse at their trembling hand is enough to betray what the markings symbolise.

"This guy." They spread their palms over the gravestone of this crossed-out page. "He was only twelve when we saw each other. In university six years later where they killed him. The only time he forget his needles, the only time, because he thought it was a hook-up." They pause, "In this book too, you'll find his friend who went to confront the gang people that killed him and I never heard from him again." More literary graves are uncovered: the guy who was found in an Agbogbloshie rubbish dump, another sex worker framed as a thief and publicly mobbed, woman killed by her husband after she'd found out he was *trumu-trumu* people and then he killed himself too. My fascination with grim stories cannot save my gag reflex from the incoming sick fucking up the ambience in my mouth. The book is tossed back into the drawer as soon as its owner realises the effect it's having on me. A window is cracked open, which does nothing for the smell of decomposing bodies clogging my nose. "But also," they speak, "if I call you for two years and you do not answer, I'll cancel your name."

"I'll not be dying anytime soon."

They stand still. "Kobby, we met in a very bad place. I don't put it down here but I know you more than I know some of these people. I've seen you grow. Even saw you at Jamestown one time with a nice white man. See, I meet people who have been sacked from their house. People who come here so sad they want to talk all day and then take my small money that I have too. But you, you won't even talk. If I don't delay you with dancing when you come to collect the needles, I'll never see you smile. If you're the one doing all these Sasabonsam killings, I don't want to know . . . everyone killed by my needles deserve the killing. I want them to die before I see any of you die."

In all the times I've met this person, a certain revelation was at hand. Their gestures possessed a secretive shrewdness that I only discerned in fleeting moments. As if they were slowly rationing their identity. As if they were undecided about whether I could endure the complete manifestation of their genius. As if, had they revealed to me just a smidgen of their malice, I'd have failed to recognise it for what it truly was: an act of subversive paternity. Wherein, they wax those parts of me others have sought repairs for, rescue me from under the vehicular weight of society's gender-roles, possess a hard-wired functioning to kill in order to protect—standards biology, with all its birthing fuss, of anti-epidural deliveries and free births, sniffing newborn scents and breastfeeding to foster connections has failed to live up to. Makes you wonder which arbitrary power above decides who gets what and why.

"Oh, you're crying?" They envelop me into a fortress that's at once strange and familial, an overdue affection that's also primal, as if it's been present from the very beginning. Into the whiffs of talcum powder and Johnson's baby oil, scents whose encounters would henceforth stimulate memories of the warmth of a father's arms, I come undone.

I pull away just to sneak in a joke, "But *wo* record-keeping *yɛ* bad."

"Kobby?" Elton's knocking on the door.

"Herh! What have you done to this Black American? What 'For Girls' did you do? *Anaa kɔte bɛn or trumu bɛn na wo wɔ n'ama man yi di w'akyi togbɛɛ-togbɛɛ.*" I laugh so hard they right me up in spite of our height difference. "Show me your tricks. Help your asexual uncle get an American Borga too. *Oyɛ sure akɛ oyɛ fine?* Don't cry again, okay?"

VII

NANA
(Day 14, day of departure)

Vincent and his friends are going back to America.

We are going to have our last food together before they go. I tell them I'll cook, I'll cook. But they say, no, they want to treat me nice, they want to take us all out to go eat at Labadi Beach Hotel, something they call Branch. They pack. I try to help. They tell me no, no, we'll pack ourselves. In the end, I just sit there feeling useless and watch them. They take the paintings I got them for cheap price. They take the wooden mask that look like what fetish priest have at their shrine. I told them it's Juju, but they didn't mind me and let the Ananse get it with them when I'm not around. The last and important thing they take is the picture frames I parcel and give all of them. Scott reads his: *To Scott, you are truly a good friend. I appreciate the friendship we've got to share in the shortest time. Come back one day and let us pick up where we left off. You have really made my days splendiferous, magnanimous, and quite interesting to say the least.*

"Aww, Nana, I didn't know you've got so much . . . (poetry) in you," Scott say. Vincent throw a cushion at his head. Vincent and Elton read their own and realise it's the same. Pastor didn't have the time to write different-different ones for them.

I wanted to write on it:

Mpaninfoɔ se . . .
ɔkwantentene akwaaba na ɛyɛ

Which if you take it directly from Twi,

it mean:

The elders say

It is good to be welcomed from afar.

But true Ashanti people know it mean:

If you return from a long and hard journey, you are re-spected. In Twi there's no word for goodbye. Even when you die, we never say goodbye. I can't say goodbye, Vincent. We say, you and God should go. You and God should go and don't forget that you have a Ghanaian brother and the promise you made him about the visa.

"Even Kobby didn't give us a (plaque)," Scott say to Elton.

Elton laugh. "We'll see him at Labadi. You can ask him for his gift."

"Thank you so much, Nana. For all this. For everything." Vincent walk to me.

"Don't mention," I say to him. He hug me hard. And slap my back.

Scott shout. Some *kotokurodu* have fly into the room. Looks like a witch someone has send to make sure Vincent and friends don't have God's travelling mercies to America; so that some-thing bad will happen to them on their way back. I do fast-fast and jump and kill it. Scott say to me that I should not come to him for sanitiser for the bee that have die *chaka-chaka* in my hands.

"Here you go." Vincent spray for me his sanitiser to clean the blood on my hands.

"Elton?" A voice shout from the outside of the room.

"Hello?" Elton walk to the door and open it with the code.

"Management wants you to pack out before we clean," a woman voice say. I know the voice. She's the woman who brought us to this room on the first day, the day Elton try to kiss me. Two weeks have passed, but it feels like it happen yesterday. Was it not yesterday that this Ananse came into the life of me and my friends when I decide not to kiss Elton?

Something they teach me that I won't tell Pastor: Buttocks sex is not really bad, in fact, it's very good, very sweet, you ejaculate faster-faster and that's good since premarital sex is a sin and you shouldn't make it keep long.

"Can we leave our things and come back for them? We're going to have *branch* at Labadi."

"No, a new guest is arriving today. You'll have to take your luggage with you."

Vincent and Scott walk to the door when they hear the woman speak. I follow them.

"There's no way around this, I'm sorry. Especially after the (complaints) management have (accrued) on your balcony behaviour." The woman tries to use that smile she use on Scott the first day we come. But Scott say this is nonsense, this is unbelievable. "I'm sorry, sirs." The woman step back to leave. "Oh, also please make sure you give out the new code to enter the (apartment) to security, the system shows you've changed it." Then she leaves with her *kronchia* shoes and the trousers only women my pastor calls Pagan wear. Nice buttocks. Bad attitude. She remind me of Mina. Her English nice too like a Fante woman.

"What are we doing now?" Vincent ask. "If we take our bags to Labadi, it'll be a lot of work (hauling) them around. Not that we can't do that. But I didn't anticipate such a hassle on our last day."

"My brother is in the prison officer quarters," I tell them. They look at me like I'm crazy. "He's brother from another mother, but same father." They still look at me with that their raised eyes. "We can go keep your bags there. It's close to the airport."

Elton and Scott and Vincent look at each other. They raise their shoulders together.

"Great, let's do that. We should get another taxi and put all our bags in there. Thanks, Nana." Vincent slap me on the back again.

We don't take long to reach my brother's place. We all put

the bags in his bungalow. Elton gives my brother some money. My brother salute at him.

"That's some (impressive) drills (display)," Scott say as we leave in the taxi. The uniform men are doing their calapartayyy attention and at-ease positions on the field. "Look at all these men, damn."

"Wishing they were at Brian's club?" Vincent ask.

"Aye, aye captain."

The taxi driver and me laugh as if we understand anything.

"These are not even prison officers," the driver say.

"Yes," I tell Vincent and his friends. "They are very bad and wicked prisoners that the government have sent to do reform: the real officers are inside their messes." I point the officers who are standing behind the iron rods in front of their bungalow. "These prisoners came just this morning to be reformed. Our president Nana Akufo-Addo is a wise man, nobody has—"

"Ei, CPS! Chief Propaganda Secretary," the taxi driver say.

It's the same driver that we pick when we were coming the first day. He gave me his number in case the Americans wanted to be driven around and see town, but I didn't call him. *Ei, Asantefo paa!* He complained to me when I call him today. I tell him the Americans rent a car and that he should forgive me. I don't tell him that if it was not for the Ananse I would have remember.

Elton asks me what's the name of the bungalow. I tell him. He text it into his phone. I tell him I'll come with him to pick it up and we'll all go to the airport together.

I look at Elton who look sad, like a dog crying for bones. He likes the Ananse, I can see. I'm happy the Ananse is not here to spoil my happiness. I don't want him to be around. I want to be the last person who sees my friends go. I am the one who brought them. So I must take them.

VIII

KOBBY

T
he role of narrators in stories can be best described by
alluding to the wind . . .'" My boss's voice diminishes,
her charcoal lips assuming the shapes of my words in
susurrations snaking the expanse of her office, which is white
and luminous, the kind of place you might encounter Morgan
Freeman cast as God. She pushes down the lid of her MacBook
and smiles at me. "How are you doing today?" I nod. "You
know, when I told you that line about narrators, I really only
intended it for journalists, and that's what I'm sure I said: the
role of *journalists* . . ." I tune out where possible, listening instead to the pleasant ASMR effect of her gestures: the shh-shh
traction of her nails combing through the melted blonde fron-
tal, the cash-counter whirring of the paperbacks (*When I Hit
You, Feel Free, Stay with Me, In the Dream House*) whose fore-
edges she flicks, and even the chinking of her ring finger over
the glass desk whenever she's emphasising a point. Her motions
are song and steel and surrender. No wonder men launch themselves at her like hopeless sailors at the hands of sirens, even
if she lives by a strict selection algorithm that embraces few:
only wealthy, only in their fifties, and very recently—an ongoing
theme she's set for this Year of Return—only "nice reparational
gentlemen," to which she elaborates, "living my best Tamera
life on the down low," and adding, for those who might get the
reference, "doing hot Queenie shit—only without the utter lack
of self-regard."

According to her, the only reason I had the job was (by no favouritism played against the suited, cookie-cutter graduates who were all pageantry cover-letters and no personality, but) for my answer to her question, What is your "awakening book?"—a term for fiction that stirs one from lifelong slumber. *What is your awakening book, Kobby, what is it? Mine's* Americanah, *for it was released at a time that I needed someone like Ifemelu to describe what I'd felt like but never been able to put into words on being both immigrant and student in one of the whitest universities. My position in the world as a Black woman, from the politics of my scalp to the politics of my skin, my identity as African, and how said identity had to be shrunk in this cold place with people of harsher interiors.* My awakening book was *American Psycho*—a response received with a pained expression, an overall anti-climatic disposition that one could equate to the feeling of purchasing an over-hyped book only to be let down on page one for its pedestrian style. As she pulled off her wig and said, *Well, at least it's not* 48 Laws of Power, raked her fingers through her cornrows—whether to convey her dismay, or to unmask this new persona she'd brought with her from the UK, it occurred to me that her literary tastes had been hammered and moulded. Radicalised. No longer the girl who, with her obsession for dark, occultist, Dan Brown-esque novels, would share stories of spirits brought from the afterlife with rituals and body-parts. The reason I rushed to hers after slamming a crowbar into mother's cheek to summon my brother's spirit, forcing into her foyer while screaming, *Yaa*, and hearing her name played back to me in echoes. *Yaa. Yaa. Yaa.* Finding a cavity where a family had once lived. Her house evacuated so meticulously I was left wondering if she'd only been as real as a friend imagined.

"Ugh." A timely interjection, as if she were listening in on my thoughts. She rushes to the windows, redirecting her concerns to the sun: "You're told, use sunscreen! But the recommended sunscreen gives you a white cast, and then you change for another that doesn't, and you're told this new one could be the possible cause of cancer. Then one Google search leaves you bombarded with more ads for more sunscreens that don't do the shit they say. This brave new world where surveillance capitalism gives you cancer. What post-industrial, post-apocalyptic mess are we living in . . ." Her language becomes indebted to a profundity where words are lengthier and meaning is tangled with overwhelming rhetoric, a verbal diarrhoea impossible to deconstruct, and with which she makes coprophagic advances, pawing through this phrasal sludge to unearth a new thread of thought. It is the silence she fears, awkward vents in our interactions when we're face-to-face with our younger selves and a slew of unresolved issues tackled through shouting matches. Like that time in Lagos '15 when I was verbally KO'd and called a rape apologist after accusing her of killing my abuser; "*. . . he was my abuser too!*" were her final words. Then, there was the Busua '18 fight, which I could only win by resorting to emotional blackmail: "*Look at me! I'm now stuck in this loop of seeking post-mortem justice against two people who were taken from me before I had the chance to fight back.*"

". . . You know," Yaa continues, having adjusted the air-conditioning temp, "through all this, I consider the silver lining, which is to say, for every traumatic experience this world puts me through, my memoir is going to be fucking banging! I'm going to cash in big on my traumas, you'll see! Which is why I'm not a big fan of auto-fiction, you know? All these writers confessing to things that'll get them thrown in jail, or worse, cancelled. But there's auto-fiction immunity now, blanket impunity to anyone who dresses crimes as fiction. So tell me why, Kobby, do you think auto-fiction will work well in a newspaper that puts out hard facts? You must have sent me the wrong file. You must be laughing on the inside right now." She hovers on the right arm of my seat like a shoulder angel, her brassiere popping into my lateral sight. "I'm not saying our paper isn't good for your writing. We're fucking global, we're the plug to the diaspora community, no matter how many times the government has refused us funding for influencers who engage in selective diasporism, who only interact with Ghanaians of their ilk having Ivy degrees, elitist pedigrees, and familial ties with the Big Six. Parties and bubbly, that's the representation of Ghana these government-appointed returnees are marketing to the world. All I'm saying is, if you've got a novel in you, write it, but this is not the kind of stuff we publish here . . ." She stretches to her desk, returns with a bundle of newspapers which she dumps onto my lap, walks back to her seat. "Now here's a story that's going to take the newspaper mainstream. From our niche audience into the hands of anyone else with a brain."

Mina and Faisal are sprawled over the front pages of each paper. They look as beautiful dead as they were alive. Their nudity, along with the mulch of maggots and feathers, money and egg yolk spread over their corpses, gives these photos an editorial quality. I imagine that if these images were in a more glossy medium, I may come upon them scattered across a coffee table and marvel at their avant-garde interpretation of death and the hereafter, as well as wonder about the artist and his influences. And Nana. Who had been kind enough to grant Mina and Faisal the grace of a bloodless death, something only afforded by monarchs, a transition from sleep into demise. One paper refers to him as the Fetish Priest Killer, a pseudonym I'm certain would be popularised like the Sasabonsam Killer.

"Kobby?" My boss snaps me out of my reverie. "Are you listening? Are you on your meds? I hope you've not been zoning out. Two deaths in Elmina. It's huge. Tourist paradise turns hell. The government is shit-scared they're going to lose a shit-ton of money if the culprit isn't brought to book . . . Luckily for us, and unlucky for them, no one has turned in this shit to any of the foreign news networks, but if this is published together with the recent Sasabonsam killings—which the government has managed to keep out of all the big local papers by imposing restraint, threatening them with lawsuits for spreading terror on the basis of hearsay, oh we will strike gold! Ghana gold. Naturally, there will be consequences, court appearances where I'll wear neat pantsuits with a smattering of breasts—*abi you know dadaa*—to confuse those judges. Oh, we'll find out the hard way what these politicians are capable of if anyone gets in the way of their Year of Return dollars . . ."

It doesn't take long for her to relapse into her "The government this, the government that" rant. She's, as always, malicious whenever she speaks on the government's ills. Ejecting from her seat, levelling her directives at me with a stabbing nail.

The gore her parents sought to correct—earning her a life abroad due to Ghana's poor clinical psychology infrastructure—has moved on from its pursuit of human lives and now lusts for the government's blood. A new anarchic insanity, which only Britain could instill in its minorities, and which, upon her return to Ghana, could have been managed if her ambitions for cronynomics had successfully steered her towards the path of governmental appointments and contracts. Once, she insisted, in endless spiel, the reason we were so close as kids was because we recognised we were both queer, and despite her parents' efforts to "straighten out her ways," nothing could be done. "Because that's what identity is," she added, "immutable, isn't like energy, cannot be converted or changed, just repressed." In my version of why we'd been close, queerness had nothing to do with it; rather, our closeness could be linked to her favourite word: malice. "Malice," according to the company catchphrase, "is inherently present in every human. We have a duty as writers to unearth it, to find that which each one of us conceals." This is the bedrock for our prevailing relationship: that we know what each of us is capable of if given the chance to unleash what evil selves our medications have suppressed. Hence, this freedom to reveal our unsavoury bits to the other without restraint or fear of being judged is—weird as it may seem—love. I love her.

"Kobby? Are you listening?"

"I'm sorry. I'm just wondering what the killer's motives were. These two people are . . . they look like the least threatening people."

She plunges into her seat, looking deflated. "I have got my own theories as to how this murder happened." She turns away from me, stares at a bin on the left of her desk. "I know the guy in the photo. I mean, who didn't know Faisal? Cambridge class of 2011, was a star. Tall, eloquent, intelligent. That Fulani success story where a boy set to take over the herding of his father's cows is granted scholarship in the world's prestigious university, saving him from a Western construct of poverty into a future of diversity lawn-photo ops for enrolment brochures and those obnoxiously ubiquitous IG higher-ed ads. Back then, you knew all the Black kids in uni, you ran into them on campus on an almost daily occurrence, and if they were Ghanaian you'd see them way too often." She chuckles, somewhat painfully. "*We were seeing each other*. At least that's what I thought until the white bitch who'd later be his wife came into the picture. Didn't even have the balls to officially end things with me. And now look at him, ended." Her face rearranges into a snarl, a look that takes me back to those seconds before she shoved my brother off Kakum Canopy walk. "That stupid piece of cadaver in those papers is the reason I returned to Ghana! Because of him I suffered a decompensation, God knows how I got through the final years of school." I reach out to clasp her hands but she bats my attempt away. "I think the white bitch killed him, which is surprising because she was such a fucking dunce. She'd tweet shit like her freckles were her body's remembrance of the time it had been African or the 'ɛyɛ original plastic chair foforɔ a aba' chant was a muezzin call.

Anyway, glad she took him out herself, because I would have done it had the opportunity risen. My theory is she caught him fucking this new woman and killed them both, modelled the crime scene like a shrine so no one would accuse her, so everyone would think it's some fucking Fetish Priest Killer. Really, she is so fucking smart now that I think of it. You should never underestimate a white woman. You need to find her, Kobby, she has the answers."

My phone buzzes, an influx of messages now surfacing because of the weak WiFi signal. All texts from Elton informing me of his whereabouts. I tap the silent icon. "I've got to leave. I'll be packing for Elmina, will set off tonight."

"I'll send you the booking information." She says this as I'm headed for the door. "Let me know if you encounter any problems. And Kobby, is your dad okay?"

"We ruined his life, what do you think?"

She nods. "Glad to have you back. Hopefully, everything's great on your end, your dates, your hook-ups, whatever it is you're doing these days. And listen, you really can stay at mine if you'd rather not go home. If you won't come over for yourself, come over for me. I sincerely miss how close we used to be in the days of Lagos and Busua. Also, a memory: do you remember when we used to call it para*sister*mol because it was the only sibling that cared enough to take away the pain—"

"Hey, so our first time in Lagos . . ." I hesitate.

"Yes? What about it? We've said all our apologies; there's no reason to reopen old wounds."

"It's not about us. I wanted to know if you've still got Chibueze's contact. I'd like to get in touch."

"What for? If this is to rekindle whatever went on between you two, trust me, Chibueze is the wrong person for any kind of rekindling. I know. I know. I've seen some of the men you date and I sometimes think that you see yourself as some—I don't know—Fairytale Jesus, do you know what I mean? Turning frogs into princes with a kiss. But honestly, Chibueze? That one's a mess—"

"You literally said he's a good choice!" I cringe, more for my incorrect use of "literally" than my sudden temper. "That night, you even put together a few couple names for us! Kobueze! Chibuby!"

"I guess I did . . . drink too much. Anyway, you were being such a moral exhibitionist I didn't think you were having fun."

Our spatial relation, along with this room and its furnishings, cautions to desist from breaching the existing boss–employee gap. I refrain from yelling. "Yaa, you're not telling me something."

"A sec." She gulps down her Voltic, rushes to the window to draw open the blinds. "It's so hot in here, gosh, or am I getting menopausal in my thirties? Where's the fucking air-condition-ing remote?" When she hears my advancing footfalls, she quits her parrying. "Chibueze likes to keep up the pretence of being a voyeur. So every few months, Dalia finds him someone, pref-erably a stranger or a tourist; to fuck in the bathroom. Someone that doesn't frequent his circles. It just so happened that our visit coincided with one of Dalia's parties."

"So you were pimping me out?" I laugh, dismayed.

"I wasn't. Dalia was. And I let her. Kobby, it really wasn't one of my best months. I needed to infiltrate Lagos's elite, so we could get funding. And there she was. Striking and well-con-nected. For the first time, I was dating someone who walked into a room and made everyone else's heart but mine skip a beat because only I knew she doesn't read—"

"Did you get the funding?"

She swats the air with repudiation, retrieves an Ankara-print uchiwa from a drawer and fans her sweat-soaked suit. "What about that guy I saw you with at the Awo Tsegah art exhibition? Tall, hefty, imposing. He's nice, isn't he? Or has he left already? He came here with two of his friends, right? One was Victor, was that his name? Anyway he, this Victor, sounded like an absolute fad: for his sake I hope he isn't. After going on and on about our ancestors selling theirs into slavery, which is the most illogical thing you'll often hear from the mouth of every Black American who doesn't know shit and won't find a book to read shit, because if we sold you, why didn't we prevent our own relatives from being 'sold,' isn't it more likely that all of us—not just 'you'—were captured? But he, this Victor, wouldn't listen to me, he just switched subjects and banged on and on about how bad he wants to invest in Africa, how he has already made a ten-year retirement plan that includes Ghana. *Mtchew*. When will he realise that this country hides behind its Internationalist front to persecute queer people, you know, just like the Israeli government's pinkwashing. Only this is reverse, we partake in something I call Lodestar-washing—positioning ourselves as an Nkrumahist haven of Black emancipation, an antidote to America's entrenched anti-Blackness, so the world doesn't see our poor treatment of gays. Not even his comfort and privilege will protect him—"

"So you did get the funding."

"You know, that kind of Black American returnee is the most dishonest kind. Bangs on about wanting to invest and then you email him a proposal and you never hear from him again. Those do not come with the intention of adding any economic value to this country, they came here to run from their own problems, escape the West, be a hermit in the woods of Africa. It's all really shit, isn't it? Not like me, who came because I knew I had too much to offer the country, and the longer I stayed in the UK, the more difficult it would have been for them to allow me to return. That's it! I was beginning to feel like looted art! I'm just saying more people like me need to return. That's what the government should be concerned about: only granting citizenship to those who are going to give back to the country. But these politicians are out here throwing lavish citizenship ceremonies for people who just want their retirement plots in

Aburi. Trust me on this, Kobby, the situation in this country will get so bad . . ."

"Yaa, I don't have time for this. I'm going to write my novel; I'm going to need you to put me on an extensive paid leave."

"Extensive paid leave? That's absolutely outrageous. God, why's it suddenly so hot in here? Or is it just me? Anyway, as I was saying. It's going to get really bad. This country's careening towards dystopian surrender. Listen to me as I prophesy here. God better help us after the Year of Return. As if returning isn't already the new opioid, see what happens after this year. Unless something huge throws a spanner in the government's works—say a natural disaster, say Ebola, which is already spreading in neighbouring countries—all of us locals will suffer! Much importance is going to be granted returnees, people with accents are going to be on top of the food chain, and those of us without the connections, who're just Been-tos and IJGBs, will suffer the consequences. And oh, for you ordinary locals, it'll be hell! You already know how worthless your degrees are when up against a Western education. The only jobs you'll get are those that are shit, or include wiping shit. It'll be the rise of the new expats, the new enemy will be the returnee who's coming back to claim what *your* ancestors stole from them when *their* ancestors were 'sold out'. I'm sounding crazy, am I not? Maybe it's true that the truth makes us all mad. Trust me. It'll happen. These returnees will take over the government. They're already taking over our traditional stools. Let's see who benefits from their return. I know I'm an unusual prophet, with her lace-front and Telfar bag. But that's always the case with us prophets, they call us crazy until they realise that we really were speaking facts that wouldn't cease to exist because they were ignored! And you're leaving as I'm saying all this? You're banging my door on your way out. Maybe it's not too late to do something about it, maybe it's not too late to paint matters on the continent grimmer than they are so diaspora doesn't return. Come back! Come back!

You'll get the paid leave, but your novel can wait. We need you. Your country needs you. God, I need to take my meds because I'm starting to listen to myself now that you've left and I realise how insane I'm sounding . . ."

* * *

My phone's still buzzing when I glide out of the cocooned office building into Accra's heat. Unpocketing it to call an Uber home, I realise all the notifications are from Elton. I tsk. Prices are currently exorbitant so I decide to cover some mileage by foot until I can afford to charter a ride.

On Asafoatse Nettey Road, there's the Ghana Post Office paying homage to our colonial era with its clock tower and hard brick walls. Its courtyard is crowded with street hawkers who've transgressed from Makola, trying to identify other opportunities, then taking off when chased by "Town Council" officers. The temperatures today make my stroll cumbersome, but I'm a man without options so I persevere with the attitude of a Panglossian tourist; until it becomes tasking to find joy when I've taken a lungful of *borla* from a passing dumpster truck.

Among the pages of my romantic travel catalogue is a 5'2" Sicilian American architect who would yank me out of his bed every 5 P.M. to take part in his pretentious *passeggiata*. "Please," he'd coerce, as he tossed a projectile of clothes which, when worn, barely grazed my navel or ankles, "all the authors I know love evening strolls." With him, I was the most authentic fictional version of myself. Pretending to be an author on the cusp of publication. Working on my edits in the cafes we transformed into an office space. And in the evenings, role-playing his favourite Shakespearean tragedy so he could be an unbothered Juliet who watched me die after I'd swallowed. These walks were undertaken hand-in-hand, spying a city whose familiarity brought with it an evaporated charm, like the man beside me whose slicked-back hair, olive skin, and broad badminton calves no longer elicited that carnal response of pins and needles pressed into my groin. "Look at that mother feeding her child with the same hands she performs her transactions," he'd speak ostensibly as though he were indeed an Elizabethan actor. "Look at the men carting around their goods, spy their legs, what beauty!" I'd smile wryly at his speeches, distracted by the catcalls hurled at him for his feminine sway. *Trumu-trumu, Trumudifɔɔ.* His whiteness was the Mark of Cain that protected us from physical harm. "All of this is inspiration, I want the buildings I make to reflect the lives of those it's made for, not like those tall industrial skyscrapers implanted in your city which hold no relevance to the people. My duty as an artist is to replicate my surroundings in my creations." I asked: *Isn't that appropriation?* "Appropriation?" he sighed exasperatingly, "Kobby, for someone who lives in a place with a Black majority, your paranoia for racism is . . . well, interesting. Anyway, when we get married, I'll have some of your Blackness to make my appropriations less . . ." He noticed my grimace and stopped, rushed to alter his course of direction: "Believe me, I was only joking." I smiled. Despite the bitterness that had sprung in my mouth for the mention of marriage and the permanence it suggested. Soon enough he was going to catch on to my pretence and I would no longer be this author. Just a boy in Accra clinging on to others to escape his dreary life. "Look," I began, releasing my fingers from his, handpicking these last words so that he'd forever be haunted by nostalgic memories of having once dated a novelist, "I think this is the end of the road for us."

I halt at a blue-tinted high-rise the Italian would no doubt have lamented over. There might be a receptionist behind the slab of glass, but I figure they've got better activities—perhaps calling a boyfriend or finding the right angle for a surreptitious selfie—to occupy their work-free intermissions instead of watching a passerby approaching an existential crisis. This city that I can no longer love becomes the backdrop to my blued reflection. Shabby buildings and smoke-puffing buses looming over an image of me that is almost thirty, with no real dreams accomplished, drugged and sad, lugging around traumas and these newspapers representing a source of (minimum) income.

A notification distracts my morose perusal. A text message from a lover who would soon be a page in a romantic catalogue:

Hey, I can't believe you're going to let us end this way! I'll be coming back, I swear. Don't ghost me! Elton x

"*Agoo-ei!*"

I step aside for a woman with a pan of crabs to pass by. My novel idleness provokes jarring scenarios, in which I picture subsequent days of trudging through similar mundanity, entertaining similar self-deprecating ruminations, as I wait for someone on Man4Man whose stories and privilege will present an opportunity to live vicariously. I turn my attention to Elton's stream of messages, sift through his pleadings with a twisted mouth, until I see location coordinates—tangible material that I too could occupy work-free intermissions with. Maybe Elton's story deserves a fulfilling resolution, something better than puns on an evening stroll or leaving him on read. What would it take to believe in him, to be a Viwe just for a short while until he leaves, to play the main character who runs to the airport to stop his man from leaving? It's a silly idea, too mushy for my melancholic configurations, but it's still a better ending than being miserable under public eyes. I wave at the glass, envisaging the receptionist applauding my immediate U-turn before an emotional breakdown.

"Taxi!"

The moment I slide into the front seat, I realise my mistake, and perhaps this driver realises it too, so he steps on the gas pedal before I can slink into the backseat to keep an impersonal distance. I'm already feeling trapped before he opens his mouth to ask how my day's going. My monosyllabic tactics do not deter him, and I'm almost about snapping when his hand clasps my knee, which until now I hadn't noticed was juddering. "Relax, everything's going to be okay." For my haste, I couldn't take in his person: broad-chested, Cleopas-headed, and wearing a grey pinstripe suit with a black tie, having the ensemble of that one employee everyone suspects was moonlighting but had no proof. His secret, as anticipated, is this taxi, converted into an Uber, then reverted to taxi again after an unwillingness to continue as a piece of data in Big Tech's profiteering manoeuvrings. All of this he'd divulged with the conduct of a man whose conscious was working overtime, judging my responses or lack thereof to tailor stories and services that should suit my peculiar needs. The perfect candidate to employ for cross-selling schemes or as a door-to-door salesman, because of his ability to function like a Swiss army knife; everything a customer wanted he had, and if they no longer wanted that too, he had something else that would be worth their time—a daisy chain of tricks, which included adjusting the client's seat without consent, blasting into the car's interior a nerve-soothing incense that could be disastrous for someone with specific fragrance allergies, switching radio stations to guess what kind of music a passenger might love even if it meant subjecting them to his psychoanalytic hypothesising. All of these transgressions would have earned a three-star rating, plus an extra two-point-five for offering me a joint, which I gratefully accept, and, as though all this isn't enough torture, for his last act of defiance, he leaves the dial set to Atlantis 87.9 whose DJ announces their next song: "Unwritten" by Natasha Bedingfield.

"Ha ha!" he cheers when I begin swaying. "I knew you were an Atlantis boy before you even got into this car! Me, I love this song too!"

At a traffic light, for the coincidental congregation of middle-class vehicles, the entire street sings the chorus of "Unwritten."

"*Today is where your book begins.*" The taxi driver wags a finger at me, "You hear? Today's where your book begins." The light turns green.

Today's where my book begins, warm tingling sensations spread to my twiddling toes as I type in this message to Aspecialkindofdouble, she who has seen all of my previous messages but is yet to compose a response. And although I'm in a good psychological space, I can't help but bristle at her silence. The "seen" markers on all the texts I've sent provokes images of parents looking on as their children take on actions whose trajectories lead to disasters through which lessons will be imparted.

"Oh is that the news of the Fetish Priest Killer on your lap?" The taxi driver notices and turns the dial to an obscure FM station. "I'm sure there'll be reports on there." On the radio comes a familiar voice from Elmina: "The locals think this is a sacrifice to appease the spirit of the bodies," the German woman talks to the presenter via phone. "What nonsense. This is a calculated tactic by the murderer to hide the bodies. We actually kept circling the place. The stench was so horrible; when we found the hen and the eggs we actually thought that was what was causing the smell. A couple of days passed and we realised that a shallow grave had actually been dug for the bodies. We're trying to get in touch with Milly, the wife of the deceased man, who also happens to be missing. I don't think Elmina can stand this. We'll need donations to revive the community . . ."

I scan the headlines of the newspapers, holding them against the waning flames of my interest. As in the instance of watching a crime documentary after bingeing episodes of its anteceding podcast, the usual magnetism for stories of this nature is amiss. I have uncovered all the mysteries. I have met the killer, ate his dinner, scared him off with my boner when he tried to strangle me. I roll down the window—

"You don't want the air-condi—No littering, boss!"

The papers fly in the wind, dance and dance, wrap themselves around street poles and slide down. Some will find themselves stuck between the teeth of the city's underground drainage, wet and useless. Others will be caught like bridal bouquets by groundnut and roasted plantain hawkers. Hopefully the important bits about the killings will go to foreigners the government protects from news such as this, expats who will stop and stare, maybe pick up the papers and go find another pair of eyes to help process the cruelty published in them.

Through Osu to airport the streets are lined with people expressing sexual and gender identities in every hue, waving rainbow flags. In comes our taxi, its driver honking, its only passenger ululating, cheering the marchers on. Somehow, a loophole in the city's contract for social conduct has been discerned, resulting in this utopia where lives dangle on the tightrope of thinly worded laws. And until these laws are axed or inundated with complex syntax, everyone's loving, everyone's living.

"Sir, you forgot your change!" says the driver relieved of his duties by the wooden NO TAXIS signage tied to the blockade at the entrance. I wave at him.

The last hook of "Pocketful of Sunshine" cedes into oblivion. Stamping boots and slammed rifles take its place.

I'm hunched over the visitors' log-in when an officer sidles up to me. "What do you want here?"

"I'm here to meet a friend . . . his luggage is in one of the quarters . . ."

He's frisking me, "*Wo ne African Americans foɔ na ɛnam?*" I nod, my eyes travelling with his hands down my lower body. He gives my calf a squeeze and asks if I have something for the boys.

I run in the direction he points, passing by bungalows with verandas sealed by prison bars where idle officers in multiple stages of undress hold buckets and gnaw on the stems of toothbrushes, their pidgins and uproarious laughter spilling onto the gravelled aisle.

"NO RUNNING HERE!" remands the voice command-
ing a battalion through their morning drill. An ensuing silence
blankets the entire barracks, amplifying the compositions of
cawing crows.

"WALK LIKE A MAN!"

I ignore the invectives of the sergeant, secure a hand onto
my hip and glide into a catwalk.

"Kojo Besia on show!"

"On show! On show!" Whistles and cheers are hurled at me
from the bungalows.

Maybe the door was hinting at something after its knob
refused to budge, a misfire in its operations which the man-
ufacturer, believing too much in omens like me, might have
included on the label's precautionary statements: *In case of
malfunction on first attempt, please beat a hasty retreat.* I enter
the officers' quarters and its smell takes me back to the casket
of my room. If my mother and brother are hiding, under the
uncreased bed, inside the chiffonier's drawers cross-breeding
underwear with USB cables and photos, within the wardrobe
that has more mosquitoes than clothes, they elude my efforts to
find them, to make their existence as substantial as their stench.
As Nana. Nana, who exits an adjoining room laughing about
something heard over his shoulder before his eyes notice mine.
The luggage he carries slips out of his hand and splits open,
sending Elton's juju masks rolling towards my feet like severed
heads. Any bystander—perhaps Nana's unfamiliar companion,
might believe each of us had thought the other a ghost, but here
I am with my nose on a stranger's garments, and there's Nana
with flashes of silver lining his neck, finger, wrist, the sights of
which spark twitches in my groin.

"*Wo yɛ deen wɔ ha?*"

"Do you know where Elton is?" I ignore Nana, addressing
this man who looks between Nana and I.

"Airport. We are going there so you can come with us."

"No! No! He's not coming!"

Nana advances towards me, kicking the masks between us. I slide out of his reach. He crashes into the wardrobe and emerges howling, clutching his bleeding shoulder. The interlocking needle sits in his humerus.

"*Wei na oyɛ* Sasabonsam Killer *no!*" The other guy, frightened by Nana's proclamation, backs into the adjoining room.

I run out of the bungalow. I trip and land on my stomach. Gravel bites into my palms and I wince. I hear the door behind me. I turn. There's Nana, a version of him I've known intimately, breathing over my face as I was being suffocated. He clutches the needle in his shoulder and wails:

"*Trumudifoɔ!*"

His voice ricochets around the barracks like a gunshot. The sound of rifles and boots can no longer be heard. He points an accusatory finger at me. "*Trumudifoɔ yi pɛ sɛ ɔne me da!*"

My phone vibrates in my pocket.

There's Elton, attempting a video-call.

Elton, on the many ways to die in Ghana, I've always skipped over the lynching of a homosexual. Always turning away before the violence begins. Scared that if I look, I'll be watching my own funeral. This is where I lose you, this is where your eyes shouldn't find mine. I must protect you from this. I kick my phone and lurch onto my feet.

With open arms, as if welcoming an old friend, I face the onrushing mob of convicts who won't listen to their supervisors screaming cease and desist orders. Death by this hand looks so serene, so beautiful. Like an oil painting, a photograph. A little, tiny head surrounded by vast humans cast onto a frame on the wall.

Everyone fails to recognise the poetry in death, but I do. Even in mine. The poetry is the stone that knocks me in the eye, blood jettisoning out of the eye socket, spraying and spraying like a burst pipe. A shoe comes into my stomach, and I bend over, more blood on gravel. I totter, another stone gets me in the neck. I feel my throat convulse, a retching from deep within. My remaining eye twitches around in its socket, searching for Nana. The world is viewed through blood until I'm knocked unconscious by something hard, perhaps a cement block, pressing my skull into the gravel. The rest of my death is what it feels like to be lifeless. Disappointingly silent. As the air blown on tea to cool before the newspaper is picked up. There I am, front-page news in my own medium. A sensitive image of my body bloodied into a pulp, contorting the surrounding text. A nice headline, I hope. Papers to toss away like ashes.

Epilogue

National Abbreviations Authority's Identification Abbreviations in 2027

LAFA—Locally Acquired Foreign Accent (both a term and a Ghanaian app for deciphering accents)

BW—Born With (a Western accent, speech formatted without bold or italics)

BT—Been-To (acquired accent by immersion and assimilation, speech formatted as **<u>bold and underlined</u>**)

WB—Wanna Be (local, speech formatted as **bold**)

Surgically-enhanced BW (speech formatted as ***<u>bold, italics, underlined</u>***)

Scott
(2027)

Nothing in her message grabs you the way her delivery does. She's like a Janet. Too much stage presence that don't match her vocals. She stands cross-legged on red platforms, wearing a red dress with a balloon skirt and red tights. She's a sight to behold. A large screen projects a doppelgänger version of her to thousands of people all over the world, majority of whom are crazed fanatics unlikely to see through the bullshit she spews. But God does she look pretty (convincing) in red.

"Ghana is a hub of opportunities for everyone . . ."

Her accent is too good, no traces of her Ghanaian one elided by the LAFA app, which points to a perfect Oxford and recognises her as a BW. I grunt. She may have fooled the algorithm, but she cannot fool me.

"In my book, I teach you to successfully repatriate." She pursues one of the panning cameras as she speaks. "Would you do it IRL, or will you keep watching me wherever you are? You make the choice: IRL or IRS." She ends her speech with the title of her memoir, which isn't as clever as she thinks it is.

I am late to the standing ovation. I pick up her book—which according to my sources was ghostwritten—and join the applause.

In the signing queue, she only makes small talk with BWs and a few BTs; everyone else is thanked for coming and reminded to follow her Substack.

"Oh, you look familiar." Her face arranges into her rendition of the Grinch's smile when I'm approaching.

"Yes, we have a thing today," I respond.

"Oh you're my two o'clock! I magnified your email's thumb-nail profile photo, which is why I recognise you."

To sign my book, she asks for my name even after our long online correspondence.

"It's Scott, but I believe we've also met in person before, at a gallery exhibition eight years ago."

"Not that I recall." She's already looking over my shoulder.

"Hey, Yaa!" Vincent pulls up next to me. About damn time. There are beads of sweat lining his upper lip. This is how I know he didn't go to the bathroom to pee. He went to the bath-room to wrap his jaws around someone else's dick. Thinks he's slick. "What did I miss?"

"My entire talk, I hope not," Yaa says.

"You're a God in this auditorium; no one can escape your voice even if they're taking a shit." He's sucking up to her. Nice. Maybe she recognises him from her old life. Maybe she's going to give up this BW pretence. But she doesn't.

"And what's your name?" she asks, then hands him his signed copy of her book. "Okay, guys, as you can see, there's a crowd behind you, hence I might be late for this meeting you two have promised—" she draws air quotes with her 3-inch scarlet nails "—will change my life."

"Though not as much as you've changed yours," Vincent adds with a private chuckle that evolves into Yaa's hammy high-pitched laugh.

"Oh piss off you two, and don't forget to follow my Substack!"

* * *

To get into our cab, we pull out our Ghana Card. Vincent opens the door for me like a man keen on grand gestures to atone for his sins. "Thanks, love."

The driver's unsurprisingly one of the talkative ones. His

conversation triggered by Vincent's courteous "boss, how you dey?"

"**Look, look, look,**" this driver points at the horde of pedestrians whose numbers might continue to grow if no one enlists the advice of every cab driver alive, "**just because they can't pay their E-levy taxes o! Their Ghana Card has deactivated and now they have to walk everywhere. Common *troski* no one can pick. Now even common beauty salon no one can go some because America people have posted on social media that doing braids here is cheap, so hairdressers have increased their prices. People are going hungry every day. People are losing their jobs every day. Common *kaya* job *kraa* is hard to find. People are always dying because they can't go to the hospital because their Ghana Card has stopped working. We need more money for more important things, but this government have gone to build a national cathedral.**"

Every time you listen to these cabbies speak it's like they're trying to hint that we, the returnees, are responsible for the country's ruin. I squeeze Vincent's hand to warn him against getting worked up by the man's words. The last time he did, the last time he got angry and cussed the fuck out of one driver, the government surveillance apps censored all of his swear words and sent back an edited recording of his offensive speech: *Nigga, if we hadn't returned things would still be bad; don't blame us because your government can't make proper legislation to keep the economy from declining.* He was charged with Serious Crimes That Could Warrant Deportation, so we were bullied into paying a penal sum into the National Bribery Fund, and another to gain a certificate which stated that Vincent had undergone necessary reforms to continue as an exemplary citizen in this country.

"*Obroni, obroni, obroni.*" The pedestrians—no longer the Nigerian kids of before—rush to the car. I look away.

"**See, see, see,**" the driver sucks his teeth, "**I had no idea that one day *paa* this Ghana will become the way it is. One dollar** is twenty cedis, one pound is twenty-nine cedis. Look at me, a graduate now driving government taxi. My engineer mates who are scrubbing toilets in New York and Germany are getting more money than me. God bless our homeland Ghana o!"

Before Vince and I decided on Ghana, we tried other countries. We would not allow ourselves to be another middle-aged American cliché, like all the other Blacks repatriating during the big DeDiasporification—a word whose inception after 2020 massive protests resulted in its overuse like its sister, decolonisation. Tried as we did to stay away, the Ghanaian government kept intensifying their DeDiasporification packages. Soon we began limiting our social media (TikTok) screen time because we'd gotten too obsessed with watching returnees talking; about their subsidised housing in Ghana while performing some viral dance; about their new Ghanaian names while performing some viral dance; about their Aburi plots, ECOWAS visa-free passports, highly-incentivised jobs with insurance covering dental and dermatologist appointments. Lots of people with kingship titles too were flaunting all of their new regalia while dancing to Beyoncé's "King Already." Fifty countries in Africa and none of them were doing the most like these Ghanaians to bring back diaspora. After spending a year in Brazil and realising it was a budget America that was slightly less racist, doing Jamaica where too many of our friends were returning to the "motherland" themselves, and briefly considering South Africa (only because of Cape Town and Pride), we gave in and Returned.

"What's the bill?" Vincent asks the driver, thankful the ride's over.

"Two dollar."

* * *

At the restaurant, Zamarana, the owner—a bleached-blonde, low-crop, five-foot tall woman—walks over to our table and asks which part of America we are from because she's struggling to place our accent which has a bit of Detroit and something from the West Coast? Anyway, she's a New Yorker herself (a lie), came to Ghana ten years ago ("Oh, we've been here for half those years," Vincent says), quit her six-figure job in Manhattan, which her friends and her parents told her she was crazy for leaving. *To up and leave just to go to Ghana? Ghana?* She mimicked their repulsion. "Glad it all worked out even though it was shaky in the beginning to turn my passion into my bread, glad that I came here before the big DeDiasporafication, a word coined by my friend who'll be with y'all shortly." She hooks her bag under her arm. "My girls will come serve you soon. I recommend the pork . . . something! Whatever these locals call it."

"Domedo?" Vincent says perfectly. "Yes, domedo." She struts out, not without adding, "How come you've managed to sound like them?"

Our order, whose preparation info says takes thirty minutes, is on our table in five. One of those middle-class Ghanaians, a BT, of the lowest duration spent in the UK according to the LAFA app, voices her displeasure, even when the waiter tries to console her by offering her iced tea ("**Forget about the tea! Fucking cup of tea!**"). She's been here for over half an hour and ordered exactly what has been given to us. She walks out.

The servers fuss over us as we eat, ignoring the calls of Ghanaian middle-class and aspiring middle-class (of income $8,000 to $12,000 a year) waving, banging their tables, psst-ing to catch a waiter. When one staff sees an opening where no BW walks in, they attend to these WBs, who copy an accent that attempts to reverse the letters of their makeup, which really is genetically impossible. But with a few surgical enhancements from that famed local plastic surgeon, Obengfo, a cheap imitation of an AAVE accent is possible. An accent that restricts the foods that these surgically enhanced WBs can order from the restaurant's menu:

"***Awish, wish, wish, Kontomire.***"
"**Coming right up!**"
"***Please, thank you.***"

Yaa walks in. Sis must think she's Naomi Campbell, catwalking to the centre of the restaurant and spinning on her platforms before heading to our nook. A storm of lights follows her every move, courtesy of those new flagship Xomian phones outfitted with DSLR-sized external flashes that only WBs find tasteful. She tosses her bag and scarf onto the table with such exaggerated airs anyone (BW) would think she was starring in a Jennifer Lewis biopic. Before she speaks, a waitress budges in to take her order, and adds,

~~"Mama Yaa, I'm a big fan, I tried applying for the job to be your secretary, but didn't get any response."~~

"Only BTs can work for me."

~~"Oh O.K., when I grow up, I want to be just like you."~~ She walks away.

Yaa takes out her phone and taps on the LAFA app.

"LAFA, LAFA, LAFA, how many times did I call you?"

"Three times, Yaa."

"Now tell me where that girl's accent was from?"

"She's a BIT—"

"What's that?" Vincent wants to know.

"A new designation: Born Into Its," Yaa answers, "For kids who grew up watching so much *Peppa Pig* they ended up picking her accent. Sadly, they can't fool the app, hence . . . she can only apply for waitressing jobs."

"She's a BIT," Yaa hits "resumé" on her app, "with a slight Kumerica accent."

"That's the one from Kumasi, right?"

Yaa nods to Vincent.

"That's interesting, how're BIT accents transcribed?" My question is directed to Yaa's app instead of her, but she shoves her phone back into her bag.

"Transcribed with bold and italics," she answers. Then she leans in, suggesting what follows is hush-hush: "The government's thinking of placing an inbuilt chip connected to our Ghana Card that allows us to easily detect people at a distance. These locals are really finding ways around the LAFA app. More foreign passports are at risk of going into the wrong hands if a BW makes the mistake of falling for a WB who's really good at faking it. What's really at stake though are the jobs and opportunities for us WBs. These locals are schooled with such rigid theory-based curricula, we can't afford the wrong jobs going into wrong hands."

The waitress interrupts. Bringing in Yaa's meal. Yaa grins at her and asks if she'd like a signed copy of her book. The girl beams, hugs the book gifted to her and cries, flips to a random page and reads:

"*'I just took a DNA test; turns out, I'm a 100% UK ballin' chick, even when I relocate to Ghana, even when I off my lace-front.' So profound and relatable in this age when the Instagram Face is dying and being replaced by the more elusive TikTok Face! You're amazing, Yaa! No wonder they made you Presidential Aide for Diaspora Affairs!*" The girl disappears at the snap of Yaa's fingers, although not before the latter has told her to follow her Substack if ever she finds stable internet connection and a debit card that can handle a monthly charge of $10.99.

"So why am I here?" Yaa asks, switching her pointed stare between Vincent and me.

"We've got a resort in Elmina—"

"Oooh, really, have you already shot your TikTok to show the world you got it cheap?"

"Yes," Vincent answers her question again before I do, "and we were hoping you'd use your influence to help a brother out, make it as packed as it was in the heyday when there were a lot more tourists coming into the country before . . . you know—"

"The disappearances in Elmina." Yaa nods, grins with mischief and flaunts that Uzo Aduba set of teeth, which in recent

years has become one of the hallmarks of the famed TikTok
Face. "Would you like to hear a fun story? I was the reason for
the disappearances. Indirectly, of course. Everyone thinks I was
made Presidential Aide to Diaspora Affairs because of my intellect—that's also true. But I was approached by the government
right when I was about to hit publish on the story that would let
the world prove these Caucasian Vanishings are an actual thing
in Ghana and not just hearsay. I should feel horrible about all
these missing white people but they, this stingy government,
paid a hefty price for my silence." She presses a gleaming ringed
finger against her lips, adds, "This stays between us, right? Anyway, why would I want to help you two with your resort?"

"So," I speak over Vincent quickly, "I want to host a yoga
retreat for all newbie and old returnees to come tap into the
power of the goddess Asaase Yaa, who, as you know, gives us
this beautiful land where our ancestors once lived."

"Oh wow, sankofapitalism in the new age." Yaa laughs hard.
"All you returnees really bringing your Western ideals here too,
can't stand y'all."

"Sankofa what?"

"Sankofapitalism," she answers Vincent. "Raking up bullshit about our ancestors to market one's product. If we're being
honest, #Beautytok and IG influencers—with melanins that are
poppin, i.e. melanins that have been Photoshopped—did the
same thing to African Black Soap. They put this local soap on a
global stage and pushed this story about our forefathers bathing with it. Before we knew it, there were European and Asian
imitations on the market forever ruining the credibility of our
own *Alata Samina*."

"Not what we're doing," I rush to say.

"Whatever," she says dismissively, "where's the business angle in all this? How do I benefit?"

"We need your influence to bring in all the BWs, even the
WBs, and for everyone referred to us through you—"

"I get a cut," Yaa finishes and smiles. "Now this is a brilliant idea, but I'm not about to put my name on a brand that I barely know."

"Oh you will," Vincent says with an emphatic fist to the table.

"Oh I see someone can't take a no." Yaa makes to leave.

Vincent quickly sets the pictures on the table. Lays them one after the other. Gently. With the unwavering cruelty of a hitman bringing a bone-knife to one's fingers, dicing them. Even I flinch at the horror reflected against Yaa's features. She sits.

"Why . . . Why . . . do you have pictures of me . . . with some guy I barely know?"

"Oh don't fucking play with me. That's Kobby, he was one of your writers. In your old life. We hear he's dead now, rest in peace to him. We know who you were before you had this rebrand. Yaa, we have information to prove you're just a BT, with just fifteen years of this accent under your belt. You should be ashamed. Masquerading as a BW, with a fucking memoir that traces your birth to a Western country."

I'm so turned on by this version of Vincent I feel an immense pride (in my pants) that he's mine. Yaa runs her hand through her scalp and offs her wig onto the table. At the sight of her cornrows, she's shrunk back to the Yaa we met six years ago, a woman with a start-up hunting for investors at an art exhibition. She's a walking testament to the benefits of social activism in the digital age. Changed her life, she has.

"Guys, I only wanted you to refine your idea and get back to me. I can't be doing influencer marketing, I'd like a more hands-on approach. I want you to extend the business to general well-being and such. Hosting events and webinars on topics such as: healing the diaspora mind from Western conditioning; restoring the diaspora mind to embody the mentalities of their ancestors. Workshops like those, plenty of them. That's the stuff I can share on my Substack. The diaspora child has to find ways to acknowledge that even though they're not born in Africa, Africa was born in them! And believe me on this, you will be providing a much-needed service! Providing what I call a *soft landing* to the recently returned diasporan . . ."

2022

We could tell everything was going to shit the moment we touched down in Ghana. Maybe the giveaway had to be the Samuel L. Jackson TSA yelling the fuck out of the line of travellers. People scurrying around like mice. Airport security doing all they could to stall the queues—for bribes, Vincent had suggested. It was the first time Vince and I had seen a set of African travellers who didn't look like they were on a layover en route to the Met Gala. "Ordinary" isn't quite the word to describe them. Maybe "shabby" is best. "Refugee" too would not be an over-the-top qualifier. All at once you wanted to give them your food together with benedictions for their long journeys ahead. I doubted they'd know what to do with the Ben & Jerry's and all the other bingeworthy contraband Vincent and I were sneaking into the country, hugging our luggages like these despondent Africans did with theirs, scared we'd be detected. And then what? "Bribe," Vincent had stated, "we'll bribe them. That shit works here, but don't go around looking like you've got something to hide. Just like they can smell people from America, they can also smell fear."

The sight of my skin, something I'd realise much later, eased our way through the queues. No long waiting, no hassle. Diplomats, is what Vincent had said about how we were treated, a bunch of diplomats hurried through hordes of sad-looking refugees. What really prevented our illegal effects from being confiscated, though, was our accent.

"Look at these proper Black American men," said the

customs officer as our passports were stamped. She pulled out pictures of her own kids in a passport-holder. "See Ama, she's only two." A little cherubic thing who made my maternal hormones twinge. "We got her to America just last week. She's going to be an African American by the time she returns, when she's thirty or so."

"Looks like you just went to give birth to her there and returned," remarked Vincent.

"Oh my brother, you have no idea." She laughed at an undisclosed memory. "Glad I work here, it was easy to push her through. All my friends here are doing the same. We all want our kids to come back and get good, gargantuan jobs. Drive big-big cars. Like the Minister of Foreign Affairs who told all Black Americans to come to Ghana after George Floyd—God bless his soul, we too saw that video. It was shared to our WhatsApp plenty times, white man is wicked! We wanted you all to come to Ghana after we watched the video, and now you're here." She belted out the lyrics of a tune we didn't recognise, "*Come to me . . . On this happy trip, into to the Promise land, oh we'll be happy and well, Welcome home—*"

"But who's taking care of these kids in America?" I voiced my concerns.

"Their aunties. They'll be maids and things in America for a while, for the small fee of taking them to school. They'll turn out fine, you see." She caught my judgy expression. "I know what you're thinking, that I'm a Patsy, but don't judge me, you don't know my story. One friend of mine's an English teacher and soon she's going to lose her job because she doesn't have your accent. We're all afraid here. We all want the best for our children. As for we older people, we're almost dead o. But this is their Ghana, and they'll suffer if they don't speak like you. So we take them instead. Over here we say, our children are our future. Michael Jackson said that too, you know."

"Surprised you've read *Patsy* though," Vincent said. Out of all her worries that's what drew his attention. This book he'd picked up because of a queer book club in Kingston. I huffed to show my annoyance for investigating and discovering that in suburban Jamaica, "book club" was no code that your husband was cheating, just grown men and women discussing a 400-page book they'd read.

"I took it from a white traveller who brought in a big plastic pipi. I made him choose between the book and his pipi. He chose the book. Immediately my mind went to that saying: *if you want to hide something from a Black man put it in a book.* So I just seized *Patsy* instead to show that white man that I was smart."

Speaking of white men, there were fewer faces in the crowds this time than we had seen during the Year of Return.

"You're the white guy," Vincent teased, laughing as we threw our luggage into the taxi Nana had secured for us. All the other taxi drivers screaming, "*Obroni. Obroni. Obroni.*" Nana pushed them back. Everyone probably thought we were diplomats, maybe even celebrities. Maybe I should have told them I used to dance for Debbie Allen.

2027

Vincent: Scott, what again? Why you gotta wake me up so early? It's the weekend and we're in Elmina for fucksakes.

Scott: I wrote a poem for our yoga retreat this afternoon. Listen: *When we left America, we left it for good. No more returning. We were tired. Even in our departure, we packed with as little energy as a kid whose mama wakes him up to prepare for church, sluggish, in between sleep and waking. Not because we were reluctant to leave. No, our souls were just paper-thin, our bodies humped over like we'd endured an extraneous exercise.*

Which indeed is America, running on a treadmill, increasing our tempos but still remaining where we began. Yearning to rise out of our skin but still remaining where we began. Fighting for our rights to live but still remaining where we began. Our minds were tired. Our skin had secreted all of its sweat. Downward dog had to stop somehow, planking in our hatred had made us so taut we could snap, and when we stood on our toes to peer at what it felt like to get a taste of white, we were shoved down. Nothing in this country would do us good. We were middle-aged, the age that sought peace from tedious jobs, reprieve from the noises of the city, retreating into the bliss of small-town living, and we knew that America didn't have enough small towns that didn't feel too big, that didn't feel like this beast of a country itself for the Black man. So we packed up and left, to an actual small country. Upward dog. In flight, the Black man reaches his peak. In flight, the Black man can finally do shavasana. What do you think, Vince?

Vincent: Just leave the poems for the bards.

Scott: (grunts) What's a Bard when you've got bars like a fucking Barb?

2022

From the airport, we were welcomed to our revamped resort by a revamped Nana who stuck his head out of the taxi and screamed to the timid maid waiting at the gates: "Go'on op'n da gates fa me."

Vincent and I exchanged puzzled expressions. The frightened girl remained sitting, confused.

"I sai' go'on op'n da gates fa me."

"Nana, that's anti-Black," Vincent reproached. "You're mocking us, aren't you?"

"Innit," was Nana's response.

We hadn't yet realised that everyone was copying our accent

and that it was quickly becoming the standard. We didn't give it much thought at the time until we were completely settled. Then it finally hit us. Really hit us one night as Vincent and I sat in silence in our bedroom after another unsuccessful attempt to fuck with a cockring and a mosquito whined nearby with neither of us making any effort to clap at it. What was once noise was suddenly becoming music. But before we could hear this music, we had to settle.

We met the German couple at the reception. The old lady's eyes, which we remembered to be a shocking blue, had been lined with red. It took us a minute to realise this was the effect of her tears. Nothing her husband said could release her death grip holding the resort's keys hostage. "We really had high hopes for Elmina," she said, "We were hoping to rake in a few donations, transform the town, but business became bad when the whites actually stopped coming in for whatever reasons . . . so what if a few people are disappearing here and there? No one knows that for sure, so why should white people stop travelling to these parts? Now there's too many Black travellers who actually do not want to live in a resort run by whites. We actually thought braiding our hair and wearing too many African prints might help draw them to our resort." She passed a hand over her body covered in a patterned maxi dress. "This is not how it's supposed to be. All of us races must learn to coexist. 'Black supporting Black' will be the death of us all."

We listened to her talk her shit. Knowing full well that when morning came, we'd place their bodies in body bags and send them to the dead enslaved.

To settle, we needed to focus on running a well-oiled machine. Finding ways to increase the resort's capital, hiring staff, luring in guests worth killing were our only priorities during our early days in Elmina.

We found a cook, who made hot spicy food, fucking shito in everything. Gave Vincent constant diarrhoea which unwittingly became the instigator of our first Elmina fight, happening one afternoon when I'd returned from beach yoga and heard the sputtering sounds of Vincent's shit. I yelled: "How do you marry a bottom and then turn around and let a man bend you over?"

"Ain't nobody bending me over."

We no longer had Accra's cosmopolitan cuisine to protect us. No more Chinese Mondays and Thai Fridays—those gastronomic routines we'd imported. Vincent was more optimistic in these early days, made me reconsider running back to our government-subsidised Villagio penthouse in Accra. He was always on some "ancestors" bullshit like the other hoteps living on the other side of the coast, those Brothers and Sisters of the Returned, whom we avoided because every effort to be more African made us feel funny. (Whether we liked it or not America had happened to us, and we had to accept this difference, or spend our lives mimicking Robin Thede's *ABLSS*'s hotep caricatures.) Vincent decided these watery stools were our bodies' way of purging all that was America so that we could fully immerse ourselves in the culinary delights of our ancestors.

This cook was no Mina, but she was her cousin and if she could make meals that would deliver our chosen guests into our hands, for the small price of giving us irritable bowel syndrome, then yes, we wanted her.

Nana's employment was by default, given he handled most of the heavy lifting around the resort. Stuff Vincent and I couldn't do without cracking a hip. 'Tis the age of arthritis. 'Tis also the age of saving up whatever waist you got for the bedroom. 'Cause the Lord was coming for us soon—so we'd heard one night after googling "life expectancy in Ghana" to find it sitting good on our ages. He's a good boy, Nana. (He'd been the one who'd overseen the reconstruction of the place before our arrival. Tearing down those awful shared bathrooms, relieving the rooms of their prison decor.) Like in the days of our first trip, he's still very dependent. He's always in need of stern direction, a father-figure, a role which Vincent has slipped into, made the boy quit spewing his church nonsense.

One day, while following his master (Massa Vincent) around like a lapdog, he saw us carrying one of the white guests into a canoe and offered to take it from there. If not for Vincent's insistence that we did it ourselves and that the dead enslaved demanded this, I'd have gladly thrown these bodies at Nana.

So we had the cook, the manager, and we thought we'd finally settled. We thought we'd heard it all; caught snatches of conversation among the fishermen on the shore in dialects that sounded different, caught a "yo," caught a "bro," caught an "I'mma" here, a "you trippin" there, but we really didn't hear it until the beautiful boy came running to us from the sea. Screaming, "Yo, yo, ain't that my mans Vincent and Scott." ("What the fuck is wrong with this town, Black people don't talk like this," had been Vincent's outburst.) This boy, something out of *Baywatch*, was buffed and bald, always sweaty despite the little work he did around the resort. He was so slow, in movements and in the head; you'd give orders about something and he'd lean in as if he was trying to kiss these orders right out of your mouth. If he wasn't asking for an advance salary to pay a brother's school fees, he was taking trips into the city to visit his "sick father" whom he'd once collected money to bury, only to use this "sick father" excuse months later. The only reason I hadn't sacked him yet was his body. No, he does nothing for me. Just the guests. He would lure them into the places they were most vulnerable, and *wham!* Shovels, body bags, canoes. To the dead enslaved!

We finally settled into coastal living, visiting the city whenever it was important. Living the dream of the American returnee, with the social life to boot: the Green Butterfly Market on Saturdays; chatting art at Front N Back's Container Gallery; Doing the Midunu pop-up dining experience. America felt so distant a life that we'd laugh hard reminiscing on those times we tried to survive in that jungle, isn't that wild? Isn't that wild?

We only truly believed this new change in language during the early months of curating our social lives, and we believed it because of the source we got this information from. This trusted source said it like it is, made it a cause for contention between Vincent and me, ruined our cockring sex later that night, gave us our first malaria too the following day.

It all happened when, like every newbie, we got entangled with funny company: this trusted source. Even though we'd become experts on who to avoid—the diasporan with a business opportunity hunting for investors, the diasporan who always had some sort of ongoing concert or other and wanted us to be in on the best events happening around the city (we were too old for that shit), the diasporan who used friendship as a front just to infiltrate your circles. Nothing, no experience we had in avoiding shady characters, could have saved us from meeting the Diasporans Who Are Revolutionists.

They had come into our lives with their flashy invites and all that flashy social-theory talk. We attended their summits and broke their bread, dialogued on race and racisms which Vincent and I found exhausting because hadn't we left America to escape such topics? Topics such as: American capitalism; American consumerism; American hegemony, for which they'd brainstormed ways to cure the imminent social order in Ghana where Americans would likely be on top. Renouncing our language, they'd decided, would solve this crisis. Vincent couldn't contain it any longer. "What's funny?" they turned to us with their mean revolutionist faces. "The American Black must acknowledge that he's been equipped with the master's tools to oppress," they said, "one of them being language."

"But how, how can we renounce what we were naturally born with?"

"We unlearn."

"How do we unlearn?"

"We learn."

"Learn what?"

"Learn Ghanaian languages."

"Which languages?"

"One language."

"Wouldn't that create a new dominance along tribal lines?"

"That's a bridge we can only cross when we get there."

2027

The preparations for the beach yoga have begun, and so have the protesters. They're lined up at the entrance of our resort with their banners and their placards, crowding the gates and inhibiting access to our guests who still force through, racing into my arms for an air-kiss on both cheeks.

"Hope you enjoy your time and sorry for all this . . ."

I always make it a point to leave it at that in case any of the attendees are sympathisers to the cause of these Diasporans Who Are Revolutionists.

"An end to American hegemony is what we seek!" they chant in their Wakanda accents.

"OMG, is Yaa in already?"

A WB filters through the protests; I keep my smile wide. She eludes my outstretched arms and rushes towards Yaa, who's walking out of the hut labelled *Abrofo Nkatie*, decked in all white, her hands up in praying-mantis style, looking like a quack new-age theologian.

"All we need is an end to the LAFA app!"

"Ahh," Vincent materialises at my side, "apparently the Revolutionists heard Yaa's going to be here and wanted to make an appearance too—"

"And here I am, the woman of the moment, the person of the year." Yaa slides an arm onto my waist. "Don't worry guys, I'm used to all the attention by now!"

"No accents, no hegemony!"

"Oh hi Peace!" Yaa beams at a new entrant, skinny and tall like her, midriff exposed, hair in a mohawk, a cowrie-choker spilling onto her shoulders. They hug.

"Yeah, surprised to see me, ehn? I was so busy at GNBC, I didn't think I'd show up, odo."

"Well, glad you did, this is going to be so much fun." Yaa points her towards the bissap stand (which is supposed to be manned by Nana) in the forecourt.

"Yaa, I didn't think you've got WB friends." Vincent's taking the piss out of her.

"And you're right," Yaa cackles. "Peace isn't WB, she's Dutch, first gen, most of her English acquired through her parents, hence the accent."

"That's an interesting dynamic," Vince responds, "but how does the app make this distinction?"

"LAFA, LAFA, LAFA, how many times did I call you?"

"Three times, Yaa. Your surrounding accents are BW American, and also a WB English accented with Ewe intonations."

"Nothing else?"

"That'll be all, Yaa."

"Humph," Yaa huffs, "identity is such a complex thing, right? Can't be categorised with AI and algorithms."

"So you admit, the app you've been funding is running a failing system."

"Oh hi Yaa, such a big fan!" Someone walks in. Yaa gives them a minor wave and points at the bissap stand over her shoulder, thankfully (and surprisingly) the indolent (but doesn't he really look beautiful today) bald guy has slipped into Nana's stead, using his charm to attend to the crowding guests.

"Seems like Scott's tense today." Yaa squeezes my shoulders.

"It'll all be fine: Black people are the same everywhere, they'll show up, they'll show up on BPT."

I shrug and pretend I'm unbothered, though secretly praying everything goes as planned, and now that the revolutionists are being taken care of—thanks to the cook who balances an ice kenkey tray and distributes its contents among them—things should take a turn for the better. These protestors accept the bottles without hesitation, screaming harder, even with their mouths full, in case we thought they'd back down for our kindness.

"How long have you been fermenting that kenkey for?" Yaa's trying to swallow back her laughter.

"Eight weeks!" Vincent says.

"Brilliant," Yaa hunches over, guffawing. "You guys have really settled in, haven't you? You know all the Ghanaian tricks now. I'm happy for you."

"Yeah, Scott and I were talking about this the other day,"— "we have indeed settled. Usually, Americans are on the extreme ends of the returnee spectrum; if they're not the Diasporans Who Are Revolutionists, they most definitely will join Brothers and Sisters of the Returned. Scott and I are just the normal, boring ones, haha."

"I see. I'll be frank with you: at first I thought your gayness would be a problem, but it seems your privilege indeed has protected you two. There are still attacks. There's still talk of tightening the laws above. Who knows? They might one day storm this place and deport you."

"Well, we're the biggest contributors to the National Bribery and Corruption Fund, so that's not gonna happen anytime soon, Yaa." I smile at her. She tightens her arm around my waist.

"No accents, no hegemony!"

"Oh God, do you know when this kenkey kicks in?" Yaa groans. "No accents, no hegemony my ass, it's not like these Ghanaians weren't already obsessing over our accents before we returned: they called this system on themselves—"

"**But it's still American hegemony, isn't it?**" We all turn to the girl called Peace, a glass in her hand, the bissap drawn out from a straw into her scarlet lips. "**I mean, think about it, if Americans weren't so keen on exporting their culture with neo-colonial fervour, all this shit wouldn't happen.**"

"Don't look at me, I'm from the *you-kayyy*," Yaa says, whipping her imaginary lace-front. Adding: "A Hackney babe, to be precise."

"So like them, you believe we should renounce our accents?" Vincent asks the new girl. "We should all be speaking like we've got a green screen behind us, and we're the cast of *Black Panther*? Listen to them, listen to how ridiculous they sound!"

"**I just think you should recognise your role in this new order and work towards shrinking your privilege, so you're not oppressing—**"

"But we're not oppressing anybody. Honestly, y'all should choose your words carefully. If we were oppressing anyone, you don't think we—of all people—would . . . Everyone makes it seem like Americans are the cause of this situation, when it's just the government, their government." Vincent's phone beeps a cautioning notification, but he powers on, "African Americans, all Black people elsewhere, have to return; we have to return in our numbers. If America or wherever stops being a home for us, we have to return."

"**I'm just asking that you make an effort to mitigate the effects of this return. Recognise that this is what your return is causing and work towards changing things. Hold on, just hold on for a sec. Let's take this example, this sobolo is amazing, but the bald guy at the stand welcomed me with this fake LAFA that made my stomach turn. He called this sobolo, 'hibiscus tea', not even bissap as you foreigners usually call it. You could tell him there's no need for him to try speaking like you. You could tell him—**"

"Yaa, omg! You look really good!" someone interrupts, a blasian in a hobo-chic wrap dress. "I didn't know you taught yoga."

"If you followed my Substack you'd know I do," Yaa answers. "But this will be my first Ghanaian class."

I turn to Vincent. He winces.

"So as I was saying—"

Yaa interrupts her Dutch friend. "Vincent, I'm so glad you decided it best that I take everyone into . . . the realm of our ancestors today. Peace, my girl, you should listen to the words I put down: *When we left the UK, we left it for good. No more returning . . .* I've got it all on a paper somewhere, let's go find it?" Yaa ushers her friends away.

"I know you wanted to do this, Scott, but the people came here for Yaa. She's got a way of reeling in everyone, especially the WBs. And besides, there was just something disingenuous about your poetry thingy, I'd rather those words came out of Yaa's mouth. The bottom line is, with Yaa, we'll be making a lot of money."

"*If it isn't the Black Americans.*"

The newcomer throws himself at Vincent, who keeps his eyes on me, waiting for some sort of reaction for this betrayal.

"*Y'all didn't really abandon me, did you? What are friends for?*"

"Kobby, is that you!"

We both turn to the sound of a crash. Yaa's bissap is on the floor, her mouth agape. Vincent and I share a look.

"Kobby?" Yaa repeats, her BT accent very obvious. "Who cut your locs? Who did this to you? And why are you fucking selling sobolo and Adinkra pie?"

The Beautiful Boy from the Sea takes off. He worms through the diasporic assemblage at the forecourt, speeds past the hut-restaurant, through the rows of coconut trees, past Nana laying the yoga mats on the white sands. He's heading for the nearby cliff, it seems. Yaa pursues him, screaming his name, "Kobby, Kobby!" We watch him cannonball into the water, screaming: **"I'm a vessel!"**

The exact proclamation he'd hurled at us having rushed out of the ocean and presented us with a suitcase of dismembered white heads, white torsos, and white limbs, all parts sealed with frosted bubble-wrap, blood thawing into the luggage's bottom where Vincent inserted his fingers to rescue a Nikon lens cap.

"You're not a vessel, Kobby," Vincent had responded. "If you were, they'd let you know where to send these bodies. But this, this, could be your leg in the door!"

Ash Hassani, Keshia Osei, Ileen Wilke and Marjolijn Hekelaar, Ngozi McCarthy, Kweku Fleming, Meghan Mccormick, Rubbina Karruna, Rose and Maud Goodhart (my London Bookseller promoters), Trish Tchume (US bookstore rep extraordinaire), Lana Purcell for all offline support: your overwhelming faith in my completion of this novel made me scared! Agent Kent Thee Wolf. I can't thank you enough for all the work you will continue to do for *No One Dies Yet*.

Reggie Bailey (@reggiereads), Akosua Peprah, Kene (@keneficent), Ashley Shaw Scott, Charlotte (@Charleyroxy), Marji Shaw, Sylvia Arthur, Kai Spellmeier, Gabriele (@Queerbookdom), Virginia (@Eatingtheirownwords), Mbama Obama, Mutisya, Nika Betuma, Makeda (@Colourlit_uk), Jaclyn (@Sixminutesforme), Akosua Shirley, @Ns510reads, @Knowledgeislost. To the author friends who came in with the advice: Saleem Haddad, Derek Owusu, Petina Gappah. More bookstagrammers such as: @Sreddyen, Simon (@BookSolace), Nana Akwasi Apau Bhavik Dohsi, Nina Chachu, Bridget Boakye, Nana Ashanti, Michelle Konadu, Rachel (@booksforbrunch), Miron Lockett, Yvonne Bukari, @Libbysbookshelf, Zanta Nkumane, Viwe Tafeni, Anathi Jongilanga and anyone else I've forgotten to thank especially those in groups as the ff: The entire Ghana Must Read (old and new members), Mom's United Book Club (Elaine Arthur and Benessa), Caribbean Bookstagram, African Bookstagram, Black (American + Brit) Bookstagram, Indian Bookstagram. I really couldn't have finished my edits without all your encouragements. From the tiniest of gestures (DM slides) to the grandest (showing up in-person to support). I felt your love. Can someone, anyone reading this help me find Jennifer Cecile? Canadian + former bookstagrammer/previously bookseller at Lunenburg Bound who introduced (read as: bought) Ondjaki and Négar Djavadi (whose book I loved so much and whose publishers—the first ever book I read from Europa Editions—would take on this challenge of a debut)?

Jen, if you knew the impact your comments under all my book reviews, encouraging me to write my own novel—really, if you knew just how much impact those short and lovely notes had on me, you'd show up and come for a big, long tearful hug. Or do I need to journey to Nova Scotia to find you? I will do this immediately I get the chance to!

For editorial/publishing support: Amyn Bala (my first ever reader who gave me the push to start querying after reading my first draft), Deyo Adebiyi (for assisting on the novel in a thematic capacity), to Aida Z. Lilly (thanks a lot for loving the work in its first draft and representing the novel for its English language rights), Christopher Potter and Eva Ferri for all your structural input and resources to get this project done. Team Publicity, Daniela and Carolina, thanks for all the hard-work.